A SPARE LIFE

A SPARE LIFE

Lidija Dimkovska
Translated by Christina E. Kramer

Two Lines Press

Originally published as: Резервен живот
© 2012 by Лидија Димковска
Translation © 2016 by Christina E. Kramer

Published by Two Lines Press
582 Market Street, Suite 700, San Francisco, CA 94104
www.twolinespress.com

ISBN 978-1-931883-55-9

Library of Congress Control Number: 2016938372

Cover design by Gabriele Wilson
Cover photo by Lisa Johansson/Millennium Images, UK
Typeset by Sloane | Samuel

Printed in the United States of America

1 3 5 7 9 10 8 6 4 2

Excerpts from *A Spare Life* were first published in *Tin House*
and the *Chicago Review*

This project is published with financial support from the Ministry of Culture of the
Republic of Macedonia, and is supported in part by an award from
the National Endowment for the Arts.

ART WORKS.
arts.gov

1984

That June afternoon on the outskirts of Skopje, in front of our apartment building, Srebra, Roza, and I were playing a new game: fortune-telling. On the steaming cement of the lane that sloped down to the residents' garages, we drew squares with white chalk and wrote the age at which we hoped to get married inside them. We would attract the attention of every passerby and, sitting on their balconies or standing by the apartment building's open windows, even the neighbors who knew us well would stare at us, because my sister and I were twins—conjoined twins—our heads fused at the temple right above my left ear and her right ear. We were born like that, to our misfortune and our parents' great shame. We both had long thick chestnut-brown hair that concealed the place where we were joined, or at least we thought so. At first glance, it appeared as if we were squatting and leaning our heads together, our bodies free the full length down. We were dressed in light strapless summer tube dresses. I was in a green dress with little yellow flowers, and my sister was in a red one with blue and white dots.

At the age of twelve, the only thing my sister Srebra and I, Zlata, were ashamed of was our names. Why would any parents name their children Srebra and Zlata—*silver* and *gold*—let alone children already marked by conjoined heads as freaks of nature in their community? These were the names of old women, cleaning ladies, or women who sold potatoes in front of the bakery. Whenever we complained to her about our names, our mother silenced us with the justification: "That's what your godfather wanted: Zlata after Saint Zlata Meglenska, and Srebra after a woman named Srebra Apostolova who killed two Turkish *beys* in Lerin."

"That's stupid," is what we always said; it was one of the few things we agreed on. Our godfather never once set foot in our house after the christening; it was as if the earth had swallowed him up. In fact, he took off for Australia to earn a living and erased us from his consciousness forever.

"Zlata's a birdbrain and Srebra's a turd brain!" children called after us, taunting us in the street; with the exception of Roza and occasionally Bogdan, no one ever played with us. Some parents, to shield their kids from nightmares, forbade them to associate with us freaks, but other kids fled from us of their own free will and threw rocks at us from a distance, shouting, "retards!"

Roza was the only one who didn't have a problem with our physical deformity. She lived on the second floor of our building; she was a year older than us, and had thick, curly black hair and dark skin; she was a little on the short side, but was sturdy. There are children so delicate, with skinny legs, pale faces, and small hazel eyes, like us, that you'd think the wind would blow them away, and then there are those that look muscular, healthy, like they'd be heavy in one's arms, with strong hands, like Roza. She was so strong-willed and adamant that we always agreed to her proposals.

That day was no different from any other; she suggested

that we draw squares, inscribe in them the age at which we wished to get married, then, above the squares, the initials of three boys we liked (potential husbands), and below the squares, the numbers one to three (how many children we might have); on the left, letters to designate how much money our husbands would have: *P* for poor, *R* for rich, and *M* for multimillionaire, and then on the right, the first letters of three cities in which we would like to live. My square and Srebra's were close to each other; Roza drew hers a little way off. Then each of us counted the characters around the edge as many times as indicated by the number in the middle of the square, circling the letter or number we landed on, and then continuing around (skipping any circled characters) until we had calculated out our circles. Here is a sketch of what the lives we imagined for ourselves looked like:

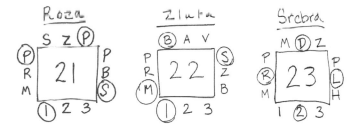

Roza was to get married in eight years, which seemed a long way off, when she turned twenty-one, as her mother had been, and she'd marry a boy whose name began with *P*. Yes, it was nice that she would end up with Panait from the Greek village of Katerini, where she went on vacation every summer with her family to stay in an old house near the cathedral that had apartments for rent. Panait lived in the house next door with a garden; he was a nice boy who had learned a few Macedonian words on account of his love for Roza, enough for shy communication in addition to glances, hide-and-seek, and swimming together in the sea.

"Sure, we'll be poor!" she exclaimed, because that was what her counting had given her: Panait would be poor, they'd have one child, and would live in Salonika, the city Panait loved more than any other in the world because he'd been born there. He had been premature, but his life had been saved, so once a year, he and his parents went on a pilgrimage to the Church of Saint Demetrius to give thanks to the saint. "Only one child," Roza said sadly, because she had imagined one day, when she was grown and happily married to Panait, she would have a house full of children, or at least two, like her and her sister, who was three years older.

For Srebra, who wished to get married at twenty-three, it worked out that she would marry a boy whose name began with *D* (she had had no particular name in mind; she had just scribbled it off the top of her head just to have three boys' names); *D* would be rich, and they were to have two children ("Good for you!" Roza exclaimed), and live in a city whose name began with *L*.

"London!" I cried, and in my surprise, tugged on her head as I jerked my own. "Why London? You don't even know what it looks like! And it's really far away! I don't want to live in London! How will you live there if I don't live there, too? You only think about yourself!"

Even from my earliest childhood I had felt Srebra was always thinking only of herself and couldn't care less that we were joined at the head and couldn't possibly lead separate lives, but only a single one, shared, as if we were one person in two half-fused bodies. We had to do everything together: eat, sleep, go to the bathroom, go to school, go out, go in, everything. Even when we were little, if she needed to pee during the night, she threw off the comforter and jumped out of bed, which meant she, with no consideration at all, tugged at me, jolting me awake and forcing me to my feet even though I was still in a haze between the dreamworld and reality. The pain was so intense in the spot where we were conjoined that I'd scream in horror, while Srebra, teeth clenched, was already running to the bathroom, dragging me with her. Once there, while one of us sat on the toilet, the other had to sit too, which meant plopping down on the blue plastic trashcan that we moved to the left or right of the toilet depending on which of us was on the seat. Into that trashcan we threw away the paper—which was not scented toilet paper, but typewriter paper my mother would sneak from her office and then tear into quarters so we could wipe ourselves after doing our business—and also kitchen waste, leftovers, all manner of garbage.

I was often cruel, too, yanking her suddenly in some unexpected direction, but I was more aware that our heads were joined, that we should be careful, every minute, how we moved so as to not hurt ourselves, because the pain in our temples where we were joined was unbearable whenever one of us made a sudden unanticipated movement. Srebra was also aware that we were two in one, but only physically, whenever her head started to ache, not psychologically; she would dream up great plans for her life, and simply took no account of my desires or of our joint capabilities. She was certain that one day, when we were grown and had a lot of money, we'd be able to pay for an operation that could separate us. She believed it so intensely that when our heads were still conjoined, she was making plans as if we'd already been separated.

It was like that with the fortune-telling game, too, when she said in an absolutely calm voice, "I've told you a hundred times I want to live in London, and you didn't write it down. Look, you put down the letter *S*. That can only be Skopje, but I'm not staying here, not for anything in the world! In London they will surely be able to separate us. They have those kinds of doctors."

My eyes were already welling up with tears. I pinched her with my left hand on her right elbow as hard as I could. Srebra raised her left arm over her head and smacked me on the head as hard as she could. Those blows on the head would hurt for days. Mom once said to her, "If you continue on like this, one day you're going to punch a hole in her brain and then what troubles we'd have!" And, as always, our father added, "You voracious creatures, you've devoured the world!"

Although our heads were not merely joined but also shared a vein by which our blood mixed—in moments of excitement, anxiety, or other extreme situations we felt each other's hearts beating in our temples—we thought differently; our brains were not conjoined. I still don't know whether this was a lucky or an unlucky circumstance of our lives.

That's why, whenever Srebra hit me on the head, she hissed, "Don't you dare tattle!" But this time, she didn't manage to say anything, because I started to cry so desperately that Roza immediately bent over us to wipe my tears away with her hand.

"Come on, Zlata, don't. Look how nicely things are going to turn out for you. Your husband will be a multimillionaire and you're going to have one child, and with all those millions, you're sure to find a doctor to separate your heads." I was crying and kneeling down, stock-still, sensing that in Srebra's mind she was already leaving for London, alone, without me, and I was nowhere. I felt I was not there, that I did not exist.

"Hey, you guys, what kind of game is this?" Bogdan called out just then, having quietly drawn near. Up until then, he had been sitting a little way off from us on the concrete wall above the driveway, leaning on the door, stealing glances at what we were doing while seemingly engrossed in solving—in his head, without a pencil—a crossword puzzle torn from a newspaper.

"You stay out of this," Srebra shouted at him. I didn't say anything. I was swallowing the mucus that had collected in my throat from the tears, and Roza just shrugged her shoulders.

"All you think about is marriage. You have nothing better to do," Bogdan called out, and then exclaimed in surprise, "Hey look, the letter *B*! That's not me, is it?"

Just at that moment, before my face turned red, a flowerpot with a cactus in it fell from one of the balconies and shattered on our fortune-telling squares. We could hear curses and shouts of indignation. The dirt scattered all over the squares we had drawn; my square was the only one now even barely visible. My fortune said I would get married a year before Srebra to a boy whose name began with *B*, that he'd be a multimillionaire, we'd live in Skopje, and have one child. That was not Bogdan, because Bogdan was the poorest boy we knew, and I couldn't imagine him being a multimillion-aire. I thought only poor girls could become multimillionaires when they grew up and that boys were either poor or rich all their lives.

We raised our heads. On the second floor balcony stood a single woman named Verka who shouted in a voice husky from cigarettes and alcohol, "You killed my mother! You! No one else! But you'll die, too!"

Auntie Mira, from the balcony above, tried to calm her down. "Now Verka, if you throw flowerpots like that, you'll hit the children. Go on, get back inside."

At that moment, our father appeared on our balcony in his white undershirt and shouted, "Wait till I come down and get you, you old drunk!" Then he turned to us and called in an equally sharp voice, "Go around to the back of the building. Your mother dropped a towel. Go and get it."

Verka went in, Roza ran home, and Srebra and I staggered—as always when we walked—to the rear of the building. There, just under the second row of balconies, we saw the towel hanging on a branch of the plum tree we had planted with Roza two years before as a symbol of our friendship. The little tree had already grown quite a bit; it reached almost to Uncle Sotir's window. We caught hold of the towel, and instead of going back around the building and entering through the main entrance, we climbed in through the basement window. The glass had been removed years ago, probably deliberately, so tenants wouldn't have to walk all the way around to get to the back of the building where they made winter preserves, or to the garages, illegally built from odds and ends, so that now, instead of green shrubs and grass, all we saw from our windows were garages: one made with a tarp, another from corrugated iron, a third with concrete, another out of boards.

Bogdan had followed us as far as the window; then he simply said, "Ciao," and climbed the nearby linden tree.

"Aren't you going home?" I managed to call out after him as Srebra pulled the two of us through the window, but he didn't reply. There was nothing to say; for a year now there had been no one waiting for him at home. We all knew that, but we pretended we didn't, ever since the day his mother was buried and our class went with our teacher to express our condolences. Before that, Bogdan and his mother had lived next to the Slavija supermarket in a small single-room shack with a toilet attached to its back wall. His mother cleaned the stairs in several apartment buildings, including ours. He didn't have a father. Although he was quite poor, he was always carefully dressed, washed, and combed. His mother, who had grown old and ugly before her time, talked constantly about Bogdan: she wanted nothing else but for him to finish his education, become somebody and something. Bogdan lived up to her expectations, both in school and out; he read everything he could lay his hands on, and he loved crosswords. Tugging at their sleeves, he begged the men who read newspapers on the benches or on the balconies to give him the page with the crossword puzzle. More often than not, he didn't have a pencil, so he'd solve them in his head, concentrating to remember the solutions he'd already figured out. The children who didn't know where Bogdan lived had no idea just how poor he was, or that he'd been starving ever since his mother was diagnosed with throat cancer.

We learned all this less than a month after his mother's death from his homework essay "When You Hit Rock Bottom." That morning, the principal came into our classroom with our teacher, and while we were still trembling from the shock of the principal's sudden appearance, our teacher asked,

"Who doesn't want to read his or her homework aloud?" Confused by the question, even though we would all rather not have read our homework aloud, no one had the courage to raise a hand. Only Bogdan did. "Ah, there's someone who doesn't want to. That's why he's going to have to," she said, and both she and the principal laughed out loud. Bogdan had no choice; he stood up and began to read in a trembling voice:

> Before she got sick, my mother bought a little pig and a little rabbit. Soon after that, she went into the hospital. It was winter and we had no heat. During the day I wandered around the streets after school, at night I huddled under three comforters. Every day I went back to the school at night to steal some of the dried flowers from the foot of the memorial to our school patron so I could take them to the pig. My mother came back from the hospital just before Christmas. She couldn't speak. She just lay there watching—first me, then the pig, then the rabbit, one by one. By Christmas our pig weighed twenty-five kilos, but its brother that lived at the neighbors' weighed two hundred kilos. The neighbors slaughtered our pig along with theirs and made us three sausages and some ham from it. Not long after that, my mother went back to the hospital. All winter, until March, I nibbled bits of sausages and ham. I was thrifty; I wanted to save for the future. In the spring, the last sausage began to get moldy, but I still tore off little pieces and rubbed the mold off; that's what I lived on until July. The

rabbit got thinner and thinner. One day I decided to pluck its fur and sell it for bread money. While I was plucking it, I pulled off a chunk of pink meat. It started to bleed. The fur hardly weighed a hundred grams. The rabbit was all skin and bones, a living skeleton. I killed it before it starved to death. I cooked it and ate it. My mother came home and died. I survived. Things can't get worse than that.

Everyone in the classroom was speechless. Behind my glasses my eyes filled with tears. From the way the skin connecting our heads pulled tight, I knew that Srebra's face was puckered up the way it did whenever she felt tears coming. The teacher and the principal muttered something to each other, then the school bell rang, and we all ran out of the classroom.

Srebra's steps and mine were never fully in sync; either I dragged her along or she dragged me. That's how it had been ever since we learned to walk: she wanted to walk fast, I still wanted to crawl. If it hadn't been for Granny Stefka's patience, we might never have learned to walk. She'd crouch on the floor holding me up at the same height as Srebra, who wanted to walk, and she'd drag herself silently along with me in tow, so that Srebra would not be stopped in her attempts to walk. When I wanted to crawl, Granny Stefka would pretend to be a cat and get Srebra to crawl all the way to a piece of black cloth that she had set down by the door, playing the part of a mouse. All of us crawling together, Srebra and I with our joined heads and Granny Stefka with her fat belly dragging along the floor.

The day after the incident with Bogdan's homework was a Saturday, and we went out to gather used paper, going from apartment to apartment, from house to house, even carrying paper out of basements. At the end of the day, the custodian and the principal weighed the paper we had collected on a balance scale, calculated what it would sell for, and, before sending it off, handed Bogdan a money-filled blue envelope—our balm for his wounds. After that, no one ever asked how he lived, what he did with the money, or whether he had anything to eat. Later, we found out that he had given the money to the salesclerk at the grocery store next to his shack for a subscription to the crossword puzzle magazine *Brain Twisters*, and now a copy of the magazine accompanied him wherever he went. Whenever we saw him doing crossword puzzles—face flushed, eyes sparkling—he looked a little crazy to Srebra and me. We hardly ever said a word to him if Roza wasn't with us. Srebra used a somewhat mocking tone, but I felt my words turn to stone in my chest; I couldn't get out a sentence from beginning to end. I was blocked as if in front of a stranger who didn't know my language: you stare at them, and don't know what to say to get them to understand you. Roza had no problem communicating with anyone; she spoke to everybody she met. She was the most outgoing girl on our street and wasn't inhibited with children or adults. Because of Roza, Bogdan felt welcome in our company, but he was never pushy; he didn't look for any special attention, didn't count on any of us. One day, Roza lost an earring behind the building. We looked for it in the tall grass between the garages, near the transformer under the apricot tree that produced delicious orange fruit in the summer—with me dragging Srebra while she dragged me. Srebra stretched her hand into the thorns by the fence separating the backyard of our building from the house of the "brothers"—as our parents called the men who lived opposite us—and pulled out the earring. Next to the transformer there was a large clump of grass called "lucky stalks." We each plucked a stem, made a wish, then pulled off all the little stems—you were supposed to be left with just the central spike. If we managed to keep the top from tearing off, we hid the lucky stalk, burying it somewhere to make a wish come true. I couldn't hide mine without Srebra seeing me, nor could she hide hers without my seeing, even though the unwritten rule was for the other to close her eyes. I was sure that our wishes would never come true and that only Roza could hope for some pleasant surprises in the future. That's why we gave in to her will, her ideas, and her ever-changing suggestions for new adventures. Every clever or dumb thing we did until two in the afternoon when our parents returned from work and her sister came home from high school we did at Roza's. In the small cupboard in their dining room next to the coffee cups and wine glasses there were two kaleidoscopes, Roza's red one and her sister's blue one. Srebra and I took them without asking permission. I picked the red one, Srebra the blue one, and while Roza rustled about the kitchen, we peered inside at the amazing designs. When I think about it, I don't believe that I ever again held a kaleidoscope in my hands for as long as I did at Roza's. Only once, in a small toy store in Covent Garden, in London, did I come across a similar red kaleidoscope, but when I stared into it, there was nothing like the checkered, angular, or cubic designs in Roza's kaleidoscope, but rather, rounded ones, with soft transitions in color. It seemed a traitor to the true meaning of a kaleidoscope. While Srebra and I each peered at the sharp colors and figures, one nearly touching the other, Roza came into the dining room holding an odd-looking plastic water pitcher shaped like a bunch of grapes; around its mouth she had tied a thin rope about two or three meters long. "Come on! Let's water the grass," she said, which meant that Srebra and I should go downstairs, behind the building, under her balcony, and from the balcony she would lower the bunch of grapes with the string, we would grasp it, and then we would water the chokecherry tree that brought springtime into the gloom cast by the garages behind the building each year. We'd also water the other flowers growing in the grass under Auntie Elica's, Roza's, and Auntie Dobrila's balconies. This was the only patch of ground, these few square meters of nature in the midst of the urban chaos behind our building, upon which no garage had sprung up. After we had used up all the water, Roza hoisted the pitcher up to the balcony, refilled it, then lowered it again, and thus we watered every bit of ground, including, finally, the hedge that grew around the green space. Then Roza would come down, having already made plans for a new game.

She decided to teach us to ride a bicycle. That had always seemed impossible to us, to our father in particular, who kept, next to his black bike in the garage, an old red Pony bicycle that he had picked up somewhere; it had an old black saddle, a chain guard painted orange, and no rear bike rack. Whenever we went down to his garage to get chalk so we could draw, we always looked at the red Pony with a vague, questioning feeling of how we might possibly ride together—where Srebra would sit, where I'd sit. And he would call out right away, "Bikes aren't for you; if you fell off, we'd be stuck trying to sort everything out." Roza disagreed. She urged us to go home, get the key to the garage, and take out the bike while she got hers from their garage, then we'd follow her instructions on how to ride. So, of course, that's exactly what we did. First, Roza adjusted the seats of both bikes so they were the same height. Then she told Srebra to sit on the Pony and me to sit on her bike, placing them precisely side by side. We had to cross our arms so my left hand was on Srebra's right handlebar, and her right hand was on my left handlebar. "Look in front of you, not down at the ground," instructed Roza, and she pushed, holding onto both seats. We rode two meters, and then smacked into an old Lada parked at the curb. We held ourselves up against the windows, and fortunately, didn't hit our heads on anything. But a small dent was visible on the front door on the driver's side, and both bikes' handlebars were bent. When our fathers came home from work, we confessed what we had done. Other than shouts, threats to send us to an orphanage, and curses, Srebra and I weren't punished. We never asked Roza whether she was punished for doing something she shouldn't have. On the days Roza didn't come outside in the afternoon, Srebra and I, not knowing what to do with ourselves, usually went to Auntie Verka's. If we weren't with Roza, we rarely wanted to play together or go to the same place. It was a constant problem both for us and for our parents that we never wanted the same thing. If Srebra wanted to go to our cousin Verče's, I wanted to stay home and watch a movie. If I wanted to go to the library and take out a book, Srebra didn't want to budge. How many arguments, pleas, bites, pinches, and stomps on each other's feet came from any suggestion, any plan in our lives. If only we could be separated for an hour or two so we could each do what we wanted. But that was impossible. The two of us did, however, like to go to Verka's. We were drawn to her—a single woman and heavy drinker who lived in one of the apartments in our entryway, directly opposite Roza's apartment on the second floor, an unusual woman who both loved us and hated us. But we didn't care. How old was Verka when we were children? When Srebra and I begged her for presents?

When she brought us the cassette *Songs about Tito* from her trade union's trip to Belgrade, along with a combed-wool doll that collected dust for years? When she gave me books by Mir-Jam, and Srebra the Fisher books? When we went to her place, and she sat on the couch while Uncle Blaško massaged her back? Even though the sight embarrassed me and disgusted Srebra, we still didn't leave, sitting at the table and passing an empty container of cream back and forth, sliding it across the table. That's how we learned that the salesclerk in the neighborhood's only bookstore—where we bought all our books and notebooks for the first day of school—had cancer and that Auntie Verka was deathly afraid she would get sick too. She once showed us a photograph of the son who had repudiated her after helping her get an apartment designated for a single person in our building.

Auntie Verka would send us to get a bottle of rakija, or a jar of mayonnaise, or cigarettes. She divided the change down to the dinar, half for me, half for Srebra. For hours, she would sit on the balcony sipping rakija, smoking cigarettes, and occasionally cursing at someone on the street, hurling abuse at a tenant seated on their balcony, or just letting out the odd shout. Srebra and I were usually in her living room then, sitting by the window on the same wall as the balcony, watching her and quietly giggling, or counting the money she had given us. Then she either shooed us away for no particular reason, swearing at us or calling down curses on our heads, or we secretly slipped out of the apartment. We would leave the building through the glassless window at the back, stepping on each other's feet, and head straight to the store for lollipops or chocolate. At times like that, Srebra and I loved each other normally, like sisters, without any tenderness; we didn't hold hands or anything, but at least we didn't fight, didn't quarrel or tease each other.

Auntie Verka was one of the rare individuals in our joint life who brought us together. Perhaps that's why, for our twelfth birthday, the only people we invited to our party were Roza, Verče, and Auntie Verka. How many arguments there were over one stupid birthday party! Our father didn't make much of a fuss; he went to the garage, to his "atomic shelter" as I called it, after the band with that name. Our mother, on the other hand, passed through every phase of disapproval, bickering, and threatening; yet in the end, she threw up her hands, because with us, there could be no peace in the house. That was clear to her from the moment we were born—as worthless as conjoined bats. It wasn't clear to her why she hadn't given us to a children's home, but she had succumbed to our father's persuasion that if she brought us home, they'd find doctors who could separate us once we'd grown a bit and were strong enough for the operation. But he'd lied to her. Where could such doctors be found if there were any at all, and besides, there was no case like ours in the whole world. I don't know if it was just Srebra and I that were unable to feel her love or if it was because, paradoxically, a child can't feel motherly love until she's grown up, until later, when she starts to analyze it. As always, we got through this fight with insults, nasty words, and spite, but in the end, we got our way: for the first time in our lives we would celebrate our birthday, against all opposition. Mom thought birthday parties were for the rich, particularly since we were born in the summer, when there was no school, and no one expected there to be a party. "Who will come to your party, God?" she asked. But on the day of our party, Mom made steamed cookies and a cake with strawberry pudding filling, sprinkled with ground walnuts. We went to the store and bought snacks and mint liqueur, and at home we made juice from sour cherry syrup. We arranged everything nicely on top of the white freezer in the big room where our parents slept. Soon Roza, Verka, and our cousin Verče arrived; Roza brought gifts—notebooks with thick red covers. Verka brought money tucked in both pockets of her skirt, and Verče came with money wrapped in a piece of white paper, just as our aunt had given it to her. We put on some music, Đorđe Balašević, the only cassette that was mine, and Srebra's Zdravko Čolić tape. We nibbled on breadsticks while Auntie Verka went straight for the liqueur. Then we cut the cake and ate it without candles or ceremony, humming along to the songs on the tapes. Our parents didn't sit in the room with us. Our father stayed in the garage the whole time, and Mom sat in the kitchen doing needlepoint, ears cocked to catch our voices intermingled with the music. Auntie Verka, who was drunk even in her dreams, could barely stand. She was sipping straight from the bottle, laughing, showing her yellow teeth among which two gold ones glittered. Roza was trying to make the atmosphere merrier by playing "one, two, three, you hit me" with Srebra and me. Verče's hands twisted a snake fashioned from small black-and-white beads which stood on the wardrobe as a decoration, but aside from the music, there was an emptiness in the room that makes me shudder even today; that birthday was so sad that we never again even mentioned celebrating one. Instead, we suppressed the shared day of our birth, even though the resulting tension lasted the whole day and was worst of all when our parents returned from work without the least acknowledgment that it was our birthday. But Verka remembered that our birthday was in summer, and for several summers in a row she gave us a present, some old thing she had in her apartment—a small porcelain horse, a chicken made of lace, small knitted shoes that had decorated the knobs of her cupboards, a book by

Tito, Marx, or Engels that she bought through her workplace until she was allowed to take early retirement due to chronic alcoholism, or money to buy lollipops or chocolate.

Mom always swore about her in the same way: "May her heart devour her," she said, although it was never clear to us why she disliked her so much, even though no one else in our building liked her. Everybody closed their doors in her face, avoided meeting her on the stairs or outside, pretended to be deaf if she asked them something. There were even those who insulted her openly, shouting, "Worthless drunk! You stink and your apartment stinks. You'll bring some disease in here! Idrizovo prison is the only place for you! Jesus, your son should never have found you an apartment; he should have just left you on the street! Why did you have to end up in our building?" All sorts of things like that. The men were particularly harsh, because it was to them that Verka most often turned for a cigarette or a sip of rakija or beer. It was only Uncle Blaško, who lived on the first floor, who didn't argue with her. He didn't smoke or drink; he just sat on the balcony, and whenever anyone walked by, he mumbled something resembling a greeting. At home, whenever we asked for something sweet, Mom always joked, "Something sweet like your sweet uncle Blaško." As a matter of fact, I think Srebra and I asked for sweets just to hear that one kind sentence from our mother, to feel that she might love us. Uncle Blaško's wife died young of stomach cancer, and on the day of her funeral, Srebra and I stood on our balcony and watched the hearse approach. On the corner, Blaško's six-year-old son stood sadly in his blue suit and pale-blue shirt, his hair combed to the side. A small, lost child without his mother. No one held his hand; he stood alone and waited for the hearse to pull up in front of our building. His father was beating his chest and crying loudly. No one else was crying. All the grown-ups who lived in the apartment building climbed into their cars and set off behind the hearse carrying Milka's coffin. In all the years before her death, Srebra and I had seen her only once, the day we had a car accident. Our aunt Ivanka had come over that day. She, too, had her troubles, because our cousin was in the hospital to have one of her ovaries removed, even though she was only ten years old. Aunt Ivanka lay all day on the small couch in the kitchen and cried, crushed from pain, grieving over little Verče's fate, that she might never have even a single child with only one ovary. Our mother said to her, "You think that my two will ever have children? Who will take them with their heads like that?" Srebra and I just stood there, mute, beside the couch. We couldn't figure out why Verče wouldn't be able to have a child. We couldn't remember what our biology teacher had said about how babies were conceived, and we said nothing—Srebra with her eyes downcast, I holding in my hands the little red toy telephone we had bought for when we visited our cousin in the hospital. In the stairwell, we met Roza, jumping up two stairs at a time as usual; she was returning from the store. "Hey, nice telephone," she called to us. I don't know how we all fit into the Škoda, but we piled in—Dad, Mom, our aunt Ivanka, Srebra, and I, as well as Aunt Milka, who was already sick and going to the doctor's in the hospital where Verče was. We hadn't driven for five minutes, when, turning onto the main street, our father hit another car coming from the opposite direction. The crash wasn't a big one, but it was enough to frighten us more than we'd ever been frightened before. Our aunt and Milka got out of the car, still shaken, and ran to the bus stop to wait for a bus to the hospital. Although we could have simply gone home on foot, we had to stand and wait for the police. We didn't get home for another hour. Dad was upset. He couldn't believe something like this had happened to him. He kept looking at the car's dented bumper. Mom simply went mute. She did not utter a single word. She was pale, and I wondered whether she might have a fainting spell, because those spells had lasted for years, when she'd suddenly feel dizzy, go pale, and then lose consciousness, all accompanied by the words, "I'm going to die." Srebra would usually cry—she couldn't keep her face puckered up in the frown she used to keep back tears—while I trembled, my body going cold as if it were thirty below. I trembled so much that I shook Srebra as well, and my hands became sweaty. But this time, she didn't lose consciousness, and when the three of us got home, she mechanically poured dried beans into the red pot and began to pick through them, sitting in the kitchen on the couch with her eyes fixed on the pot—picking and picking over the beans. Srebra and I sat down by the small table on the wide chair our father had made for us a long time ago from some boards he got some- where, with a cushioned seat. We just sat there, saying nothing, handing back and forth our only doll, its crying mechanism long since removed from its belly, naked, its head bald on top, with one arm that kept falling off. We passed it back and forth as if it were a real baby: slowly, gently, without a word. It was deathly quiet in the apartment. Suddenly, the front door opened, and our father came in with another man, a mechanic I supposed. They sat in the dining room, we didn't move a muscle; Mom didn't get up but continued picking at the beans. We heard our father ask the man whether he would like a glass of rakija. He must have nodded in agreement be- cause we didn't hear a response. Then Dad went into the big room where the glasses and rakija were kept. When he came back, Srebra and I peeked from the kitchen table through the opening between the kitchen and dining room, as Dad said to the man, "Here you go, old pal." That was the first time in my life that I heard the word *pal*, and it has remained in my memory, stitched in embroidered letters. I was thrilled with the word; it filled me with hope. They drank the rakija and went out again. We still hadn't spoken. Srebra had to go to the bathroom, so we went, and while I sat on the trashcan holding my nose so Srebra's excrement wouldn't stink so much, she began to giggle, shaking my head also with her giggles. "He said 'old pal'—that's ridiculous! Dad doesn't have any old pals, since he doesn't even know anyone from where he came from. He's talking nonsense." I knew Srebra was right, but didn't say anything. Our father hadn't been in touch with his family for years. When he and our mother got married, they lived with his parents in the house that, our mother said, he built when he was still a child, lugging the cement and mortar himself. Our aunt and uncle were little then and played hide-and-seek while he worked excruciatingly hard, but they're the ones living there now. Put simply, his mother and father treated the newlyweds very badly. They were unhappy that their son had married a village girl; while our father was at work, our pregnant mother stayed home, in rooms with small barred windows in the basement of the house. Grandpa would insult her, chase her outdoors, and then call her back inside. Several times, he even hit her with a broom. Grandma acted as if she didn't see anything. Our mother cried every day, and maybe that's why we were born with conjoined heads, with this inoperable physical deformity. When our grandparents saw what kind of children their daughter-in-law had produced, they just threw us out onto the street. Dad managed to take his only coat along with a pink coatrack that had a mirror and a shelf for hats, which stands in our hallway to this day. With us—infants just a few days old—the coatrack, and their bags, they hopped on the first bus that came along and begged the driver to take them with all their baggage. The coatrack's mirror banged against the handrail throughout its journey on the bus, and cracked down the middle. Finally, we reached the last stop, at the other end of the city. We got off the bus, and the driver took pity on my parents and helped with the luggage. They asked the first woman they met whether she knew of a room for rent nearby. The woman, Stefka, lived in a small house at the edge of the neighborhood. She was a widow whose son had gone off to Germany, so she happened to have an empty room. Stefka picked up Srebra and me, thinking we were normal twins, and would have pulled our heads off had our mother not explained that we were born with joined heads, God save and preserve us. Granny Stefka gave us a small room in her house anyway; she found a woven basket for Srebra and me, and we stayed there for three whole years, until our parents were able to buy an apartment on credit two bus stops away. Our father never forgave his parents for what they did that day, and they literally forbade their other son and daughter, and all the other members of the extended family, to have any sort of ties with him. Our father was left with no family, no loving touch of a parent's hand. Our aunt and uncle felt no compassion for their older brother, erasing him from their lives. One day, though, when Srebra and I were six years old, a young woman came to our house. The darkest brunette we had ever seen sat in the big room on the couch where our mom and dad slept. She picked up the belly-shaped hot-water bottle that was lying on the bed. Srebra and I had won it in a school lottery and christened it Hermes; we played with it, rocking and hugging it before bed, when we filled it with hot water from the small green pot on the oil stove. But it was our parents who slept with it. The young woman turned the water bottle over, looking at it from all sides, then put it down and took from her handbag two chocolate bars with crisped rice—the biggest ones we had ever seen—and gave them to Srebra and me. "This is your aunt," our father said with a shaky voice, his hands trembling like slender branches. We just stared at this aunt of ours. She sat there awhile and cried a bit, without uttering a single word; then she stood and left. We ate the chocolate bars with crisped rice over the course of a whole month, square by square. Nobody ever mentioned the visit again. After that, our father's hands never stopped trembling, and he was so nervous that he shouted at every little thing. In fact, his moods changed every five minutes: He'd be polite and gentle with us, calling us his little chicks. He would buy us chocolate bars with pictures of animals on the wrappers, but then he would shout at us: "Get lost!"; "You voracious asses, you have devoured the world!"; or "Beasts, I'm going to take my belt to you!" One day, when we were in the dining room making models of traffic lights and signs for a school assignment, he got totally fed up and began reeling through his repertoire of insults. I tugged on Srebra with all my strength, because I couldn't stand the torrent of words dirtying his mouth. Srebra cried out in pain. We went out onto the balcony, and below, Lazarus Day singers were strolling by with a bear. The air was wintry and melancholic; the large room was cold. In the dining room, Dad glued the models together as he shouted, "You have devoured the world!" Saint Lazarus was nowhere to be seen, but the bear was walking on its hind legs. And on that day, Srebra and I once again ate sole, flour-dusted and fried—that whole winter we ate sole—I liked the shape of the fish, like an inflated heart. Srebra poked the body with her fork, making the form of a cross, and then ate it with her hands. Our mother and father ate boiled ham that came from the five-kilo tin fried with eggs, but the pieces of processed ham didn't stick, they just lay there beside the eggs in the pan. Our father had bought both the fish and the ham through his work, along with a large plastic container of plum jam. He would drink some of the red wine he kept in the basement and his anger would fade away. I could hardly wait for the electricity to go out, which usually happened in the afternoon, due to rationing. Then all four of us would squish together on the small couch in the kitchen, Srebra and I would ask Mom and Dad common expressions in French, and they would dredge up something from their school days, or make something up and we'd all laugh, while around us there was total darkness, and it wasn't unpleasant to sit next to one another, huddled up, not only for me and Srebra, but for them, too, for our parents. It wasn't unpleasant to love one another and be happy. Those afternoons without electricity were beautiful in their illusion of family happiness. But when the lights flashed back on (I always imagined a man sitting in a large room filled with on/off switches who alone determined when the lights would go on) and we could see one another, we all got up right away. Srebra and I, as if on command, jumped to our feet. We'd busy ourselves with something we could do in the same place, or argued, or simply sat and watched television in absolute silence, each of us already closed into herself, already alienated, loathing one another again.

That New Year's Eve, as usual, our father decorated the holiday tree while Srebra and I crouched down and watched him put up the ornaments, wind the frayed red garland around the tree, and place a few puffs of cotton here and there on the green branches. The tree was small, a half meter tall, with just a few meager decorations. He decorated it himself so we wouldn't break the ornaments. There were only six of them, each different. Then he picked up the tree and brought it into the large room, their room. He set it on the small table in the middle of the room, and our mother immediately placed a bowl of Russian salad with mayonnaise to its left and a plate holding a cake filled with pink strawberry pudding sprinkled with ground walnuts to its right. And so the New Year's Eve atmosphere was created, though not in the dining room, where we sat on hard wooden seats around the table to watch television, nor in our room, where Srebra and I slept on a foldout couch, with Mom's sewing machine in the middle of the room covered with an embroidered sheet on which stood a vase filled with plastic flowers. No, there was no New Year's Eve festivity there, only in our parents' cold room, in which Srebra and I spent just a few minutes a day, just long enough to have a look at the tree and nibble a bit of the cake.

While they ate lunch at the small table in the kitchen— our father seated in our large chair and our mother perpendicular to him—Srebra and I, who had already eaten, stood in the dining room listening to a Serbian song playing on the radio: "They're asking me, they're asking me, apple of my eye…" Our hearts pounded wildly in our temples. Srebra's face seemed clouded over; I think she wanted to cry, but I was somehow elated, as if enchanted. I could hardly wait for 1984 to pass so we could enter the new year, which would surely bring us something new, a new life, perhaps new hope for our future. The children's magazine *Our World* had wanted to publish a photograph of us with the caption, "The new year will also bring hope to Skopje's twin sisters conjoined at the head." Our teacher, however, wouldn't allow them to photograph us. "As it is," she said, "everybody gawks inquisitively wherever we go. If you turn up in the papers, there will be no end to the photos! Everywhere we turn, there will be journalists. My mother-in-law lives with us, and she's a village woman. If she saw that, she would gossip with the neighbors about me and the kinds of students I have. Over my dead body will they photograph you, and that's that!"

So, on account of the gossipy habits of our teacher's mother-in-law, the media did not find out about us during our childhood, and the editor of *Our World* was too kind a man to wish us any harm.

That evening, right at midnight, we had planned to perform the play *Alphabet Soup!* on the front steps of the apartment building with Roza, but when Srebra announced it, our father snapped, "Whoever feels like watching can go ahead and watch; I'm staying inside." Mom added, "Really, we're not going to go out there and freeze for some stupid thing. You just do whatever you think up, and now it's a play you want to perform?" Srebra and I slipped silently out of the house and rang the bell at Roza's. Her sister came to the door all dressed up, about to head out for a New Year's Eve party; we told her that the play was canceled, and she shouted to Roza while putting on her coat, "Roza, the play's canceled." She came out, smiling, and pinched our cheeks. Then she closed the door behind her, and the two of us, tugging at each other and jumping up the stairs two at a time in tandem, ran home in our stocking feet. We went into the bathroom. It was bitterly cold; the little bathroom window was never closed. Standing in front of the mirror, we each pulled our hair into a ponytail with a red rubber band. When we pulled our hair back into ponytails, the spot where our heads were joined was visible right above my left ear and her right. The skin passed from one to the other. There was no scar, nothing. Our temples drifted into each other's like desert sand. There was just enough space between the fused spot and my ear to poke the temple of my glasses through. We were so similar that if I didn't wear glasses, no one would have been able to tell which was me and which was Srebra. We looked at each other in the mirror, our gaze fixed and powerless. We stood there a long time without saying a word, Srebra with her sullen face, I with tears streaming down behind my glasses. Finally, Srebra dragged me over to the toilet. After she flushed, we unlocked the door and went out.

New Year's Eve smelled of roast chicken and potatoes. Srebra and I ate first, and when we got up from our big chair in the kitchen, our father sat down in it; our mother sat perpendicular to him, and they ate. Then Srebra and I went into the large room to see the New Year's tree on its little table one more time. We stood for two or three minutes trembling with cold, nibbling a bit of the cake with the pink filling and sprinkled with ground walnuts. We waved to the tree and left the room. Later, the four of us sat around the table, each of us with a little yellow plate of roasted peanuts, and watched the New Year's Eve program that was broadcast from Belgrade. A half hour before the start of 1985, our parents lay down, and Srebra and I snacked on the last of the peanuts and quietly counted down to midnight. Then we quickly turned toward each other as much as we could and exchanged fleeting air kisses, murmuring, "Happy New Year." Right after that, a movie began in which Demi Moore had both a male and female lover. They were emitting shrieks and lying on top of each other. The women were touching each other's breasts, and when Demi Moore was with her husband, he put his hands over her hips, grasping as much of them as he could. She was moaning with pleasure. My heart was pounding like crazy. I felt an excitement between my legs. Srebra must have felt it too, because she kept gulping down her saliva. Suddenly, the door to our parents' room opened. Our father stood in the doorway. He stepped into the dining room, turned off the TV, and said sharply, "Go to bed. That's not a movie for children." Srebra and I went and lay down. Usually we slept on our backs with our hands alongside our bodies and our legs stretched away from each other's. That New Year's Eve we lay on our stomachs, with our faces in the pillows. I was on her side of the bed, she on mine. We moved our bodies as far from each other as possible without causing pain in the spot where our heads were joined. My left hand was tucked up under my stomach, and Srebra's right hand was tucked under hers. The two of us were thinking of the day when our summer game of fortune-telling would come true, when we would have husbands with whom we too could cry out in pleasure. We didn't dare think about women. Sleep overtook us in that position. When we awoke, it was the first day of 1985.

1985

That year, January 6, our Christmas Eve, fell on a Sunday. Early in the morning, you could hear knocking on doors as carolers went door-to-door singing traditional carols. Srebra and I never went out caroling on Christmas Eve, not even when we were younger; we couldn't stand it when people opened the door and gasped when they saw our conjoined heads and then, confused and not knowing what to say, they'd shove a few chestnuts into our hands before locking the door after us, crossing themselves in horror at the encounter, some even spitting on the spot to prevent something like that happening to them. We were conscious of the fact that it was best if the coordinates of our lives moved between home and school—to the store, around our building, and no farther, not to other buildings or neighborhoods—just to places where people already knew us, though, even there, we weren't really accepted. That is why on Christmas Eve we stood silently in the hallway, listening as carolers sang and knocked on the door, while our hearts raced like mad. We did not open the door even for Roza, because there was always some other child with her. If our parents were home, our mother would open the door and give each caroler an apple, even as our father asked, "Why are you opening the door?" Although we didn't open the door ourselves, we wanted Mom to tell us how many children had been there, whether they were older or younger, boys or girls, what they were carrying in their bags. But on that January 6, by the time our mother got around to opening the door, the carolers were already gone. Srebra and I were still lying in bed and, just like every other Sunday morning for the past several months, listening to a Tina Turner song that reverberated from the neighboring apartment. It was always the same song, every Sunday morning for months. It was Christmas Eve and our mother made a leek pita pie, and the traditional round loaf with a coin baked inside was small and soft. Srebra and I sat on our chair, Mom and Dad stood as Mom divided up the loaf, and the coin was inside the piece that had been set aside for God. Then we shared walnuts, chestnuts, apples, dried plums, and figs. Just as it did every year, the ritual lasted about two or three minutes. Our father muttered, "OK, OK, that's enough," then took a step back toward the divider between the kitchen and the dining room, stopping with one foot there, one here, arms crossed, ready to sit down on the chair in the dining room and turn on the television. Srebra and I were eating the Lenten leek pita along with cheese, even though it was a fasting day. We didn't scarf down all the leek pie so there would be some left for our parents. When we finished, they sat down to eat, and we stood, leaning our elbows on the back of one of the dining-room chairs, staring at the television screen. This is how Christ was born in our house: quickly. I always thought of him as a premature baby lying in an incubator. Srebra and I went to our room, sat down on the floor, and turned on the yellow heater behind our backs. I asked her what she thought about God. She said that she did not think about him and that God didn't exist, that we had evolved from monkeys; after all, weren't the two of us absolute proof that man descended from monkeys? Surely some simian mistake had caused us to be born with conjoined heads, because if God were perfect, as they say, why hadn't he made us normal and not like this, disfigured for our entire lives. I didn't know what to say; Srebra was convinced that, while my God may have created other people, he certainly hadn't created us; we were clearly descended from apes. I wanted to go to bed as soon as possible. I needed to scrunch down under the quilt and move my body as far away from Srebra's as possible, as far away as our heads would allow, so I could be alone with my thoughts. I had one specific thought that helped me fall asleep on my most difficult nights: "my" house, the house I would have one day in a beautiful Skopje neighborhood, after Srebra and I had been separated and each of us was able to live as she wished. The house had two floors, with rooms and furniture that never changed in my imagination; for years, I always pictured it the same way, the rooms clearly laid out: tables, beds, pictures on the walls, dishes, everything. I would live in that house with my husband, who would be named Bobby—I really liked that name—a doctor, and he would have his office in the back part of the house. Our bedroom would be on the upper floor between the bathroom and the children's room. I would sit for entire days in the armchair in my large library, reading books and writing novels. Since we would have lots of money, every month I would visit a poor family on the outskirts of the city and bring them everything: food, clothing, medicine, toys for the children, anything they needed. And I pictured their house in detail as well, always the same, and I pictured them too, always the same, as if they really existed, as if we had known each other for years. What didn't I imagine before falling asleep? I went deep inside that house of mine, until the sweetness of sleep overtook me.

But that night, as soon as I fell asleep, Srebra elbowed me in the ribs to wake me up. "Mom's sick! Hey, Mom's sick," she whispered. I opened my eyes in the dark and pricked up my ears to hear the voices coming from the dining room. "Let's go," said my father. Then my mother, in a tired voice, said, "Take my bag." They left; they locked us in and left. Where? To which hospital and why? Srebra and I lay on our backs, silent. We swallowed the spit collecting in our throats. We lay there without saying a word, without moving, as if frozen, until an hour or two later when they returned. They went to bed quickly, got up at the usual time, five thirty, went to work, and we went to school a bit later. On our way home from school, we had the same thought: boil some water in the little pot with the red cover (the one that came with a packet of Vegeta seasoning, one of socialist Yugoslavia's rare marketing successes), shake in the chicken soup packet, add noodles, boil it, pour it into small deep china bowls, chop up some stale white bread, and then deliver this pleasure to our stomachs, which, during the day, only ever had a roll spread with margarine, *ajvar*, or a small cheese-filled bun for a snack. We'd slurp up that soup as if it were human warmth while Mom, pale, distracted, or sick lay on the couch in the kitchen and watched us silently, absently, or worked mechanically on her needlepoint, pushing the needle through the small openings. Our father would be rustling down below in the garage. Srebra and I sat on our chair, and all our sadness, shock, and concern floated in the chicken soup with the crumbled stale bread, which, homeopathically transformed into a transitory feeling of security and happiness, caressing our souls like the soft warm blanket we didn't have in our childhood because we were covered with heavy quilts, or roughly woven covers, scratchy shag wool throws, or small tattered blankets that smelled of dust and decay. That soup from a packet, served with boiled beans, was one of our favorite, but also one of the most unavoidable, meals of our primary-school years. As we slurped our soup greedily, we glanced, either surreptitiously or openly, under the couch on which our mother was lying, where, ducking our heads, we had hidden the small first aid booklet, and during moments of our mother's dizzy spells, when we were not sure what was happening to her, we madly turned the pages with trembling hands, hearts in our throats. Although we tried to remember how to do artificial respiration and revive a person, nothing stayed in our heads, and we never really learned how to give first aid. When our mother got up to use the bathroom, Srebra and I, as if on command, would sneak into the pantry, open the refrigerator and, one after another, quickly take swigs from the blueberry juice that was purchased only when our mother was sick—on those days when she wore her blue robe with its yellow-green flowers. That's how we knew for sure she was sick, and we felt a tightness in our chests, and in the spot where our heads were conjoined it felt like the striking of a wall clock. Her robe covered her body almost to her feet, protecting it with cotton, and announcing to her surroundings that her body underneath was weak, vulnerable, and sick. On the days Mom wore her blue robe, she was drowned in a world of her own. She had the unhappiest face in the world, and never smiled. What was it: depression, nerves, or some other illness? Or was it only tremendous pain? Reliving the memories of her first year of marriage when her father-in-law beat her with a broom and she was pregnant with us, and then nursing babies with conjoined heads? All the torments, all the human evils that had injured this poor typist? Whenever she felt she was at death's door—we knew that by the whispered sentence, "I'm going to die"—our dad would start the car and take her to the doctor. When she felt like that he would shut us into the big room so we wouldn't see it if she died. And outside, the hit song "Julie" echoed, filling the air with light-heartedness and sadness at the same time. One day, several years later, when we returned from school, our mother was sitting on the balcony doing "The Gypsy" needlepoint pattern and crying. At moments like that, neither Srebra nor I knew what to say, what to do. We stood, leaning on the balcony and turned toward her, silently, our hair hanging loose, intermingled, our two heads with one head of hair reflected in the window of the balcony door. All at once, our mother stood up, left everything behind, and went out. We saw her from the balcony as she hurried, nearly at a run, down the street that led to the store. She returned with a bar of chocolate. She opened it and ate it herself, without offering us a single small square. That day, Srebra and I ate beans without meat again, but she ate chocolate, in silence. Then her sickness went away. Surely, the fortune-tellers and seers to whom she went also had a share in it. One of them had "foretold" that the thermometer from Ohrid in the kitchen behind the door had mercury in it and was making my mother's blood pressure drop, so it had to be changed. And that she had to drink English ivy tea. Black magic? Several times, we found rags burned black and sooty in front of our door. Who had left them there and why? Did something from that ominous magic touch us? Srebra told me, "Magic does not touch those who are descended from monkeys, it touches those who are descended from God." I felt faint with fear.

But that January in 1985, I just wanted the days to pass

until winter break when we'd travel alone with our cousin Verče on one of the Proletariat bus company buses to the village and directly into the embrace of our grandmother. The fire blazed in the only warm room in the house; while Srebra and I sat in our grandma's lap, Verče had already found something to amuse herself—she had pulled a lead pellet from her pocket and was sticking it into the woodstove with tongs to see if it would melt. "Tomorrow we will go into town," our grandmother said. "We'll see the girl your uncle wants to marry. But don't tell your mother, she'd yell at me, asking why I took you along and brought shame to us in front of the in-laws." "We won't tell her," said Srebra, but I had a gigantic lump in my throat. We could hardly wait. Grandma, Verče, Srebra, and I went to the house of the girl our uncle, our mother's brother, was in love with so we could have a look at her. She and her sister were standing at the window—the chosen one was a brunette, her sister a blond—like a picture of angels and divine brides in heaven, although the only thing that our prospective aunt-to-be had of that image was the plump body of a woman in a baroque painting of paradise. At first, when her parents saw Srebra and me, they could not help their open mouths uttering "Oh!" Then they scowled, but, finally, her father smiled as broadly as possible. He stood behind Srebra and me and hugged the two of us, placing his hands on our breasts. He ran his hands across them, as if by accident, while we stood, stunned, looking at the tapestry hanging on the wall. His wife went out to bring some juice; Verče sat in front of the television set; our grandmother settled down next to her and looked around. When our prospective aunt appeared, her father let his hands drop from our breasts. Our cheeks burned with shame. "Were they born like this, or did it happen to them afterward?" the mother asked our grandma, pointing to us as she served the juice. "That's how they were born; it's fate," our grandma said. "What's your sign?" asked our potential aunt. "Your uncle and I have compatible horoscopes, both our signs and rising signs." "You have beautiful, beautiful granddaughters, even if they are like that," her father laughed again. He had a leering expression, white teeth with a few gold ones interspersed. Later, as we were waiting for our grandmother to put on her shoes, he passed Verče in the hallway and grabbed hold of her by the breasts, too, as if by accident, while helping her put on her coat. Verče was twelve years old and as flat as a board, but we were a year older and almost unnaturally mature, our nipples obvious under our blouses. And in all our future meetings, at the engagement party, at the wedding, at every family event connected with our uncle and aunt, her father always greeted us warmly with his firm grip, immediately throwing his arms around our necks and literally taking hold of our breasts. Srebra and I would freeze, red with embarrassment. We hated him and we hated ourselves, while his wife, smile in place, chatted on about nothing. They were the owners of a fabric store called Makedonka. On occasion, our aunt gave us a meter or two of some material or other—I remember one that was a dirty white color, with a brown and orange palm tree in the middle, or maybe two palms: our aunt sewed us skirts with elastic waistbands and a flounce. They didn't look great on us because of the elastic waistbands. We usually wore them with light brown tank tops that stretched enough so, like all our tops, we could pull them up from our feet.

From the very beginning, our grandmother did not like our uncle's choice. For a daughter-in-law she had wanted a nurse, someone hardworking and as cute as pie, with long hair, a fair complexion, smiling, beautiful, and blond. The woman our uncle had selected was the diametric opposite of Grandma's ideal. Our uncle cried behind the house when our grandmother told him she was not the girl for him, then took off somewhere. Our aunt cried sorrowfully, "My poor little brother. He's the only one with any education, and now look…" she sobbed, then set off after him. Srebra thought it was funny, but I cut off her laughter with a sharp pinch to the hip. Verče suggested we take a walk through the village. No sooner had we set out than we met Vida, our grandma and grandpa's neighbor. Granny Vida was most interested in whether our father had settled things with his family. She always asked when we saw her, and Srebra and I always said we didn't know anything about it, that the topic was not mentioned in front of us. "So what about you? Are you looking for a cure, or do you plan to stay like this?" Granny Vida asked. Srebra and I did not know anything about that either, because Srebra and I didn't know where to find a cure, and it always seemed to us that our mother and father weren't looking, and that we'd continue on with conjoined heads to the end of our lives, old maids, scorned by everyone. Perhaps we'd end up like our neighbor Verka. Deep down, our grandma also seemed to think we'd be old maids, because she frequently told us about an old maid in the village. "She gets her paycheck, eats, and drinks; she's like a buffalo. What does she need a husband for? A wife with a husband doesn't eat or drink; she just slogs along looking after children, who then bring home lazy, unwashed daughters-in-law." Another old maid in the village was Slavica, the agent who interrogated our grandfather that winter, though about what no one told us. Thin, tall, bony, with dark skin and hair, a gold tooth, and eyes that blazed with malice and power, she was the queen of Yugoslav Communism in the village, a member of UDBA—

the secret police—dressed in a long leather coat. Who made those leather coats the UDBA agents wore? For years, even after the breakup of Yugoslavia, they wore them over their business suits. Every time Slavica showed up at the house, Grandpa, as if on command, threw a heavy wool jacket over his shoulders, and with peasant *opanci* on his feet, grimy from working in the animal stalls, went off somewhere with the agent. When he returned, he didn't want to eat dinner or sit with us in the room with the woodstove, but lay down in his room, where he pulled the quilt and heavy woolen blankets over his head and trembled like a branch. Several years later, they found him, beaten, not far from the vineyard. He spent several days in the hospital and then came to Skopje. Srebra and I were alone. We had just returned from a book fair we had gone to with our school and were at Auntie Dobrila's; she made leather slippers at home on an industrial sewing machine. We sat on the couch and watched her. She was not bothered by our appearance nor was she ashamed of us. She jokingly referred to us as the "ass and underpants" as if we chose to be together all the time rather than being forced to. Our grandfather arrived at our apartment and rang the bell over and over until it finally occurred to him to ask Auntie Dobrila where we were. We unlocked the door to our place and let him in. He came in and sat on the couch in the kitchen. He was confused, anxious, his head bandaged. This was not our grandfather from the village; he was like some other person. We didn't know what to talk about. We left him there and went back to Auntie Dobrila's. We returned after our mother and father came home from work. We read the court decision aloud several times, but still didn't understand whether our grandfather had been charged, or had brought charges against someone else. The next day, he left on the first bus, and we went to the Prohor Pčinski Monastery with Roza's class—her teacher taught history—for Roza had begged for us to be taken along to see the monastery where the Anti-fascist Assembly for the National Liberation of Macedonia had met. Srebra and I sat in the front seats of the bus, across from Roza, and all three of us looked straight ahead, through the bus's windshield, while the radio played the Serbian pop song "Those Green Eyes Were Mine." Our grandfather never came to Skopje again, and we never went to Prohor Pčinski again. Nor did he allow our grandmother to come to Skopje more than once every two or three years. It made him angry that she sat on the balcony where everyone could see her. Was he jealous? Or did he think that it wasn't her place, a villager, to be out on the balcony? Or was he afraid that, in his absence, our grandmother would seek out her first love, a man named Kole, whom she had loved for seven years before she married our grandfather? She hadn't known how to write, so her sister, Mirka, had written letters for her, which she sent to him baked in loaves of bread. He appeared to her in a dream just before he died, and now that he was dead, she was more sorry than ever before that she hadn't married him and sat in a city garden in Skopje enjoying herself, rather than being tormented by village chores. Unrealized love, a life of pain. Her stomach ached until the end of her life. Every evening she licked sugar in place of morphine.

That winter vacation, after we met our prospective aunt, our aunt Milka told us that our father had telephoned from work to tell her that our mother was in the hospital. "She was feeling sick to her stomach," our aunt said. "It's a good thing it's vacation and you're here, or who would have taken care of you?" That evening, while Srebra and I were sleeping with Verče in the bed in the room with the woodstove, our grandma lying at our feet like a dog, I began to run a fever. When she noticed that I was sick, Srebra got really angry. We hated each other most when one of us was ill, because the other one also had to lie there as if she, too, were sick, and, more often than not, would get sick herself. And now, of all times, while white snowflakes blew outside and Verče had already asked Grandfather where the sled was, I got sick. I was burning with fever and almost delirious as I drank yogurt our uncle brought from town especially for me. Srebra covered her nose and mouth with a handkerchief so she would not get sick too. Verče kicked about the room, turning the cassette player on and off. Finally, she put on a Riblja Čorba tape and left the room, and all day, between dreaming and waking, I listened to songs from their album *Buvlja pijaca*. Srebra looked at the ceiling with her mouth and nose covered, fists clenched. At such moments, she hated me more than anything in the world. I hated her too, because I felt her hatred. Our mother was far away; we didn't even know which hospital she was in. Most of all, we were afraid she would die. I quickly recovered, and before the end of vacation, Grandma took us to the village center. We stood on the path near the village school and looked downhill toward the small river, where, when she was younger, our grandmother had washed clothes with the other women from the village. The village priest threw a wooden cross into the shallow, partially frozen river, and several men and boys dressed only in leggings, naked from the waist up, jumped into the water at the same time and poked around until one of the younger boys pulled the cross from the water. The priest called out, "Blessings upon you, Jovan! God bless you!" He patted the boy's shoulder, which was turning blue, sprinkled him with basil, and presented him with a small grayish-black radio-cassette player. "Grandma, how come

Grandpa didn't come to jump in after the cross? Or Uncle?" I asked, but, walking along behind us, she said, "Oh, they're not keen on such things." Grandpa only went to church on Saint Nicholas Day, and our uncle was a young Communist. It was Epiphany, and the Blessing of Water, a celebration of Saint John the Baptist's baptism of Jesus in the Jordan River, when God presented his beloved Son to the people while the Holy Spirit, in the form of a dove, flew above their heads. For years I asked myself, and once I asked Srebra: "Why in the form of a dove, and not some other bird?" Srebra said that monkeys loved to catch doves, and that is why the Holy Spirit appeared to them in the form of a dove. I didn't believe her. But really, why in the form of a dove? And was it because of the Holy Spirit that Uncle Boro, who lived on our street in Skopje, kept a dovecote filled with such beautiful white doves? The only dove we ever had, which our uncle in Montenegro gave us, suffocated in our Škoda just as we pulled up in front of our building. That was an emptiness nothing could fill, a dove that was impossible to replace, not even by one from Uncle Boro's dovecote. Was it the loss of my personal, private Holy Spirit? Two days before we were to go back to Skopje, our grandma said, "Your uncle is going with you. He'll stay in Skopje till the summer; he's taking a language course. Look after him. He's the only uncle you've got. Let him eat whatever you're eating. Give him whatever he wants, so his weenie doesn't fall off. He's a grown man, after all." Our grandfather yelled, "Come on, stop it, don't go prattling on, he's not a child." Our uncle spent so long in town saying goodbye to the girlfriend who was to become his wife that summer that he barely caught the bus we were on. Perhaps Grandma thought that if he weren't with her for half a year, he would forget her. Did they really sell a cow so our uncle could study a language that he was never going to need, or was it to distance him from this girlfriend, whom they did not want as their daughter-in-law? We arrived in Skopje. Our father was waiting for us with the car at the station. First we dropped Verče off; then we went to our apartment. Our uncle asked whether our mother had returned from the hospital. "No," answered our father. "They're letting her go Friday." Srebra and I said nothing. What awaited us at home was the little woodstove, its fire burned down, and a pot of beans our father had boiled. First Srebra and I ate with our uncle sitting perpendicular to us; then Dad ate by himself. Our uncle had to sleep in the big room, on the foldout couch by the door, in the room where our parents slept. Together, we somehow made up the bed. We'd have to wait for Mom to return from the hospital so she could empty a few things from the cupboard and give him space for his clothes. The next day, our uncle went to visit her. We did not. Dad said we shouldn't go to the hospital; a hospital is no place for children. When our mother got back two days later, she brought dolls made from felt: one pale yellow, the other orange. The dolls were long and attached to wooden sticks. Someone had been selling them in the hospital. They were not for Srebra and me; they were just to have around the apartment. We put one in our room on the shelf; the other sat in the big room on top of the old television. After our mother put on her blue robe, she lay down on the couch and silently looked at us seated in our chair. What concerned us most was whether she would laugh as she had before. Her laugh was the only thing that eased our anxieties about being unloved children. When our mother laughed, it gave Srebra and me confidence; we grew more sure of ourselves. In those moments we heard her laugh—and she laughed loudly, almost hysterically—Srebra and I felt close to each other, and carried our misfortune more easily. Our father almost never laughed; he only let out a sound that was supposed to resemble laughter, a sort-of laugh released as an exhale, as if he were clearing his throat, a laugh he had second thoughts about. As it turned out, for a whole month after her return from the hospital, where they had removed a cyst from her ovary, Mom didn't laugh in her usual fashion. It was not until she went to work again and was once again able to tell us who said what and who did what, in particular about "Comrade Director," that she was able to laugh as she had before. One evening, before going to bed, our uncle, wrapped in a heavy wool blanket and shivering, accidentally broke one of the globes on the lamp that hung in the big room. Afraid of what our father would say, he opened his drawer (the top one was his our mother had decided), took out his pants, and got himself ready in case our father should happen to kick him out of the house. My heart was beating like crazy because I loved him and was worried and afraid for him. Srebra loved him too, but she argued with him, calling him an idiot whenever we played a pinching game and he pinched us too hard. Our father did get very angry, but he controlled himself and didn't kick Uncle out, but that evening in front of the television, he muttered the same thing for hours: "As if people like that should study languages, the bastard; because of people like that the country will fall apart…" Our mother sobbed silently on the couch; Srebra and I watched the quiz show *Kviskoteka*, but both our minds fled to the big room, where, scrunched down under a quilt and thick wool blanket, our uncle's body trembled. What we loved most was when mother vacuumed and shooed Srebra, me, and our uncle into the hallway, where we sat until she was done. In the hallway, we played hopscotch on the brown carpet with its brightly colored lines. Srebra and I held each other tight under the arms and hopped each on one foot, while our uncle hopped on two. We laughed until our uncle turned completely red in the face, including all of his forehead, and then Srebra would toss at him: "You look like a monkey's ass." Something oppressed my spirit, though, something indefinite, but our uncle said, "And you look like a witch." In the evening, Mom boiled some noodles, and we grated the cheese that was brought from the village. When our uncle wasn't lying in bed, he sat in the dining room and watched television, silently, trying to be invisible. Mom always asked him if he wanted to eat, as if it were not quite clear, since, during the day, he ate in the student cafeteria, and for some reason all of us expected that he would never be hungry at home. I think we all secretly prayed that he would say no so there would be more for us. Also, Dad often yelled at him, like he did at us. Our uncle was nearly full grown, the only one in our family to finish university, and was now enrolled in a foreign-language course. He was a man on the verge of marriage, but our father treated him like a child. When our father insulted him because of some minor thing even Srebra felt sorry for him; I could hear her swallow the lump in her throat. I wished we had a caged lion on our balcony, so every time Dad screamed the cage would open and the lion would charge, frightening him. Those six months with our uncle in our home hardened Srebra and me. We became more decisive, more contrary. And our hope grew that one day our heads might be separated, because our uncle told us he had read in an English textbook that in London there were many talented doctors, who, many years ago, had separated two babies whose heads were joined. "I told you," Srebra threw at me. "I knew it." In Skopje, we didn't know any doctors like that, although every doctor and nurse we met in the clinic hallways—eye clinics for me, and ear, nose, and throat for Srebra—stopped and approached us. They asked our father what had happened, how we had been born with conjoined heads, whether it hindered our development, whether we had one brain or were our brains conjoined. Always the same sophomoric questions. Srebra and I, first one then the other, would silently twirl our father's car keys, while he answered the curious doctors and nurses: "Their brains are separate, but they share a vein; I don't know, I don't really understand it, but that's what they told us. This one has sinus problems, and that one doesn't see well. There is no one who can perform the operation. It is a very difficult operation." And then we would go into the office of either an eye doctor or an ear, nose, and throat specialist. Sometimes at home, Srebra and I played patient and ophthalmologist. We would stand a ways back from the wall calendar. I couldn't see the numbers and letters on the calendar, but Srebra could. We hadn't known how to tell our mother and father that I didn't see well, so we didn't—it was discovered during the first routine school checkup. Srebra often called me, "blind idiot," and in those moments, I was grateful to her. I thought Mom and Dad would ask why she was calling me blind, but they never asked, because all the ugly words spoken during a quarrel were understood merely as symbols, part of the war of words, not as expressions of reality. Later on, over the years, we would go to the eye doctor, and I would sit in the special chair for my examinations, and Srebra, attached, would sit in a normal chair, while the doctor with questionable personal hygiene would breathe in my face and fit glasses, often missing the opening for glasses between our joined spot and my ear, poking us with the glasses right where it hurt the most. Srebra, keeping her lips firmly pressed so as not to inhale the doctor's bad breath, covered first one eye with her palm then the other, silently guessing the letters and numbers on the chart. Then she would whisper them to me when I couldn't get them. The doctor appeared not to notice her whispering, or, perhaps because of it, he prescribed thicker and thicker lenses, which stuck out of the black frames, the cheapest ones possible, which my father selected. Every trip to the doctor was followed by complaints: "This is becoming intolerable. All we do is go to doctors' offices. Screw the two of you. You voracious beasts! You just know everything. You think you're just smarter than everyone. You've devoured me." Srebra wouldn't put up with it for long, saying, "Who else is there to take us to the doctor? You're our father." That would make him even angrier, and he would swear all over again. I felt terrible that we exhausted him with our ailments. I was embarrassed that he had to take us to the doctor's, take vacation days from work, get up at night to make tea when we were sick, rub skin cream on our behinds when Srebra and I, in a gust of cold wind, backed into the gas stove, and when he had to give Srebra nose drops every eight hours, which he usually gave to me as well, just in case. It was as if we were someone else's children hanging around the house, not knowing what to do in their world, with insufficient light for my eyes and insufficient heat on winter nights for Srebra's sinuses. Her nose ran in torrents. To wipe it, she needed two or three handkerchiefs a day, which our mother hand-washed and dried on the top of the gas stove before returning them to her. Only radiation of the sinuses would help—a ten-day treatment in the clinic by the Bit Pazar. But when they saw us, the clinic staff did not know what to do. They would have to cover my eyes with the red cloth, too. They bound our heads with one long cloth, wrapping it around twice, over my glasses. They pointed a red-hot lamp at Srebra's face. We had to close our eyes and stay like that for twenty minutes. But I peeked stealthily at the red lamp with one eye. My glasses were pressing on my nose and I quickly got bored with the red of the lamp, so I lifted the cloth a bit more, and, through the other eye, a view through the window unfolded. Outside, I saw the red city buses raising dust, and on the grass by the side of the road sat Albanian men with white felt caps on their heads and Albanian women wearing raincoats and headscarves, while children ran everywhere. Where does their desire come from to sit wherever there is grass on the slope by the road with its constant flow of traffic and spewing gas fumes? Did they feel like Americans or tourists in Central Park sprawled out under the trees with a sandwich or can of soda in their hands? The veiled women and old men with felt caps spread along the road breaking bread and nibbling onions. There was freedom in their sprawled figures that didn't apply to us. We sat on chairs without backs, side by side in a clinic by the Bit Pazar, in front of a red lamp, eye to eye with the glow. It would be lovely if we, too, could lie on the grass by the road, look at the sky, and eat sunflower seeds. I thought how pleasant it would be to sit on the grass with Roza, who would surely dream up all kinds of new games and funny sayings, or with Auntie Verka—how many interesting things would happen between her and the Albanians on the grass, how many arguments, but then again, maybe not, because Auntie Verka, unlike us Macedonians, liked Albanians and Roms and drunks and whores. She didn't like ordinary people, *provincials*, as she called them. That's why she picked a Rom as her lover, a guy named Riki—"The Gypsy," we all called him—who moved in with her, with his big belly and huge behind. They sang and drank together in the apartment. They fought or cried out in pleasure. It was never as loud in our building as those two years when Riki lived with Verka. During that period, Srebra and I did not dare go to her place, and she no longer sent us on little errands to the store. After the radiation treatment for Srebra's sinuses, we discovered when we got home that there was no power in any of the apartments, because Riki had cut it off. He was angry that no one ever said "Good morning" to him. Curses, howls, everyone shouting—he, Auntie Verka, all the apartment residents. Someone called the police. Two older policemen came into the building and grabbed him, and at the bottom steps they kicked him, beat him with their truncheons, and swore at him. Along with our dad, we barely got past them. Roza was sitting on the railing of the upper stairs, eyes wide. "This is a madhouse," she said as we went by her. "C'mon, let's go somewhere," she whispered, and we needed to get out of there so badly that, without saying anything to Dad, we sneaked past the gathered residents and ran outside. We headed automatically toward the store. Roza said she wanted to buy some snacks. As we left the store, we ran into Bogdan, who was going home to his small shed attached to the back of the store. "Hey, Bogdan, what are you up to?" Roza said, "You're never around; you don't hang out with us anymore." We stopped. Bogdan turned red, then got up his courage and said, "Well, I'm going home to pack." "Where are you going?" she asked. "I'm moving in with Auntie Stefka," he said. "How did that happen?" Roza asked. Srebra and I just stood there silently. Bogdan shrugged his shoulders, mumbled something, and then went into his house. We returned home, wondering about what he'd said. Bogdan was moving in with Auntie Stefka! Stefka was a single woman, like Auntie Verka, a decent person, quite young, our parents would say—though she seemed old to us, if still pretty, with long black hair that she wore in a bun—who lived in our building. There were also single women living in the building next door—twin sisters on one floor, and an older woman on another. It wasn't clear to us why each entryway had an apartment for an unmarried woman, sometimes even two women, *singles*, as we called them, because that's what we heard our parents call them. "My sister says Prime Minister Milka Planinc has decided that each entryway should have a single woman, and she gave them apartments so they, too, could have a life," Roza explained on the way home. "A woman who doesn't have a husband or doesn't want to get married can send an application to Planinc, and she gives her an apartment, and that's how she becomes a single," and that seemed logical because we'd heard that Auntie Verka's son had arranged for her to get the single woman apartment in our entryway. "But why was Bogdan going to live with one of these single women?" That was not clear to Srebra. "You know, my parents said something about how children can now adopt a mother for themselves," Roza recalled, adding, "older children, like Bogdan, whom no one wants to adopt." It seemed pretty weird to me that a child, even an older one, could pick out a mother for himself. Somewhere deep inside me a thought crept in—which mother would we select if we did not have a mother? "Grandma," was my internal reply, but Grandma was not a *single* woman, and among the singles we knew, we were only close to Auntie Verka, but she was a drunk, and thus not allowed to be adopted, and Riki was living with her. I knew there was a special home for children without parents, which is exactly what it was called: Home for Children without Parents. From time to time, our parents threatened to send Srebra and me there. They'd take us there and then we'd see, Lord only knows what, that that was a place for the likes of us. But no one ever mentioned that Bogdan should live in such a home, even though it was logical that a ten-year-old child, which was how old Bogdan was when he was left motherless, shouldn't live alone. But Bogdan had been living alone for three whole years since his mother died. He ate in the school cafeteria, wore clothes the store clerk gave him, and when he had to go to the doctor or some other official place, our classroom teacher went with him. It had seemed to all of us that Bogdan didn't want to leave his place. He spent hours there, solving crossword puzzles in *Brain Twisters*, to which he'd subscribed with the money that we had raised for him by collecting old paper. And now, suddenly, Bogdan was to move in with Stefka, the most entrancing, but also the saddest, single woman on the street, always in high heels with her hair in a bun that revealed a white face with large dark eyes. At home, we told our father straightaway. He didn't say anything. He went down to the garage to kill the day he had taken off work to take us to the doctor, but when Mom got home, we also told her, and she turned to our father and said, "I told you. Didn't they say on television that it had been decided? Each child whose mother and father died simply has to select a new mother and adopt her. Good Lord, save and protect us, instead of grown-ups adopting children, now children adopt parents. A new law in Belgrade, that's what they said, because there were many single women, and since the state pays for their apartments, they can at least look after a child." That afternoon, Auntie Dobrila came for coffee. She always came when she needed tweezers to pluck the three hairs that grew near her mouth; she had no tweezers at home, so she used ours, which had been bought at a fair. All us females sat in the kitchen, Srebra and me on our chair, Auntie Dobrila perpendicular to us, and our mother across the table, where no one ever sat when we were alone. That chair was for the dishcloth that Srebra and I used to wash our faces in the evening before we went to bed, using the last of the warm water from the kitchen boiler. On the table stood a yogurt container we used as a bucket for scraps; Srebra and I spun it around to read the label for the hundredth time while our mother shot us a look telling us not to. That used to happen sometimes when Auntie Zorica came to visit, too. One evening, we were looking for our mother to give her our key, and she was visiting Auntie Zorica who was seriously ill and who died a few days later from cancer. I wanted to go into the bedroom to see Auntie Zorica one more time, but Srebra was against it. The death of a neighbor was announced from the balcony of the deceased in the form of a loud cry and weeping, and soon the entryway bell would ring. And that's how we found out about Auntie Zorica. But now, sitting with Auntie Dobrila, the only conversation was about the singles in the neighborhood. Auntie Dobrila also confirmed that it was true; children without parents could adopt a mother—any single woman—and move in with her. "Now, how did that child come up with Stefka?" wondered my mother. But Auntie Dobrila wasn't surprised. "She's the youngest, the prettiest, the healthiest; she earns a good salary. The child will live better and better!" "Well, you never know, maybe she likes young children for...well...for those things..." commented our mother. "Anyway, that's who Bogdan chose; Mara from the Slavija market took him to the town hall, where all the singles from our neighborhood had been summoned, all except Verka, because she's a drunk and couldn't be selected, and Bogdan saw them all and liked Stefka the most, so he chose her. People were waiting all day; there were so many children and singles." Bogdan was lucky to have gotten a mother from our neighborhood. When they heard he was an excellent student, they took pity on him and said, "This child has a future," so Bogdan will move in with Auntie Stefka. "What won't they think of," said Mom. "Children adopting their own mothers. That didn't exist in our time; how could a child know how to adopt a mother?" "No, seriously, believe me, it's better for a child to adopt his mother, rather than have some pervert—excuse me—adopt him and turn him into an addict," Dobrila assured her. There was nothing bad to say about Stefka. A single woman, she had some education, having completed a commercial high-school course. She did not have parents. Their house, in a village in eastern Macedonia, had burned to the ground, and when she heard about it while living in the student dorm, something severed within her; she was beautiful, young, but sad, very sad, just work then home again. She didn't have friends, or a boyfriend, or anything. When her sister was still young, she had gone off to England, and that sister was all Stefka had left. Now at least Bogdan might heal her wounds a little. She would have someone to converse with. And she had money; she could take care of him. That's what Auntie Dobrila thought, and Srebra and I agreed with her. But we were still curious which other children would adopt which other singles: Who would adopt the sister-singles, twins but not Siamese like us? Who would adopt the single woman who lived in the yellow building, or the one in the prefab house on the road to school? "She's not that sort of single," said Auntie Dobrila. "No one is going to adopt her. She was left alone because her husband died a few years ago. The woman went out of her mind, and people say that on the bedroom wall there is a big splotch of blood. Who knows where it came from? Maybe she killed him and then went crazy when he appeared to her in a dream, but the police didn't pursue her; they just left her there like that, and now she barely walks, dragging herself along, not wearing underwear under her dress, and if you don't believe me, lift it up sometime, and you'll see." Really? Was that possible? I wondered, but Srebra started laughing hysterically, and her laughter shook my head. She laughed so hard she had to pee, and we ran to the bathroom. Auntie Dobrila went home, and our mother scolded us all evening, telling us we were crazy and that we didn't know how to appreciate what we had.

A couple of days later, Bogdan moved in with Auntie Stefka. Now we lived in the same building, almost neighbors. In the building next door, the twin single ladies were adopted by two Rom girls. They never went outside, and we never hung around with them—following the wishes of their "mothers," they still went to their old school. Every morning, all four of them took a bus to a different neighborhood where the school the girls attended was located. Then their mothers continued on to work, and in the afternoon, they all came home together. At the time, we had such an intolerant attitude toward Roms that we simply didn't want to be around them, not at school or outside in front of the building. "Gypsified" was the word grown-ups used when something was ugly, unclean, not how it should be, and we once heard our mother say on the phone to our aunt, "To tell you the truth, it would have been better if I had given birth to Gypsies rather than these two." When she heard her say that, Srebra began to sob, shaking me, but I scolded her, even though I couldn't look her in the eye: "What are you crying about? You know they don't love us." With something approaching envy we looked at the happy face of the single woman who lived in the building next to ours who had been adopted by a stout girl with mild developmental disorders. The girl wore glasses with thick black frames and walked with her feet pointing outward, limping with both legs. Her hands were fleshy, white like snow, and she always held her adopted mother's arm, and the single woman, with a smile in her eyes and on her lips, supported her new daughter. There was something heavy, solemn, almost tragic in her gait; her whole being displayed a sense of concern. And that is how it was for years, until the most tragic moment in her life and in the life of her new and only daughter.

Most important, however, is that in March of 1985 we went on a three-day excursion to Ohrid. On the bus, Bogdan sat behind us, solving crosswords. There were ten of us to a room at the children's resort. Srebra and I always had to share a bed, and the beds there were particularly narrow. On the first night, I dreamed that our mother was falling from the eighth floor of a building. The girls were sleeping. Srebra did not move when I opened my eyes in the horror of the night and the loneliness in my soul. At the moment in the dream that my mother fell, I felt I was also falling into an ever-greater emptiness, that I had broken something that could not be fixed; that my soul was broken. When I told Srebra the next day, she screamed at me in our reflection in the cupboard mirror: "Really, it seems like you want Mom to fall in real life. And then we'd have to figure out what to do." I could barely wait for the three days to pass to go home so I could tell Roza what I'd dreamed. Roza always understood other people's dreams: "That's odd," she said. "I also dreamed I fell from the eighth floor. But how can that be, when our building only has three floors? Forget it; it's all nonsense." I don't know why I've never been able to forget that dream. Not so much the dream, in fact, as the emptiness into which our mother fell, and I along with her (and, whether she wanted to or not, Srebra). It haunts me in my sweaty hands, in the beating of my heart, in the pain in my head. "My head hurts, too, because of you," Srebra would say angrily, because a reaction in one of us gave rise to the same in the other. If one of us laughed, the other laughed; if I was upset, so was Srebra; and when Srebra was hungry, I felt hungry as well. We did not know how to explain it any other way than the way our grandma put it: "Your blood mixes. That's why."

Roza suggested that we go to the movies, to a Bruce Lee film. We had never been to the movie theater before. We dressed nicely, begged our parents for money, and set off to the neighborhood theater, which was in an old building from before the earthquake that also housed the district registry department. There was nobody else there. The cashier covertly spit into her blouse to ward off the evil eye when she saw us, then called through the window, "They won't show the film. You're the only ones here!" We were terribly disappointed. I begged Srebra and Roza to at least go to the church, a two-minute walk from the theater. Srebra wanted nothing to do with it, but Roza agreed. "Why not?" she asked. "Maybe they'll give us a communion wafer." I hoped that as soon as I went in, all the anguish that had taken root after my dream about our mother's fall might disappear, that everything in my soul would be as it had been before, and all memory of the fall would vanish and never return. Whether the priest caught something in my look behind my glasses, I cannot say. It was clear that he recognized us from the few times we came to church with our mother and aunt. I smiled at him. He gave me a thin chain with a cross. He only had one, he said, and Srebra and I should take turns. Srebra immediately said she didn't need a cross, but Roza asked, "When will you have more? I'd like one, too." The priest smiled and said he'd surely have them by Ascension Day. On the way home, while

Roza walked in front of us deep in her own thoughts, Srebra whispered, "You think God created us and that's why you want the cross. I don't need one. I'm certain we're descended from monkeys." Roza turned and shouted, "C'mon! Don't you two know how to do anything but fight all the time?" I wore that chain around my neck day and night. I didn't take it off even when I bathed, huddled with Srebra in the beat-up old bathtub, or during radiation treatments for Srebra's sinuses. I wore it to school, even though we weren't supposed to wear religious symbols there. Even when we began wearing lighter clothing, I still wore my white turtleneck blouse that had ten buttons up the back so I could pull it up over my legs, and beneath the blouse, stuck to my skin, were my chain and cross. It was like a rope to save me from falling. I rescued myself with it when I felt something pulling me down toward an unclear abyss that I sensed almost physically—deep, dark, black.

One morning, we spent the first hour of the school day in front of the building, lined up in rows, listening to the director give a speech about the life and works of the national hero in honor of whom our school was named. There were many green-uniformed soldiers in the schoolyard standing around with their smooth faces and attractive eyes. The morning was very cold. It was the first of April, and we were celebrating our school's namesake. Srebra and I were wearing espadrilles—black with decorative yellowish buttons. Our toes were so cold we stamped our feet the whole time, but the cold spread upward, throughout our bodies. We shook like branches, and it was more obvious than with the other students, because our heads shook in unison as if someone gave them a shake every five seconds. Even if one of us tried to stop, the other's head would go on shaking. The director continued reading his speech. A soldier approached us from behind. His head touched our hair as he said, "Hold out a bit longer and I'll take you somewhere." Srebra and I were taken aback, but said nothing. Each of us sank into the cold and our own thoughts, which were definitely the same that day—thoughts of our mother, who, during the night, had felt sick again, just as she had throughout almost the whole year, and our father had taken her to the doctor yet again. That morning she hadn't gone to work, and our father told our uncle to stay at home with her in case something happened. The pain in our toes was like the pain in our chests—sharp, unbearable, devastating. Finally, the director stopped talking. Since it was a holiday, they let us go home early. The soldier behind us said, "Come on. Let's go someplace and drink something warm." I liked the soldiers a lot. They all seemed good-looking to me. They infused me with trust. They conveyed something protective. Perhaps I would have agreed to go with him, but Srebra dragged me along the path and said we were going home, our mother was sick. The soldier tried to persuade us that she would get better. He said we could go home soon, that he was alone and wanted female company to pass his two hours of free time, and we were extremely nice girls, despite our conjoined heads. "That's nothing," he said. "I've seen people with two bodies and one head. You at least have hope that one day you'll be separated, but for those with only one head and two bodies, there's no such hope." "He's lying," Srebra whispered to me while dragging me as hard as she could toward the road, and finally, we set off at a run, staggering left and right as if drunk, leaving the soldier alone by the school fence. Halfway home, we caught up with Roza, who was also hurrying home. "Do you know that last night, my sister Mara and I played the fortune-telling game? Mine came out the same as last summer." "Well, of course! How else should it come out if you did everything the same as the last time?" Srebra laughed. "No," said Roza. "This time I put the number *33* in the square so I'll get married when I turn thirty-three, and everything still came out the same." "Are you crazy?" Srebra shouted, and it wasn't clear to me either why Roza wanted to get married when she was so old. "Well, that was the age Jesus was when he was resurrected," she said. "I want us to be the same age on the most wonderful day in our lives." Good Lord. It didn't make sense that Roza would wait so long to get married, and more importantly, if her P would even wait that long. What if he wants to get married earlier? "I'll explain it to him," Roza said. "I'm going to Greece with my grandma and grandpa on April 15. Mara wants to come too. Grandma and Grandpa haven't been for almost forty years! They've been told they can go for one day, and we want to go with them. Mom and Dad don't want to let us. They say what's the point of going for just one day, but Mara wants to see where Grandma and Grandpa lived before. We've never been—we always just go to Katerini—and I want to call Panait; it's cheaper if you call from a village to a city within Greece." Srebra and I were, I think, jealous of Roza, because, at least for one day, she would go abroad, to another country, unknown to us, even though it was so close, a country with which we shared a border. We arrived home. Mom was lying in the big room, half asleep. Our uncle said, "It's a good thing you're here. I have three hundred things to do, and I can't sit here all day." When it came time for lunch, Mom got up, fried some chitlins with eggs—my favorite—and chopped up a bit of garlic for the dipping sauce. She was feeling better. That afternoon, our father said, "Come on. Let's go to the Hippodrome. Let's get some fresh air." It was the only time we ever went to the Hippodrome, our only family outing in the fresh air, unless you count the one trip we took to the city park in Skopje when our cousin Miki was at our house, and, to show that his aunt and uncle were good people, we all went to the park, where our parents bought him a candy apple on a stick, but nothing for us. While we walked around, I remember the feeling that washed over me: pride that we were walking in the park, even though everyone gave us a wide berth and talked about us, horror-stricken. But at the same time, it was unpleasant for me, the way it is when strangers pay too much attention, or when you think that someone does something because they have to, not because they want to. Still, in some way, that walk in the park, our one and only, was lovely. Before going to the Hippodrome, our mother put on a dress and nice shoes. She put on her gold necklace, too. We put on our espa- drilles and, after a ten-minute drive, arrived at the Hippodrome. We got out of the car. It was a beautiful April afternoon, and it was no longer cold on our legs. We stood for twenty minutes beside the car, not knowing what to say to one another. We were embarrassed that we were there, and sad, and soon wanted to end the outing, get back into the Škoda, and go back to the safety of our home where Dad would sit in front of the television set, Mom would sit on the couch in the kitchen with her embroidery, and Srebra and I would sit at our table by the window with the book about Heidi. The light there had a forty-watt bulb. On the table, some crumbs from our lunch scratched our elbows. The wall clock counted the time covertly, with regular silent beats. It was a white wall clock with the inscription "YU Auto Re- pairs" that had been presented to our mother at work on March 8, International Women's Day, after which the noisy old wooden clock disappeared under one of the beds in the "big" room, becoming a clock in suspended animation, entombed in an archive. On those April afternoons, we played with Roza every day somewhere inside the building, or we played pachisi on the steps (but then we'd also call Bogdan so the four of us could play), or dodgeball in the street out front, which Srebra and I would always lose, because we couldn't coordinate our running. Or we simply walked through the neighborhood, and the early spring breeze caressed our bones. It carried to us the scent of love, but we knew nothing of that. We thought, however, that Roza might know, because she was in love with Panait, and he with her. No one was in love with me or Srebra, and we were not courageous enough to fall in love. Srebra really liked Enis, a young Turk in our class, while I preferred his brother, Orhan, who was in Roza's class and occasionally came to our class during recess to sing the Croatian hit song "Oh, Marijana," accompanying himself on the guitar. Neither Enis nor Orhan paid any attention to us. We sat at our desk with the chairs pushed together, and then Bogdan would come sheepishly over to us, stopping in front of the desk to ask us the name of the composer of the ninth symphony, or something similar, but neither of us had any idea how to solve crosswords, and we'd just shrug our shoulders, looking sullen or sympathetic. But it was like Bogdan didn't notice. He circled around our desk, taking our pencils, comparing his eraser with ours. Now that he was living at Auntie Stefka's (that's what he called her even though she was his new mother), he had a proper set of school supplies, much better than ours—a pencil case with colored pencils, markers, a pencil, an eraser, a pencil sharpener—while we had only one small case with two pencils, two pens, one sharpener, and one eraser. "Look how stuck-up he's acting," Srebra said to me as we walked to school and saw him in front of us, alone, in clean pants, a nice jacket, his bag over his shoulder. I wanted to hurry and catch up with him, but Srebra pulled me back. She had no desire to walk with him. His presence always annoyed her, both when he had been poor and now that he was rich, and it was only because of Roza that she agreed to let him be part of our group when we played in front of the building. In our red orthopedic shoes with yellow-white plastic soles, me with the ugliest glasses in the world, the two of us in checkered skirts and long blouses fastened with belts around our waists, heads conjoined at the temples, surely we were a grotesque sight from which old women would shield their gaze, while children shouted, "retards" at us.

The day they took class photos in the courtyard, one class at a time, Srebra and I looked down when the shutter clicked. The atmosphere was light, playful, as if only the insects flying about had any weight. The cross on my chain sparkled in the sunlight. I touched it from time to time to see if it was still in place. As Srebra and I were walking home from school, a young Rom kid ran up to us and unexpectedly blocked the path, stretching his hand toward the chain, but without even thinking about it, Srebra and I pushed him away. He staggered, fell backward, then quickly stood and lunged again, but I had already hidden the chain under my blouse and was holding onto it with my hand. He had to give up, but still called us cunts, sluts, a two-headed dragon, scarecrows. He ran off toward the small houses in the Rom quarter, crammed off to the right side of our school. How we hated the Roms who lived there; how afraid we were of them. Now Srebra and I trembled as we hurried home. I was on the verge of tears, and Srebra was on the edge of a nervous breakdown. "They should build some sort of district, a camp, and gather all of them and put them there so we won't need to see them anymore!" Srebra said, but I didn't say anything, although at that moment, it seemed like a good solution. We were still in primary school! Where did we get such monstrous thoughts and wishes? Whose fault was it that we had those ideas in our conjoined heads? The school? Our family? Our upbringing? The state? Our own character? Grandma bought spindles and sieves from the Gypsies in the village, or she sold them bread and sheep's milk cheese. Our classmate Juliana—with shiny long black hair, beautiful complexion, and deformed legs; first alphabetically in the attendance book—had low grades but a good soul and a beautiful voice. She transfixed the whole class on every bus excursion with a Serbian song that began something like, "I wander the streets…," a song I've missed all my life. Juliana later became a member of a dance troupe, and saw the world many of our classmates never saw. The last time we saw her, at the fair in Skopje, she was selling blouses and skirts. We recognized her, but we didn't say anything, I don't know why. In her childhood, she had the most colorful orange-yellow-green fur coat. Another girl, Šenka, from the neighboring class, had lice more often than anyone else in the school. On Sundays, we went with Roza to school so we could watch Rom weddings from a distance, but more interesting still were the Rom circumcision rituals: a young boy perched on a horse cart decorated with red ribbons, scarves, and gold chains, seated on blankets of the most picturesque colors, and two horses slowly pulling the cart as young girls and boys sang, played, and danced around it in colorful clothing and jangly earrings, necklaces, and belts. The music drowned out the car horns; the father of the brave boy who had been circumcised walked alongside the cart with a bottle of beer, and every few seconds passed it to the child to drink. The boy was already woozy from the alcohol and surely from the pain between his legs as well, but everyone distracted him, entertained him, slapped him on the shoulder, on the ear, and he didn't pass out while the procession wound its long way through the streets. After a while, we'd go home, embarrassed and horrified by the thought that his weenie had been cut, but too ashamed to ask anyone why it was done or how. And that was the sum total of our relationship with "The Gypsies," unless we counted Auntie Verka's Riki, with whom we never spoke, or the young Rom girls who adopted the unmarried twins in the building next door as their mothers but with whom we never played, even though they dressed twice as nicely as we did and were twice as clean, certainly bathing more regularly than our once-a-week Sunday bath.

At the beginning of April 1985, Greece was mentioned often on television. Mom said, "Well, they're saying Aegean Macedonians will be able to enter Greece. It seems Papandreou will open the border, and they won't require visas. Just imagine how many people are going to go. Every living Aegean Macedonian will go, from as far away as Australia and America." "Roza's going too," said Srebra, "with her grandma and grandpa." "Oh, that's right, they're Aegean, so they will come from Germany and then head down to Greece. They probably still have a house there; maybe some land. People left all sorts of things behind when they fled." Neither Srebra nor I were clear on who fled, why, or from whom. At school our history teacher never explained it clearly. We only knew it was very significant, and the evening news didn't open with the war between Iraq and Iran but with the agreement signed by Greece and Yugoslavia to open the border for one day so that people who had been child-refugees could visit their homes. What's more, they wouldn't need visas, which they had purportedly been unable to get precisely because they had been child-refugees. We weren't sure how they could be child-refugees: Roza's grandparents were old. They were going to come from Germany and continue on to Greece with Roza and her sister. It's all Roza talked about. The afternoon her grandparents arrived in Skopje, Roza came to the front of our building and stopped resolutely in front of us. "Zlata," she said, "can I ask you to do something for me?" "Yes," I said, surprised by her tone. "Will you lend me your chain to wear in Greece? Just for a day. We're leaving tomorrow at five in the morning. In the evening, when we get back, I'll give it back to you." I looked at her, surprised. Srebra yawned. "This isn't like going on vacation. We're traveling with our grandparents, who haven't been there for almost forty years. I want to have something with us, something Macedonian," she added. I wasn't certain the chain the priest had given to me was Macedonian and not bought from the Bulgarian sellers of halvah, rose perfume, and pendants. Still, carried away by Roza's enthusiasm, I took it off and handed it to her, "Just until tomorrow," I told her, feeling its absence from around my neck. "Yes," said Roza, and turning, shouted, "Ciao!" and went inside.

The next day, before lunch, Srebra and I were working on our math homework at our table in the kitchen, while Mom, who had come home from work, was cooking some ham for our dinner, when suddenly, loud cries came from the stairwell. "That drunk again," Mom said, and we, too, thought Verka and Riki were fighting. But these cries weren't angry, but cries of pain, screams the likes of which we had up until then only heard in films. We heard doors open, then someone knocked sharply on our door, and Srebra and I jumped up, tripping over each other's legs as we ran to open it. In the hallway we saw the crazed faces of Auntie Dobrila and Auntie Mira, and from the floor below came loud groans. Our neighbors looked at us with ashen faces, and we, in shock, went to the railing that overlooked the floor below, and Auntie Magda, voice worn out from pain, moaned, "Aaaah, Roza." The moment we heard that, Srebra and I literally couldn't move. It was as if we had been turned to stone where we stood. Then our hearts began beating as hard as they could. I could hear the rapid beat of Srebra's, and she could hear mine, and at the spot where our heads were joined it was like the roar of an ocean, a pain so entirely unexpected, a pain such that one could not imagine that such pain existed. But what roared most of all were the words we heard. We stood pressed against the railing, horrified, mute, and it was only due to our conjoined heads that one of us didn't fall, keeling over the edge in madness, in the sharp sensation that sliced our bodies. Mom came and pulled us from the railing, then pushed us into the apartment, whispering as quietly as she could, "Come on, come on." Then she stepped out alone. Srebra and I stood in the hall, right where our mother left us, glued to the wall, opposite the small cabinet with the mirror, petrified, speechless, without making the slightest sound, only our hearts beating loudly, uneven as the lines of an erratic EKG. We caught sight of our faces in the mirror: eyes wide, ears alert, foreheads creased, lips partially open. Our faces were not children's faces, but the faces of old women. A person in pain is either the most beautiful or the ugliest on the planet. We were the ugliest. We heard a cacophony of voices. We recognized the voice of Uncle Kole, who was crying like a baby. Nearly everyone was crying and Srebra also began to cry, crying like she never had before. But I couldn't cry. The eyes behind my glasses were dry, drier than they had ever been in my life. Srebra was shaking me with her crying, but I held myself against the wall and stared in the mirror at myself, at Srebra, and again at myself, unconscious of what or whom I was looking at and whether I was looking at anything at all or whether everything was merely an illusion, a nightmare that would pass. But it did not pass. After a while, our parents came in, our uncle right behind them. No one said anything. "God forgive her…no, there's no need for forgiveness. She was a young girl," Mom said at last. "But how could she have died from lightning?" asked our uncle. And that's how we heard how Roza had died. We had been so frozen by the very thought that she had died, that she no longer existed, that we hadn't thought about the cause. "She was wearing a small chain. Her grandmother and grandfather were at the spot where their house once stood. Roza and Mara were running around in the fields when it suddenly began to pour, and the children ducked under a tree to hide. But then the lightning came and a bolt struck the cross, killing her on the spot. Mara just fell down, disoriented but not hurt, though she's in terrible shock." I think my mother said all this in one breath while taking the roasted ham hock from the oven. The scent of cooked meat emerged from the oven and wafted through the kitchen and dining room. Our uncle stood between the two rooms, our father behind him in the dining room, Srebra and I supporting ourselves by holding onto the kitchen sink. Our legs had been cut from beneath us. My head spun. I felt our common vein pulsating in my temple, but only into me, as if it had shifted from its channel and coursed into my head alone; with her right hand, Srebra kept me from falling and pulling her down on the couch along with me. "Give them some sugar water," our father said, and the next moment, we were sitting on the couch drinking sugar water from the same glass. "I gave the chain to Roza; I lent it to her; it was my cross, the one the priest gave me," I managed to get out. Mom said, "Fine, so you will carry that on your soul your entire life," quickly adding, "Come on, get up and eat, the ham will get cold." I didn't know if those who are suffering could eat, whether the body can even take in food when the soul is undergoing great torments. Can you reach for food when your conscience bores into your spirit? Can you eat lunch when you've lost someone you love, and the guilt is within you and no one else? Srebra and I dragged ourselves mechanically to our chair. On the table, the ham hock, almost blackened, stood in the small circular baking dish of gray aluminum. On the bottom, the fat had congealed into small black crumbs. We ate meat and bread on the day Roza died. I mechanically pulled off a small piece of meat. When I put it in my mouth with a bit of bread, I felt as if I were committing a sin—something inside me resisted. But the sin had already been committed; the meat was already traveling down my throat toward my stomach. Roza was dead, and we were eating meat. As if we were eating her flesh. That is the sensation I had, along with the memory of my grandmother once saying one shouldn't eat meat when someone dies. Srebra also put bits of food mechanically into her mouth. The meal lasted two or three minutes, but it seemed like the longest of my life. Srebra and I felt as one that we had to go see Auntie Verka. We went quietly up the stairs. Though there was no longer anyone in the hallway, we heard sobbing from Roza's apartment, interrupted by despairing cries of pain. We couldn't bring ourselves to go in, even though we had made a tentative motion toward the door. I felt that I had to go in and tell Roza's parents that I had killed her with my cross and chain, that had I not given it to her, she would be alive. But I lacked the strength, lacked the courage, and the tremendous pain in my chest suffocated me. We stood in front of the door for several seconds. Srebra seemed to be waiting for me to go in, but I suddenly turned and dragged her, stumbling, without knocking, into Auntie Verka's apartment. She was sitting by the table in the living room. Alone, she stared at a point on the wooden table. Riki wasn't home, but we didn't even notice. Auntie Verka raised her head. The bags under her eyes were dark and more sunken. We sat on one chair, each with a hip on the seat. She said, "Children, you know, Roza can come back. It happens sometimes with people who have died. The first and second days they're dead, but on the third they come back to life. The day after tomorrow, Roza will surely be alive. I'm not lying to you. There have been cases like that." I will never forget the feeling her words provoked in me. Never. I grasped at her words as if at a straw, a real, actual straw with which I would save Roza. Roza was always so decisive, so brave. If she did not appear now among the living, when she had to, then when? My soul was filled with hope I would never feel again. It made perfect sense that Roza would come back to life on the third day. Just like Jesus. Better for Roza to be resurrected like Jesus than to marry at the age he was resurrected, I thought. And while Srebra looked at Auntie Verka as if at a ghost, I looked at her in that moment with all the hope that existed in the world. We went back upstairs to our apartment. All night, Srebra and I lay on our backs looking at the ceiling. We fell asleep at dawn. When we awoke, our first class at school had already begun. But we didn't go to school. We went out on the balcony. There was hardly anyone outside. The warm April morning was unaware of the tragedy that shrouded our lives. Srebra and my conjoined heads seemed like only a minor misfortune. We were alive. But Roza was not and it was my fault. Suddenly, Srebra whispered, "Roza went by." I hadn't seen anything. Srebra whispered again: "She just went inside. I saw her. She came around the building, in red pants and a green tee shirt. Didn't you see her?" It didn't occur to me that she might be lying, making it up. But I was infinitely sad that I didn't see her, and kept looking. Auntie Verka had said Roza would come back to life on the third day, but it was now only the second day. Anything seemed both probable and improbable. I dragged Srebra down to the front of the building. We went to the slope in front of our garage, where we had played the fortune-telling game last summer. Roza was supposed to get married to Panait at twenty-one or thirty-three; they'd live in Salonika and have one child. Oh, the irony! The irony! Roza died at fourteen, in a village near Salonika, a child herself. We set off from in front of the garage to a spot under Roza's balcony. The balcony door was closed; everything was quiet. We stood on the slope, and children from the street slowly gathered. Bogdan came. He hadn't gone to school either. His eyes were red, puffy from crying. He stopped next to me. It was as if he wanted to reach out and touch my shoulder, but he stopped. We were standing on the drive when Nena said in a muffled voice, "According to the almanac, people born in August die at four, fourteen, or forty-four." I felt Srebra and I would also die at fourteen, in a year, because we, too, were born in August. But the small hope that Roza would come back to life smoldered within me. The residents of the apartments would go out onto their balconies, look around without saying a word, and then go back inside. Only Auntie Verka sat on her balcony, head resting on her hand, looking around absently, or perhaps at us, without calling out, as was her habit, without waving her hand. We children stood on the sloping drive, also without saying a word. We weren't silent for just a few minutes, but for a long time, until the arrival of the police car, which parked on the street corner. Two police officers emerged, one younger, thinner, tall, the other older, stouter, with white hair. They walked past us down the street, and before going into our building, they both took off their caps. At that moment, I knew Roza was dead, and that she wouldn't be coming back. I knew people took off their hats when someone died; my grandfather had told me. That's how one pays respect to the dead. The policemen vanished up the stairs. We stood on the sloped drive in front of the building all day. From time to time, the door to Roza's balcony opened, and some unknown people dressed in black stepped out. Toward evening, a black car pulled up. Two men took a white coffin out and carried it quickly inside. In the evening, our mother said that we were going to Roza's parents' apartment to convey our condolences. "I can't," said our uncle. He was packing. The next day, we were taking him back home to the village, because he no longer wished to study a foreign language, but wanted to go home and prepare to marry his girlfriend. Srebra and I wore pleated skirts of brown viscose and brown blouses. We didn't have black clothes, so brown ones were the most appropriate. We went to Roza's apartment. Her aunt and uncle stood in the dining room greeting everyone. First, we went into the small room. Roza's father and sister, Mara, sat on the bed crying, heads on their knees. "We've lost Roza, Daddy, we've lost Roza," Mara repeated. Her father cried uncontrollably, hunched over like a child, his face yellow as a lemon. Mara wept in fits. I wanted to stroke her head, but didn't have the strength. Srebra gently pulled me into the other room. It was packed with people, everyone weeping aloud. At the end of the room, nearly flush against the wall where the balcony was, on a table, stood Roza's white coffin. Inside, in a white wedding dress, lay Roza. Her face was covered with a veil. Her black curls poked out from under the veil. On her feet were white shoes with low heels. Her hands were lying on her chest—pale, limp, soft. She looked like a sleeping doll dressed in bridal clothes. Her toes pointed upward, and her white shoes cleaved the air with their luster. There are images that a person never forgets: if they were photographed, they wouldn't be as real, as true, as they are embedded in our consciousness. Roza, dead, in a wedding gown, in a midsized white coffin—neither for children nor for grown-ups—in the big room with two foldout couches and furnished with a wall shelf unit similar to ours. Motionless, Srebra and I stood in front of her body. Why didn't we bend down to kiss her? Why didn't our mother push us toward the edge of the coffin to stroke her veil? In that moment of such intense sorrow, did our conjoined heads shatter the moment with their grotesqueness? Did they lessen the pain? I don't know, but we said our farewells to Roza without a kiss. But my longing to kiss her, or at least touch her, broke my heart forever. We pushed our way out to the balcony, and stood looking down at the sloping drive. We re-entered the room. We went up to Roza's mother, who was held by two women to keep her from collapsing onto Roza's body. I don't know if she recognized us. I wanted to tell her that the chain was mine, that I had killed Roza. I wanted to beg her forgiveness, to offer her my life, to let her kill me, beat me, spit on me. But I had no voice. Nothing came out of my mouth, not a sound. Srebra said nothing. We left and stood for a long time outside in the night, looking up to Roza's balcony. Early next morning, at four o'clock, our mother shook us awake, whispering, "Get up, get up, come on, we're going." We left the apartment silently. Our steps were as quiet as if we were tiptoeing barefoot down the stairs. Our uncle carried the bags; our mother closed the door, and crossed herself. We got in the car and set off for the village. We were fleeing Roza's funeral. For the three days we spent in the village, Srebra and I hung out in a room with iron beds, reciting from memory "Eyes," Aco Šopov's poem about the death of a female partisan, our homework assignment for Macedonian class. "Three days we carried you huddled up…" The blood in our temples pounded, and I couldn't imagine the poet's partisan. Instead, I saw Roza lying on a stretcher, my chain around her neck hanging over her right shoulder. The small cross swung back and forth, striking the stretcher with a barely audible thud. "Auntie Verka lied to us," said Srebra. When we returned to Skopje, our mother brought us the evening newspaper. Inside was an obituary for Roza signed by her mother, father, and sister, alongside a small pale photograph. Our entryway was quiet. The residents moved almost silently. Not a sound came from Roza's apartment. When Srebra and I came home from school, we hesitated on the stairs, but we didn't have the courage to knock on her door. Every night I struggled with my conscience. I was certain that the next day, I would tell Roza's parents I was guilty. But during the day, Srebra would unravel my nighttime resolve. "I don't know how wise it is to tell them," she said. She didn't know, however, why it would be unwise to tell them. We didn't go to Auntie Verka's anymore, although she once called to us from her balcony, "Come, let me give you charms to protect you from evil." We didn't go. Deep inside, we were angry that she had lied to us about Roza coming back to life. One day after school, I made Srebra turn toward the church. A powerful force dragged me there; I had to go in to find the priest who had given me the cross. We didn't have enough money for a single candle. The priest was walking through the courtyard. He stopped when he saw us. He remembered us immediately. No one who had seen us once in their lives failed to remember us, and perhaps we even appeared to many of them in their dreams, in nightmares along with other strange beings that only vaguely resembled people. The priest stopped, blessed us, and asked, "Why are you dropping by church now, after school, where they teach you that God doesn't exist?" He laughed, pleased with his joke, then added, "Bravo, bravo! This is how it should be; you should come to church." "Father," I said with the last of my strength while Srebra shook her head, shaking mine along with it, "that chain with the cross you gave me—I lent it to Roza, the girl that was with us, and she was struck by lightning that hit the chain. She died." The priest was alarmed. He had heard about the accident, but didn't know that the chain that killed Roza was from here, from his church. He stared at me and Srebra so rudely, his mouth wide open, his belly big beneath his frock, gasping deeply. "God keep and protect her," he whispered, frozen, powerless, flushed. After a while, he collected himself, and with a quick gait, he nearly leaped up the church's stairs. He disappeared inside while we stood in the courtyard and waited for him; he soon reappeared, and from under his frock he took out a miniature wooden icon, handed it to me, and said, "Here. This is an icon of Zlata Meglenska, so she can pray for you, so you do not carry your friend on your soul. What you are given in church is not to be passed on to someone else. The Devil drove you to lend her the chain. But this icon, don't give it to anyone, not for your life. Through it alone will you be delivered from the sin that lies on your soul." I grasped from what he said that I really was guilty of Roza's death. I took the icon, and Srebra and I looked at it, seeing for the first time what Saint Zlata Meglenska, for whom our godfather had named me, looked like. A strange-looking saint, with a long kerchief on her head, neither tied under her chin the way our grandmother wore it, nor wound and tied at the forehead, the way other women in the village did. A kerchief-veil as if from a folk costume. She also wore traditional clothes, with embroidery on the sleeves, around the collar, and on the blouse under her dress. Her right hand held a cross, nearly identical to the one I'd had. I tucked her in my pocket, and with rapid steps, Srebra and I set off. "At least she's pretty," said Srebra. "Who knows what Srebra Apostolova, whom our godfather apparently liked so much, looked like?"

From that day on, I kept the icon with me always. I only wore clothes with pockets, leaving all the rest to Srebra. At night, I put it under my pillow, and was disappointed that I couldn't sleep on my side at least once to press my cheek to it and be merged with my protectress. I felt it would bring me closer to Roza. I still could not believe that Roza was truly dead. Unable to accept the truth, and therefore unable truly to mourn for her, I couldn't shed tears. One morning, Srebra woke with a cry—I opened my eyes at the instant her head jerked mine upward and then downward toward our toes. Her two big toes were swollen, yellowish green, with pus oozing from under the nails. I immediately looked at my own, but there was nothing amiss. Srebra shouted while wiping at the pus, which flowed like blood, with the sheet. I had never seen anything like it. It was dreadful and Srebra's pain unbearable. Mom and Dad were already up, getting ready for work. They came into the room and saw Srebra's toes. Our mother said to our father, "Go and tell Goran that you're not going to work. Tell them you have to go to the doctor." Dad left and returned ten minutes later. He was boiling with anger. "This is unendurable. We go from one doctor to another." Mom put on her shoes and left. Dad rubbed Srebra's feet with rakija and tied them with a bandage, and after we got dressed, only I put shoes on, then we went down the stairs, Srebra walking barefoot on her heels. Dad brought the car right up to the door and somehow stuffed Srebra inside, while I, dragged along, plopped onto the seat beside her. When we got to the hospital, I gripped Srebra around the waist while Dad supported her on the other side until we got inside. The patients looked at us with mouths agape. People stood up from the benches in the corridor so Srebra and I could sit down. One woman said, without thinking, "Just when you thought you had seen everything…" Our father returned a short time later with an orderly, a gurney, and the doctor, who gaped in surprise when he saw us. The cot was too narrow for both of us to lie on, so we sat while the orderly pushed us to the operating room. There, they pulled over a small cabinet that was the same height as the bed, stretched Srebra's legs onto it, gave her a local anesthetic, and pulled out her toenails, which evidently had abscessed cuticles. Srebra automatically turned her head to the wall, and the two of us saw a poster that read, "Tito gives blood. Give blood, too." Below which was written the date: January 3, 1980. We stared at that poster, which apparently had hung on the wall of the operating room a full five years. Srebra moaned the whole time, even though the doctor told her to quit faking—it couldn't hurt with such a powerful anesthetic. After a while, he said, "All done. You can go." Dad supported Srebra, grasping her around the waist as firmly as he could, nearly carrying her while I attempted to keep up and prevent our heads from hurting at the spot where we were joined. An older woman opened the door for us. Somehow, we got ourselves into the car, and off we went. We went to the brewery so Dad could buy himself a crate of beer. Then we picked Mom up from work and drove home. She hurried ahead to unlock the door of the apartment, and our father, breathless and worn out, supported Srebra while I bobbed up and down next to her; several times our legs nearly tangled, and we would have fallen had I not been holding firmly to the banister Roza had slid down so many times. Dad cursed, "Screw you all." Waiting for us at home was the first postcard we ever received, addressed to Srebra and me from our uncle, who was on a trip to Ohrid. For days on end we lay on the couch in the big room where our uncle had slept. Our mother was sick again, and she lay on the other couch, dressed in her robe, moaning. Srebra moaned as well. We barely said a word for hours. I read Lawrence's *Sons and Lovers*. Then *Nana* by Zola. And *American Tragedy* by Dreiser. It seemed to me that I understood everything, but nothing was clear. Srebra read *Das Kapital*. My novels and her *Kapital* knocked against each other. Occasionally, our pages overlapped. We slipped pages we didn't want to read under the pages of whatever the other was reading, then glanced at sections of each other's books. Mom stopped moaning, took a thick book with a red cover from a drawer in the side cupboard, and gave it to us. "Read this," she said. It was a book written in Serbian, *A Book for Every Woman*—a housewife's handbook. The book was full of all sorts of information. Srebra and I read it silently together; she read one page while I read the other. I thought about how, when I was grown and had a family, I, too, would divide the family budget into several blue envelopes as the author suggested, and on each would write what the funds were for, and that's how I would take care of the money in my family. When our father returned from work, we'd all get up and go into the kitchen. Our mother would quickly fry something— liver with eggs, tomatoes with eggs, or spicy red sausages with eggs. Srebra walked by rocking back on her heels, as I walked slowly beside her. We ate at our table in the kitchen then returned to bed before our parents ate. In the evening, our father turned on the television, which was draped with a lace doily and sat in an opening of the wall unit. We watched the news, short advertisements developed by the Economic Propaganda Program, the cartoon *Teddy Floppy Ear*, boxing matches with Mate Parlov or Ace Rusevski, or soccer games, and then it was time for bed. Srebra and I would go to our room, to our shared bed, Srebra on her heels while I walked quietly beside her. I wanted my footsteps to be as silent as possible, so they couldn't be heard and I could hear how a person's steps echo when she walks alone. But Srebra walked on her heels, so her footsteps thudded dully on the floor.

Soon we were on school break, and Srebra had new nails, wavy and curved like talons. We wandered through the neighborhood for days. Without Roza, everything was empty and pointless. The shed where Bogdan used to live before he adopted Auntie Stefka had been knocked down, and a merry-go-round had been brought in from Luna Park and put on the empty lot. Two large speakers at the base of the merry-go-round blasted music until midnight. Over and over again the music of the Bosnian folk singer Šemsa Suljaković played. Srebra and I couldn't ride the merry-go-round; there was no place wide enough for the two of us to sit. Watching the others spin, the voice of the singer penetrated our bodies with longing, a vague desire, but there was nothing for us to desire. Bogdan came over. He stood with us and silently watched the merry-go-round, which he, too, never rode, and from time to time he said, "Now Roza's gone." Srebra couldn't stand it. She felt he was making himself important, as if he had been Roza's best friend and wanted to tell us that we had forgotten her while he hadn't. I wanted to talk about Roza, but the words always came up against an unbreachable dam in my throat. Whenever anyone mentioned her, I stuck my hand in my pocket and squeezed the small icon, my hand sweating and oily from the wood. If we saw Roza's sister, we hid so she wouldn't see us, and when we left the building, we first listened through our front door to determine whether anyone was on the stairs, perhaps Roza's mother or father—to whom we had no idea what to say if we were to run into them. At the time, it seemed like Srebra felt the way I did, but perhaps I alone fled from confronting Roza's family, and Srebra wasn't thinking about it at all. We no longer walked along the main road that summer, writing down license plate numbers. We were already getting big, but if Roza had been alive, we still would have done it, because when we were with her, we felt young enough for that sort of silliness. We puttered around the apartment or outside, around the buildings, and one day, we nearly ran into a young guy on the stairs carrying over his shoulder a big bag filled with shoes. We realized right away that the shoes belonged to the people who lived in the apartments in our entryway who always left them in front of their doors day and night. We blocked his way and shouted, "Thief! Thief! Help!" Mičo immediately ran out of his apartment, and when he saw us holding the stranger, biting him, scratching him, he grabbed the bag and threw it to the floor. Soon everybody came running out of their apartments, except for Roza's parents. "I need to pay for my girlfriend's abortion," the thief defended himself, crying like a small child. "Let me go, please, I don't know where to find the abortion money." I knew what the word meant, but I didn't know that boyfriends paid for their girlfriends' abortions. After a while, the residents let him go. Everyone took their shoes and went home, but the young man, tearful and frightened, slunk up to us and hissed, "That's why your heads are stuck together." I had no idea why he would say that, but that night, I slept badly again. Instead of putting the icon of Zlata Meglenska under my pillow, I pressed it with my hands to my belly. "At least now he'll have a child," a voice whispered to me, but it was my own voice, no one else's. Srebra was snoring in her sleep while I squeezed the icon, exhausted. The next Saturday, our father took us to a village near Skopje so he could fix some woman's window. We hung around in a yard that bordered a muddy stream. Butterflies flitted about; the scent of the flowers was intoxicating; one could sense a happiness in the atmosphere. We were too big to play, but too small to sit and make conversation. That's what we thought, anyway. When it was time for lunch, the woman came out onto the balcony and called for us to come up. She brought out a baked bean casserole and fried fish. We ate lunch with our father and the woman, who had a sunken face. She said that the window was working properly and our father was a real master. The beans were the tastiest in the world. And what a wonderful combination: beans with the fried fish, which we only ate at home with fried potatoes, never with bean casserole. Our father smiled somewhat charmingly, almost with embarrassment. That was the first time we ate with him at the same table, with the unknown woman who was no relation of ours but had prepared a family-style meal for us.

That summer, a very lovely family moved into our building: two three-year-old blond boys, Zoki and Sašo, and their blond, long-legged mother, who stood at the ground-floor window for days on end, most likely not waiting for their father—a young, smiling, somewhat shy man, a policeman by profession, who had a mirror on the inside door of his garage—but for Nenad, a hefty young man with a full dark red moustache, black eyes, and curly hair, who wore baggy sweatpants, was younger than she was, and lived in the neighboring building, and had immediately set his eye on her...and she on him. That lovely family soon fell apart dreadfully: she took the children one night and ran away with them and Nenad to some unknown destination. Her husband killed himself with his service pistol. I was stunned by the events, but Srebra just kept repeating, "I knew it." I couldn't figure out the world of grown-ups; I couldn't figure out the world of our parents or other families. The single women who adopted Bogdan, the girl with delayed development, the two Rom girls, seemed happy, and their new children even more so. Bogdan always smelled of baby soap, and we envied him that smell, because we always smelled unwashed, a smell whose meaning we discovered years later, by chance, on a walk over the stone bridge, where homeless people gathered. They never bathed, except in the Vardar River in the summer. Srebra and I had to wash our faces in the kitchen if there was warm water left in the small boiler after our mother had washed the dishes. We bathed only on Saturday or Sunday evening. After the water heater was turned on, our mother carefully monitored it, checking the water several times while barking at us, "OK, go get your clothes." Our father would shout, "Hold on, wait a sec, it's not hot yet," but she'd just go on saying, "It is so. It's full of hot water!" Srebra and I, huddled in the tub, washed ourselves with a barely flowing stream of water, always surprised anew by our naked bodies, the ampleness of our breasts, which had grown to dimensions we would never have dreamed of when we were younger. Each of us rinsed herself, passing the shower hose back and forth every ten seconds. Soon there'd be a knock at the door: "Come on! What are you doing? Have you drowned?" Mom would shout. If we wanted to wash during the week, we turned on the small boiler in the kitchen to heat the water, then placed the water in the white five-liter tub and carried it to the bathroom, where we let it cool in an old beat-up green pot. We hopped into the tub and took turns pouring water over ourselves with the small yogurt container. Then we'd shiver in small frayed towels, because we didn't have bathrobes. Our mother had an orange bathrobe she never wore from her trousseau; she kept it in a bag with a bathing suit that Srebra and I secretly tried on when our parents were at work. We'd dress quickly, as quickly as we could, pulling our clothes up over our legs, and then, soothed by the smell of some generic soap or other, we'd go out on the balcony to dry our hair. In front of the building, residents from the apartments would be washing or drying their carpets. The heat was typical in Skopje. That year, for our vacation, we went to the town of Pretor, on Lake Prespa. The day before we left, Mom sent us to the store to buy peanuts and sunflower seeds for the road. In the store, we could only find peanuts, so we bought a small bag of salted peanuts and went to another store to look for sunflower seeds. We left the peanuts at the entrance, by the window, so as not to go in with something we had bought elsewhere. While we were paying for the sunflower seeds, we saw a neighborhood drunk take the bag, quickly open it, and start shaking the peanuts into his mouth. We were so flustered that we couldn't say a word. Trembling with anger, we started after him, but he just chomped the last peanuts in his mouth. If Roza were with us, I thought, she surely would have yelled at him, and we would've found the courage to confront him. We saw Bogdan across the street. He waved at us. I waved back. The next day, we left for Pretor. One day, a group of brigadiers in blue uniforms, gold scarves around their necks, came into the camp where we were staying, and a blond boy, Ismet, three or four years older than us, appeared in front of our beach bungalow. He said he was from Kagne in Bosnia. Anyway, that's what we thought he said, and for years, we looked for a place called Kagne on the map of Bosnia and Herzegovina at the back of our *Geographic Atlas* where there were maps of the former Yugoslav republics, with Montenegro last. We became obsessed with the town Kagne, especially later, during the war in Bosnia, when we were constantly upset by the thought that Ismet might have been killed. He was our joint crush; we didn't let him kiss us, but he was the first boy who'd ever wanted to touch us, the boy in front of whom, even with our conjoined heads, Srebra and I wanted to be beautiful, though we didn't know whether we were, dressed in brown tank tops under which our prematurely developed breasts were evident, and skirts with elastic waistbands and two palm trees and flounces that our mom had sewn from the bits of fabric our future aunt gave us from her parents' store. Ismet said he liked both of us and wanted to come into our bungalow, but we got scared and didn't let him. We waved to each other a lot. Srebra and I waved from the beach, where we lay on a military tent fly that our father had attached to a beach chair (which shone in the scorching heat with what seemed to be glistening beads of oil), and Ismet from the bus that was taking him home. The children of our family friends, who were also our friends, drank chocolate milk from Tetra Pak containers, but we were poorer than they were. We teased them, saying they were spoiled little mama's boys. Even though we understood chocolate milk was a luxury we couldn't allow ourselves, we envied them anyway and were certain that their parents Viki and Jovan loved Jovče and Drakče more than our parents loved us. But all those small displeasures were nothing compared with the event that marked our summer vacation in Pretor: bumping by chance into our uncle, our father's brother. They hadn't seen each other since the day our mother and father left his family's home with us infants, driven out by the grandma and grandpa we had never seen. When our uncle saw his brother, he grew pale and green, and didn't utter a word. Our father also said nothing. Our uncle and his wife disappeared into their camper, pulling a young girl who was evidently their daughter. The next day, there was no sign of them, although a trace of them remained with us, particularly with our father. Who knows what pain he felt, what fury? He didn't say anything about it. Nobody said anything about it. Ever. Was he able to sleep that night? What was he thinking while lying on his bunk in our bungalow? Mom was in the bunk below him and she moaned all night, but Srebra and I lay in the big bed, trying not to let it squeak and reveal that we were awake, while, for the thousandth time, we pictured the faces of our would-have-been uncle, our would-have-been aunt, and our would-have-been cousin. We would never know that side of our father. What had come between us to keep us forever estranged from him? We felt uncomfortable that we were living at the same time, that we were contemporaries with our own father. With our mother, we at least argued. We acted as if nothing had happened. Other than that incident, the most important event, like on every vacation, was the purchase of toy trucks for our little cousins. We stood for a long time every evening in front of the stalls where tourists gathered, while Mom picked something out: toy trucks for her nephews, and for Grandma, a souvenir thermometer or decorative plate with a motif of the place where we were vacationing. No toys or souvenirs were bought for us. When we got home from vacation, we saw that the fish in the aquarium we bought just before going on vacation had died. Our uncle, Aunt Ivanka's husband, was supposed to feed them. Mom also discovered that, in the cupboard where we kept the bedding, the small envelope under the afghan with their engagement rings was gone, and two rakija glasses made of thin green crystal with gold engraving were missing from the china cabinet. She and our father cursed our uncle all day. Finally, our father took the aquarium with the dead fish into the bathroom. We heard the toilet flush and then the apartment door opening. Later, we'd see the empty aquarium collecting dust on a garage shelf. Mom hand-washed all the clothes we had taken with us to Pretor, and when they dried, she packed them into several bags and suitcases, and we set off for our grandparent's house in the village. Our uncle was supposed to get married at the end of August. Grandma who'd said she wanted to give her son a wedding in a *kotel*—Srebra and I laughed and corrected her: *hotel*—now expressed no such desire. She and Grandpa didn't have any money. They'd spent it all on the foreign-language course our uncle took, and no one knew whether he had actually learned any English during those months. The wedding had to be held at home, upstairs and out in the courtyard. Srebra and I weren't included in the wedding preparations. Our mother and Grandma chased us out of the house so they could bake dinner rolls, make Russian salad, and prepare steamed cookies. Srebra and I wandered around the village and ran around on the threshing floor, bumping into each other, recalling two summers prior, in our childhood, when, on this same threshing floor, we had played with a beat-up, blue-colored brass plate while Grandma and Grandpa threshed. Our family's mule, Gjurče, was now old and worn out. The heat, the sharp hay, the two of us playing with that brass plate under the apple tree made us feel happy and safe, although, at the time, it was still not yet clear to us why we were the only ones with conjoined heads. We tried to play the game again, but it no longer held our interest. I recall my feeling of sadness, nostalgia, and a certain sorrowful pang that I'd grown up, that I'd outgrown the game. I felt a vacant place in my soul. Srebra said, "This is so stupid, as if I'd play with plates. I'm not a little kid." That same feeling had flooded over me the previous year in Skopje, the last summer of Roza's life, when, as in previous summers, we pretended to make winter preserves. Our parents were making preserves outside. Roza carried a platter of coffee to the grown-ups. It was the first coffee she'd made in her life. Everyone complimented her on how good it was. We waited for her to serve everyone so that we could play together, but as soon as we set up the dishes and pots for our preserve-making game, Roza suddenly stood and said, "I don't want to. I'm too big for such games." And I was flooded with emptiness and sadness, as if I had lost something valuable that would never return. That is how it was that summer in the village. Every game Srebra and I had once played together, whether we'd wanted to or not, was now distant, lost in time. In those moments of melancholy— though we hadn't known the word then—something pulled us again and again to the house of a distant relative, our mother's cousin, whom almost no one went to see, because he had a child, two years old already, who, people said, was retarded, adding: "God save and protect us. God forbid this from happening to us." His wife was a tall woman from the next village with big green eyes and red cheeks—a very warmhearted woman. Although she was young, she acted more like a grown-up aunt, giving us money whenever she saw us. Srebra and I had been feeling guilty since the boy was born, and we happened to be in the village and were the first to go visit him. "Don't stand behind the baby's head," the wife said to us when we saw the baby for the first time. But we did, and soon the child fell ill and became retarded. Srebra and I secretly blamed ourselves, because if you stand behind a baby rather than facing him, he rolls his eyes to see who's there, and it scrambles his brain. For years, we cursed ourselves, thinking the baby's mind had been affected by our behavior, until one day, years later, he died at the Bardovci Psychiatric Hospital. Our mother's cousin came to our apartment in Skopje then, chilled to the bone, and he sat on the chair in the dining room closest to the television, watching a program about the Slovenian Communist Edvard Kardelj. Srebra and I sat on the small couch in the kitchen, ears pricked, listening to him talk to our father. He spent the night at our place, and the next day went to see his dead son for the last time. How did he feel? How could he talk about politics with our father, about work in the paper plant, about the town wiping out horticulture in the village? His son had died, paralyzed, with a diagnosis we never learned. And he never visited the grave. His wife didn't even know where the grave was. They erased the child from their lives, and gave birth to other children, but did they forget him? He had a big head that fell to his shoulders and immobile arms and legs that were soft, as if they had no bones. And all of it was, apparently, due to a shot of penicillin. Srebra and I loved the child. Still, when we were in the village and had visited him we sometimes cried out in our sleep, and our mother or father woke us and scolded us, saying because he was disturbed, we were getting disturbed as well, and our heads were already messed up without that. The day we learned the boy had died, Mom told us, "Little Igor has gone," and in her voice we heard relief. Was erasing the stigma more important than the life of the child? It was. But when he was alive, Igor was a part of our village life: we had conjoined heads and he, a big floppy one that fell every which way like a rag doll's. His mother went from house to house with a woven basket, asking for eggshells. Everyone saved them for her, and she ground them with a bottle on the table-top, as if rolling out cookie dough, and gave little Igor ground eggshells mixed with milk by the teaspoon, because she had heard that it could help children like him. She once gave us a spoonful mixed in cornelian cherry juice, saying that our heads could surely be separated if we ate eggshells. Our heads didn't separate, nor did Igor survive. Yet life continued. When we went with our grandmother for a visit and a coffee with her oldest sister, Mirka, who lived in the upper part of the same village, Granny Mirka told us not to look into the well—"the devil's down there and he'll call you down to him"—but we looked anyway. Staring down into the well was sort of like a primitive black-and-white television, but when I told that to Srebra, she said the small television we had bought in Skopje for May Day, so we could watch Eurovision, was much better. During the summer, we didn't bring it with us; Dad said there wasn't anything interesting on. But we were bored. The children in the village didn't want to play with the "weirdo girls from Skopje." We could just barely hold on until our uncle's wedding, after which we would return to Skopje. When our parents were with us in the vil-lage, Grandma didn't have much time for us. Once she'd fin-ished all her chores in the evening, it was too late for us to sit for hours in her lap and cuddle. During the day, we knocked around the village or strung tobacco, or, from time to time, went to Granny Mirka's. She was nearly blind and was terri-bly attached to her daughters, especially Aunt Vaca, who lived in Skopje and sold needlepoint kits and tee shirts at fairs throughout Macedonia and Serbia. All the children in the whole extended family wore tee shirts with characters from the TV series *Calimero* that Aunt Vaca had given us when she saw us at a fair; our mother even sent us to the fair saying, "Go on, Aunt Vaca's there; she'll give you a shirt." Aunt Vaca even made shirts with extra large openings that we could slip up over our bodies: red for me, white for Srebra. For years her husband quietly and humbly sold her tee shirts and needlepoint kits at markets and fairs, his wife's excessive attachment to her mother filling his soul with bile. She spent the winter with them in Skopje, and sometimes stayed all spring, in the summer taking her daughter back to the village with her so she wouldn't be alone. One day, the son-in-law took off, moving into their summer place in Bistra. He left everything behind and never returned to Skopje. At a wedding, Mirka screamed at our grandmother, "Why did you bring the children? So people can make fun of them?" Srebra and I wore yellow dresses with red dots and large zippers up the back. Our grandmother wasn't ashamed of us. But when Mirka went half-blind, she wasn't ashamed of us anymore either. On the contrary, she was happy when we visited her, and gave us the dark purple plums or white cherries that hung in clusters from the tree in her yard. Little by little, Srebra and I got up our courage, and even walked into town, to our aunt Milka's or to one of our other relatives'. As if we didn't care if someone laughed at us. We found it most interesting at Granny Vera's—yet another of Grandma's sisters—who lived near the arched bridge where the town suicides took place. She had a son who was a barber, the biggest drunk in town, which was just something noted by everyone who mentioned him, but no one ever did anything to get him sober. His wife, Elica, with her long black hair—quiet, calm, like a princess in a story—wore her bathrobe and joked around when we went to visit them. The barber was never at home. They had a daughter, our age. Just a few years later she would be raped by someone in the center of town as she was coming home at night from a birthday party, and then she got married in another town. One day she got fed up with her long curly hair and wanted to cut it, but her father-in-law and mother-in-law (who stood in the hallway door every morning to watch their daughter-in-law brush her hair) jumped in and told her it was only on account of her hair that they had accepted her as their daughter-in-law. Several months later, she visited her parents and grandmother. She took barber's shears from her father's drawer and cut her hair as short as possible. A few steps and she was on the bridge, and then she threw herself off. "Well, perhaps it was for the best," wagged several evil tongues in town. "How could she have had a family if she spent her whole life thinking about the night she was raped? A young girl shouldn't walk alone at night. It happened because her father drank and her mother, well, she never seemed to notice anything."

Srebra and I stayed only a short time at Granny Vera's, just a few minutes; everyone looked at us with kindness or with pity, but no one said anything, so we went running down the street to Milka's—our favorite aunt. She and our uncle Kole rented the lower floor in the old white house that belonged to Jovan and Pavlina, who had been the godparents at their wedding, both teachers at the high school. The window frames were painted the same blue as the double front door. Our aunt and uncle had two rooms, in one they had a woodstove, a table, and couch; and in the other, two beds pushed together and a third against the wall. Our uncle's civil defense uniform was spread out on the bed by the wall. When Srebra and I stayed there, we slept in their double bed, our aunt in the bed with the uniform, and our uncle on the couch in the living room. They didn't have children for several years after their wedding, and when we were returning to Skopje and stopped in to say goodbye, our aunt came out to the car in her green dressing gown, gave us a big hug, and cried and cried. In movies young brides were in love and happy, but our aunt was sad. On the second floor of the house lived Grandpa Jovan and Grandma Pavlina, as Srebra and I called them, and we particularly liked Grandpa Jovan, because when he came to our grandmother's house in the village, he always gave us money, and once, when we were little, he gave us twice as much, at least that's what our grandfather—who understood about money—told us. In return, Srebra and I had to give our pacifiers to him, and on his way back to town on the bus, he threw them out the window into the little stream that flowed beside the road.

When we were at our aunt's, Srebra and I had the most fun in Grandpa Jovan and Grandma Pavlina's apartment, which they left unlocked when they weren't home, because there was nothing to hide from our aunt and uncle. Our aunt and uncle never went upstairs to their place, but Srebra and I, very carefully, taking care in the hallway darkness not to trip over each other, and with not only our heads stuck together but our bodies as well, climbed the stairs and went into their bedroom with its wide bed covered with a red satin coverlet. Then, kneeling in front of the drawer and glass shelf in their nightstand, we each took a book and carried it down to our aunt's and leafed through it on the couch in the room with the oven where something delicious-smelling was always be-ing prepared. Why didn't our aunt ever notice that we went upstairs to the landlords' apartment and took things that didn't belong to us? Sometimes we took the books with us to the village, and even to Skopje. *Heart* by De Amicis, *Luka the Beggar* by August Šenoa, *Dubravka* by Ivan Gundulić, all these books that belonged to people who never mentioned the fact that we were book thieves when we saw them. Nor did they say anything to reproach our aunt. Perhaps they didn't notice the books were missing from the shelf. More often, however, we stole books from a tiny room on the landing, in which every inch was flooded with books as if they'd been poured from a sack onto the floor. We would open the small wooden door with extreme care, and then Srebra and I would take the books that spilled off the heap and across the threshold. Among them were old atlases, books on arithmetic and biology, novels by Dostoevsky, a blue-covered edition of Njegoš's *The Mountain Wreath*, and many, many others. Every summer, we each returned to Skopje with five or six books from Grandpa Jovan and Grandma Pavlina's library, but no one ever discovered this fact. Years later, after Grandpa Jovan died of sorrow over his daughter's death from cancer, Grandma Pavlina in her old age began planting marijuana in the fields above the town, and not only planting it, but also selling it to the young people in the town. Until the day her former student, then a policeman, popped her in jail where, with nothing and no one to her name, she died from sadness. While they were renting, Aunt Milka and Uncle Kole built a new house, and they moved there and had two sons. No one spoke about Grandpa Jovan and Grandma Pavlina's house anymore, but Srebra and I continued to dream about how it might have been: I always imagined it with the sign "Drug-store" on the blue double door that was always freshly painted, but Srebra told me that she pictured it with a sign saying

"Self-Serve Market." Srebra and I argued about what the sign might have said, and she added, "A 'Drugstore' sign is ridiculous. There was only one drugstore in town, and it was in a different place. How could that house have been a drugstore?" Drugstores are supposed to be the cleanest places in the world, but that house didn't even have a bathtub or toilet. Still, our aunt and uncle's rooms were sparkling clean, but completely wiped from our minds was where we went to the bathroom when we visited, where they bathed, or where our aunt washed the dishes. "What you're saying is nonsense," I said. "How could it have been a store when there wasn't a salesclerk? We just took the books and didn't pay anything for them." Several hours later, Srebra added in a serious tone, "Didn't you learn in school that that's what Communism is? Take everything you need for free?" Srebra was right, but I hadn't thought of that. I always thought someone would catch us stealing and, at some point, we would end up in an orphanage as punishment. Perhaps in some way that's what I wanted. Our conjoined heads often awakened in us feelings of victimhood, but when no one pitied us, I thought that we could at least pity ourselves. Like our grandma pitied herself when our uncle, her son, found himself a good-for-nothing wife, and the day of the wedding had now arrived. So many preparations! Uncle Kole knew better than anyone how to chop vegetables for the salad, and so, for our uncle's wedding, no one else could do the chopping; we all waited on him. He took a day off without pay to chop all the sacks of cabbage our mother and father had bought at the market in the city. He took a head of cabbage in his mountainous hands, placed it on the cutting board, and quickly and artfully cut it up. On the day of the wedding, he prepared a dressing of oil, vinegar, and salt and stirred it separately with each plate of cabbage.

Our father was amazed that our uncle would do woman's work like that. He was happy to carve the pig with an apple in its mouth. Srebra and I set the table with the dishes, forks, and napkins borrowed from the neighbors. Knives weren't put on tables then, but we set out big platters of dinner rolls and pieces of pita stuffed with leek or spinach, plates of cheese, salad, and other appetizers. Srebra told me that she wanted to climb onto a chair in front of the hallway mirror so we could have a look at ourselves. We took a chair, placed it in front of the mirror, and climbed up, both of us holding onto the wall. We lifted our dresses up to look at our legs: we both had slightly crooked legs, but beautiful knees and ankles. We were disgusted by each other and ourselves. We were thirteen years old, still young, but with the bodies of maturing girls, me with glasses and she without, and hair that fell to our shoulders, intermingling at the inner sides of our heads. When we were ready to get down from the chair, Srebra knocked into the mirror with her elbow; it wobbled and fell. It broke. Our mother, who was at that moment carrying shot glasses filled with rakija, heard the crash. She set the glasses on the ground, came over, and struck each of us as hard as she could on our heads with her index finger and said, "I wish you'd bang your heads together. This is no life with you." She gathered up the shards of glass, stuck the mirror frame under the bed in the bedroom, said nothing to the others about the mirror, and no one noticed it wasn't there. The spot where our mother struck me hurt, as I'm sure it hurt Srebra. Seven years of bad luck in love, I thought, asking myself which of us would be cursed by the broken mirror: me, Srebra, or our uncle, since it broke on his wedding day. We sat at the table in the room that had been set up for children, and while all the other children gaped and nudged each other with their elbows, pointing at us, Srebra and I spoke with our cousin Verče and stole sips from the small glass of rakija we had grabbed from our mother, who, after smacking our heads, had brought the glasses into the room with the longest row of tables. We dug in, filling our stomachs with everything on the table, and when they struck up the dance in front of the house, and later in the village center, we took spots at the head of the dance, singing, shouting, dancing, kicking our legs to all sides. We were so loud and pushy that the villagers gathered around to watch us, rather than the bride and groom, crossing themselves and nudging each other. Our father cursed loudly, but Grandma told him to leave us alone; we were children, so let us enjoy ourselves—we only had one uncle. When the wedding was over and our aunt and uncle went to their room and closed the door, we stood in front of the door with Verče, calling out under our breath: "Three cheers for sex! Three cheers for sex!" And giggling as never before. That night, Srebra got her first period, and I puked. I vomited blood. Our mother had to get up. Instead of a sanitary pad, she gave Srebra several torn rags from our grandmother's sewing machine, and she made me drink water with baking soda. It was one of the worst nights of our lives. Our father cursed all night, while our mother tried to calm him. "Don't shout. The newlyweds are next door." "Fuck your whole tribe," our father repeated. "Fuck your whole gypsy tribe." The next day, he fired up the car, and we quickly got in and set off. We skipped the traditional honeyed rakija, and Verče told us later that the women said there wasn't any blood on our aunt and uncle's sheet and, because of the shame, they not only burned the godmother's underwear, as was the custom, but they also didn't give her any new ones, so she had to go home without any. Verče, Srebra, and I giggled hysterically, thinking about our uncle's godmother, twice as fat as our aunt, going home through town, probably on foot, with nothing under her skirt. Our mother could have just kicked herself that she missed the honeyed rakija at her brother's wedding. When we got home we heard that Bogdan and his adopted mother had moved to her sister's in England. "They got their asses in gear," said Auntie Dobrila. "Just as soon as they got their passports. The child waved as he climbed into the taxi. You should have seen the suitcase he was carrying, a black leather case like olden times. Who knows what was inside?" Both Srebra and I thought of his crosswords, all the issues of *Brain Twisters* and clippings from the newspaper. We were pretty much convinced that was what Bogdan had taken with him to England. I squeezed the little icon in my pocket, jabbing my fingers into its soft wooden surface. Why was I so upset, but Srebra not at all? Why did Srebra say, "As if I care that he gets to go to England; we're going too, someday. Doctors there will separate us." I remembered that Srebra wanted to marry someone in London, some unknown person whose name began with a *D*. Bogdan was gone; Roza had died; Srebra and I were left as we'd been before: with the awareness of our misfortune growing along with our bodies, with the curves of our hips, and with the breasts that grew and began to ache when we ran up the stairs, one of us holding the railing, the other the wall. A distant relative was visiting and we thought he, like everyone else, noticed our growing breasts and stared at them. In an old *Rosica* children's magazine that we had kept since nursery school there was a picture I liked of a many-tracked train set in a boy's room. It gave me a feeling of home. Srebra said she wanted to buy a train set with tracks that completely covered the floor of our room one day. We became conscious more than ever of the smells our bodies excreted: the sweat that moistened the hair in our armpits; the grease that crystallized on the tops of our heads; the blood that flowed to our vaginas as if from a hidden well in our wombs. When I got my period, Mom also gave me cloths sewn from old underwear and our father's undershirts. I had to make pads out of them, and over that I put on a pair of special underwear, of which there was a single pair for both Srebra and me. "Thank God your periods fall on different days, so we don't need a second pair," our mother said. The cloths quickly turned red from the blood. They soaked up the liquid blood, but the clots, pink and dark-red, stayed on top like snot, and, while Srebra covered her eyes with her hands, I changed the rags with ones that had been washed. I threw the dirty ones into a green pot in the bathtub, on top of which we kept a white plastic bowl with violets at the bottom. When Srebra next had her period, she'd use the same cloths, laundered, but with stains that couldn't be removed. We were only able to change the rags once or twice a day, even if they were soaked with blood, because Mom said she had cut up all of the old clothes she had, and we should be careful not to run, because blood would flow more heavily. Srebra's periods were heavier than mine, so she had to change the rags twice a day, and one time, as she threw the dirty one into the green pot, she screamed, "Cockroach!" My head hurt from her sudden tug. I yanked my hands from my eyes and peered into the pot, where a fat black cockroach sucked blood from Srebra's pads. I was nauseated by the sight and began to cry. Our mother came into the bathroom, saw what was happening, and said, "Oh, big deal, a cockroach." Later, we took a bath, but with water carried in a white tub from the boiler in the kitchen rather than water from the bathroom heater. We were filled with powerlessness, shame, and anger as we splashed ourselves with water with the yogurt container, and the towels we wiped ourselves with smelled of flour, onions, and mold. It was hardest to tolerate each other when we were naked, sitting in the bathtub, passing from hand to hand the greenish bar of soap that our parents also used, and pouring water over ourselves from the yogurt container, which we also passed back and forth. Our souls boiled with anger and helplessness and hatred toward each other, or perhaps shame in front of each other. "Wash yourselves well," our mother said, "I am taking you somewhere." It was September. We had turned thirteen. We had started the seventh grade, and were the most developed in our class, really, like mature women with breasts and hips. That first Friday in September, our father had gone on his first and last business trip to Mavrovo, to a hotel that was under construction and needed a glazier to finish off the work. Our mother took advantage of the occasion. She ironed our skirts, which had large openings in front through which one could see our white slips underneath, hemmed with silky trim. She handed us our blue tee shirts with palms on the chest and large neck holes so we could pull them over our legs without stretching them, and said, "We're going somewhere special." We were burning with curiosity, since our mother never organized any surprises, not nice ones, that is, and this seemed like it might be a nice surprise. We took the bus as far as the Engineers' Club, and from there, walked to Roosevelt Street, where we turned onto a small street lined with beautiful old houses with gardens. In front of one of them, a white house with stairs leading up to the front door, Mom said, "This is the house your father grew up in. Ring the bell. I'll meet you in two hours at the bend in the road. She turned and quickly set off. Srebra and I stood in the yard, frozen, confused. I had my hand tightly wrapped around the icon in my skirt pocket. Srebra was biting her nails. Her heart pounded in my left arm and mine in her right. We squeezed close together and barely made our way up the stairs, which led to a small porch with a door that was half glass, half metal. We rang the bell. An older man who looked a lot like our father opened the door. He stared at us, took a frantic step forward as if he might close the door, collected himself, and asked, "Yes?" "We're Stanko's daughters," I said, rather loudly and decisively, feeling the tapping of my finger against the icon, and that tapping brought strength to my voice. Srebra just stared at him, uncontrollably, so intently that my face was also pulled forward. Our grandfather, our father's father, whispered, "Come in," and once inside, in the wide hallway, he grasped our heads, mine in one hand, Srebra's in the other. It felt like he was deciding if he should kiss us, but he just held our heads in his hands, then let us go. He took us into the room where our grandmother, the uncle who, two months prior, had fled with his family from Pretor when he saw us there, his wife, and their young daughter, our cousin, were watching television. "Look who's come to see us," our grandfather stated, pretending to sound happy, but his trembling voice was filled with concern. The room filled with silence which was then cut by the girl's shout, as she dragged her mother toward us: "Look at their heads! Look!" Our aunt, whom we had fleetingly seen in Pretor, was young and beautiful. She smiled sincerely and greeted us, and only then did our uncle and grandmother greet us. Our grandmother was very dark, thin, all skin and bones, with black hair that peeked out from under a brown headscarf tied in the front. She was identical to the aunt who had brought us the chocolate bar with rice, only much older. They made coffee, the first coffee of our lives. Our grandmother read our future in the grounds of our Turkish coffee; our grandfather asked whether we had a car, whether our father was still working as a glazier, and whether we had been to a doctor about our heads. Our uncle kept quiet, watching us. Grandmother kept repeating, "Oh, children, children." No one asked about our mother. Nor did they ask how we had found their house, or who had brought us there. At one point, I wanted to tell my grandfather that he was an idiot for beating our mother, but the words stuck in my throat and refused to be spoken. Srebra kept hiking up her skirt then jerking it down toward her knees while answering their questions. The little girl ran around, pointing out objects she played with: an old wooden pestle with red embroidery around its handle, an orange juicer with a rusty sieve, a beat-up, three-legged wooden stool. I thought that perhaps our father had sat on that stool when he lived here. And perhaps our grandmother had strained tea through the strainer with the rusty bottom for him when he was sick. But nothing recalled that, years earlier, our father had lived here. In this house, which, our mother had said, our father built with his own hands when he was still a child, there was no history of him; his past did not exist. Srebra and I looked at the clock on the wall, and in the extremely tense atmosphere of quiet with spurts of words that cut the air with exaggerated weight, we wanted those two hours to pass quickly so we could leave, tear ourselves away from our might-have-been relatives, from this family that was not for us, and go back where we had come from, to our home, such as it was. As we were leaving, our grandfather gave us money, a thousand Yugoslav dinars, and our little cousin gave us a kiss, but the others said goodbye with just a handshake and a big smile. They did not say, "Come again." Nor did our mother ever say we should go there again. Her goal had been accomplished: those grandparents, our aunt and our uncle, and our little cousin most of all, had become part of our thoughts, of our lives. We were aware of their existence, aware that there were people living in the center of the city, in the house that our father had built when he was a child, out of which our grandfather had driven Srebra and me when we were only a few weeks old, and these people, in some way, belonged to us, as we did to them. Before we met them, we had not considered them part of our lives, but now, now that we had met them and were certain that we did not want them to be part of our lives, they had become a part of it. And we had become a part of theirs. That was the most significant. They could no longer sleep peacefully, let alone live, without also thinking of us. That's what our mom said. Years later, we heard that our grandfather died in great agony, suffering, on the brink of death for days, neither here nor there, neither in this world nor the next. As for our grandmother, she nearly died of hunger, locked in one of the basement rooms where our grandfather had mistreated our mother when they lived there, from where he had driven us. Our grandmother died sick, racked with pain, unaware of anything going on around her. Shame on our uncle's family— they fed her bread and water and left her to die with our father's name on her lips. Much too late, much too late. Not even after our grandfather's death did she gather the courage to seek out her son, to see him. She died like a dog. They say a man dies in the manner in which he lived. The one who lived in inner agony would die in agony; the one who thought of life as a game would die playing; the one who suffered his whole life would die of illness; and the one who loved greatly would die of love.

1986–1991

The years spent at school desks must be examined under a microscope. Not only the substance that made up our bodies, but also our souls should be viewed through the eye of a magnifying glass. Everyone noticed, and some even wanted to help us get rid of, the first bouts of acne that broke out on my forehead and chin and on Srebra's nose and cheeks; our biology teacher said that if we forced out some blood with a needle heated in the flame of a cigarette lighter we could be cleansed and would no longer get acne. "A sewing needle," she said, "Clean it first with rakija and then prick your fingers to let out some blood and you'll see, there's no better cure for acne." "Use acid perm," said the hairdresser, who trimmed our hair while we stood, because there was no hairdresser's chair on which both of us could sit. "I'll rub it on with a cotton ball, and it'll burn the acne off." Both the hairdresser and the biology teacher laughed at us when we were too afraid to try their methods. "Well, if you're afraid of a needle and acid now, then how are you going to be able to have your heads operated on some day? They'll actually slice you to separate the spot, though how can they, if you're not brave?" "We will be under an anesthetic," said Srebra. They just shook their heads and had the same answer: "Perhaps, but you never know how you'll react to anesthesia. Some people wake up immediately, and others never fall asleep." My hair stood on end at such thoughts, even though I never imagined Srebra and I would really be separated. How? Who would pay for it? Where? Would our parents actually take us abroad? And how would they? Drive our Škoda, in which one of us—and most often both—always threw up during the two hundred-kilometer drive from the city to the village? Could we really travel to other countries by car, and if operations to separate Siamese twins were done only in London, could we even get there by car? Over the water? And the bigger question: With what money? Our parents constantly complained about how expensive everything was—how those damn prices were so high—and how there was no money for anything, least of all for luxuries. "That's a luxury," our mother would say if we wanted to buy sweat suits and sneakers for gym class so we could at least run, even if we couldn't play volleyball or basketball. Instead, we wore dark blue cotton pajamas that our mother insisted were sweat suits and black ballet slippers instead of sneakers. These were just more of those things we lacked in our obviously terrible situation in relation to our classmates, who had already begun falling headlong in love with one another, who went out at night to sit on the benches in front of the school or stroll about the neighborhood chewing sunflower seeds. We rarely hung out with them; we spent most of our time with the girls from our class who were considered clumsy and clueless, though not retarded, which is how the other students viewed us. It was typical among our classmates to stand around in a doorway because we couldn't socialize inside our homes, where the majority of us were alone since our parents were at work. It was as if there was an unwritten parental rule not to let anyone in the house. If a classmate came by to borrow a notebook, we wouldn't invite her in but stood at the door, even when it was cold out, sometimes for more than half an hour. The same thing happened when we went to someone else's house; we almost never went inside. Kids only came inside when the parents were at home, and then only if they said, "Come on, come inside. Why are you standing at the door?" I sometimes thought about the fact that Roza was inside our apartment only once in her life: the time we celebrated our birthday with her, Auntie Verka, and Verče. Only once, and even then, she didn't go into our room but stayed in the big room, our parents' room, which they considered more appropriate for a birthday party. We never stood in the doorway at Roza's; we always went inside; it was understood we could wander freely around the apartment— lie on the bunk bed in her room, where Srebra and I were naturally on the lower bunk, and Roza on the upper; sit in the armchairs in their big room, nibble figs at the dining-room table, take the kaleidoscopes by ourselves from their shelf; or go to the bathroom where one of us sat on their yellow trash-can while the other did her business. We could do anything in Roza's apartment when she was alive. But now she no longer existed. Whenever her mother saw us, she called out for us to visit, and once she gave us each a *gevrek*, a baked sesame ring. We forced ourselves to eat them—each mouthful sticking in our throats while we stood in the hallway in their apartment, unable to enter the dining room—then turned and ran out. Srebra coughed loudly, choking on a bite until I pounded her on the back. I stuffed half of mine into my pocket, thinking Saint Zlata Meglenska would have something to eat. The gevrek stayed in my pocket until it dried up and Mom found it when she told me to take off my skirt so she could wash it.

Later, whenever I ate a gevrek I would gag and cough. My eyes would tear, and I would squeeze the icon I kept in my pocket or in the small shoulder bag I carried when my clothes had no pockets. Why didn't I gather the courage to tell Auntie Magda that Roza had died because of my chain with its little cross? Everyone said it was fate that a young girl was taken so early, at the threshold of her life. "What is fate?" I asked Grandma. "What is written for you," she said, and I understood fate to be something already written, perhaps in one of the big books the priests read from in church. "Does everyone have a fate?" I asked. Grandma said there was no person without a fate; God had thought up a fate for everyone. "So," she said, "your fate is to have conjoined heads; that girl's fate was to be struck by lightning; another's is to have no mother or father." "Do you have a fate, Grandma?" Srebra asked, and the two of us burned with curiosity. "Your uncle is my fate: my only son, married to a woman who doesn't call us Mom and Dad, who doesn't know how to make coffee or cook a meal." Her fate caused her such an excess of pain that we considered it our whole family's fate. Our uncle's response was, "What sort of fate is that? What kind of God is that? That's just nonsense; people know what they want. I took what I wanted. So whatever your grandma wants, she can ask for it." We heard a third view in church, where the priest who had given me the icon of Zlata Meglenska and before that the cross and chain, said, "There's no such thing as fate, only God's will, but you also can't forget human will." None of what he said was clear to me. "Then why did Roza die?" Srebra shot back at him impudently. The priest was about to say, "It was written," but he caught himself and said, "You think she died, but now she sits with the angels and watches you and laughs, living her life up there." When we left the church,

Srebra said the priest was talking nonsense and I should never drag her to church again—she was sick of all that and I was a naive idiot for believing in silly old tales. "The fact is," she said, "Roza is no longer alive, and let whoever wants to, say: 'Roza no longer exists.'" That was the first time she used the word "fact," and the whole way home, the word echoed in my mind, as if it had crossed through the connection of our bodies, passing from her mind into mine, and it became a fact for me that Roza was no longer alive. It was a fact that she would not come back to life as Auntie Verka had promised. Just as it was a fact that we had conjoined heads and well-developed breasts, as the neighborhood women said, and men on the street would call us Samantha Fox One and Samantha Fox Two after the British pinup girl, snickering as loudly as possible, though others called out, "Yeah, but with faces like pickles." It was a fact that we were growing up and were already young women, and, although the years were passing, not a single boy had paid any attention to us with affection or tenderness, only out of curiosity or malice. It was a fact that Bogdan was also gone from our lives, having seemingly vanished overnight, with not a single trace of the sound of his voice remaining.

Toward the end of eighth grade, Caci, who sat in the back, called all the girls over and told us with wide, glistening eyes and burning lips, "You won't believe this, but I fucked someone for the first time last night! It was amazing! You've got to try it. It's the best thing ever." We all blushed, nudging each other with our elbows and stepping on each other's feet. My heart was beating like crazy, and I thought everyone could hear it. Srebra poked me in the stomach with her elbow, lightly, but enough to bruise my spirits, if not my body. All day long, I couldn't get Caci's words out of my head. Srebra and I had seen grown-ups making love on television, but had never seen a porno film, only romantic scenes between couples. In those films, people always said they *made love*, but Caci said that she'd *fucked*. How could she say that word? I felt such trembling inside; it was like someone had poured cold water over me, but my cheeks burned. That afternoon, Srebra wanted to go visit our cousins Verče and Lenče. When we left, Verče came with us as we started off for home, stuffed with Aunt Ivanka's piroshky, and Verče pointed out a small store that had opened in the neighborhood. "It's a toy store," she said. I convinced Srebra to go in to see what they had. We always carried a small red wallet with our joint funds, because we didn't each have our own, and it was now in Srebra's pocketbook. Srebra only agreed to go in because she liked to shop more than I did, to look at things, and buy things if she could. It was rare, though, that we went to stores. We didn't have money for that sort of thing, and got embarrassed when salesclerks stared at us as if we had fallen from some other planet, asking us, without hesitation, if we had been born this way, what had happened, how long we would stay attached. The same sort of salesclerk awaited us in the toy store, and while we answered her questions with a yes or no, we looked at the stuffed bears and dogs, the plastic dolls, the buckets with shovels and rakes, and the assortment of other things. Our childhood had contained none of these things, and in our inexperience, we wanted to touch everything, to stroke them, look closely at them. Verče said it was too bad that we hadn't brought Lenče, too, so they could pick out a Hula-Hoop together. My hand was drawn to a clown on the shelf, his legs hanging down, his cloth cap twirled up into a point and stiffened with shellac, his long arms hanging alongside his body. He didn't have a typical clown face; a small nose not a big red one, cheeks rosy rather than red, eyes not covered by makeup. I liked him at first glance and decided to buy him. Srebra was surprised and voiced her disapproval, but I yanked the purse to my side and shook out all the money in front of the sales-clerk. Hugging the clown close, I dragged Srebra outside. As Verče turned to head back home, she laughed, "Well, Auntie will be happy you got something you'd been missing in your life." A bit worried, we wrapped the clown in a bag, but the tip of his hat poked out. Our parents yelled when they saw it. "You're fifteen years old, and you're still buying yourself toys! I'm telling you, you won't amount to anything," our mom said. "Just screw the lot of you," our father added, "You voracious creatures, you've devoured the world! You don't know what it means to earn one's bread; that's why you buy such nonsense. You'll just go on with those heads of yours." They said all sorts of other things. But inside I felt more and more aroused; shivers of excitement passed through my body; I felt something in my lower body unfold like a poppy, and droplets dampened my underwear. I wanted night to come quickly, so I could lie in bed with Srebra and wait for her to fall asleep. But that night Srebra had difficulty falling asleep, as if she too were caught up by my wakefulness. The clown lay drooped over in the narrow space between the wall and the pillow. I slept on the right side and Srebra on the left, with our legs pointing not toward the door but away from it. When I was certain Srebra was sleeping, breathing deeply with her mouth open, I pulled the clown on top of me with my right hand; I laid him on top of my body; I positioned his legs up toward my head and his head down; I poked the pointed cap between my legs, and—without moving out of fear I would wake Srebra—I clenched my legs around the clown's head. The tip of the cap seemed to cut through my pajamas, penetrating me. Sexually aroused for the first time, I clenched the clown's cap tighter and tighter, turning it left and right, but rather than the point of the cap, it was my pajamas, and my underwear beneath, that went deeper and deeper into my vagina. I was afraid to pull down my pajamas, because although Srebra fell asleep quickly, she also awoke quickly. I felt pleasure, but it was incomplete: an emptiness remained between my legs; bliss was located somewhere deeper than I had imagined. As quietly as I could, I tossed the clown over my head onto the floor. I called him Bobby. He was my first lover. I fell asleep with dissatisfaction in my body. I awoke with dissatisfaction in my soul. When Srebra woke up we got out of bed and I saw that the clown had been lying there all night with his arms crossed, as if in prayer. I took my icon from under the pillow. Srebra had to run to the toilet. The door nudged the clown aside as we went to pee. All day I thought about the incident with the clown. I passionately wanted his pointed cap between my legs, but, somewhere deep inside me, I burned with shame before God, and most of all before Zlata Meglenska, with her serious, worried face on the small icon. I had been given the icon as comfort for Roza's death so I could ask the saint to pray for Roza's entry into heaven. And that is how I prayed silently to Zlata Meglenska while pressing the icon in my pocket: "Holy Zlata Meglenska, pray for Roza so that she may rejoice in the Heavenly Kingdom with the angels." But, I confess, I also prayed for myself, for this or that, an A in mathematics, a pair of jeans, for God to bring our father to his senses when he shouted and cursed, for our mother's health so she wouldn't lose consciousness again, and, in moments of despair over our conjoined heads, I begged Saint Zlata Meglenska to pray to God to separate us, and if he did, we would serve him the rest of our lives. My first encounter with the clown burrowed into my mind, and unconsciously, I asked myself, "Will I do it again tonight? How will I feel when I get up? What if Srebra finds out? Is it okay? Is it a sin? What is a sin? I'm not sleeping with a man, but only a toy clown, so I am not tempting anyone. The Lord's Prayer says: 'Lead us not into temptation.' But what if a person wants to be tempted?" There were so many questions with no answers. Day has its order, and nighttime its own. Daytime was shared with Srebra, every movement, every slight shift was shared, unavoidably, locked within the physical coordinates of our existence, fixed in the bond between our heads, in the piece of flesh covered in skin and hair, where the blood intermingled, pulsating in our brains. As much as we hated that spot, which from the moment of our birth, had destroyed our lives before we became conscious of it, we considered the spot sacred, untouchable. We preserved it for skilled, miracle-working hands in some future time; we allowed no one to pull our hair aside to look at it, much less touch it. But there were countless times people tried. Everyone who offered advice wanted to pass their hands in the space between our heads, to examine how we were joined, what the connection looked like. They wanted to see why it couldn't be removed, or perhaps dried out in some way to simply fall off, or be cut with a sharp knife, okay, not at home, but at a doctor's office—any doctor could do it. Doctors have diplomas after all: Can doctors really receive so much schooling and still not know how to separate heads? Our neighbors and our aunts and uncles on both sides of the family to the second and third degree, everyone wanted to help, everyone had some idea how you could separate Siamese twins, but if someone tried to touch our holy place, Srebra and I would go crazy, our faces would turn red, our eyes sparking with rage. The power of Amazons rose up in us, a power that destroyed everything in its wake. Usually, we ran out of the house, or grabbed the person trying to touch us in our painful spot, shouting loudly to leave us in peace. Only once, long ago, in a moment of complete trust and friendship, we let Roza briefly touch our Achilles' heel. We put ourselves in her firm hand, which gathered all the tenderness from every cell in her body so she would not hurt us, and she just lightly passed her hand along the skin mixed with strands of hair that covered the vein in which I often thought I heard our blood streaming, merging, flowing from one brain to the other, one heart to the other. Her touch was a light breeze, and she said, "There's nothing to feel; it seems like the vein is deep inside. Like you have a spare vein." We found it hardest to stop our grandmother from touching us, because the village fortune-tellers had passed on various recipes for separating heads, and she often made us drink mixtures of herbs steeped in homemade rakija or slurp soup made from the heads of pigs, goats, or lambs sieved through gauze and spiced with paprika that was kept hidden behind the small altar door in the village church. When those remedies didn't achieve the miracle, everyone blamed us, saying such things couldn't work if they weren't done in combination with the spot getting rubbed with various homemade creams imbued by God's breath—or the fortune-teller's at least—with healing power and miraculous effect. There was no way we would let a living soul rub cream on the spot where we were conjoined, although there were moments I wanted to give in, to abandon myself to these folk doctors in the hope that they might actually succeed in separating us. But Srebra was convinced that one day, when we were grown and rich (although I don't know how she thought we would become rich!), we would go to London, where there were doctors for such an operation, although I personally was not convinced there were any. And why London and not New York or Paris? Someone said even in Zagreb we could have this kind of operation, and another said it was possible to find a specialist for us at the Military Medical Academy in Belgrade. "There's one in Skopje, too, apparently. He's the best; maybe he could try," Auntie Dobrila once said. I was almost ready to try, but Srebra said that she wasn't an idiot and would not take the risk. "We're not going to be someone's guinea pigs," she said. "It's different in London; they'll have experience with cases like ours." "That costs money. Who's going to pay? And how do you know the operation will be successful? It's not that simple," our mother said whenever anyone started in on the topic. Dad was even more convinced that the time wasn't right, that there was simply no chance of success. "Perhaps children of some rich bigwigs can go and find that kind of surgeon. But we're working class; we don't know the language or how to make ourselves understood there; and not just there, even here, where would we find the money for that kind of operation? Who would give it to us? Anyway, they're used to the way they are; they've been that way since they were born." "No, we are not used to it," we wanted to shout, each thinking that we still did not know each other the way our father thought we did, but in his presence we always felt embarrassed and could not utter a word. We gave in to our fate, but our souls gathered bitterness, anger, pain, and rage. That's why I preferred nights to days, when Srebra and I lay next to each other on our backs, each in her own darkness, her own world, her own quiet; separated from each other on the verbal, spiritual, and existential planes, we felt we were separate, almost as if we were physically separated, even though any time one of us turned a bit the other felt it and the link between our heads would ache like a tooth, like an inner ear, like the sting of a wasp. We knew this feeling quite well, because we shared the long pillow our aunt sewed especially for us, filled with stuffing from two Lio brand pillows, each of us positioned for maximum comfort, Srebra with her knees raised, and I with one leg over the other. In the darkness we immediately fell silent. We were not like sisters who chatter and tell secrets before falling asleep. On the contrary, even if we both had our eyes open long into the night, we remained silent, each in our own world. It was only the swallowing of saliva, the scratching of noses, or sighs that revealed that we were awake, but we still maintained our silence and fell asleep like two strangers compelled to sleep in the same bed. After I bought the clown, it always sat on the bed, pressed against the wall, head lying on the part of the pillow by my head, where it was simple for me to pull him toward me, or on top of me, once I sensed Srebra was asleep. Before lying down, Srebra would tell me to get him off the bed—he was taking up space, and the foldout bed was narrow enough to begin with—but I didn't give in. I told her that since I had bought him, I would sleep with him, period. "Well, then, why's he always on the floor in the morning? He takes up your space, too, so you throw him off in the night." I told her he fell off by himself. After several attempts to have sex with him through my pajamas, I got up the courage and one night slowly, silently, with the most controlled movements of my right hand, I stretched the elastic of my pajamas and underwear, and pushed his head between my legs so the tip of the cap poked inside me. I pressed with all my strength, and the tip went deeper and deeper inside, and although I felt a pain similar to that in our connected spot, I also felt pleasure like I never had before—bliss spread through my body, all the way up to where we were conjoined. I had the clown penetrate me three times that night, and then, in exhaustion, shame, anger at myself, and unable to bear the pleasure, I tossed him off. I felt a certain disgust, and, breathing deeply but taking care not to be heard, I fell asleep with my legs spread out, one leg touching Srebra's. In the morning, I noticed a drop of blood on his cap. I was stunned, but ignored it. Srebra also noticed it. She was surprised and thought we had gotten it dirty somehow. "But how," she asked, "since we don't even look at him? He just sits here all day; you bought him for no reason." I suggested that perhaps the stain had been there when we bought him, but we hadn't noticed, and now that the sun's rays were coming through the window directly onto his head, the spot was visible. "Yes," said Srebra, "the salesclerk sold him to you like that, and he was so expensive." We went to pee, and it was my turn to go first and Srebra's to sit on the trashcan. There was also a red spot on my underwear. Srebra noticed it too, although she usually looked at the ground while I sat on the toilet. She shouted madly, "You've got a red spot that matches the clown's!" "Well, so what? Maybe my period is coming," I said, but that was impossible, for it had ended just a week prior. "No, it's not your period, you idiot! You're doing something with that clown; you're doing something!" Srebra shouted, and she jumped up from the trashcan, dragging me by my underwear toward the bathroom door. I was barely able to pull up my pajamas. Our parents were already at work, and we had to go to school. Srebra kept shouting at me, insulting me with words that I had never heard come from her mouth before: *dirty whore*, all the while shaking me left and right. I was silent the whole time, but finally, a moment came when I couldn't contain myself, and I screamed, "You know, it feels really good! There's nothing more pleasurable than that!" Srebra dragged me into our room, grabbed the clown, twisted his head with all the strength she could muster, and ripped it off. Scraps of cloth and bits of foam fell from his neck. The clown's head emptied and it flattened, but the cap was still hard and full. With her teeth Srebra ripped the seam connecting the head to the body. From the split seam spurted bits of rag and small balls of foam, like pearls. "Now let's see how you screw yourself!" Srebra said to me as she kicked the clown. I cried; tears poured silently down my cheeks, large and fast. I cried, but not only about the clown. I cried about everything, about myself, about Srebra, about everything. A flood of emptiness drenched my heart; pain spread through my entire body. I cried that I no longer had the clown, I cried that I no longer had Roza, I cried that I no longer had Bogdan, I cried that Grandma and Grandpa were so far from us. I cried that our uncle had married an unsuitable woman, I cried that I no longer had little Igor. I cried for all the losses that occurred to me; I remembered all the sorrows that I'd hidden in my heart. I cried that Srebra was my sister, I cried that I, Zlata, was Srebra's sister, and I cried because our godfather had given us those names. I cried because our mother and father had daughters like us, and because we had parents like them; I cried because I was alive. Srebra had likely expected I would get angry, that I would argue and shout, but now she was completely bewildered. She fell silent and didn't know what to say; she did not know whether it was better to say something or remain silent and wait for me to calm down. I cried for a long time, sobbing, until my lips were dry and purple, and I shook and shook Srebra's head with my sobs, but she remained silent, and we somehow dragged ourselves to school, late for the second class of the day. Along the way, I kept repeating silently, "Our neighborhood is in Gazi Baba,

Gazi Baba is in Skopje, Skopje is in Macedonia, Macedonia is in Yugoslavia, Yugoslavia is in Europe, Europe is in the world, the world is the planet Earth." I repeated the sentence over and over while pressing the small icon of Zlata Meglenska in the pocket of my light jacket. Was that my mantra, my strange prayer? I know that I always repeated it when I was at the nadir, when I saw no escape. I repeated that sentence the morning when we left for the village on the day of Roza's burial. As I'd looked at our mother's back and the windshield in front of her as we passed through forests that had turned green, I repeated my geographic mantra, only changing the starting point—in place of our neighborhood, sometimes it was Grandma and Grandpa's village, or Pretor, or Lukin Vir.

That day we grew distant, but also the most connected we had ever been. Nothing was said in words. I felt we would be closer if we could separate, but now, trapped by the fusion of our heads, we remained strangers, almost enemies. I felt as if a channel had closed within me, as if I had become as distant as possible from Srebra and our connection had become merely a physical defect, not a spiritual one. Inside, I felt freer than ever, thinking I could fly away if there weren't that senseless physical impediment. I felt Srebra close into herself as well; at moments it resembled contempt. We went out less and less. We sat at home, on our chair in the dining room. I read a book; Srebra watched television. That is how we spent our free time.

On February 15, 1987, Uncle Kole brought us an invitation to Mara's wedding, which was to take place on March 1, at the Olympia restaurant. Our parents went, but they didn't take us, just as they usually didn't take us to the weddings of more distant relations so people wouldn't look at us and talk. "It was lovely, just lovely," Mom said when they got back, "but

there were a lot of tears; everyone cried; everyone cried themselves out, and Mara, poor thing, was such a beautiful bride,
but sad and pale; it isn't easy for her without Roza." For two
nights, I dreamed of Roza in her wedding gown, her white
shoes with the toes pointing up. Srebra softened a little. She
suggested we go to the theater. On March 3, 1987, we went
to the theater for the first time, to see *Sarah Bernhardt*. Srebra
made me promise that if we went to see *Sarah Bernhardt*, we
would also go see Jordan Plevneš's play *R*. I promised. I loved
Sarah Bernhardt. The story tore me apart; her life seemed
unique. The woman sitting behind us asked us not to sit with
our heads together; "I can't see anything," she said. And we
turned toward her the way a wolf turns with its whole body;
with our two bodies and our two heads, and we stared at
her. "And what's more, you're impudent," she whispered as
we swallowed the saliva in our throats so we could answer
her. "Our heads are conjoined," Srebra whispered as quietly
as possible, but several people turned toward us nonetheless.
No doubt, several of those people remember that they saw the
play *Sarah Bernhardt* only because they remember two girls
with conjoined heads sitting there. Whether we wanted to or
not, we became a memento in the albums of unknown people.
R was scary; at one point, I was restless and wanted to stand,
but Srebra was engrossed in the performance; her eyes devoured the stage set and everything happening on it. I closed
my eyes and just listened to the dialogue; it seemed different
from anything I had ever heard spoken aloud, different from
anything on television, as if it were a language that first had to
be learned. I recognized the words from books, but not from
sentences spoken aloud. We did not go to any other theatrical
productions for the rest of 1987, but at home, we alternated
reading *Sarah Bernhardt* and *R* several times. On March 21,

our father brought the *Vujaklija* dictionary home from the city for us. Milan Vujaklija's dictionary of foreign words and expressions was 1,050 pages long, with explanations of more than 260,000 words. Srebra and I set it on the bed, then lay on our stomachs to read the words, each of us reading a page at a time. That was also how we learned English, by reading dictionaries. When we returned from school on March 26, another surprise awaited us—our father had bought a dual-cassette deck. It cost twelve million old dinars, he told our mother, and was made by the Italian company Lancio. "You only buy nonsense," Mom said. "As if they need books and a cassette player." Father just replied, "Well, don't you know everything," and nothing made him mad that day. But in the days that followed, his mood changed three hundred times an hour. Once again, there were times I wanted to address him using the formal *vie* form for "you"; the thought overtaking me whenever I was angry or hated him. For years, our father had bought us Animal Kingdom brand chocolates, and he called us "beasts." He collected the little stickers that came with the chocolates in a blue envelope he kept in the cupboard beside their bed. Sometimes when they were at work, Srebra and I secretly climbed up on a chair to get the envelope from among the other things hidden in the cupboard. We never bought the album you were supposed to stick them in. We never even sorted the stickers on the table; our father just collected them in the blue envelope our mother had brought from work. When we wanted to see the pictures, he would shout: "Great, now it occurs to you; I'll have to go rummage around." And I would really want to address him formally, to show him that I despised him, that we were not father and daughter, but strangers. Srebra, it seemed, didn't have that desire. I used that formal pronoun to punish the people I despised (some of them, like our father, whom I also loved). I wanted to pull away, to distance myself from their viciousness, and in so doing, protect myself. I was also formal with Uncle Boro, our neighbor who hadn't spoken to our mother in years on account of some minor quarrel the year we moved into our apartment, and because he would yell to Srebra and me, "Where are you, two-heads?" When he died, Mom went to his funeral with the rest of the neighbors. I was overtaken by uncontrollable crying that entire afternoon while all the people from our building were at the funeral and Srebra and I were left sitting in the big room—Srebra putting cards in order on the table and minding her own business, while I put my elbows on the table and wept, accidentally knocking her cards all over the place. I don't know whether I was crying specifically for Uncle Boro, who died just a few months after returning from an engineering job in Kuwait, or because I imagined the deaths of all the people I knew: those I loved, those I didn't, and even those whom I addressed with the formal pronoun *vie*. "Don't be a hypocrite," Srebra said. "You didn't even say good morning to him on the stairs, and now you're crying because he died." I cried the same way when Desanka Maksimović's "A Bloody Fairy Tale" was broadcast on television. It was a morning program bringing back memories of the National Liberation War. The murder of schoolchildren in the Serbian town of Kragujevac during the Second World War was described in detail. One of our aunts, who lived in Kragujevac, had given us a small statue of the V-shaped monument commemorating that event—white, uneven, on a black base. I ran my hands along the small statue and waited for Srebra to touch it as well, but she only said, "How can you cry for people you don't know, when you barely shed a tear for Roza?" She was right; I found it easier to cry for people I didn't know, like peeling an onion; the tear ducts just opened and the tears poured down my face, but for those close to me, it is more difficult. You think there's something stuck in your throat, something throbbing in your head, your heart beats in your temples, but your eyes are dry, dry, too dry, like an iron dam holding back a reservoir. So tight not a single tear can pass through the cracks in your soul. But once it does, there's no end—your whole body weeps, your entire being, not just your eyes. I even wept when Indira Gandhi was killed by Sikhs, although I knew her only from television. Since then, something has bound me tightly to India; I feel an attraction to that country. Years later, I dreamed of marrying Rahul Gandhi, the extremely handsome grandson of Indira. But neither the letter *R* nor New Delhi had occurred to me when Srebra, Roza, and I were playing the fortune-telling game. "That game doesn't mean anything," said Srebra. "Roza's fate didn't come true, did it? If it had, Roza would still be alive." True, I thought, the game didn't mean anything; perhaps I should try a different game. Better to play the game of waiting for the hands of the clock to align and then thinking of a three-digit number, then adding up the digits to see what letter of the alphabet it corresponded to, and someone with that initial would think of me. It wasn't *A*, or *B*, or *C*. Emptiness took hold of me, body and soul; after Srebra ripped the clown apart I felt an emptiness between my legs at night, and I had to poke my fingers into that space that longed to be filled. I didn't know whether to pity myself or Srebra, who didn't know the secret of corporal bliss. When I read books about love, I could imagine what the main characters were doing, how they felt. But Srebra could not.

Who knows what was going on with our father then, but he was more generous than he had ever been. Once, we heard him tell Mom that he had become president of his union. Maybe that's why he had a bit more money, and in addition to *Vujaklija* and the cassette player, he bought us each a digital watch and a midsized red accordion that looked like a toy, but was a real accordion. "It's for sharing, so take turns," he said. First Srebra took a turn. She let out a couple of sounds, stretched it several times, turned it all around, counted the keys and buttons, played a few more notes, then shoved it into my hands. I was holding an accordion for the first time in my life. I dragged Srebra to the kitchen table. I set the accordion down on it, and took a sheet of the typing paper our mother brought home from work from the pile that stood on the chair on which no one ever sat. The paper, cut in quarters, was what we used in the bathroom for toilet paper; I put the sheet in a slit in the accordion, and began to pound on the keys as if it were a typewriter. I never did play the accordion, but I used it as a pretend typewriter. Srebra would play a few random notes, but I would immediately lay it down horizontally on the table and type on it, banging as if I were writing something very important. "Do you at least know what you're writing?" Srebra asked me scornfully, breathing rapidly. "Do you think you are Agatha Christie or Mir-Jam?" "No, I want to be like Zola, or Dostoevsky, or Lawrence." "You can't; they're men." "Then I'll be like, like…" I wanted to reel off the names of several female writers, but the only name that came to mind was the Macedonian writer Olivera Nikolova. "I want to be like Olivera Nikolova," I said, but Srebra shot back, "Dream on!" One day, our mother brought home a real typewriter in a cloth bag. "It's from work. It was just sitting there and no one was using it," she said. I immediately christened it Ljubinka. We set it on top of the sewing table in the middle of our room. We shifted the vase to the left side and put the typewriter on the right, next to the sewing machine. Srebra and I couldn't sit in chairs to type, but had to stand. We stuck in a sheet of the paper from our mother's office and typed, me with my right hand, Srebra with her left. She had become left-handed when she was little and saw that it would be difficult to draw and write with her right without bumping into me. The typewriter completely pushed the accordion into oblivion or, more precisely, into the corner between the shelves, the wall, and the bed in our room. The typewriter became as important to us as the cassette player and the dictionary. What a salvation that typewriter was when unexpected guests arrived. They'd show up on Saturday evening or Sunday afternoon—our mother's cousins with their spouses and children, all dressed up, with a box of little cakes or wafer cookies in their hands—determined to spend part of the day visiting, while the hosts—us, that is—were unprepared, either not yet washed or just preparing to bathe. We'd all be sitting in front of the television dressed in old clothes or tattered pajamas, staring at some film or other, when all of a sudden the bell would ring, once, twice. Dad would turn down the television as the bell rang a third time, assuring him it wasn't some beggar or Gypsy selling something, but rather someone we knew. Mom would stand up, shouting, "Go see who it is." Dad would get up, flick on the light in the dining room, clear his throat, turn on the light in the hallway, turn the locks—one, two—open the door, and there before him would be the guests, simultaneously joking and looking a bit uncomfortable ("You weren't lying down were you? Oh dear; it's not too late for guests, is it?") but also full of self-assuredness ("Even if you were lying down, get up—we didn't come just to stand in the doorway. It's Saturday, it's Sunday, it's a day for a visit") and in they'd come. They'd shake hands with our parents in the hallway, then take off their shoes and coats, while our mother quickly changed out of her robe, but didn't manage to slip her bra on before the guests entered the dining room. She'd say warmly to them, "Oh, it's been so long since you've been here; how nice that you thought to come," but at the same time she'd be angrily thinking, *Really, why didn't you call first? Is this how one comes for a visit?* She'd take the box with the cakes or wafers, toss it on the couch in the kitchen, and get busy taking out cups while the guests in the dining room would greet us, kissing us three times on the face, first me, then Srebra, then me again, looking us over as if something had changed in us. We'd giggle; Dad would head to the basement for some cornelian cherry juice and wine; Mom would take out salami and cheese, chop it, and place it on the table, fretting that there wasn't anything else. Srebra and I would already be on the way to our own room; we'd quickly push the door shut; meanwhile, the guests would sit by themselves in the dining room and watch the movie we had been watching; finally, everyone would be seated. They'd nibble the cheese and salami, chattering on about this and that—about how expensive everything is, about politics. Srebra and I would type away on our typewriter standing in front of the sewing table; we typed unconnected words, both of us too embarrassed to write anything concrete in front of each other, a sentence with a beginning and an end. Years later, I'd understand why I couldn't write, even though I carried the urge within me: I was never alone. People can't write when they are not alone. It's impossible to write with your head connected to another head. Writing is a private act, but Srebra and I did not have privacy for a single moment in our lives. As a result, I forcibly turned away from writing, but inside, I wrote and made note of everything that happened to us, everything I noticed, and everything I felt. Just like Bogdan, who solved crossword puzzles in his head because he had no pencil, I wrote internally because I had no space. In any event, when we were typing mindlessly on the typewriter, none of us—not the guests, not us—felt particularly at ease. The guests would finally leave, we would lie down, and as Srebra and I listened to our mother and father gossiping about the guests through the wall, I would be overcome with a feeling of emptiness before falling into a dream; our blood was diluted with cornelian cherry juice, our father's with wine, but our mother's blood was water. In truth, sometimes we went visiting, although much less often and to fewer places than those who came to visit us. Srebra and I were happiest when we went to visit Viki and Dragan, our second cousins on our father's side. The only relative who kept at all in contact with our father was his cousin, a lieutenant in the Yugoslav National Army who had lived in Belgrade and married Snežana there, and then, through high-up connections (and machinations, most likely, as our mother said), they moved to Skopje, where they were given a large military apartment in the Gradski Dzid, the central apartment block, right downtown, where they had two children, Viki and Dragan. From time to time, our mother would say, "We're going to Vančo's this evening," and Srebra and I would get dressed up as nicely as we could, and then, slumped in the back seat of the Škoda, we would turn our heads in unison, first to look out the left window, then to the right. Outside in the dark, the street lamps shone, flickering like lanterns all around us; the atmosphere of the city center, which we so rarely saw, opened before us like a magical arena; the cars honked and rumbled; the red buses puffed at the stops. We wanted the trip to last as long as possible, and then when we entered our hosts' apartment, the children went straight to the kids' room, which had its own balcony, just for our cousins. We stood on their balcony and peeked onto the one opposite, where, according to Viki and Dragan, a "pervert" lived. We stifled laughter while staring into the pale light of the pervert's balcony door, waiting for him to appear, so we could see what he was like. Up till then, neither Srebra nor I had seen such a person, but Viki and Dragan had seen him; they said that he sometimes smoked out on the balcony, and there was another man, another pervert, who leaned up against the railing with him. "It's not just one pervert there," said Viki, who was five years younger than us, and Dragan, "There are two—they stand outside when our parents aren't home." "Do you even know what a pervert is?" Dragan taunted her, though I didn't know whether he knew himself. "Doesn't it mean *homosexual?*" I asked with some embarrassment, because I knew what a homosexual was, but the word *pervert* could refer to many things. "No," said Dragan, "these perverts aren't the same." Srebra seemed like she wanted to add something, but remained silent. I think she was thinking of the time, one day when we were still little, when we were waiting on our balcony for our young uncle to take us to the village on the bus. We could see as far as the house on the corner of the street that led to our school, and in the other direction as far as the iron crossbar that was used for hanging carpets when they needed to be beaten or for chin-ups, with the dumpster next to it, and a linden tree beside them, and Srebra asked me whether I knew what a "pervert" was because once she had heard Riki the Gypsy, Auntie Verka's lover, shout to Bogdan, "Where are you, you little pervert?" I hadn't known what a pervert was. I thought it was a child without parents, and so I told Srebra that that was probably what it was, and then, on the bus to the village, I thought about "the little perverts," and was happy that all the children without parents who now had adopted the singles in our neighborhood were no longer perverts. But today we were laughing with Dragan and Viki because their neighbor was a pervert, though it still wasn't entirely clear to us what a pervert was if not a homosexual. Plus, he had a mother and a father. The next time we saw Dragan and Viki, at our house, we played "I spy with my little eye," and when it was time to go, Uncle Vančo stood up, gave my father his hand, and told him quite loudly, curtly, almost militarily, "It's no big deal, cousin, but I have to tell you that we won't be coming to your place again, and don't you come to ours, because after last time your father called me and told me that everyone had turned against you. He asked me what the hell I was doing seeing you, and told me to tell you that we wouldn't see each other again. So, don't show up again, even though you're my only cousin on my father's side." Then our aunt Snežana, who had never properly learned Macedonian, added, in a mixture of Serbian and Macedonian, "What can you do? That's how people are." Our father blanched, his lips trembling, and only managed to say, "If that's the way it is, Cousin, I won't force you; you know best." And we all said goodbye, shaking hands, without hugs or kisses, even us children, and we never saw them again. "Pervert," whispered Srebra; I knew she was thinking of Uncle Vančo, and I pictured our grandfather's face. I never wanted to see either of them ever again.

In the summer of 1987, after we finished primary school, our mom and dad told us that we would be vacationing in Montenegro, in the village of Lukin Vir on the Lim River, at our Grandma Stana's house. All we knew about her was that she was our great aunt, Grandma's sister, and they hadn't seen each other since childhood, since the day Grandpa Ljubo came from Montenegro to get Grandma Stana and they eloped on horseback to his village, somewhere far, far away by the Lim River. Who knows how many days they rode? And they lived happily until the end of his life. Grandma Stana was the most happily married old woman in our family, the only one who had married a prince on a (white or black) horse. Mom had a telephone on her desk at the state-owned company where she worked as a typist, and she often used it for personal calls to friends and relatives she would not otherwise have wasted money calling. From her office phone our mother maintained connections with friends and family, near and far. No one else called our relatives in Montenegro, in Kumrovec, in Zaječar, in Pančevo, or in Kumanovo, only our mother, and after she called, everyone would know how everyone was, what they were doing, which of the men or women were getting married, who was building a house, who had gone abroad, and that sort of thing. And so, since Mom kept up these ties with Grandma Stana's son, her cousin in Montenegro, they agreed that summer to go to Ulcinj for a week, while Srebra and I stayed at Grandma Stana's in Lukin Vir, where we would spend our vacation with the second cousins and aunt and uncle we hadn't met before, and the grandma and grandpa we had only heard about in conversation. Things turned out both good and bad. Our uncle, a traditional patriarchal husband with a Montenegrin father and Macedonian mother, wanted a son; our aunt, a tall thin dark-haired teacher with the warmest eyes and voice in the world, gave him five children, four daughters and the youngest, a boy, who was born the same year as Srebra and I. They lived in the city, but spent summers in the village in a big three-story house. The first floor had no walls or separate rooms; every-thing was one large space: kitchen, dining room—with the longest dining-room table we had ever seen—and the living room in an extension to the house. On the second floor was Grandma Stana and Grandpa Ljubo's bedroom: under his pillow was a shiny black pistol that we secretly looked at and picked up. It was strange to Srebra and me that anyone could sleep with a pistol under his head, but it was completely normal and understandable to our second cousins. "What? Your father doesn't have a gun?" our cousin asked in amazement. But Srebra and I wondered why he would keep one and what our life would be like if our father slept with a pistol under his pillow. I think the two of us thought at the same moment: "A pistol, that's all we need." Our aunt and uncle's bedroom was on the same floor, and, of course, our uncle also had a pistol under his pillow, a brown one with a gray handle. Next to their room was another, with five beds for the kids. Above, under the roof, there were two large guest rooms, each with six iron hospital (or prison) cots and nothing else—no chair, no table, no little cupboard. We slept there with our mother and father; Srebra and I squeezed into one bed, even though it wasn't very comfortable—when we pushed two together we saw one of us would be sleeping in the gap between the mattresses on the iron bars, which sent shivers up our bodies. During the day, we went to the beach on the river, always on the side that looked across to a strange house the color of ocher with symmetrical windows and a front door that looked more like it belonged to a building than a house. Grandpa Ljubo would gently hold Grandma Stana by the arm; with the other he leaned on a cane that glistened in the sun as though it were made of gold. Grandma Stana would lie down on the sand, and we children had to cover her so only her head stuck out. "For my rheumatism," she would say, "It's good for my bones." Grandpa Ljubo sat in a plastic chair beside her, with his cap and sunglasses, always in a long-sleeved shirt. At home, he sat at the head of the table at every meal in a suit, tie, and hat. We each had a plastic red cup with our name written on the bottom in ink, and from those cups we drank water, juice, or milk. Meals were eaten in silence. During our first days there, some of our cousins got sick during lunch and lost their appetite, and I saw Grandma Stana whisper something to them while glancing at me and Srebra, after which everyone tried not to look at us while they ate, and their appetites returned. Grandma Stana would slip us two halves of a boiled egg or a piece of chocolate on the sly. One morning, while we were standing in the yard, we noticed a car parked in front of one of the neighbors' houses, and a man got out with two girls our age. The man let the girls out, kissed them, and immediately drove off, while they took their suitcases, climbed up the steps to the house, knocked, and went in without anyone opening the door for them. Grandma Stana crossed herself three times, then turned to us and said, "Don't let me catch you going out with them; they are not suitable friends for you." We were surprised and kept asking her why we shouldn't get to know them. "Did you see their father? He's not even allowed inside. He's a Shiptar, a damned Albanian, that's why! Svetlana was such a beauty, but she went off to study in Prishtina, where she found him and bam—she was pregnant. For years now her mother and father haven't talked to her; they disowned her in the paper, and don't ever want to see him. They feel bad for the children, though, so they take them during the break. If I were their grandma, I wouldn't let them come. She fell in love with a Shiptar—let her take care of them herself. I don't even want to catch so much as a glimpse of her. That's why I don't want to catch you with them. No one here talks to them; they'll hang around at home for two weeks, and then their father will come to pick them up—he's not allowed to set foot in the house." It was all pretty incomprehensible to us, the lack of brotherhood and unity among the peoples and nations of Yugoslavia. Srebra, who already attentively followed politics on television while I read, whispered, "Wow! Grandma Stana doesn't know what she's saying." On the afternoons when we didn't go to the beach, our cousin Tanja got her harmonica and played for us the Macedonian folk song about Biljana bleaching her linen, the only song that connected them to Macedonia, the land of their grandmother. They had a strange attitude toward their grandmother's origins, and she had forgotten the Macedonian language. It was hard for her that not one of her four sisters in Macedonia, among them our real grandmother, had luck like hers, to live life with a husband who carried her in his arms, loved her, and respected her into their old age. "Macedonian husbands are dreadful," she would say, "There isn't anyone there like my Ljubo." Yet our mother would tell us, upstairs in the room before we fell asleep, "Poor Nada, with that Stojko. He's got her trained. She's like his dog, and whatever he says, goes." During the day, Srebra and I paid more attention to our aunt's behavior, and watched to see whether she was, in fact, so well trained that she was like a dog. In some ways, it was true: she worked from dawn till dusk, cooking for thirteen people, washing the dishes, making apple strudel and cakes sprinkled with grated nuts, plus finding kind words for each of us. Every morning, she beat an egg yolk for Srebra and me to drink. She said, "It's not for separating your heads, if that's why you think I'm giving it to you. It's so you'll have lovely voices, because whoever has a beautiful voice is beautiful, even if they have three heads." The middle daughter liked to lick Vegeta herb salt, and would get up secretly at night to lap it up. Once, Srebra and I went downstairs for a drink of water, and we found her sitting on top of the dining-room table, with her legs on the chair she had sat on that day, and in her hands, she held the small white container with the red letters spelling "Vegeta." She was licking the yellow-green dust from her fingers and sighing in pleasure, in delight—the sounds reminding me of the sounds I couldn't release, that remained in my throat and excited me, on those nights with the pointed cap of the clown inside me. Suza experienced that sort of pleasure licking Vegeta, and when she noticed us, she let the jar fall from her hands. It rolled and fell to the floor with a sharp clang, shaking the condiment all over the place. Srebra and I immediately ran upstairs, Suza muttering something after us, not daring to call out for fear of waking the others. The oldest cousins, Vesna and Sonja, were only ten months apart, and behaved maternally toward Srebra and me. They sewed us slacks out of red material that our uncle had bought in the city. He just about ordered them to sew us new pants, noting that we were always in the same pairs of green shorts. They cut pieces of apple strudel for us, showed us the village, took us to visit their neighbors, and in one way or another protected us from the overly curious or hostile glances of the people we met at the beach or around the village. Someone dubbed us the "two-for-one Macedonian," and that's what we were called until the end of our stay. Our male cousin, our uncle's only son, the same age as us, had two ways of behaving: usually, he was good and called us "sisters from my auntie," but one day, he tricked us into going inside the outhouse behind the house, which was used only when someone didn't feel like going indoors. And when we got inside, he locked us in, dropping the bolt, and began to laugh loudly, calling out, "two-for-one Macedonian, double heads, double asses, I laugh and laugh myself to pieces." And that wasn't all—he untied the dog that was lying peacefully in its doghouse and tied it to the outhouse door, so that, from a distance, nobody could hear us over the dog's barking. Our mother and father were in Ulcinj, and we were alone in Lukin Vir, left, of course, in the trusted care of our relatives. Other than eating and sleeping, no one worried about anything else: we children were always outside, at the beach or in the yard, and Srebra and I most often lay in the grass in the yard on our stomachs. She turned the pages of old editions of the Serbian *Evening News* or *Politika*'s entertainment section while I read the collected works of Maupassant that Vesna had ordered for me. Now, as Srebra and I languished in the outhouse, there wasn't another sound to be heard: our cousins had gone to the river, Grandma Stana and Grandpa Ljubo were dozing in the house—likely glancing occasionally at the kettle with beans boiling on the woodstove—and our aunt and uncle were in the city, visiting our aunt's brother, who had suddenly been taken by ambulance to the hospital. For a while, Srebra and I shouted and pleaded for someone to open the outhouse door for us, but as time went by and we realized no one was coming, we grew angry, and the two of us, with a strength that we did not know we possessed, pushed on the door. The bolt gave way, one of the boards splintered, and the door swung loose, pulled from its upper hinge. We went out, stinking of excrement and urine. The dog was barking his head off, though he didn't know why he was barking and why he was tied up there. Just then, our uncle's car pulled up in front of the house. Our aunt stepped out, a black shawl over her head. She was crying silently; pearl-shaped tears were running down her face, and without making a sound, she entered the house with small, tired steps, while Srebra and I set off quietly after her. She paused as if about to nod, her face pale and sallow, then went directly to her bedroom on the second floor. She closed the door, and we didn't hear her until our cousins got back from the beach. No one went up to check on her, not Grandma or Grandpa, nor our uncle—no one. At the time, that seemed strange. I asked myself how it was possible that no one went up to her to ask how she was, or what had happened; everyone left her alone, and the house was filled with a deathly quiet. Years later, I saw people behave that way in films, leaving the sad people in peace so they could pull themselves together, and that it was the right thing not to pour out sympathy onto the person in pain. How incomprehensible that was to me at the time! "Oh, just wait till Mom hears," said Srebra, and we no longer knew how to behave there. We gathered with the others in our cousins' room; they were crying and looking at us askance as if we were somehow guilty of the death of their uncle, whom we had never even met. "There are outsiders here who are useless to us but not our uncle who is gone," said our cousin, sobbing. Sonja and Vesna gave him a sign to be quiet; he looked us directly in the eyes, and he didn't hate us or like us, it just wasn't clear to him what we were doing there right then and what we wanted in their house, from their family, we, relatives who had been absolutely unknown to them until then, intruders on their pain. We also wanted to leave as quickly as possible. Mom and Dad returned from Ulcinj on the day of the burial, when everyone except us had gone into the city; it was the date of our birth, Srebra's and my birthday, but they didn't remember. We were alone in the house, and when our parents found out what had happened, they decided we should leave as soon as possible. Our mother wanted to iron some clothes for the road, and got the iron from behind the couch in the living room, but when she began to iron on the bed, the iron overheated and there was instantly a strong smell. "Oh, dear Mother, it's burned out," she said. The iron, probably the only one in the house, had overheated. Our father cursed a few times, and Srebra and I felt the blood pound in our temples, our shared blood; it was as if our heads wanted to explode, each in its own direction. Our noses and backs were peeling from being out in the sun for days at a time without sunscreen. Dad was also sunburned. In Ulcinj, he had spent a lot of time lying on the tent fly during the most intense heat, and now he was peeling too. The four of us stood in the living room, Mom muttering about the iron, Dad clearing his throat and occasionally cursing, until Mom said, "All right now, that's enough. What's happened, happened; the people here don't know where their heads are from the grief, and they don't need to hear that from you on top of it." Still, no one remembered that it was our birthday. That evening, everyone returned from the burial. We sat in silence; the pale faces of the children and grown-ups merged with the black mourning clothes they wore. Our grandmother got up, went into the kitchen, brought back some bread and cheese, and said, "You need to eat something," offering it to us. Although we were really hungry, we couldn't eat; the bits of food stuck in our throats, and our cousins were looking through us as though we were invisible. Why didn't we express our condolences? Why did our parents only express their sympathy to our aunt? And we didn't even do that! No one had taught us that one expresses sympathy to a person who has lost someone close. We lay down early to sleep that evening, and the next morning, even before Grandma's rooster crowed, we set off for Skopje. Our uncle had shoved a shoebox with a pigeon in it into the car. It died just as we arrived at our building. The first thing we did on our return to Skopje was buy an iron. Our father wrapped it in pages from the evening paper *Večer* that our mother brought home from work after her director had finished reading it, sealed it with tape, put the package on his black bicycle, and took it to the post office. He mailed it to our relatives in Montenegro. That is how our summer in Montenegro ended. After that incident, Mom rarely mentioned that she had spoken on the phone with them. Still, they remained in our lives, and perhaps we did in theirs.

On December 3, 1988, a demonstration was held in front of the Greek consulate to protest the Greeks' failure to recognize us as Macedonians. A mass of people, flags, banners, shouts, cries of support, well-crafted speeches, and various other events. And then we jostled in the smoke-filled rooms of the Boni and Ani Café across from the consulate with glasses of vodka cut with fruit juice in our hands. Srebra and I went into town quite rarely, to avoid being laughed at, as our mother said, and that made each such outing a special event. We were already high-school students, with free monthly transit passes, so it was easy to get downtown. That evening, when we returned home, our uncle Stojko from Montenegro was there; he had come to Skopje to get his degree in physical education from the university. Why he chose the university in Skopje was not entirely clear to us, but for the first time in his life, he had officially acknowledged his roots on his mother's side and had decided to get his degree in Macedonia. "I'll bet he brought his pistol," Srebra whispered when we got into bed. I, unaccustomed as I was to talking when the light was off, said nothing, but shivers ran through my body: on the other side of the wall our uncle slept with a gun under his head, across from our father in the other bed. After our mother had arranged everything in the kitchen, she came to our room to sleep in the other bed, which had been empty for years; it had been bought as a package deal with our bed, because it was cheaper that way. Cushions from our mother's dowry decorated with butterflies and kittens lay on top of it. I think no one except our uncle closed an eye that night. He left early the next morning. We didn't mention him again for a long time. Nor did we ever consider going to Montenegro again on vacation. Then, in December 1989, our mother came home from work one day and announced as she came in the door that Stojko had been taken by some idea or other and had gone to Romania to fight either for Ceauşescu or the opposition. "There's good money to be had," she said, but several days later, we saw on television that the Romanians had killed Ceauşescu and his wife, and though we tried to find our uncle in the crowd of people, we couldn't see him. On December 31, the squares in Poland, Czechoslovakia, Romania, and Germany were filled with people welcoming the new year with shouts of "No Communism in 1990!" Srebra said to me, "Do you know what countries are still Communist?" I wasn't sure what the answer was. "Yugoslavia, the USSR, and Albania," she said. "That's not so few," I said. "No, it is a lot," Srebra responded. The next day, January 1, 1990, we received a call from Montenegro, not to wish us a Happy New Year, but to tell us that Grandpa Ljubo had died. Our father's eyes filled with tears. He dressed and put some things he would need in a suitcase. Our mother gave him money for the bus and for while he was there, saying—because she took charge of the money for both of them—"So you can buy candles and flowers," and he left on the bus to Montenegro for Grandpa Ljubo's burial. Grandpa Ljubo's son, our uncle, arrived at the same time as our father, directly from Romania. In Romania, the dictator and his wife had been buried in secret, but in Lukin Vir, at Grandpa Ljubo's funeral, there were lots of people—the whole village—and countless wreaths, flowers, and all sorts of other things, crying and wailing of young and old, our father among them, and our cousin took his grandfather's gun and shot over and over again into the air, down to the last bullet. Now he would sleep with the gun under his pillow. "God forgive him," our mother said, and crossed herself three times. I pressed the Zlata Meglenska icon in my pocket; Srebra pursed her lips. We were very sad for Grandpa Ljubo, for Grandma Stana, and for our aunt, but less so for our uncle, even though he had lost his father, because it seemed to all of us that Grandpa Ljubo might not have had a heart attack if his son hadn't gone off to Romania as a mercenary.

And that wasn't the end. Several years later our uncle and our cousin went to Bosnia to fight with the Serbs. That was the last thing our mother heard on the phone; after that, the phone lines were down for a long time. Our cousin was the same age as us, but he was already killing people. Our mother sent Srebra and me by bus to Montenegro to bring our relatives flour, oil, sugar, and noodles. "Why are we going and not Dad?" "You're young women; they'll let you across the border," she said, not worried that something might happen to us—to us in particular, given how we were with conjoined heads but bodies already those of young women. That was the first time we crossed a Macedonian border and not a Yugoslav one. It wasn't regular border guards who entered the bus, but soldiers with machine guns. First, they stared in shock at our heads moving at the same time as if mechanical, then they grabbed our passports and disappeared for a full two hours, while the driver of the bus swore at us, saying they had been stopped solely on our account, because people with pumpkins instead of heads didn't cross the border every day. "Fuck those heads of yours," he said, and Srebra wanted to yell at him and spout off a few hundred choice expressions, but I squeezed her hand and said, "Don't, don't, or we'll be stuck here at the border until hell freezes over." The soldiers carrying machine guns returned and asked us where we were going; I proudly said our uncle's name; he was considered the best physical education teacher in Ivangrad. "Berane," the soldier sternly corrected me. "In Berane," he repeated, and I repeated the word, and it was quite strange to me that we had set off for Ivangrad, but in the meantime, its name had been changed to Berane. He gave us our passports but couldn't resist saying, "What's with your heads?" We only shrugged our shoulders—what could we tell him?—and we continued on and reached Berane, where our uncle was waiting for us. With a firm masculine handshake, he said right to our faces in Serbian, "So, Macedonia, it seems, is separatist? You don't want to be with the Serbs, with us? You want to be like the Slovenes and Croatians? If so, Macedonia will collapse; it will totally collapse!" All the way from the bus station to their house, in the car, he kept repeating that we were separatists, and that there was no one like Slobo Milošević in the whole world. Our aunt hugged and kissed us; our cousin blushed. His forehead and cheeks had deep furrows that didn't correspond to his youthful face. Our oldest cousins had resettled at their aunt's in Pančevo; they found work there, and one of them a husband—the middle cousin got married to a soldier who had fought with our cousin in the war in Bosnia. As for the youngest, she was at work, volunteering at the hospital. Srebra and I watched two long videos of our middle cousin's wedding with all the traditional customs, the fathers' speeches, the winding line dance, and the departure of the bride from her father's house when everyone yells, "Don't turn around, Suza, don't turn around!" which reminded both Srebra and me of a film that was shown on Macedonian television, *Don't Turn Around, Son*, but our aunt explained that if the bride turns back toward her father's house, she will give birth to a girl. And she said that when she got married to our uncle she had turned around, four times even, because it was so difficult for her to leave her father's house, and that's why she had four daughters, and only then a son, "May he have a long and healthy life." Afterward, our uncle took us to the attic to show us all their reserves. There, covering the floor, stacked on top of each other, were bags of flour and sugar, boxes filled with oil and vinegar, bags of noodles, conserves, and who knows what else. "We have provisions; everything is here if we need it," our uncle said, and we were ashamed of the few kilos of flour and sugar and two liters of oil in our bag that our mother had us bring to them in case of a crisis or war. "We're not waiting for Macedonians to supply us," our uncle said and smiled. "But the time will come for us to provide for you." And then, in a serious voice, he continued to talk about Macedonians as cowards and separatists, how they wanted their own republic, but what would they do with it, what's a republic for a nation like that? It would be much better for the Macedonians to have stayed with the Serbs and with them, the Montenegrins, to live under Milošević. "And those guys to the north can just fuck off," he said. He then began telling us at length what great warriors the Serbs had been in Bosnia, how each true Serb—even if he were a Montenegrin—was more honorable for having fought in Croatia and Bosnia and how he had not even considered that his son might not sign up for such a thing. He said, "You should have seen what a good shot Kolja was; he was such a great soldier that he amazed everybody!" Srebra and I stayed silent, our fingers fumbling with our cousin's black wool cap with a cross in the middle, which our uncle had shoved into our hands, and we could barely wait to get outside for some fresh air. Outside, below the house, flowed the Lim River, the same river as in the village a few kilometers from the house. Srebra and I went down to the river, and some force from I don't know where swelled my breast, and I began to sing the Macedonian song "Tell Me Why You Left Me." At first Srebra was silent, but then she joined in, and we sang that song loudly, as loudly as we could. As we kept walking along the river we sang, "Tell me why you left me and drenched me in sorrow," and a sorrow spread through our bodies—from our toes all the way up to our shared vein—and the river roared in our heads and the blood rushed in our hearts and tears poured from our eyes as if someone really had left us right then. A pain, almost like a love pang, spread through us from the sound of the song in our throats. That evening, our middle cousin, who was married to our other cousin's comrade-in-arms, made dinner in our honor. On a table stretched across the whole room were roasted lamb and pans of rice and potatoes. Everyone gathered, except our cousins who had moved to Pančevo. When we had eaten our fill, our aunt and uncle stood up and said, "You are all young. Enjoy yourselves; we're going home." And after they left, our cousin's husband put on a cassette, and the traditional Serbian *kolo* burst forth, and everyone leaped from their seats, hugged each other, and pulled us along with them as they danced the kolo, and it wound around with thunderous repetitions of the words. They sang with unwavering voices—both the men and the women—and spun around, spinning us too, and our cousin's husband's hand slipped from my shoulder and slid down to my breast. I felt him squeeze my breast, kneading it with his hand, singing along, and in the midst of the frenetic dance, the words "Serbo, Serbo, Slobo, Slobo" rang out. I couldn't stand it any longer and screamed as if someone had struck me. Srebra shouted, "Enough, enough. Stop it!" and once everyone had stopped, Srebra began to cry hysterically, and I right along with her. We shouted over and over again, "We want to go home, we want to go home," and tumbled to the floor, banging our conjoined foreheads, shouting, "Go home, go home." Finally they somehow got us outside, stuffed us into a car, and drove us to our aunt and uncle's; the next day, we caught the first bus, having waved hastily to our uncle at the station. We never saw them again. Our uncle died a few months later of a heart attack, and I heard, years later, that our aunt was still alive and had twelve grand-children each with a name more interesting, more Slavic, and more Serbian, than the last.

But that was many years later. When Srebra and I spent that summer in Lukin Vir for the first and only time, we were in our first year of high school. But the high-school years are not worth recalling, because it was a minimal life, one reduced to traveling to school by two buses in the morning—in the greatest possible crush of people—and the daily smirking of a group of high-school students who pushed and shoved each other on the bus and always banged into us out of malice. Some were so rude that they'd try to push between us, intentionally ignoring the fact that our heads were conjoined and they could not get through. We endured so much physical pain over those four years while traveling on the two buses to school and two buses home, so many jokes because of our deformity, and were constantly singled out. That time wasn't comparable to the years at primary-school desks in our neighborhood, although even during those eight years, someone always teased us about things that weren't our fault. But leaving our neighborhood, joining the passengers on the city buses and later our classmates and teachers in school—most of whom were initially shocked and then revolted by our physical handicap—we saw that in primary school our introduction to society had been extremely limited compared with others at that age, and now it was as if we had been thrown into a boxing ring but didn't know how to box. "You'll learn, and then you'll see how to do it," the psychologist told us when we went to see him on my insistence, because I felt, two months into high school, that I could not cope with my appearance, which was so critical to being included by the others. "Dress as nicely as possible, be as clean, modern, and attractive as you can. You are beautiful girls, and they'll stop teasing you, you will see. Distinguish yourselves as much as possible in your classes, learn English, speak up in every class, and they'll look at you differently. Even more important is not to argue between yourselves, don't hate each other, and don't give them occasion to hate you. In short, young ladies, love yourselves more than anything so that others might love you." That is what the psychologist, a chubby man the same height as us, said. The part about studying and distinguishing ourselves was not a problem; both of us were excellent students, and although Srebra wanted to enroll in the social-science track in our high school, things turned out my way, and we enrolled in language arts. Until then, we had never attended any English or French courses, but we had always loved to learn foreign words on our own, lying on our stomachs on the bed and reading English words from the dictionary. That's why, even from the beginning, we distinguished ourselves in class, industriously studying all the new material and responding to every question. When we both stood or went to the board but only one of us answered, you could hear giggling, sometimes muffled, sometimes loud, from the back desks. The teachers seemed to need time to get used to our duality; it would surprise them every time both of us stood up but only one of us answered. Over time, they got accustomed to it. It was much more difficult for us to follow the first bit of the psychologist's advice: look our best, wash regularly, sparkle with beauty. How? At home, we continued to have a real bath only once a week, on Sunday evenings, so we were clean at the beginning of the week. On Wednesdays we heated water in the boiler, poured it into the white tub, and then carried it to the green cracked pot in the bathroom, and then with the yogurt container, poured the water in turns, first me, then Srebra. Acne broke out on our faces, our backs, and even on our backsides sometimes, and, ashamed or not, we squeezed our pimples and wiped our hands on the insides of our blouses, or, if we were lucky enough, on a handkerchief. When we got our periods, never at the same time, instead of pads we used rags that our mother boiled on the stove in the same green pot and ironed after each washing to get rid of any bacteria. Instead of ordinary underwear, we shared the same single pair of nylon feminine hygiene underwear that didn't leak but did soak our skin, leaving red lines. We only rarely got new clothes, so we wore what we found at home, sometimes even our mother's old skirts and dresses, which were old-fashioned but not yet retro. We didn't get an allowance, and except for when our aunts or uncle gave us a bit of money, we couldn't sit in cafés after school with an iced coffee or hot chocolate attempting to befriend our classmates. We practically had to beg for money for toothbrushes and a tube of toothpaste so we could finally switch from rubbing our teeth with salt on our fingers, as we'd done until then. We had learned the technique from our father, who, when we were young and had to go to the dentist, took the salt shaker out of the cupboard in the kitchen, wet his right index finger under the faucet, dipped it in the salt, and then rubbed our teeth. Our mouths burned from the salt, and we rinsed them with water as tears came to our eyes from the taste chafing the roofs of our mouths. Now, finally, we had toothbrushes and a gold box of Kalodont toothpaste. Also, the dentist in the state hospital, a young and energetic woman, wasn't disgusted by our looks and had us lean against the wall; then she climbed on a chair and carefully examined our teeth, all the while talking and pointing out the problems with our teeth to the students standing around us. A few of them gaped at our conjoined heads, but most of them were so in love with the dentist that they didn't even consider laughing. The most difficult to follow was the psychologist's third bit of advice: to love each other most of all. How can a person love herself if she is never alone, if she is not independent both physically and psychologically? At first glance, Srebra and I were only physically attached, with the shared vein covered by skin and hair just below my left temple and her right. The doctor at the general clinic told us that through this shared vein our shared blood flowed and we both had A positive blood, and that both our brains and both our hearts were fed by the nutrients our shared blood delivered to them. He didn't see any possibility of separating our heads. As far as we were concerned that was the opinion of an "unschooled doctor" who didn't know all the things that were being done abroad, and even in greater Yugoslavia. "In Macedonia, you can die having your appendix out, let alone during an operation like separating heads," our aunt Ivanka would say. She knew several nurses at Skopje clinics, and even a medical technician in the state hospital, and everyone said to her, "Don't let your nieces even entertain the idea of having that kind of operation in our country; we don't have specialists like that." Still, we had heard that there was one, but there was simply no way to get to him, so it was easier for us to believe Aunt Ivanka. We were to be physically marked forever. But our lack of physical independence was not the only impediment to our individuality. The physical spot that joined us had psychological consequences as well. We couldn't do what we wanted; we couldn't fulfill our own desires, because we always had to depend on each other. I knew that the decision to enroll in the foreign-language track in high school was my choice alone, but it compelled Srebra to study the same thing even though she had wanted to study the social sciences. She wasn't satisfied with the choice and wasn't satisfied with herself. We did not like ourselves most of all, nor was there love between us, although we did feel some amorphous closeness—we were twins, born at the same time, with the same eyes, the same faces, the same bodies. We knew that should something happen to one of us, it would by necessity happen to the other as well. We would warn each other when crossing the street or walking along a narrow sidewalk. We would say, "Be careful" if a car passed close by, or if there was something in our way we could bang into. We would have been very happy, beautiful young twins if we had not had that physical connection. We would have belonged to each other more had we been able to live each according to her own will, desires, and interests. We would have loved ourselves, as the psychologist had advised us, if we had been "normal" girls, and we would have been normal girls with crushes, boyfriends, young friendships, and new life experiences had we been two separate people, each for herself. What gave us strength during those high-school years? For me, it was surely books, and, most significant at critical moments, the icon of Saint Zlata Meglenska tucked in my pocket or in my purse. Her face, scraped, peeling from the wood, always looked directly in my eyes, but her look was stern and sad. Sometimes, it bothered me that she didn't look at me more tenderly, that she never smiled or closed her eyes, but always stared directly in my eyes; she absorbed me with her look, cut me with it, penetrating through me, sternly and sadly. On the other hand, I rarely looked at her; more often, I just wanted to feel her with my hand, hold her in my pocket, and sometimes squeeze her so hard I'd draw blood, to feel her presence physically in my life. Srebra didn't have that kind of dependence on anyone or anything. She was happiest when we sat and watched television, or when I read with my elbows on the table while she stared at the television with her elbows also on the table—my left elbow and her right pushing against each other. She watched the daily news reports, which spoke about the social structure of Yugoslavia, the post-Tito government, and problems in Kosovo. She wanted to read the *Young Fighter* and *Communist* newspapers, and one day she even begged me to go to the post office with her so she could subscribe to the Slovenian liberal review *Mladina*. The social turmoil in our country attracted her attention, as did wars and social movements throughout the world. It wasn't clear to me whether Srebra was right-wing or left-wing; I don't think it was clear to her either, because she liked positions and ideas from both the left and the right. One day she said, "Yugoslavia is going to break apart." Our mother, wiping the glass table-top upon which Srebra was reading a newspaper and I the fifth book of *In Search of Lost Time*, said, "Of course it won't. It's not going to fall apart; Slobo won't allow it." At the time, many people called Slobodan Milošević by the nickname

Slobo, but they had no idea what he was doing, whether he was good for Yugoslavia or for Macedonia, and the grown-ups' opinions were tossed around like odd mismatched shoes. If the person they were talking to said something positive about Milošević, everybody else agreed, but if someone said he was a mafioso, everyone agreed that he stole just like the others, caring nothing about the people. Our parents were among those who didn't have their own opinions about him but changed position depending on which guests were visiting. The first thing that came to my mind was that if the situation was as Srebra said it was and Yugoslavia would collapse, then we were too late—we should have gone to Belgrade or to Zagreb for the operation. "Maybe it's better," said Srebra. "We'll have to go to London." London had been turning around in her head since childhood. I don't know where she acquired such faith in London, but she had been convinced forever that one fine sunny day, when we were big enough and rich enough for the complex operation, we would definitely have to seek a solution in London. I think it came from the time we were playing a game and Roza mentioned that she had heard there were doctors in London who would revive the queen if she died. Did Srebra wrap up the idea of London back then and hold on to it all these years as a refuge for her hopes? Even though I believed Roza when she said there were doctors who could revive the queen if she died, London had never become a refuge for me. We were two absolutely ordinary girls from Macedonia, children of a working-class family, with no connections, money, or opportunity to gain access to those London doctors who could revive the queen. "If Bogdan ever comes to Skopje, we could ask him," I said, and Srebra was surprised that I had thought of Bogdan after the two of us had erased him from our minds following his departure for London with his newly acquired mother. He had never contacted anyone, no classmates, no neighbors, not us who had been, after all, his only friends besides Roza. Yes, were Bogdan to come, we could ask him whether there was a doctor in London who could ease our suffering. But waiting for Bogdan was delusional. Sadness pricked my soul when I thought of Bogdan, because he was inseparably connected with Roza; they were our only friends from childhood, and both had disappeared from our solitary world. We were all together in only one photograph from our childhood: a small faded black-and-white photo in which we kneeled and stared off to the side, at someone or something. Roza, in a white dress with lace, Srebra and I in red dresses with white dots, and behind us, sitting on a bench looking at the camera, are Bogdan, Mara, Viki, and Vesna, all dressed in holiday clothes. You have to wonder when the photograph was taken—was it Easter or Patron's Day at our school? And who took the photo of us? Srebra said she recalled that Uncle Dobre took our picture "before his operation," because for us kids, Uncle Dobre's life was divided into before and after the operation on his eyes; through some sort of injury he had been left blind in one eye and from then on, he didn't laugh as he had before and didn't tease us while making animal sounds before laughing so long and so loud, so tenderly, that it made all of us children love him. A real misfortune befell us when, after his eye surgery, he stopped laughing and teasing, instead going quickly past on the stairs with a sad and stern face, like that of my Saint Zlata Meglenska. How he cried when Roza died; how many tears fell from his blind eye. The evening of her wake when she was dressed in a child's wedding dress he wept as if she were his own child.

Left to ourselves, without friends or boyfriends, I felt that

Srebra and I spent our high-school days reminiscing about our childhood, which had irrevocably passed, trying to connect our present life with what had been—and nothing was as it had been. Auntie Verka continued to drink and sing, swaying on the stairs, sometimes alone, sometimes with the Gypsy Riki, who came back to her time and again, until the fateful evening when he disappeared forever from our building—first to the police station, and then who knows where. That evening, as Srebra and I returned from school, we stumbled upon some commotion in the entryway, and then our curious neighbors approached from all sides and two police officers came with clubs in their hands. We were surprised but not frightened, because the police had their hats on, which meant no one had died, and we grasped that Riki had tried to rape Auntie Dobrila. He had frightened her and she had attacked him with a flowerpot and a stick of wood, so he had run to Auntie Verka's, where no one would open the door under any circumstances. Everyone finally dispersed without the police doing anything concrete, but two hours later, we heard shouts again, as two new police officers grabbed Riki under his arms, led him outside, and shoved him into a blue van. We never saw Riki again, and Auntie Verka never mentioned him. She drowned herself in alcohol, until one day, shortly before we finished high school, her son came and carried her out of the apartment in his arms; he locked the apartment, and we never heard anything more of her. The apartment remained locked and empty for several years, and when a young family with a small child moved in, it was as if the story of Auntie Verka was erased forever. None of the neighbors ever mentioned her; no one asked where she was or what had happened to her; everyone seemed to breathe more easily now that she was no longer there—now that the stench of cigarette smoke, rakija, and burned food no longer wafted from her apartment. That's how people from our childhood disappeared. Our high-school years, which, by definition, should have been the most frenetic and exciting, were, in fact, the most boring, following the well-worn path of home—two buses—school—two buses—home, and on Fridays or Saturdays, though not every week, to the Central movie house, the theater to see a play, or, rarely, to a café, and only twice to a disco, once to Hearth and once to Tourist. At both places, the bouncers told us they would let us in that once, but the next time, they would let us in only if we had gotten pretty enough to attract other young people. I don't know why they had to do that, since even without any special events, there were long lines in front of the discos, and they let in only girls or couples, but not groups of young men, and the only time we went, two guys immediately attached themselves to us so they could get in. Once inside, they got lost in the crowd, and we bopped along with several other girls from our class, one next to the other, swinging our heads first left, then right. Everyone who passed by, drink in hand, stared at us, pausing for a moment and nudging each other. One group of three guys and two girls crashed into us, as if by accident, crushing our fingers and shoving us in the groin, and then, pretending to apologize, they moved on, laughing, but we just pulled ourselves together and kept dancing until midnight; then we caught the night bus at the Record stop, and, still subjected to sneers and tasteless jokes, we arrived home at last.

The custom of not celebrating birthdays in our family hit us hardest in 1990, when we turned eighteen. We bought a red candle in a red glass jar with a lid from a woman at an improvised market in front of the Žito Luks bakery. The candle seemed so unusual that we wanted it for our birthday, but when we got it home, our mother shouted not to light it because it would be a shame to burn such a beautiful and expensive candle; it would be better if we kept it as a souvenir. So the candle stood in the bathroom for years, on a plastic decorative dish on top of the shelf where shoes were kept, and it was only later that I realized it was a memorial candle, like those placed in Catholic cemeteries. Sometimes, we were drawn by some magic force to the drawer in our room where the almanac with its horoscopes, fortune-telling guides, and perpetual calendar was kept; it was still open to the page of our uncle's birthday. It was noted that he would be married twice, which had been our grandmother's hope for years, that he would find a better wife than our aunt, maybe a doctor or a nurse. We wanted to read about ourselves in the almanac, but I told Srebra that it might be better if we didn't, because the text would apply to two people, and did she really want us to continue this same joint life, with no hope of separation? "You're right," said Srebra. "It's better that we don't know what awaits us." Also in the drawer was the book *Mara's Wedding*, and inside it was a matchbox with Marjan's address; he had been writing ever since he first wrote to us as pen pals in primary school, addressing the New Year's greeting card to the "male or female twins." In the card for 1985, in addition to the wishes for success in the new year, he had written a postscript that read, "Write to me," along with his address in Jegunovce, near Tetovo. At the time, Srebra and I couldn't control our laughter, but also our anger that some kid from Jegunovce had sent us a New Year's card, and what's more, he wanted to exchange letters with us. We ripped up the greeting card and threw it out the window onto the driveway behind the building. Our mother scolded us and ordered us to go and get it, because Marjan had the same last name as a well-known cardiologist at the state hospital in Skopje. "That might be his father," Mom said, "but even if he's his uncle, that would still be good; we might need him. You never know; you have to stay in contact with a family like that." So Srebra and I went downstairs and climbed through the glassless window frame in the basement, and found the torn and scattered pieces of the card. We gathered up the pieces, which were wet with snow and dirt, and Roza, who had just scattered scraps on the balcony railing for the hungry sparrows, urged us to put the card back together, but we hadn't found all the pieces. For Mom, it was most important for us to find the piece with Marjan's address; we absolutely had to write to him, we had to, and she would send the card through the courier at work. I don't know why we obeyed her, but we did, and for years, Marjan wrote us letters and greeting cards at regular intervals. Then all at once, he stopped, and we no longer wrote to him either. Each time he wrote, he invited us to Jegunovce to visit his parents so we could actually meet each other, but we always found an excuse, and we never invited him to come; we never sent him our photograph, so he never found out about our handicap. He must have thought we were two normal twins with strange names, though names like ours, he wrote, were not a rarity among Macedonians in the Tetovo region, and there were even many boys named Srebre or Zlate. We never asked him whether the well-known cardiologist was a relation of his, and, thank God, no one needed him.

In 1991, at school the day before the Yugoslav selection for the Eurovision song contest, which Srebra and I followed every year without exception, our geography teacher spoke about the position of each republic within Yugoslavia: "Yugoslavia is a mother with six children and two stepchildren. Mother and stepmother." Our teacher, with her great pregnant belly covered by a dark blue dress, leaned despondently on the table, her elbows resting sideways on the lectern, her blue eyes washed out, her skin pale, her hair short and greasy. From a classmate in Macedonian class we had learned that a year earlier, her husband ran over their three-year-old son while backing the car out of the garage. The son had died. Now she was pregnant again, just on the verge of giving birth. She could barely walk; she barely spoke. I was obsessed with her story in the days before she gave birth, just before our graduation evening. I asked myself whether it was possible, just three or four months after the death of one's child, to conceive another child. A second child, after the first no longer existed. At night in bed, conquering the sadness, the pain, the consciousness, the emptiness, the hate, the resistance, the loss, the memory, motherhood, fatherhood, for one's body to feel arousal, carnal desire, for the clitoris to tremble, the penis to harden, and for two despondent bodies to merge into one in orgasmic joy, in relaxation, relieving the stress and depression, and in that moment of conjoining, for them to conceive a new life? The child's room is empty; there is no one there to awaken. Does the new child replace the old one? Will it be a simulacrum of his brother, wear his clothes? Will it have the same name? Will it sleep in his pajamas in his little bed? Will it be loved because of what it is, or unloved because of what it is not? Will it be a child or stepchild to its own mother and father? What drove me to think about that, I do not know. I had my sorry experience with the clown doll, the only sexual probing of my body, not counting my own fingers, which from time to time I poked under the elastic of my pajamas and underwear while Srebra slept, and entered my body, for a moment; I would reach the climax of sexual arousal, of ecstasy, but immediately afterward I was disgusted by myself, and instead of falling asleep in sweet bliss, I would be unable to close my eyes, thinking of my misfortune, of Srebra's misfortune, of our inability to have our own lives and sleep with our own, real boyfriends, spread our legs to a man's sexual organ like all our peers. I envisioned our geography teacher in that act, only three or four months after the death of her child, spreading her legs to her husband, and him entering her and conceiving a new child, and in that moment of union, they are infused with joy and pleasure. Perhaps for a moment, they forget their dead son run over by the family automobile through the inattention of his own father, the little body still disintegrating in its tiny coffin in the earth. And perhaps afterward, they don't feel happiness, but disgust. Perhaps they cry in the night, their backs turned to one another, filled with self-loathing, hatred toward each other, she with her unspoken, smothered reproaches that bubble to the surface from time to time during the day, causes him to run from her, stay longer at work just so he doesn't have to hear that he was guilty of the death of their son, and she shuts herself up among her geography atlases filled with photographs of their child, crying and moaning, while in her womb a new life kicks. O God! O holy Saint Zlata Meglenska, is that life? What awaits us? In my mind I could see the past, I could see the present, but the future had no color, no scent, no sign, no omen, no beacon, nothing. We only thought about tomorrow's trip to the village and how we would take the small black-and-white television set so we could watch the Eurovision song contest taking place that year in a hall in Sarajevo. The songs of the six republics and two provinces played one after another, immediately following an advertisement for Nivea face cream and the evening news, which had broadcast demonstrations against the government of

Slobodan Milošević that took place all day in Belgrade. Our father clicked his tongue without saying anything; our grandmother crossed herself three times; our mother only said, "Good God Almighty." But we quickly forgot about the unrest in Belgrade when the Yugoslav singers began to sing. The group Baby Doll won. On Monday, our art teacher asked whether we had watched Eurovision. She quoted the saying: "The village burns; Grandma combs her hair," then asked: "Did you see what's happening in Belgrade? It has finally occurred to people that they need to stand up to Milošević." Srebra, who followed the news and made connections between events happening elsewhere in the world and in our country—and thought about them but rarely shared her thoughts with me—said, "Yes, finally." The art teacher looked at her in surprise. She was the only teacher in our whole school who cared about our situation. We called her by her first name, Lala, which is what she told us she would like to be called. "I must do a drawing of you so you will have a picture as a memento once you are separated," she had said to us, and her words infused us with an assuredness that we would be separated some day, and both of us were stunned by her confidence. "Do you think so?" Srebra asked her uncertainly. "Yes, we live in the twentieth century," she replied. "Do you know how far medicine has progressed out there in the world?" "I don't know," I said, but inside, I felt I believed her, and it was in that instant that I began to like her, or to put it more precisely, began to respect her more than any other teacher in the school. Srebra liked her more, but I respected her more. After the matinee showing of *Dead Poets Society* at the Kultura movie theater we raced down Partizanska Street toward her, and when we caught up to her, the last person in the entire school going home, we nearly ran into her. She wrapped our heads in a hug and held us and we cried, out of sympathy, enchantment, admiration, sadness, joy, everything. That evening, we sat in a café in the Leptokaria mall, and while we drank juice, she told us about how, one day, she got totally fed up with everything: maintaining her ideal weight; her firm, smooth stomach; her smooth, hairless, cellulite-free legs; sick of all the care she had given her body in her youth; sick of the young men she changed like socks; sick of the high heels she wore to the receptions famous artists invited her to. She was fed up with being young, beautiful, blond, so she lay in bed for months. She just lay there and ate and didn't shave her legs, didn't color her hair, didn't paint her nails, didn't iron her clothes, didn't exercise; she just lay there and ate everything that came to hand. She emptied all the shelves in her mother's pantry, shook out all the boxes of crackers, snacks, and cookies, licked all the jars of jam and Eurocrem. Within a few months she had eaten more than she had in her entire life, and she got fat—three times as heavy as she had been; she fought against her own body. "And now," she said, "Look, I'm fat, but happy. I don't have a boyfriend, no one looks at me, no one bores me, I don't waste money on makeup and creams, I don't worry about what I eat, I'm free, free. I draw and I live." Srebra and I, our mouths full of the baguette sandwiches she had ordered for us, listened and nodded as we ate. We never bought ourselves baguettes, but we liked them more than anything. After rehearsal for the children's show *A New Year's Tale*, in which Srebra and I played a two-headed star who made children's dreams come true, Lala brought us the leftovers of the baguette sandwiches and talked openly to our classmates: "What makes Srebra and Zlata different from you? Is it the one small spot where nature joined them? Is that it? Is that enough of a reason to exclude someone from your group of friends, from society?" They kept quiet and bowed their heads, swallowing mouthfuls of baguette with mayonnaise and ham; it was unpleasant for Srebra and me. Lala was aware of that, so she asked us, "Why should it be uncomfortable for you? It should be unpleasant for the majority, not for the minority." We performed the show at the retirement home in the Zlokukani neighborhood, at a hospital for sick children, and at the Drugarče library. For a long time thereafter, some of our classmates called us the two-headed star, but Lala had given us self-confidence, which seemed to make us stronger, and we only smiled at the joke with pride. Before our eyes hovered the pale cheeks of the children from the hospital as they clapped for us with their little hands and waved with tears in their eyes when we left. Lala taught us it was more important to give than to receive and that everyone was good for something. Both Srebra and I thought of her when, on May 4, we watched the Eurovision contest and the group Baby Doll sang a catchy, but extremely dumb, song entitled "Brasil," which received only one vote. "The village burns; Grandma combs her hair," Srebra said, intentionally quoting Lala. "Yugoslavia won't exist anymore." To my shame, the first thing that came to mind was that if Yugoslavia ceased to exist, it would no longer have an entry in Eurovision, and that made me sad.

On May 6, 1991, the lead news story was a broadcast video of the murder in Split of Sašo Geškovski, a Yugoslav National Army soldier from Kavadarci. He was killed before everyone's eyes, mowed down by a Croatian Army bullet. Geškovski was the first official casualty of the Yugoslav conflict. That night, someone kept calling our phone. Srebra and I answered, but all we heard on the other end of the line was a strange rumbling sound. Someone was apparently dialing the wrong number, and we heard our parents in the big room saying, "Someone got our number somehow, and now they're pestering us." The ringing stopped. Sašo Geškovski had died; Yugoslavia collapsed. For the first time, Macedonia found itself affected by the events in Yugoslavia that had led to its collapse. Many people adopted an anti-Croatian, anti-Slovenian position, and in so doing, took the side of the Yugoslav National Army. They chose the side of Serbia and of Slobodan Milošević. This was just the beginning of an evil that we knew from our history textbooks was called war, but we had never thought it would happen in our lifetimes.

It wasn't long before we celebrated our graduation at the disco on the Kale fortress, but as usual, no one asked Srebra or me to dance. We hung out in a booth in the corner, waiting for the evening to end. Lala, dressed as usual in a black skirt and long black-fringed tee shirt, kept us company. She hugged us and said, "Now it's up to you to take charge of your lives. Know that I'm always here for you." She took two hundred English pounds from her pocket and shoved them into my patent leather purse, saying, "To help get you to London." Although both of us protested and wanted to give the money back right away, she said, "It's only a loan, that's all." We didn't know what to say; we simply felt how much this young woman meant to us, how close she was to us. It was the first concrete step toward our lifelong dream, the first bit of capital that Srebra and I would save in our drawer, tucked into the almanac with the perpetual calendar. Those two hundred pounds, more than anything else, awoke in us the hope that we really would be separated one day, that a solution could be found for our conjoined heads. After that, for a long time, we did not see Lala. We thought she would now have new special students in her new class, so we felt uncomfortable seeking her out. We didn't go to London. The money rested in the perpetual calendar and waited for the fine sunny day that, as Lala had said, must surely come. In the meantime, we saw her on television from time to time, always modest and positive— she had developed an entire film school for young people. Several years later at the airport, as we set off on our fateful trip to London, fate wanted us to meet Lala again. She was waiting for a flight to Turkey. "I'm looking for sponsors to buy movie cameras," she said. "The children need to shoot films. Good luck to you on the operation; I will see you later, separately, at Café Leptokaria." With her two hundred pounds in our hand luggage, we saw her for the last time, and she us.

A difficult decision awaited us after graduation, when we were to submit applications to universities. Srebra said, "I gave in when we enrolled in high school, now you need to give way." Over the years, I had sometimes thought about the day when we would need to choose a department, and knowing Srebra, I knew that she would say precisely this— that I needed to give in because she had given in and had allowed me to choose our high-school courses, but now we were facing the real decision: What should we study? We already knew other languages, and besides the general resistance Srebra felt toward the study of languages other than just learning enough to make ourselves understood, she didn't want to consider studying literature or languages, or anything like that. "No," she said, "I've had enough of things that don't interest me. Yugoslavia is disintegrating, but you still want to study something for pleasure," which is what she called those subjects. "Aren't you aware that you need to study something more specific, something important for society, and for the world? We'll study law, period," she said. If there's anything I don't like to read, it's legal records and legislative documents, and if there's something I don't like to write, it's appeals, testimonies, requests, and other administrative texts. And now Srebra wanted us to study law! "If you don't want to study literature, why don't we study ethnology or psychology?" I said, attempting to offer a new suggestion. "Because all those disciplines are egotistical, directed toward the individual. They are only concerned with an individual's being, his soul, or his nationality, but law is a discipline about everyone, about humanity. Everyone is the same before the law; there is no subjectivity, there are no personal thoughts and desires but rules and laws that must be respected, regardless of whether the question concerns one person, an entire community, an entire nation, or the entire world." We always spoke parallel to each other, because we couldn't look each other in the eye; our words disappeared as if carried off by the wind. I knew that Srebra was a good orator, and had, therefore, the foundation for being a lawyer, though I didn't know who would want a lawyer with the kind of physical deformity that Srebra and I had—to sit opposite not one, but two people, who were inseparable due to a bodily defect. For me, this was all so distant, so foreign, that for the whole night after our conversation, I lay with eyes open, cursing my fate. In fateful moments, Roza always appeared to me, and I now envied her that she was dead. I wanted to die as well, so I wouldn't have to face this dreadful choice. I didn't know how I could study something I did not like, how the knowledge would even enter my head at all. I would likely fail the exams, I thought, and Srebra and I would have to withdraw, or at least I would have to withdraw and then stay physically present in the classes and exams waiting for Srebra to finish. "What do they need to get a degree for?" we once heard our father say to our mother, "What then? Even if they do graduate, how will they find work? Who will take them with their heads like that?" Surprisingly, this time our mother was the more sympathetic: "Oh come on, let them finish something. You never know, maybe someday they'll open their own law office and support themselves. Maybe they'll be the bosses and people will work for them, and they'll earn the money. It's different with schooling. Besides, what will they do without it? When we die, they'll be out on the street." And in my private self-irony, I saw the name of our law office, "Two-Headed Star," and inside, Srebra and I sat on a double-wide chair, meeting clients, who stared and didn't know whether to turn and leave or sit on the chair opposite. Some did run off as if they'd had their heads cut off, but others sat down, and we took their cases, and whenever we went to court, there was always a crowd in the courthouse. They came out of curiosity, wanting to see the two-headed lawyers. And there were always many journalists, and every legal case we conducted received publicity, and…all sorts of other things as well. It was decided without my being asked for consent: we handed in our documents for admission to the Faculty of Law. And we were accepted.

The lead story on the news the next day was that Slovenia had broken away from Yugoslavia and voted for independence, and the next story was that Croatia had done the same. "I told you," said Srebra. "Yugoslavia doesn't exist anymore." "What do you mean? Yugoslavia can exist without them," Dad said, but Mom's first comment was, "Oh no, poor Tomče! Who knows what he's up to? He'll never be able to return." Tomče was one of her first cousins on her mother's side, our mother's youngest cousin, who as a child had gone to live with his uncles in Slovenia after his father died in a mining accident, and who now worked there. He had an apartment, money, but what was all that to him now that he couldn't return to Macedonia?

Would the Slovenes permit him to leave, now that they had separated? She said she would call him the next day at his house in Jesenice, and she really did try to get him on the phone all day from work, but the lines were cut; she couldn't get a connection. Tomče became the primary topic of conversation at home, because he was our only tie with Slovenia, which had been attacked by the Yugoslav National Army. He was our only connection to the war that had begun as if it had fallen from the sky. It seemed to me that we only followed the news about the war in Slovenia because of our distant cousin left outside the borders of Yugoslavia, not a trace of whom remained; he hadn't been in contact with his brothers either, who remained in Macedonia and had quarreled over the house that was left to them when their mother died. Except for the times in his childhood when Tomče, who always wore a woven wristband, came to our grandmother's in the village to help with the reaping and haymaking, Srebra and I had only seen him once since he left for Slovenia—when he came to visit us and his other relatives in Macedonia. He was indeed a young man, the youngest of the relatives we called "Uncle." He was very handsome, blond, nicely dressed, and he brought us a present: two wide umbrellas with long wooden handles and cords for carrying them over your shoulder. It seemed he had forgotten that our heads were attached and, logically, we could use only one umbrella, under which we always got wet down one arm and one leg. He was a bit upset that he had brought us two umbrellas, so he said he'd brought one for Verče, though he hadn't seen her since childhood. We were delighted with the umbrellas; there was nothing like them in Skopje then. "They don't have them in Slovenia, either," he said. "But every Saturday, I bike to Austria to go shopping."

That was incomprehensible to us, going abroad on a

bicycle, to Western Europe no less, where they had everything that was unavailable in Yugoslavia. "Maybe he fled to
Austria on his bicycle," said Srebra, but our mother worried
about him and always talked about him, though prior to that
she had spoken of him only when she got on the phone to ask
about his life there: whether he had a girlfriend and when he
would be coming to Macedonia. She would tell him about his
brothers' arguments, how one had taken to drinking, how his
mother was turning in her grave because of them, and that
he was the only clever one in their family and should stay put
where he was and not even think of returning to Macedonia.
Let the brothers kill each other. But now, now that he was cut
off from the world, she complained that he wasn't here: "You
see? We're not fighting each other here, but they'll pluck each
other's eyes out over there; people are going to die." The war
in Slovenia lasted a few days, and when it ended, our father
started up the car and we drove to Grandma and Grandpa's
in the village. We no longer went on vacations together; it
was shameful for such grown-up girls (not to mention those
with conjoined heads) to go on a vacation with their parents.
Our cousins Verče and Lenče came with us, but their mother
and father had to go by bus. Our grandmother was happy the
whole time, and kept repeating, "Lawyers, lawyers. Now we'll
have people to defend us, too." Grandfather added, "from flies."
Srebra laughed loudly and said, "You'll see, Grandpa, you'll
see. We will put that Slavica in jail, you'll see," which made
Grandpa angry; he got up and left the room, saying, "Both
you and Slavica can just go to hell." I tried not to think about
the fact that I was going to study in the Law Department. I
wanted to spend the summer before university as wonderfully
as possible, if, that is, it was possible with our conjoined heads.
While our grandfather, father, and uncle, and sometimes our

younger uncle (that is, when he was allowed to by his wife, who did not like anything or anyone—and we didn't like her either) went into the field to work, reaping and baling the hay, and doing all sorts of other things, the women, sitting on the floor in the large passageway called an "earth cellar" because it had a dirt floor, would string tobacco leaves. Leaning against the walls, dressed in old clothes and woolen vests because even in the summer it was as cold as a refrigerator in the cellar, we threaded the tobacco, talked, and drank coffee, our mother and aunt reading the grounds in our coffee cups. We gossiped, and sometimes laughed. Everything was easier when our aunt and grandmother were present, because Srebra and I felt that they loved us, and that our aunt Ivanka didn't differentiate us from our other cousins. Leaning our heads against the cold wall, Srebra and I often got our needles and thread tangled, and tore some of the leaves, and our mother would say, "Just leave it alone; you're not fit for stringing tobacco. You're going to tear all the leaves." But our grandmother would say that it wasn't our fault that our threads got intertwined and that it was nothing too serious; the tobacco wasn't worth much anyway, there wasn't hardly any point in stringing it, the work caused us nothing but trouble, and in the end, it wouldn't bring enough money for medicine, let alone bread. One day, while we were stringing the tobacco, our aunt said to Grandma, "Verče hasn't had her period this month. I'll bet she was out among the hazel trees. Just you wait. She might be pregnant." Verče was at the store at that moment. We had sent her to buy some bottles of Strumka so we could slake our thirst a bit. Twelve-year-old Lenče asked, "Can a woman get pregnant by walking through the hazel wood?" And right away, I could imagine the scene in Lenče's head—she had serious psychological problems diagnosed as manic depression, and sometimes, without knowing why, she would beat her mother until she drew blood and afterward wouldn't remember it—Verče walks on and on, passing the clearing, then climbing up the hill on the right side of the road to reach the hazelnut forest. She sits under the lowest tree, tears off some hazelnuts, breaking some with a stone, some with her foot, and others with her teeth. She crunches them with relish until all the spaces between her teeth are filled with ground bits of hazelnut, and when she feels there is no way to eat even one more kernel, she fills her pockets, for the others—that is, for us. She stands up, her belly heavy, pregnant, and drags herself to Grandma's house in the village. She gives us the hazelnuts so we can also become pregnant, and she waits for her baby and ours to be born from the hazelnut pregnancies. But no one answers Lenče. No one thinks she needs to know about such things. When Lenče was born, she was completely normal, a sweet girl who developed like any other kid. In first grade, they even enrolled her in the folk-dance group at the Pioneers' Club. How she liked to dance! She learned the dances faster than anyone, even the most difficult ones. We always asked her to dance for us when she came to visit, and she would twirl around the dining room with our mother, who also knew all the dances, while Srebra and I watched, laughing, carried away by a warm pleasure, by some measure of closeness. Lenče took the bus with two older girls to the folk-dance group for three years, and as long as she didn't have to pay for the bus, everything was fine. But when she was in the third grade, the city bus drivers warned her that she, too, would have to start paying the fare. Lenče told her father, and he decided to pull her from the program. After she was withdrawn (*Extravagances*! How her father loved that word; now the bus fare has to be paid and the price of membership has gone up!) Lenče fell into a depression and suffered nervous breakdowns that consisted of hitting (especially Aunt Ivanka), screeching, falling into a trance, and later of missing her periods, not eating, visiting doctors, taking medicines, and finally, the consequences of such events on such a young organism: curvature of the spine, difficulty walking, weakening vision, abrupt weight fluctuations, and nervous crises in which she lost herself completely and had to be taken to the hospital, where first in the children's clinic and later in the adult psychiatric ward, she refused to eat, bathe, or allow anyone to visit her. She swayed like a branch in the hallways in an indescribable languor and sense of hopelessness. Nothing helped her, and Lenče never danced a single dance again. Her mother, fearing her younger daughter's violence, became increasingly possessive of her, and began to control her, to rule over her in every possible way: what she ate, how she dressed, where she went, what she did, when she bathed, how she combed her hair.

Lenče's father was even sicker from various psychological points of view. He went around on his black bicycle collecting old bottles, which he stored on their balcony. He loved to shove politics and healthy living in your face, constantly gathering herbs and spending his solitary afternoons in the shadows of the village of Katlanovo. He was a man who would destroy the kitchen water heater on purpose simply to conserve the maximum amount of energy, water, and money. A man from whom cousins and brothers borrowed money, but was never paid back, a man who even had money stolen from his coat that was hanging in the hallway when he went to visit his youngest brother. A man who bought the first computer model, but kept it unopened on the shelf for better times. A man who boxed up the television set when Verče started school because she was to study and not watch television, but would then come to our place and sit for hours in front of our television while our father boiled with rage. Once, Uncle Mirko was at our house when my toes were itching, and he heard me scratching and complaining, while Srebra shouted: "Stop it! That's enough!" He got up, took a handful of herbs and grass from his pocket, went into our bathroom with the green pot, and filled it with hot water from the kitchen boiler. He put the plants in it and barked at me: "Go on, sit here, put your feet in." I don't know how, but my feet were already in the pot, with Srebra's beside it. We sat on the couch in the kitchen, while Mirko sat in our chair by the little table, Mom moving around, Dad watching television. The water was pleasant and aromatic, and I recalled how Aunt Milka once scalded our father's feet with hot water in this same pot when we were little and she had come to visit for a few days. Srebra and I had been quite frightened, and I think that was the exact moment when both of us understood that, despite all the aversion we felt toward our father, we did, in fact, also love him. And once, Milanka, our uncle Milan's wife from Berovo, when they came to sleep at our place, filled this same green pot with hot water from the kitchen and went to the bathroom, most likely to wash up. She and our uncle Milan had slept in the big room with our mother and father. They were all unusual in their own way, but no one surpassed the extremes of our uncle Mirko. He was a man who, when in the village, loved to sit on his old wooden bed and drink milk from sheep, cows, or goats but would not help with a speck of village work, not even carrying a stick of wood. A man about whom our mother said it would be best if someone "just whacked on the head with an ax" and maybe that someone should be our father, though it would be a shame for him to be stuck in prison. Mirko was a man to be sneered at, quoted, and joked about in our family. This was the same uncle who didn't even feed the fish in our aquarium when we were on vacation and let them all die. A man who, according to our mother, stole the rings from the shelves in the big room when he watered the plants while we were on vacation. He was a human parasite. "May his heart be devoured," our mother cursed him. But the curse didn't strike him. He was as healthy as an ox. While we strung tobacco, he was out with the other men in the field, but he just lay in the shade and enjoyed the scent of the hay. That's what our father said, and he cursed him with every phrase that came to mind. Grandfather had called to him, "Come on, Mirko, it's getting dark." But who knew exactly what went on in the fields while we women were at home. One evening, when they returned from the fields, our grandfather said, "From now on, you will kiss my hand." This intrigued the grandchildren, and whenever we saw him, we ran and kissed his hand, Srebra and I at the same time, bowing our heads to touch his coarse hand with our lips. His hand was rough, wrinkled, and withered, but firm—a villager's hand. Our grandfather had a nickname in the village—*Blood*. He had really tough blood, they said, especially when he was harassed by the secret police from UDBA; he was a tough guy. So we were called Blood's grandchildren, although some village women secretly called us "the ones with the heads." Blood's hayloft at the edge of the village was well known; behind the barn was where the extramarital lives of the villagers took place, and our grandfather's barn had been critical for many types of love affairs: affairs between young women and men from the village; between men from the village and young women who came to visit from far away, especially during holidays and summer vacations; and between villagers and those from the nearest town. And it wasn't rare for adulterers from neighboring villages or the city to make love behind our grandfather's barn. Sometimes, we went with Verče to see if anybody was behind the barn, but in the blackness, you couldn't see a thing; you could just hear muffled voices—sighs, moans—and the crunching of soil and small pebbles on the ground. All those sounds in the dark seemed frightening, like in a film, and although we knew what the people were doing behind the barn, we didn't laugh, but ran away as quickly as possible, dragging Verče along, each of us thinking about what we had heard but hadn't seen, longing for something un-known, yet known. I asked myself whether Srebra knew what sexual desire was at all, if maybe while I slept, she, too, poked the corner of the blanket up between her legs, or perhaps her own fingers, and if maybe she, too, was no longer innocent. Or perhaps neither of us had been innocent since that afternoon in childhood when, right here at our grandmother's, Srebra and I lay beneath the grape arbor on a small rug while Grandma was baking bread in the oven. To keep the sun from burning us, we opened Grandma's little golden umbrella, which was probably a child's, but that she still carried when it rained, and, lying with our backs on the narrow rug under the little umbrella, pressed against each other, rubbing my left thigh and her right, my left breast and her right, until a faint arousal and trembling spread through our bodies. I had long forgotten that event from early childhood, and who knew whether Srebra remembered it. I never mentioned it to her, but having recalled it, whenever I thought of that scene under Grandma's umbrella, I felt shame in my soul. We would find scattered bits of paper and condoms behind the barn some days—how disgusting it was to see the remains of passion left by unknown people who had chosen this bare patch of ground behind our barn, or against its wall, as their oasis and who, before leaving, never gathered up the garbage, but got their asses out of there as fast as they could before anyone saw them or a car coming down the road beside the barn shined a light on them. Verče, Srebra, and I had to sweep behind the barn to keep our grandfather from getting angry and lying in wait the next night for some impassioned couple to appear. He'd wave his ax or pitchfork at them, and our grandmother would say, "He's going to end up in jail." So every afternoon, we went to the barn and swept with the straw-bristled broom; nobody thought about a clean environment or about ecology, so we just swept the garbage down the hillside behind the barn that was no longer our property but didn't belong to anyone else either. It was sort of a village dumping ground in the midst of the harvested fields. Srebra, Verče, and I remained in the village all summer. Grandmother saved the cotton balls we used every morning and evening to clean our faces. "Just in case," she said as she gathered them up in a plastic bag that sat by the pitcher set on the sill of the closed window in an unfinished room. The cotton balls smelled of acne medicine, face-cleansing lotions, and cucumbers dirtied by Revlon powder; there was a whole bag of them, because Srebra, Verče, and I cleaned our faces in the village more often than at home, but we were always covered in acne because there was simply never enough hot water in the yogurt container filled from the pot on the woodstove for us to wash. From time to time, we would go into town to sleep at our aunt Milka's, and on those days, we would stroll through town, and regularly go to our uncle's for coffee, because our aunt, despite her faults, knew how to read coffee grounds and horoscopes, interpret omens of the afterlife, create spells for seducing men, and do lots of other newage things. She spent hours interpreting astrological charts, but there was nowhere in the room to sit; clothes and socks were strewn everywhere—on the couch, on the chairs, on the table. There were puddles of honey or dried milk; cupboard doors were on the verge of falling off; there were burn holes in the carpet; the curtains were moth-eaten and dusty. To the critical eye, the pinnacle was to go to the bathroom to do one's business, which was not done sitting on a toilet bowl or even squatting over a Turkish toilet, but on top of a big empty paint or varnish can with the bottom removed and placed over the privy hole. Neither our aunt nor uncle was shocked by it—they lived day to day—but all of us, their relatives, worried about our university-educated uncle. He had completed the foreign-language course—our grandparents' only son, in whose honor our grandfather had sold a cow when he was born and feasted the villagers in the village restaurant for three days and three nights—our much-beloved uncle, the one who, to Grandpa's great sorrow, hadn't been able to find a wife up to his standards, but had selected the biggest lazybones in the village, the worst wife in the world. When our aunt read Srebra's and my fortunes and saw a knife, a surgical knife, in the grounds of both our cups and saw that our heads would soon be separated and everything would be as it should, those were the moments we loved her and were somehow convinced this really could happen after all the years of our shared misfortune. "If countries can be separated, surely people can," said our aunt, and we felt something like love for her, because her words seemed to carry truth. When two whole republics could be separated from Yugoslavia, something that had been, up to that moment, the equivalent of science fiction, why couldn't two heads be separated by a surgeon's knife? How could our heads not be separated?

1991–1995
SREBRA

Macedonia separated from what remained of Yugoslavia. That week, on the eighth of September, I was angry with myself, Srebra, and my mother. The previous Saturday evening, when I had taken off my wide, deep-pocketed Bermuda shorts to put on my pajamas, I had left my small icon in the pocket. This had never happened before; it was just automatic that I took it from my pocket or its special little purse and placed it in another pocket or under my pillow before I went to bed. But as soon as I got undressed, Srebra pulled me toward the door of our room to listen to something she heard on television. As she opened the door, I yanked her sharply back, embarrassed that my father might see me in my underwear. Srebra pressed us against the door so she could hear more clearly the announcement on the television that there would be a referendum the next day on Macedonian independence and that everyone over eighteen should go vote yes. "So what? They've already said that a hundred times today," I muttered. Srebra had heard it, too, but she wanted to hear it again. Once the announcement ended, we moved away from the door, put on our pajamas, and got into bed. As soon as we had pulled up the covers, our mother came in, and although she didn't turn on the light, light filtered in from the dining room. She snatched something from the armchair and went out. The next day, I noticed that I was missing both my shorts and my icon. Mom had hand-washed them with Srebra's shorts, along with the icon, which she had pulled out when she felt something hard under her fingers. Saint Zlata Maglenska had been soaked, drenched down to the smallest splinter of wood and darkened by the water. It was drying on the sheet metal on the balcony, where my Bermudas and Srebra's already bone-dry shorts were hanging on the line. I was angry and hurt. I wiped the little icon, which was dry on the outside, but still heavy with moisture inside. Srebra and I put on our shorts and walked to the school to vote. People were pouring in, in groups of two, three, or more. Our mother and father said they would go vote after lunch, which is why we went after breakfast. Unless it was unavoidable, we did not go anywhere with them. That day, our aunt Ivanka invited us to lunch. We could hardly wait to see Verče and Lenče. Our aunt was considered the best homemaker in the entire family even though she lived under the worst conditions because of Uncle Mirko—he was the biggest cheapskate in the world—but she did wonders with what little she had. At our aunt's you would eat the best piroshki, the tastiest fried pastries, the sweetest beer cookies. At our aunt's, there was sliced wholesome black bread and the salad had lettuce, though our father called it "rabbit food" and refused to eat it, so our aunt always made him a tomato and onion salad. She knew how to make the best moussaka, the tastiest chicken and rice. For this lunch, she greeted us with her specialty: the honey semolina cake she usually made for Easter. "Today is a holiday," she said. "This is the first time we'll have our own country." "What are you talking about?" our uncle said. "We had a country before, one as big as you could hope for." Mom chimed in, "You just listen to me—we'll be wishing for Yugoslavia. Mark my words." But Dad, as usual, said, "Oh come, now, like you know everything." "Please, I'm begging you. Can we not talk about politics?" Verče protested. She had been traumatized by politics, because of what happened to her best childhood friend, Dzvezdana, who had just returned from Sweden, where she had lived with her parents up until Tito's death. She hadn't really known who Tito was, and while watching his funeral at their neighbors' house, she had said, "So what if he died? There are other people." The neighbor went out and was gone just a short time before coming back with two policemen, and they said to Dzvezdana, "So you don't care that Comrade Tito died?" and while Dzvezdana tried to compose herself in all the commotion, they grabbed her under the arms and carted her off in their van to the police station, where they held her until night, after she'd apologized a hundred times for what she had said. Her eyes were swollen from crying when she got out, but her parents were waiting for her. At home, her father gave her a beating, and her mother sat her down and lectured to her all night about Tito—where he was born and everything he had done—thereby etching forever in her daughter's brain everything she should have told her in Malmö, Sweden, while Tito was alive rather than now in Skopje, a day after his death. Soon after, they sold their apartment in Skopje, went to Sweden, and never came back, although Verče waited in vain for them every summer vacation for an entire decade. When they announced the success of the referendum and showed Kiro Gligorov congratulating everyone gathered in the square celebrating the news of a sovereign and independent Macedonia, we were not among them, because it was Sunday evening, when we heated the boiler and took a bath.

Srebra and I both felt our spirits filled with happiness mixed with pride, and Srebra kept repeating, "I knew it, I knew it."

That fall, however, the battles in Croatia eclipsed Macedonia's independence. Every day prior to the vote for independence, we had watched news clips from Vukovar, and for several weeks after the vote for independence, all anyone talked about was Dubrovnik. That lasted a long, long time. All through the fall and winter, people talked about Dubrovnik, and everybody had their own story and stuck to their beliefs. Once, Uncle Mirko said the Croatians were lying about Dubrovnik being set on fire; that it was the Croatians themselves who had set tires ablaze to make it appear as if the Serbs were burning their city. Srebra became upset, and I wondered who would be stupid enough to burn such a beautiful city as Dubrovnik. We heard all kinds of things at that time, especially during the first month of our studies, October 1991, when several Macedonian soldiers died in Croatia.

The amphitheater classrooms were always filled with students, and at first glance, we blended in with them. The students were, at least, more cultured than our high-school classmates and didn't cry out in shock when they saw us or ask, "What's with the heads?" or "Is that possible in real life?" We usually sat in one of the back rows so the professors couldn't see us very well, and from a distance we probably looked like two students with their heads leaning awkwardly against each other so they could whisper or read from the same textbook. The lectures were as boring to me as they were interesting to Srebra. She listened, took notes, got excited or upset, smiled, and I felt our joined vein throbbing above our temples, even though I was calm, yawning from boredom. Srebra thoroughly enjoyed each new subject, each new bit of information. Although it was unspoken, it was clear she would take the lecture notes, remember the important things, and drag me to the bookstore and library for materials. It was clear that I would be physically present and like it or not, I would go through the motions of studying law, but she would really study it with consistency and dedication. What a waste of time it was for me to sit in those lectures in the cold amphitheater of the Law Department and listen to material that had no relation to me, that neither interested me nor repelled me; I was absolutely indifferent to the legal system. To me, it was remote and foreign, and although I was aware it was important and would be even more important now that we had our own country. I was much more drawn to literature and ethnology, which Srebra considered egotistical because of their focus on human nature and individual differences, as opposed to the rules governing society as a whole, which were so precisely defined in the legal system.

Srebra assured me I was mistaken if I thought that law wasn't applicable to the individual; on the contrary, law was precisely the discipline that was dedicated to both the individual and the community, and it was vitally important in our lives. "Let's take ourselves, for example," she said. "We could sue the state because it hasn't found a solution to our medical problem, or our parents, who didn't ensure that we weren't stigmatized from birth." Srebra said all sorts of things, all of it vague and remote to my concerns; I only knew that the country of Yugoslavia no longer existed and Macedonia was too small to assume any responsibility for the lives of its citizens, and what's more, we were adults and were responsible for looking after ourselves. "Even legally, we've now been left to ourselves," I replied to Srebra ironically, and I felt the desire to scratch and scratch and scratch the spot where we were joined, to scrape away the skin covering our shared vein until it bled, and in this attack, driven by passion and rage, tear it apart. I would tear through that irrevocable connection, a connection we despised, didn't need, and loathed from the depths of our souls.

What was happening in Croatia and more generally throughout Yugoslavia was discussed at the university, often in connection with soldiers from the Yugoslav National Army—many of whom were deserting and returning to Macedonia. We all followed the mothers who set out by bus to search for their sons across Yugoslavia, and who burst into the assembly shouting, through tears and rage, "Bring our children home!" New students turned up at the university who seemed older than the rest, with deep bags under their eyes and hollow faces, confused and frightened, or rude and impudent, or drunk; tears ran down some of their faces during lectures, and it was clear where they had come from. While we were all dying to know, no one was brave enough to ask if they had killed someone, if they had been ordered to kill someone, if they had been imprisoned, if they had been tortured, if they had tortured someone else. Once, one of them said, "Fuck it all. How did I end up in the wrong place at the wrong time?" And it was true for all of them—a lost generation that found itself in the wrong place at the wrong time. When we heard about the shelling of Dubrovnik, our colleagues clicked their tongues, happy that they weren't there, but here, at their desks, secure and protected. Some of the professors adopted a pro-Serbian stance, which sparked emotions in the amphitheater. Mostly, however, everyone just wrote down what the professors dictated, forgetting what was happening a few hundred kilometers away. At times, there were even gales of laughter, especially in the middle of lectures, when our old professor of criminal law checked out the female students from head to toe and joked to those wearing short skirts, "*That* is more suited for washing than airing in public." Srebra and I tried to avoid sitting in his field of vision, in anyone's field of vision, but it was sometimes unavoidable. Still, I think all the events taking place somehow blurred our "oddness," and it became rare for someone to ask during our breaks what had happened to us, if we had been born this way, if we were going to have an operation, and other questions like that. Most often, it was those from the interior of the country, far from the urban center, who were stunned, and stared at us with frozen expressions, mouths agape, but soon they, too, stopped paying anymore attention than the others.

When classes ended, we went home, while many others went to the school cafeteria for lunch or off to their dormitories. I felt like Srebra's appendage: I followed her to the photocopy shop, to the library, to the bookstore. I did everything necessary for us to be ordinary students, but Srebra wanted more than that. She wanted us to start preparing for our final exams as early as the first semester, and we sat at the dining-room table at home with piles of notes and thick books to read out loud. First she read for a while, and then I did. The material seemed to go in one ear and out the other. I would yawn, annoying Srebra with my lack of interest, as she wondered how I would pass the exams, and whether I knew this wasn't how to study. "You have no idea how aware I am," I said to her, "but you were aware that this stuff didn't interest me when you wanted us both to enroll in law." "Well, you have to," said Srebra, "because you don't have a choice. We don't have a choice, and if we enrolled in something else, I would be the bored one." "Great. Couldn't you have found something that interested both of you?" our family chimed in, bewildered. We had not considered that when we enrolled in the university; law was all Srebra wanted—nothing else—and since she compromised when we picked our high-school focus, it was now my turn. "Sure, but high school and university are not the same," our uncle, the only member of our family with a university education, said. "You should have asked me for advice. This isn't how one goes about studying at the university." There were moments I was overcome by violent sobbing. I was in a hopeless situation; I did not know how to live like this—how to get used to studying law, how to force myself to accept it. Literature attracted me more and more, as did religion. When Srebra finished getting her books from the library, I would drag her to the literature section to grab novels and poetry collections. From time to time, I got up the courage to drag Srebra to the card catalog to find books on spirituality, and I would take out texts on the Akathist Hymn or the Church Fathers. I was pricked by the edges of the Saint Zlata Meglenska icon in my pocket; it was a presence that marked my life, a refuge in case of danger. I knew she was with me, which made it easier for me to live my life, to sit through the lectures. While the professors, men in ties and suits and women in suits and high heels, spoke dryly or animatedly, waving their arms and pacing in front of the blackboard, I thought about the past, about eternity, about God, and about art.

We spent New Year's Day of 1992 in bed. Now that our father had finally bought us a small television set—if only a black-and-white one—before the last Yugoslav Eurovision Song Contest, we could watch television by ourselves. We set the small TV on a shelf opposite the bed, after our mother, unleashing a whole host of comments, removed from it the porcelain teapot and cups, various porcelain roosters, lions, a hen with seven small chicks with red beaks and covered with dust. Our father removed the two glass doors in front of the shelves and placed the small television inside. Srebra and I had our own television at last. We watched lying under the blanket because we weren't allowed to keep the heater blowing while the television was on.

Just like every previous New Year's, the tree stood on the small table in the big room, along with pink pudding cake, steamed cookies, and Russian salad. But now that we were grown, we didn't even think about the tree. We tirelessly watched TV, stretched out comfortably on the bed after so many years of watching from the stuck-together chairs in the dining room. In the days after New Year's, the lead news story was that the war in Croatia might end. Surely there wasn't a single normal person who did not feel relieved by this news. But, in fact, the farce had just begun. Things were now beginning in Bosnia. The information one could glean from the news or from other people—most often professors or students who had relatives dispersed throughout Yugoslavia—was always contradictory, and always tragic. The fact was that there was killing, rape, shooting, torture, everything. God alone knew how and why this was happening. The wars coincided with our studies, grotesquely filling our time with the weight of death. Refugees from Bosnia poured into our oasis of peace, as Macedonia called itself. Most often it was veiled women warmly dressed with small children in their arms, carrying bags and suitcases, who sought asylum with their lost looks and worried faces. Some treated them with sympathy and compassion, directing them to the offices of the Red Cross and the UN Refugee Agency; others wanted to drive them away. A third group openly disapproved of the flow of Bosnian refugees. Aunt Ivanka told us a woman in her building was a refugee inspector, and every day, Aunt Ivanka saw her taking boxes of oil, flour, and laundry detergent from her car to store in the basement. Then a racketeer would come, put the boxes in a cart, and sell them at the market. "They ought to be ashamed of themselves," we said, but our aunt's neighbor wasn't the only one who took advantage of the Bosnian refugees' misfortune. There were many such incidents, most of which were only discovered after the war in Bosnia had ended.

Somewhere around March 1992, a telegram arrived for Srebra and me: "Be in front of the shopping center tomorrow at noon, please." It was signed Marjan Siljanovski. We looked at the telegram, turned it every which way, but couldn't make sense of it. It was the same Marjan with whom we had corresponded when we were still at our primary-school desks, though we had never met him. We had spoken to him only once on the phone, a full three years ago when he called from Belgrade, but we hadn't received a letter for at least four years, since our first year in high school, when he wrote to us from Belgrade on bright red stationary, including a photograph of himself in uniform. He had written that he was studying at the military high school and that all was well with him, except he was lonely and begged us to write to him more often if we could; that our letters always meant a great deal to him, and that, on his way home on leave, he would get off at the railway station in Skopje so we could finally see each another and get acquainted. "And who knows, maybe I will fall in love with one of you." That's what he wrote to us. At the time, Srebra and I laughed at his letter and didn't answer it, but then, he called from Belgrade. He'd had a free afternoon and was walking around and wanted to hear our voices. Srebra and I could not have been more confused. Srebra was overcome with hysterical laughter as he was saying something into the receiver; she couldn't stop laughing, and I, also choking with laughter, told him we were late getting downtown and hung up on him. I remember our shared laughter as one of the most pleasant in our lives—young laughter connecting us in that moment and overcoming all our misunderstandings and misfortune. Marjan didn't call again. After the war in Yugoslavia began, I thought of him, and said to Srebra, "I wonder what Marjan is doing now?" And she said, "He's probably in a battle somewhere; after all, he was studying in a military school." Now, a telegram had arrived from Marjan with the word *please*, and we thought we had to go see him right away, as if his life depended on us. It was absurd to run to meet a person with whom we had only corresponded as children (and only because our mother realized his last name was the same as that of the best cardiologist in the municipal hospital), a person we had never met before who was not only unaware that we were Siamese twins but also that it was by our heads that we were conjoined. We did not know why we should meet him and what we would say to one another. We were strangers who had nothing to connect us aside from those occasional childhood letters, the last one from several years ago. All afternoon, we turned the telegram over and over in our hands, and that night, we both slept badly, pulling our legs away from each other's, covering and uncovering them, until we fell asleep in the early morning and didn't make it to our first class. We left school after our second class. It was already 11:30. "We're going to go, right?" I asked Srebra, although I had already decided we would, and I saw that Srebra wanted us to go as well. "I'm curious to know what exactly he wants," Srebra said angrily, and with small steps to avoid bumping into each other or the passersby—returning from the market with their plastic bags and satchels along the thawing sidewalks from which the snow hadn't been cleared—we reached the shopping center. It was only then that we stopped to consider we did not know at which end he would be waiting. In my backpack was the photograph he had sent us from Belgrade. We circled the stores in front of the entrance facing the Workers' Technical College, but there was no one there who looked like Marjan. Then we walked through the entire mall until we reached the far exit, but there was only one person there, a blond guy who was evidently waiting for someone else. And, indeed, before long an extremely good-looking woman wearing a red cape met him. They kissed, and arm in arm, ducked into a small bookstore.

We stood there a while, then wandered around; we were growing annoyed that we didn't know exactly where he meant when he wrote, "In front of the shopping center," but then we saw him. We recognized him immediately, because the Marjan in the photograph had the face of an old man: wrinkled, a worried face, not like a child's, and now, as a young man, his face still carried the same wizened look, the same concern. The person walking toward us also had the gate of an old man; he seemed barely able to drag himself along. He was dressed in blue jeans and a black leather jacket. In his right hand, he carried two rabbit-eared cardboard boxes of popcorn that he had probably bought in the square. He carried them carefully, so none would tumble out. Srebra and I were dressed in black duffle coats, red berets on our heads that, from a distance, probably looked like one big hat. We wore corduroy pants and black boots. The winter was cold and had seemed to last an eternity. Before we left the house that morning, I had thought we looked like Little Red Riding Hoods, two in one, and the image had brought a smile to my face. We stood woodenly, motionless, on the stairs by the entrance to the shopping center; we knew he recognized us, though he had never seen us in real life or in photographs. He came closer, looking at us, and the smile on his face turned to surprise. We waved to him. He was now standing before us, with the two green rabbit-eared boxes filled with white and yellow popcorn puffs. "Zlata? Srebra?" and we smiled at the same time and answered, "Marjan?" He couldn't get out another word. He stared right at our heads, gaping at the spot where they were joined, where our red berets touched, and his gaze cut through our shared vein like a knife. "Are those for us?" Srebra asked, breaking the silence. She took the popcorn from his hands, passed one of the boxes to me, stuffed some in her mouth, and then began to cough. I only held the cardboard rabbit-box; I couldn't eat. Finally, I said, "As you can see, this is how we are. I'm sorry we never wrote to you; we were children then and were embarrassed." "Yes, yes," he stammered, "yes, of course." "Come on, let's go somewhere," Srebra proposed, and we set off toward the square and the stone bridge. He strode along beside us, confused, lost, concerned. "Let's go to Café Arabia," I suggested, because Srebra and I went there once when we were finishing our first semester after seeing an announcement pasted on the front door of the Law Department inviting everyone to gather in Café Arabia and drink tea to protest the war in the Persian Gulf. We had really enjoyed ourselves; we drank black tea and ate falafel, while Ali, the owner of the restaurant, spoke, in beautiful Macedonian, against the war. Srebra and I almost never went anywhere, and the outing to the café filled with young people rumored to be comparative literature students, was an incredible experience for me. That night, I had strange dreams: a large pyre in the square, and in the fire—a chair. All the children in the world had been gathered there, and one by one they were put onto the chair in the fire. And they burned. All that remained was the charred body of the last boy in the world, but it was intact, pinkish gold, the color of light meat. And then the torturers broke his arm, his leg, his skull. It was a terrible dream. Still, I wanted to take Marjan there; at that time of day it was empty with only Ali inside, straightening the tables. He remembered us, because no one forgot us once they'd seen us, and he was happy that we'd come. He put us at a table by the window, and brought us tea and a plate of falafel, then went off to the kitchen. Srebra began, "Why did you send the telegram for us to meet?" Marjan hesitated, not knowing whether he still wanted to talk, but then told his story. "I didn't know you were this kind of twins, but you and my mother saved my life. You were my guardian angels." We couldn't figure out how we could have saved his life and just looked at him quizzically. "You remember how I once wrote and called you from Belgrade when I was at the military school? You didn't write back, so I decided not to write to you again. But I thought of you, and dreamed that one day we would see each other, and I might fall in love with one of you. In February of '91, my entire class was sent to Croatia, to Zagreb, and then on to Split. We were told to be on alert and that we had to fight the Croatians. They made me a sergeant, even though I hadn't finished the military high school. They gave me an apartment in Split and a big salary. I was living well, and nothing happened until May. On May 6, Sašo Geškovski was killed. You probably saw it on television. That night, I called you, but you couldn't hear me. I called several times, but you just said, 'Hello, hello,' and you couldn't hear me." Yes, we remembered that night when someone called several times, but the telephone only crackled, and whoever was calling gave up. "That was me. I was calling you, because

I didn't know who to call. There is no telephone in my village. I was so frightened and wanted someone to be thinking of me. I know my mother didn't sleep at night and protected me from death, but you were also my guardian angels, because my future was connected with yours, and I stayed alive so I could come back and fall in love with one of you." "And then what happened?" Srebra asked, moving quickly past that last sentence, "How did you save yourself?" Marjan drew close and said extremely quietly, "I fled. I deserted. I left the apartment and everything I had inside: money, furniture, clothing, I left everything. I put on an old pair of pants and a jacket I still had from home. I hid day and night until I crossed all the road-blocks. I arrived on foot from Split. For two months I hid in bushes and behind rocks. And now here I am." "You're crazy!" Srebra shouted, and I thought the same. "Yes, I am crazy, but alive. When I got home, my mother almost had a heart attack. She hid me in the basement. Meanwhile, the postman found out, delivering several orders demanding that I return to the Yugoslav Army, and if I didn't, I would have to answer to the military court in Belgrade. I couldn't stand it any longer. I got dressed and went to see the mayor of Tetovo. I told him what had happened and that, if necessary, I would condemn myself, but I would not return to that army. He replied, 'Bravo, young man. There's no reason for our children to die for foreign interests. Don't worry a bit. Macedonia is putting together its own army. We'll give you a job, and you will get an apartment and a salary.' So I'm a free man now, and I came to tell you." "Yes, to tell us," Srebra repeated. We looked at him across the café table, and there was something childish and naive in his wizened face cut through with wrinkles, deeply lined, and pale. His eyes were dark brown, almost black; his eyebrows were thick; his hair was oily and black. He was about twenty, the same age as us, but his body—though built up from his military training—trembled, slack and sick, under his V-neck sweater. This man opposite us was so fragile; his hands shook as he slowly drank his tea; his lips were narrow and pale in a fixed sweet smile. He looked at us with childlike trust, open to our gaze, our judgment, to us. This was the first male, the first young man, with whom we sat and spoke as young women. We fell silent and looked at one another. "Evidently, you don't like me," he said with an accusatory tone. "Maybe I don't look so great now because I'm tired and run down from everything, but everything is going to get sorted out. I'll get an apartment and a job in Skopje; I am going to be able to support a family." "Support a family?" I said, surprised. "But you're only twenty years old. What do you need to support a family for? What family? Your mother and father?" "I want to have my own family," he said. "A wife, children—I want to live a normal life and not hide from anyone, to live here in Macedonia." "And how can we help with that?" asked Srebra. "Yes, what are you expecting from us?" I asked. He was clearly uncomfortable; he blushed, his lips began to tremble, he could barely speak. "I had never imagined that you had a problem. I thought one of you would like me and you could be my girl-friend, my wife." "And now?" Srebra curtly put in. "What now?" "Now...now..." Marjan stammered, but Srebra added, "Now, nothing. Now nothing, right?" Marjan fell silent; he didn't know what to say. He got up, went and paid Ali, quickly put on his jacket, swaying back and forth several times behind his chair, and said, "Okay, well, goodbye. Just know I'm always here for you if you need anything." He turned and went down the stairs, but Srebra yelled after him, "Goodbye, goodbye to you, too," and then quietly added, "We'll certainly never need anything from you." Now that we were alone, I could sense how angry she was, while I was just confused and inexplicably sad. "Cretin," she said, "cretinous soldier," and she poured the popcorn on the table, and pulled me so hard it hurt as we stood up. Ali waved as we went down the stairs. I couldn't get my thoughts together. I did not know what that had all been about; what that strange situation resembled; whether Marjan was guilty of anything, and if so, of what. For the image he'd made up of two young twins, his guardian angels in the Yugoslav battles? For his illusion of a future filled with love and happiness? For his desire to have a family, because he was mature, nearly grown old, though only twenty? I felt sorry for him, and I silently prayed to Saint Zlata Meglenska, touching her with my fingers, to pray for Marjan, so he could find happiness.

We could not find happiness as long as we were the way we were. But even if we had been normal, I wouldn't have loved Marjan. He wasn't my type. He was too timid, too submissive; his aged child's face posed no challenge. I knew exactly how life would be if I were a normal girl and married him: He would work on the military base; I would be a homemaker and the wife of a soldier; we would live in an average apartment; I would give birth to at least two children, probably not have a job outside the home, because military men were committed to the idea that their wives should not work. On Sundays, we would go to his parents' in the village for dinner, and during the week, he would be tired from work and would watch television all evening or play with the children (sons if possible). That is what our lives would be reduced to, because it was rare to find men with military educations who were interested in the arts. He would find excuses for why he would not go to the theater, why he could sit through a movie with Sharon Stone but not a Dutch film, why he yawned through poetry readings, why he didn't read literary books, but only crime novels and things like that. Perhaps I wasn't being fair, but that is exactly how I imagined life with Marjan—monotonous and provincial. I wanted to ask Srebra how she imagined life with him, but she was too upset, and we never spoke another word about him.

In the examination session of June 1992, Srebra passed all her exams, but I passed only one, and that by sheer will. All the other students had written exams, but ours were oral, to prevent us copying from each other—that is, so I couldn't copy from Srebra. After the professor entered the marks on our report cards, he told me: "You, unlike your sister, do not like law. It's obvious you're forced to study it on account of your sister. That's a serious problem: both for you and for us. You should withdraw. Either study seriously or withdraw and just come along to the lectures. Read something that interests you. Enroll in some other department as a part-time student." It was good advice, even though I had become indifferent to what I studied, or whether I studied at all, given the overall outlook from the news and other reports about the war: the horrible pictures of a young girl marrying her fiancé who had been killed in the marketplace in Sarajevo; the images of the swollen eyes of refugees; the viewpoints and attitudes of those around us sympathetic to the Serbian position; the atmosphere at home, where our father and mother understood nothing but commented on everything about the former Yugoslavia in their own idiosyncratic way. Srebra and I were already mature young women with big breasts and hips, though our conjoined heads were viewed as grotesque, perhaps even revolting. There was no indication anywhere that it was possible to realize our dream of an operation. It was a luxury to think about something like that and egotistical to want a solution for our personal problem under such conditions, with the barriers, new borders, death, death, and death. I knew my parents would be furious if I withdrew and switched to the Philology Department and studied literature part-time, because I would have spent a whole year of my life supported by them with nothing to show for it. No, from that moment on, I decided to force myself to truly study law. For the fall exam session, I registered for three exams. I studied all summer, even when Srebra and I went to the village to our grandmother and grandfather's. There, we shut ourselves in the room with the blue table, blue chairs, and a blue vase with plastic flowers. We settled comfortably on the couch and crammed. We studied together for the exams Srebra hadn't passed yet, reading aloud from our thick textbooks. There was no TV in the village, but the old radio picked up things we couldn't get in Skopje. Every station spoke of the war. On August 26, 1992, a barely audible station announced that the Serbs had set fire to the library in Sarajevo. Everything was burned. Grandma and Grandpa only said one thing about the war: "Ordinary people die, but the big shots sit around and devour everything."

On September 1, 1992, we returned on the Proletar bus to Skopje, and a man of about forty, with bright red cheeks, wearing a light brown suit and holding an old map of Yugoslavia in his hands, was seated across from us. He kept his eye on us, but he watched us less with surprise than curiosity. We were accustomed to being looked at with much ruder and more impertinent glances. He would look out the window, then at the map, then at us. Srebra and I looked straight ahead. I usually felt nauseous when we rode the bus. After a while, the man got up the courage and spoke to us in English. He asked how to get to Belgrade from Skopje—whether there would be an evening bus. Srebra and I didn't know. Then he asked where he could spend the night in Skopje, where it would be least expensive. Srebra and I didn't know that either. He laughed, unperturbed, as if still expecting we would help him somehow, give him some sort of advice. But in fact, we really didn't know where he could sleep cheaply. Even though he was asking about Skopje, we had never slept in a hotel, and we'd heard that both the Continental and the Grand were expensive—hotels for foreigners. He was foreign, but judging from his worn shirt, he wasn't wealthy enough to stay in an expensive hotel. We didn't say anything; we just giggled, looking straight ahead all the way to Skopje, our heads swaying left or right in response to the curves in the road. At the bus station in Skopje, something inexplicable rose forcefully in my breast, and just as we got up from our seats, I said, "Come with us." Srebra heard me and started, but he only asked, "Really?" I merely replied, "Yes." "My name is Gary," he said, and it was only then that we introduced ourselves. We got our bags and started off across the stone bridge. "*Slebla*, *Zhlata*," he repeated several times with a wide grin. Srebra didn't say anything the whole time, and she pulled me left and right out of spite, causing us to walk as if drunk. There was hardly anyone on the bridge except for a few people who were actually drunk, staggering along submerged in themselves—meditative drunks turned inward, not outward.

Gary walked self-assuredly with small hurried steps, trying to follow the rhythm of the four legs and two conjoined heads—now quickly, now slowly. Little by little we made our way to the Record bus stop. We had to wait for the night bus. There were other people waiting as well, young people with cigarettes or slices of *burek* in their hands, loud, drunk, filled with summer-night self-confidence. There were women our mother's age, as well as other, older women wearing skirts below their knees, viscose blouses, sandals with low heels, handbags over their shoulders, and shopping bags in their hands, evidently returning home from their jobs in cafés or some other odd business that stayed open till midnight. Gary looked at them discreetly, with curiosity and intensity—not with the gaze of a tourist but of someone who really wanted to comprehend how life was lived here, why people lived the way they did. The bus finally arrived. We got on and I took enough money from my purse to pay for Gary as well; night-time tickets cost double the regular fare. Gary thanked me several times, touched by what he understood to be Balkan generosity, but what was simply a normal gesture for us. As always, the other passengers gaped at us wide-eyed, elbowing each other. Those who were our age laughed out loud, but this time, they also looked at Gary, with his big red Adidas bag with white lettering and pockets with zippers. We were speaking English. Our neighborhood's main street happened to be under repair that summer, and all the buses stopped at an improvised stop a bit farther than our usual one, and we had to get home somehow with all our bags, guiding Gary through the small, dimly lit neighborhood streets. Srebra unlocked the door and we went in. We brought Gary straight to our room. Our bed was made; from time to time, our mother surprised us by setting up our bed. Until that moment, we hadn't thought about how we were going to arrange everything: where Gary would sleep; how to tell our parents that we had a guest staying over; how they would react—whether our father would get angry and shout or whether our mother would be the one shouting. We left Gary in our room, and went into our parents' room. Mom was always a light sleeper, and she often woke up during the night and stood in the bathroom or sat on a chair in the dining room when one of her strange dizzy spells took hold of her. She got up immediately, asked what was the matter, whether we had gotten home all right. "A foreigner came home with us, a guy from England. He had nowhere to sleep," I whispered to her. "What? What sort of foreigner? Why?" our mother asked, a bit confused, getting out of bed as if she wanted to see him immediately, to see why he was here, but then she remembered she was in her pajamas. So first she took off her pajamas, put on a bra, threw on a viscose blouse and a skirt, and just as she was ready to confront our guest, she remembered something. In the half darkness, she fumbled for something in the ashtray on the little table and then placed around her neck her gold chain with a half-moon clasp, saying, "A foreigner has come to our home. Let's not let him think Macedonians are unrefined." She woke our father, but he couldn't grasp what was happening, so our mother explained everything to him in a whisper, and then she followed us out of the room, knocked on our bedroom door, and the three of us went in. Gary was sitting on the other bed, confused, not knowing what to do or say. Mom approached him, greeting him warmly and saying in Macedonian, "You're from England? Such a large country. What brought you to Macedonia?" Srebra translated for him, but didn't translate the bit about England being a large country. Gary smiled. He said he'd wanted to see Yugoslavia once again as it had been, but he was too late; the country had already disintegrated, even though there was no war in Macedonia. "We're an oasis of peace," Srebra interjected, and I had to explain that that was what our first president, Kiro Gligorov, had nicknamed Macedonia. "An oasis, a holy oasis of peace, but there will be shooting here, too, and won't we be surprised then," our mother said, but Gary only smiled kindly, exhausted from his trip. Mom quickly took our bedding out of the room and remade the bed with a white sheet, white pillowcase, and blue blanket, the complete set she kept for guests. We said good night to Gary and left the room. We lay down on the empty bed in our parent's room. The next morning, our mother got up early and made fried dough pastries. The whole apartment smelled of cooking oil and yeast dough. After Gary woke and washed up in the bathroom—it didn't occur to any of us that there wasn't any hot water in the boiler—we led him out onto the balcony. Mom had put out quite a spread: warm pastries, yogurt, tomatoes, even ajvar—probably the last of this year's pepper relish—kashkaval, bread, salami; everything in the refrigerator was arranged on the balcony table, and we all sat on the brown plastic stools. Our father was already down in the garage, but Mom kept appearing on the balcony and then disappearing again. She made coffee, brought out glasses of juice, fluttered around our overnight guest from England, sparkling, decked out in all her gold jewelry. After breakfast, Gary pulled a pocket edition of the Bible from his bag and begged us to find our Macedonian edition. Then he asked us to go to the book of Ruth and to read it aloud with him. First he read a section in English, then we read the same verses in Macedonian; that is to say, I did, because Srebra refused to read. Then we took him downtown, and after a walk through the Old Market, Gary had to catch the bus to Belgrade. Before he got on the bus, Srebra asked him in a hoarse voice from the depths of her soul, "Gary, do you know if there's a doctor in London for our heads?" "London has everything, so there is probably that kind of doctor, too," Gary said, and then, waving for a long time, a smile on his red cheeks, he left. We went home in a strange mood, a bit sad. We knew almost nothing about him, except that he was from the Beatles' hometown, Liverpool, and that he was married with three sons, the youngest a three-year-old. He left us a family photo to remember him by, which pleased our mother. "He's a serious person," she said. "It shows. It's no small thing to have three children, though what was he thinking, traveling here during the war?" Our father added, "God save and protect us from such people." The incident with Gary was discussed for a long time at home, whenever guests came or Mom spoke with our aunt and uncle on the phone.

The fall examination period was approaching. We didn't have time for anything except studying. Before each exam, Srebra and I made a big hot chocolate with lots of sugar. I always sensed I passed those exams thanks to the energy-producing cocoa that we drank before taking them. Our mother left for work before us and so couldn't do the custom of pouring water on the stairs to give us good luck, as she had done for our uncle when he was living with us and attending his foreign-language course. We took exams and went to lectures, then took more exams and listened to more lectures. Everything was the same and everything was new at the same time. Macedonia already had its own governmental structures, while in Bosnia, more and more people died. One cold November day, it was announced that Croatian forces had destroyed the old Turkish bridge in Mostar. "What a bridge that was!" our father sighed. "It was so old!" Then, just before New Year's, we finally got a call from Tomče, our uncle in Slovenia. Our mother scolded him on the phone: "You disappeared for three years. We thought you died. You didn't think to call? I tried so many times to find you, but I couldn't understand the Slovenians. The whole time they were shouting *Ni*, *Ni* at me." This is how we learned that, when the war broke out in Slovenia, Tomče had fled to Austria, to Graz, fearing he would be drafted, and he found work as a mechanic in an auto-repair shop run by a Slovene from the Austrian region of Styria. He had been living well, but didn't travel to the former Yugoslavia, because he was afraid he would get stuck in some army or in a camp. But now he was going to come back to Slovenia, he said. Things had been better for him there—he knew Slovenian, had friends, and his relatives were there. Everything would be as it had been before. It was unlikely he'd come to Macedonia, he said, until all the conflicts ended. At the end, he added, "I hope you are not siding with the Serbs." Our mother didn't know how to answer, so she just said, "As if I care about who's for the Serbs and who's against them; what's important is that you are alive and healthy."

At the university, Srebra and I mingled more and more during our breaks with the other students. We would sit down for a while with a group and attempt to participate in their conversations. Some were still distant, our physical defect bothering them, but we were sufficiently mindful to notice and to keep our distance from them. During the breaks, there was one group in our department that was always the same: a slim, almost bony, young woman with long thin hair, a blond beauty with large blue eyes and a modest body, a tall guy with a ponytail and small beard, a shorter guy with glasses and long bangs. There was also an older woman with a long braid down her back and a man who likely had some illness, because his left hand constantly shook and the left side of his face grimaced strangely. They were gentle and calm, spoke quietly and discreetly, always keeping off to the side. They dressed modestly, but neatly—the women didn't wear makeup and wore long skirts or wide pants that appeared old-fashioned somehow; the men wore blue jeans and inexpensive shirts. When any of them encountered Srebra and me or simply met our glances, they smiled, almost imperceptibly, discreetly. I liked this group and felt they must be good people. During one break, I dragged Srebra over to where they were seated on the top steps of the amphitheater. The older woman was holding an apple and a small knife in her lap. She was cutting slices and sharing with the others. When Srebra and I approached, she immediately offered us slices as well. We took them, thanked her, and right away they all asked us how we were, how things were going. We all already knew each other; we had been in the same department a long time, but only now were we formally acquainted. They were talking about what they were going to take with them to the monastery. They said they were planning to go to a convent for New Year's to see Sister Zlata, and to avoid the New Year's Eve craziness. They would spend the night there in peace, and then there would be a vigil. This was the second year that they were going to the convent on New Year's Eve. It felt to me as if Saint Zlata Meglenska moved in my pocket, jumping with joy when she heard their conversation. "What about you? Will you celebrate New Year's Eve?" the slim student asked kindly. "We never celebrate. We just watch television and eat peanuts," Srebra laughed. "It's hard to celebrate New Year's Eve with joined heads," I said, laughing at my own expense. And they burst into laughter. "Everything is good for something," said the older woman, and we all laughed again. How good I felt in their company! Later, Srebra said that each of them was a bit eccentric, and that if they weren't such zealots, they would really be ideal. For me, it was precisely because of this that they were ideal—they believed in God, or at least tried to believe in God. Although my relationship with God was undefined, I felt we were on the same wavelength.

"Hey, why don't you come with us?" proposed the young man in glasses. "You won't regret it." Srebra and I felt a rush of warmth flood our shared vein. At that moment, the professor came in. "We'll see you later," I told them. "A convent? Are you crazy?" Srebra muttered when we got back to our desk. "Please, I'm begging you more than ever before," I whispered, and for the entire class I drew crosses, chapels, and saints with halos on my notepad. Srebra couldn't contain herself, and quietly hissed at me, "Don't you see what priests are doing in Serbia? They give their blessing to believers to go slaughter women and children in Bosnia, and you want to go to a convent." "Sister Zlata is surely not like that... Surely... they are not all the same," I said, defending her, even though I hadn't met her, because I wanted, more than anything, to go to the convent. "We are going," I told Sneže and Ivan—the blond woman and the guy with the ponytail. Later, we learned that they had been a couple for years, as were the slim young woman and the guy with long bangs. On December 31, 1992, we found ourselves at the train station early in the morning. There was another young woman with the group, who had a beautiful white face, olive green eyes, and a limp in her right leg. The older woman from our department had a nine-year-old girl with her, her daughter. Another young man had come, our age, short and nice-looking, with glasses and a trim beard. We could barely find an empty compartment. The women took seats, and the men stood in the corridor. The train was loaded with passengers, and one immediately noticed the refugees from Bosnia with their small children clutching their skirts. It was loud and crowded. The train was unheated, and wind blew from all sides; only the air that we exhaled warmed us slightly. "Why are you studying law?" I asked Sneže, Marina, and Kristina. "Ah," said Marina, "we are all children of long-established Skopje families, and, you know, we always become lawyers, judges, or jurists. Tradition! We didn't want to break the chain, so we obeyed and enrolled in law." Sneže added, "And that's how we met each other—forced to study law rather than something better, like theology or literature." "I've already completed theology," said Kristina, "I'm not a student. I just go to classes. I like feeling young again, and I keep them company. Besides, I don't have a regular job." "That was truly an ascetic journey," she said when we arrived. Her little girl had already befriended us and dubbed us the "Double Lottie," from her favorite children's book about Lottie and Lisa. We climbed into three taxis, which took us up a steep, snowy road to the monastery.

We unloaded our bags in front of the convent and entered the church. All of them, except Srebra and me, bowed three times before the main icon, kissed it three times, and crossed themselves three times. I wanted to do the same, but I was afraid to pull Srebra over only to have her not want to bow and for us to teeter and perhaps even fall. Sister Zlata was reading the midday prayers. When she finished, we crossed ourselves and went outside, where everyone kissed her hand and said, "Mother, bless us." That's what the others said to her and that's what I said. Srebra merely extended her hand, but did not kiss her. Sister Zlata smiled at us warmly, her big blue eyes sparkling like lakes. How unearthly she looked in her long black mantle: tall, firm, humble, and dignified. She was our namesake—mine and my icon's—and I felt such pride because of it. She led us into a reception room connected to the kitchen, where a warm hearth awaited us and the aroma of linden tea. She drew tea from the kettle with a ladle and offered us tin cups. A jar of honey stood on the table, and everyone served themselves as much as they wanted. "We also have coffee," she said. "But no one reads the coffee grounds here," she laughed, and we laughed along with her. I poked my hand into my pocket and caressed the icon. *Look,* I said silently, *her name is Zlata, just like us.* Had Zlata Meglenska brought us here, to Sister Zlata? Was this God's plan? Three Zlatas in one place. In the distance, we could hear the New Year's Eve commotion: firecrackers going off, music reverberating from all directions. We sat in a large room with a small chapel in one corner, and each of us was occupied with something: Sister Zlata was teaching Srebra and me how to make candles, Sneže and Ivan were quietly reading a prayer, Kristina and her daughter were attempting to pick up the melody of a hymn, Marina and Kosta were reading the lives of saints, and Darko, the young man with the trim beard, kept us company by making candles with us. When we finished, Sister Zlata called Srebra and me into the kitchen and said we were going to make pita. We scooped boiled beans from a large pot, while she chopped an onion, fried it, salted it, and then mixed it into the beans. Srebra and I blended the mixture. "Have you eaten pita with beans before?" she asked, and Srebra and I shook our heads. "There are many temptations in life, but pita with beans is the greatest. Even so, we monastic people don't give it up for Lent," she said, laughing. My eyes devoured her cheerful figure. I even gathered up the courage to ask her how people who lived a monastic life slept, so if they died during the night they wouldn't be found in some unsuitable position. "That's a good question, but it's a secret. However, since you are Zlata and Srebra, and we are namesakes, I will tell you. We sleep on our backs," she said, "and hold a cross in our hands. If we die in our sleep, our soul skips along the cross and departs—poof—straight to God. The cross is the soul's stairway to God." When I heard that, I immediately thought of Roza and my cross that became her soul's stairway to God. But too early, too early! "But those who marry," she said, glancing around the room to where the others were gathered, "cannot easily hold a cross while they sleep. It's sufficient for them to sleep with their arms crossed." "We always sleep on our backs because of our heads," said Srebra, "but without a cross, and we can't cross our arms because our elbows knock into each other." "You carry your cross inside," said Sister Zlata. "You don't need another one." Is that why Roza borrowed my cross? Is that why? She skipped along the cross to God, leaving us to mourn for her. I felt this was the right moment to show her my icon, our shared Saint, Zlata Meglenska. I pulled it from my pocket and offered it to her. I had never done that before. She held it gently, almost sacredly. She looked at it, crossed herself, kissed it, and returned it to me. "You and Saint Zlata Meglenska are already one," she said, taking the pita from the oven. It was the most wonderful pita in the world. Just before midnight, we went to bed: the women on couches or borrowed mattresses in the room with the small chapel; the men in the other, empty, room. All night, the sounds of New Year's Eve reached us, but from a distance. They were not loud and distinct, but more like echoes of the wildest night of the year. The world was outside, but we were in a convent. Srebra and I lay on our couch by the door, and a candle in the corner illuminated the icon of the Holy Virgin. Somehow, I managed to cross my arms on my chest, and after a while, I sensed that Srebra had as well. But it wasn't easy to sleep with our arms crossed, because our elbows constantly touched and our noses itched. Our arms inched their way down beside our bodies. We had trouble falling asleep. Early the next day, the clang of

Sister Zlata's bell woke us. We dressed and entered the church, read the morning prayers, crossed ourselves, and bowed our heads. Srebra and I were new to all this, but everyone was patient, and everyone was enraptured by one love. I finally felt I belonged somewhere—that this was the world I needed. The others performed the Saint Basil's Day custom for good luck—crawling beneath the icon of Saint Basil. The small table was narrow, and I didn't think there was enough room for Srebra and me. As if reading our thoughts, Sister Zlata waited for everyone to finish, then took the icon, kissed it, and placed it on the table where the church books were kept. Now Srebra and I could crawl underneath. Srebra did not want to, both on principle and out of embarrassment, but Darko came up and said, "Nothing is by chance in this world. Everything is God's plan." Srebra gave in and pulled me under the table, and while we passed underneath, I prayed to Saint Basil for love. I listened to my inner voice praying for health, for happiness, when all of a sudden I heard myself praying for a man. I was ashamed of myself. I was certain that Srebra prayed for only one thing, for us to be separated, for us to be freed of one another at last, but that hadn't occurred to me. Then we had free time. We went to the library, and among the many books, Srebra found Eliade's trilogy on religion, and I found Dostoevsky's story "The Meek One." We took the books and sat on a bench at the large carved wooden table, spending some time reading. Later, all of us peeled potatoes. Sister Zlata spoke: "There are many temptations in this life. It's easier to be delivered from some, while from others it is more difficult. But we saved ourselves from New Year's Eve didn't we?" We all laughed. "And now, sitting and peeling potatoes, we think there is no temptation, but look where our hands are; they are not in the air, or on our chest, or alongside our bodies. They are between our legs, just where the devil loves! Something starts to tickle, a desire we didn't seek, but which comes unbidden, and the mind goes astray into the world of pleasure, the soul falls asleep, and there you are…sin is not far away. So, it is best if our hands never rest between our legs, but are always busy away from our bodies. See, we should sit like this." She sat down with her back straight and lifted the potatoes into the air, not touching any part of her body. We all tried to sit like that, but there was no way Srebra and I could sit so straight, because our heads pulled one of us toward the other; for years, we'd had pains in our necks and our backs, soothing them with our mother's Chinese balm. "It's not easy," said Kosta; "my hands ache. It's better if I stand up." "Exactly," said Sister Zlata. "A person should stand, rather than sit, to work and to pray. To avoid sin, a person should stand upright." "How much can you personally resist temptation?" asked Boro, the man with the misshapen face and the hand that constantly waved back and forth. Sister Zlata thought a moment and said, "Very little. It would be more difficult for me if I lived in the world. Here, I can pray all day, but out in the world, everything comes before prayer. If only God had had mercy on me and made me worthy of a life spent wandering, rather than a life in this palace, then, like Saint Seraphim, I would sleep not in warmth but in the cold, eating roots. If He had only given me the strength to be like Saint Catherine in the desert! If I could glorify the faith as Zlata Meglenska did…" and she turned toward me, adding, "who, for Jesus's sake, was flayed, hanged, and cut to pieces. But my children, I am far too weak for such adventures of the soul and body. For years, I have been tormented by rheumatism, and at times I get dizzy." A hush fell over the room. I squeezed the icon tightly in my pocket. On January 3, everyone was getting ready to leave. "Come on," said Srebra, "let's get ready." But something was compelling me to stay. I wanted us to spend our January Christmas with Sister Zlata, in peace and love, and not at home in Skopje, where, once again, Christ's birth would need to be celebrated quickly on Christmas Eve, where, once again, we wouldn't open the door to carolers, and where, once again, Srebra and I would eat alone before Mom and Dad sat down to eat.

I gathered my courage and asked Sister Zlata, "Could we stay for Christmas as well?" Srebra recoiled, stunned by my suggestion. "Of course you can!" exclaimed Sister Zlata, happy as a child. Srebra didn't have the heart to protest. So we said goodbye to the others, thanking them for bringing us to this heaven on earth, and waved to them from the enclosed wooden balcony as they left. Darko turned around a few times to wave at us, and then they were lost to view down the path below the convent. Each of them had taken away a small leather pouch with a small wooden cross inside. We were told we'd also get one when we left. "Darko is kind of strange," I whispered to Srebra, "wanting to hang around us the whole time, even drying the dishes while we washed." Srebra only said, "I don't know why we didn't leave with them." That whole day, we cleaned the monastery, read the psalms of David, and learned to sing hymns. For as long as I could remember, my favorite hymn had been the *Cherubic Hymn*. It now entered my dreams, in Sister Zlata's voice. Those days at the monastery were lovely. We had time for reading, for prayers, and for cooking, our first such experience, since at home, Mom never taught us how to make anything. Often, when she was making dinner rolls, or steamed cookies, or a cake, she would kick us out of the kitchen so we wouldn't get in her way and cause her to burn something or make a mistake in the recipe. Sister

Zlata prepared food with ease, leaving part of the work for us, laughing, "Who has helpers as good as mine!" I added, "And two-headed ones at that," and we laughed. Suddenly, Sister Zlata began to sing a new hymn aloud, and it echoed through the monastery, and our spirits were filled with beauty and happiness. Is this what is called *bliss*? I wondered. As though Sister Zlata had heard my thoughts, she said, "God is a blessing; there is no greater blessing than He."

We laid down straw in a dark windowless spare cell, and in the middle of the room we placed a good-sized oak sapling decorated with bits of cotton in a flowerpot. A man from the village brought a small lamb that raced freely around in the straw, gamboling about as if it, too, rejoiced in the imminent birth of Christ. On Christmas Eve, early in the morning, children came to the monastery singing a different version of the traditional Christmas Eve song than we knew, and we gave them apples, pears, walnuts, and three candies inside little pouches made from curtain material and tied with interwoven white, blue, and red threads. "I make them gifts every year, and they seem delighted with them," said Sister Zlata. When the last child left, we went into the church. We kissed the icons, read several prayers, and then withdrew to the convent—Srebra and I to the room with the chapel where we were sleeping, and Sister Zlata to her cell. On the wall in our room hung an icon of Saint Christopher. I dragged Srebra over several times to look at the saint with young Jesus Christ on his shoulder. We had learned of Saint Christopher in a volume about the lives of the saints, and I read his story aloud. A wonderful story about a man who wanted to serve God in a special way, and, unknowingly, carried Christ across the river. As Christ became heavier and heavier, Saint Christopher said to him, "Why are you so heavy, child? It feels as though I am carrying the whole world on my shoulders." Christ told him who he was, blessed him, and baptized him. The story fascinated me. I hadn't heard it before, nor had I known that there was a saint with that name. When I finished reading, Srebra said she wanted to shower, since that evening was Christmas Eve. We went down the stairs to the washrooms, which were a bit like school, a bit like camp. We opened the door to the shower, and recoiled, frozen by the view: Sister Zlata drying herself with a towel. She was naked, having just showered. Her hair was down; it was wet, black with threads of gray, and long, almost to her waist. "Oh!" shouted Srebra as we slammed the door shut. Inside, Sister Zlata merely said quietly, "God grant forgiveness, God grant forgiveness." We fled upstairs to our room. Both of us were quite rattled. Srebra began to laugh quietly, as if her nerves had given way, and I crossed myself repeatedly, not able to stop. I was embarrassed. It made me feel ashamed, but also surprised. I had never considered the fact that monastic people also took their clothes off, washed themselves, that they, too, let the hair they never cut down. I don't know if they ever combed it. "Okay, quit it, now," said Srebra. "You quit, too," I told her, and we finally settled down.

When we went downstairs again, Sister Zlata was no longer there. We washed as quickly as we could, with our eyes closed. Because of our heads, we either had to bend down together or not at all, and in a standing position we were never able to see our legs or our vaginas, just the tops of our breasts and our nipples, which stiffened when the water was a bit cold. We hadn't been embarrassed in front of each other for a long time—we couldn't be, we simply had no choice. But now, we both closed our eyes, because we were taken by an unpleasant feeling of intimacy, as if we had broken some rule in looking at Sister Zlata naked, with her hair down, which had otherwise always been covered by her nun's felt cap and veil. Sister Zlata didn't say anything when we saw her in the kitchen. She was making a vegetable pie and Lenten beans; Srebra and I fried fish dusted with flour, the way we had seen our mother do it. We had Christmas Eve dinner in the cell scattered with straw and a fireplace in which the gold and orange fire danced along the five-century-old walls of the monastery. It was truly a feast. We didn't have a round loaf with a coin inside, though, because Sister Zlata considered it a relic from pagan ritual. Instead, we had dried fruit, apples, pears, leek pita, fish, beans, and homemade bread. Sister Zlata sang Christmas carols all evening, and the lamb scampered around the cell, licking our palms as if it, too, rejoiced in the birth of Jesus. It was the most wonderful Christmas Eve of our lives. On January 7, 1993, at the boundary between night and morning, Sister Zlata woke us to go to church. Since she was a nun, she couldn't celebrate the Christmas liturgy alone. In capes and boots, we went down the snowy path to the village church, where every single person sang, those who could and those who couldn't. That togetherness in God was beautiful and grotesque and primordial. When we returned to the monastery, it was mid-morning. As always, Sister Zlata lay on the floor, hands crossed over her breast, as if she were lying in a coffin, prepared for heaven. We lay down in our monastic cell, and were as gladdened by the birth of Christ as we would be by the birth of a child.

Before evening prayers, just as we were about to enter the church, someone in the courtyard called out, "Hey, Zlata, Srebra!" We turned—as we always did when someone called to us, not just with our heads, but with our whole bodies like wolves—and at first, we didn't know who was calling to us.

Then we recognized our aunt, our uncle, and our cousin, who was now a young woman. We hadn't seen them since that one and only visit when our mother left us in front of the door of the house where our father had grown up. We hadn't gone there since. And now here they were, in the courtyard of the convent, and we hurried to greet them, but with no hugs or kisses. We were extremely reserved with our uncle, and unnaturally cordial with our aunt, who immediately asked us what we were doing, how we were, and why we happened to be there. "We came for New Year's and stayed for Christmas as well, but we're leaving tomorrow." "That's really great. We came to see the convent, since we're here on a ski trip and decided to take a walk, but it's really cold, so we went inside to light candles and were just heading out," our aunt continued. Our cousin stood bashfully off to the side, her cheeks burning. Did she like us; had she missed us? Was she aware that, just like us, she had, and simultaneously didn't have, cousins? "You know, your grandmother died," our aunt said. We simply nodded. We knew she died because someone called to tell our father when the funeral was, but he had merely said, "God forgive her," and didn't go. By the next day, I had forgotten that she died; I felt nothing toward the woman, except an ache that she had not been the grandmother to us she should have been. Srebra even said, "She croaked," but we didn't laugh. Our father continued to watch television, spend time in the garage, get angry and swear, or call us by our nicknames. Nothing changed in our lives. And now here they were, standing in front of the church, our would-be aunt and uncle, and our cousin, with whom we shared no cousinly feeling. We said goodbye one more time, and went into the church as they climbed into their white Lada and vanished down the path below. The entire time I was in the church, I prayed for my father; for the first time in my life I didn't think of him just fleetingly in my inner prayers, but I prayed to God to help him find peace while he was alive, to make peace with his brother, his sister, all of them, and to go at least once more to the house he built when he was still a child. When we left the church, Srebra said in a hushed voice, "I never want to see them again," which was a bit shocking, since I thought Srebra was flooded by the church's blessing also and had only good thoughts for everyone. *Temptation*, I thought, but said aloud, "What about Dad? Do you think he doesn't want to?" Srebra pursed her lips. The next day, we had to leave. Sister Zlata said to us, "You can come whenever you wish. Also, you should know I've decided not to give you your small crosses and chains, but will save them for next time." She was sad we were leaving, because it was clear we got along together well. We had formed a kind of family, even Srebra, who always resisted anything related to the Church, had felt relaxed there. Sister Zlata didn't say it, but we could almost hear the unspoken sentences: *And where else, but in a convent, will people like you be loved? You are beautiful to God, and it's God's brides alone that you can possibly be.* She asked me to show her my small icon one more time. She crossed herself and kissed it. I pulled Srebra over to the icon of Saint Christopher one last time, and I patted the heads of Saint Christopher and the baby Jesus he carried.

On the train, I said firmly to Srebra, "If we never manage to get separated, the best thing for us would be to go into the convent." But she responded more firmly, "We will get separated!" Once we were on the train, I began to think about life outside the convent. All the days there, we had heard nothing about what was happening in the world; we hadn't even thought about the war in Bosnia, or anything else. Now, at the railroad station we saw women with children waiting for someone, for a train, for anyone who could help them, someone to take them to a refugee camp or other place of asylum. "I wonder what has happened?" said Srebra, and indeed, after we got home and quickly wished our mother and father a Happy New Year—fleeting kisses on the cheeks, which we only did at New Year's or when we were going to leave to stay more than two months in the village—we heard on the evening news about new horrors in Sarajevo and throughout Bosnia. I think we were less pained by what we were seeing on the screen than shocked, asking the question, "How is it possible that this is happening? How is it possible?" The January examination period began, and at some of the exams, we saw the friends with whom we had traveled to the convent. They told us they went to the church in Krivi Dol every Sunday. They said the most beautiful liturgy in the city was held there and one had to go early because there were so many people and the church was quite small. Sometimes not everyone could get inside, so some had to remain outside in front of the door to take part in the service. But that winter of 1993 was very cold, with black ice and heavy winds, and it was difficult to get up early on a Sunday morning and endure our mother's questions: "Where are you going? How can you be so foolish as to go to church in such a storm? The bus doesn't go there, and the snow isn't cleared; someone will grab you and take you off somewhere. Who goes to the church? If you need a church, there's one here…" and on and on. In fact, we didn't get to experience many Sunday services because the boiler hadn't been turned on on Saturday night. I longed for a real liturgy, for angelic singing, for my *Cherubic Hymn*, for communion in God with people who were spiritually close to me. For a while, I somehow forgot about the church in Krivi

Dol. It was Easter service when we went there for the first time. We climbed uphill a long way, past the skating rink in the fortress, past the closed disco, looking from the heights down on the Vardar River and the city stadium surrounded by the spreading greenery of the city park. We walked on and on while buses rolled past us. One even stopped, and the driver, a young man, asked, "Aren't you going the wrong way? This isn't the way to the nuthouse." Then he and his co-driver had a good laugh; another kept honking his horn as if it were a wedding, but we finally made it to the church. As soon as we entered and heard the melodious voice of the priest and the small choir accompanying him, we forgot our exhaustion, our anger, and our shame, at least I did, because in the depths of my soul, I gave myself over to the liturgy, which pierced straight to my inner unrest. All the school friends with whom we had traveled to the convent were there—Boro, Kristina, her daughter, and Darko, who winked when he saw us and shifted his position several times in the crowd. The women stood to the left, the men to the right. Most of the women wore headscarves and long full skirts. Srebra and I had neither headscarves nor full skirts. We could only wear shallow hats in winter that reached down to where we were conjoined. Perhaps we could have tied a scarf over both our heads. But it wasn't important. We all floated in a kind of bliss. At the end, we received a wafer, and many of the others also took communion wine. We didn't, because we hadn't fasted, gone to confession, and repented for our sins of thought, word, or deed. The priest drew wine from the chalice with a spoon and placed it and bread in each person's mouth; we sang. Later, at home, Srebra said, "How can everyone use the same spoon? It must be a hotbed of bacteria," immediately adding, "I know what you're going to say, sickness doesn't spread to those who believe in God." "What do you know?" I retorted. After the service, everyone greeted one another in the churchyard with hugs, saying, "Christ is risen. Truly, He is risen." It was lovely. Darko brought us back downtown in his car. He asked, "Will you come regularly?" "Yes," I said. "No," said Srebra. "No?" asked Darko. "But I thought I could see you here." See *you*, he had said, thinking only of Srebra. "See *you*, he said; he was only thinking about you," I said to Srebra at home. "He must have been confused," said Srebra. We didn't mention it again until the following Sunday. Darko drove us home again, but we didn't want him to drop us off in front of our building, because someone might see and then gossip about it, especially our parents, and then we'd have to explain who he was and why he was bringing us home. Men were *a priori* excluded from our lives, and it would be, of course, absurd for anyone to be interested in us, especially in one of us, as Darko now was in Srebra. Was he blind or weird? And how could he be interested in one of us, or even both of us for that matter, when we were predestined to be alone, or more precisely, because we were already a pair we could never be a couple with a man? Darko studied architecture, and, in addition to religion, he was also interested in politics. He told us he was a member of the opposition party. Srebra attentively followed all the political events in Macedonia and the former Yugoslavia. Although I was always forced to watch television with her, my thoughts were not on what was being shown on the screen, or I simply read a book, and events seemed to slip past my attention, so I didn't know that the new Macedonian parties had young members, and not just middle-aged men and the occasional woman. In our family, politics were talked about in the most reductive, and I would say, populist, manner. Our mother and father changed political views whichever way the wind was blowing: If they listened to Serbian news, they were convinced Serbs were dying in Bosnia, rather than Bosnian Muslims. If our president, Kiro Gligorov, said the acronym FYROM—Former Yugoslav Republic of Macedonia—that was fine as long as we were granted entry into the UN; then they agreed with him, but they also thought opposition members Ljubčo Georgievski and Branko Crvenkovski were young and bright. It was only about Albanians that they had a single point of view, which was negative and stereotyping, as it was in so many families, even those with educated parents. For years, nothing changed. The general politics of compromise, a remnant of the one-party system, ruled for a long time in our family, in which, except for our uncle who changed from a Communist to a liberal, there were no parties, nor even party sympathizers, but only commentators on the things that had a direct effect on our lives. The fact was, Macedonia was becoming more and more of a country with its own national symbols, its own money and government structures. The fact was, the war in Bosnia wasn't ending, and we had all become accustomed to that; people were dying, but we lived more or less normally, carrying on with our own joys and sorrows. Srebra had found herself in the study of law, and I studied as much as I had to, but the rest of the time, while Srebra delved deeper into supplementary readings, I immersed myself in novels and poetry. Books were my best friends, and that was not just an empty slogan taught to school kids. When I thought of friendship, I grasped that we had rarely had friends in real life. As kids, we had Roza, but she died, and it was my fault—that was clearer to me now than ever before, and I had never, ever found the courage to admit it to her parents. Most likely they knew, because Roza hadn't had a chain of her own, so she must have borrowed it before going on that fateful trip to Greece. On the stairs, whenever we saw her mother, father, or sister—who now had her own little daughter who looked so much like Roza—we greeted each other warmly, with sadness in our voices, especially noticeable in her father, who was never again quite himself. He dragged himself around in black clothing, his face sallow; he spoke quietly, timidly. The loss of his daughter had caused his shoulders to sag, and seeing him so bent, so sad, made you sad, as though Roza had died yesterday. No one in the building ever mentioned Roza anymore; everyone had closed that chapter in their lives, or more precisely, from our everyday experience. The changing years swept everything before them. No one spoke of Auntie Verka either, whom we could have also counted among the friends from childhood. And everyone had forgotten Bogdan. New people lived in the apartment of his adopted mother, a young couple with no children. For a long time we didn't have friends, until our New Year's trip to the convent, when we became close with Sister Zlata and the colleagues from the university who had invited us. The loneliness of all those years had become a natural condition, and I have always felt that it was the books that kept us from going crazy, regardless of whether they were legal tomes or novels. When I read entrancing novels, I felt aroused almost every night, even though, in the novels, characters rarely made love. I was particularly aroused while reading *The Kalevala* just before bed. It wasn't obvious why such an erotic charge came from such a spirited work. Given our age and the whole situation, I felt entitled to self-gratification. I poked my fingers inside or twisted the end of the blanket on my side of the bed and slowly, so as to not wake Srebra, rubbed it against my vagina, pressing it inside and feeling bliss spread throughout my body. I would fall asleep, but then would wake up several hours later feeling like a monster. I knew God saw everything, and I was ashamed before Him, so I'd recite the Lord's Prayer ten times to myself, until I fell asleep again. A new schism was growing in me, a division between my longing for God and my longing for a man. What would it be like to be with a man, to be under him, on top of him, to be one body joined from two, not by our heads but by our sexual organs? Some of the other students at the university were already pregnant, and I thought about the way in which they became pregnant. During exams, they frequently used pregnancy as an excuse for their lack of preparedness. Srebra and I never spoke of these things. I don't know how she controlled her sexual needs or whether she even felt such things at all. She usually slept peacefully through the night. And during the day, we heeded Sister Zlata's advice not to put our hands in our laps lest the devil lead us into temptation. Sister Zlata! Sneže and Ivan told us that they had heard she'd been thrown out of the convent and sent to a village near the Greek border, to some small abandoned convent, and that the convent we had gone to was now a monastery, with new monks. How difficult that was for me! But why did they throw her out? She took such great care of the convent. She was so good! Kristina said she'd heard that she had begun to go out, that's what the villagers said. She would go walking about, singing, crying, or laughing hysterically, and once, she threw herself on the ground in front of the convent doors, thrashing her legs. She was unable to stop until a priest from the village sprinkled her with basil, and he then managed to pull her back inside. She had gone mad, the villagers said. But, poor thing, she was just a holy fool, nothing else. A holy fool! How I loved that expression. I had read an entire book about holy fools in Russia, and after that I couldn't be apart from *God's Pauper* by Kazantzakis or *Narcissus and Goldmund* by Hesse. Srebra seemed to want to say, "I knew it," but if she had, I think I would have dug my fingers into her side. She kept her peace. We continued to go to services in Krivi Dol regularly, Srebra saying that she wasn't affected by the singing, that she only went out of a desire to see the other parishioners, to see how they reacted, whether they fell into a trance, whether it was a collective delusion, and to hear what the priest said in his sermon: Would he mention the war in Bosnia? Would he take sides? Many Macedonian priests were allying themselves with the Serbian Church that held the view that Serbs were the victims, not the torturers. The Serbian priests sent soldiers into battle, marking their foreheads with the sign of the cross more to symbolize the Serbian eagle than the Christian cross. Srebra approached services analytically and objectively; I went subjectively. I was the one who experienced the blessing in the prayers and hymns, the wafer and the candles. Once I even took communion. I dragged Srebra into the line and, with her walking beside me against her will with her arms drooping, I, with arms crossed, opened my mouth as far as I could to not spill a single drop of the communion wine. I had managed to eat no fats for a whole week, which irritated our mother and father terribly. I only ate boiled beans, not fried, bread and onions, peppers, tomatoes, and cabbage with a little red pepper and salt, but no oil. Still, I didn't go to confession, because we didn't have our own spiritual father, unlike most of those who went to Krivi Dol. "I don't have one yet, either," said Darko, who always drove us back to our neighborhood, and, when it was cold, insisted on picking us up. More and more often after service, we went for coffee at Café Kula just the three of us, and we two would sit on chairs pushed together in the garden outside with him across from us, or in winter, we sat on the banquettes in a booth. We drank coffee or tea and talked about this and that. He wanted to build a church in his neighborhood someday, where, he said, there wasn't a single one: "I can't see why they wouldn't build one; there will be more and more churches now," he said. "People are returning to the faith, and it's high time, now that we have our own country, and everything belongs to us." He did not talk much about the party, unless Srebra asked him specifically. We learned that his father was vice president of the party and was on television sometimes. It seemed to me that most of the time, in fact, we were silent, drinking our tea or coffee. Darko would occasionally take Srebra's spoon and hold it and, as if unobserved, lick it, before returning it to her plate. He would help us put on our coats, always brushing Srebra's hair from her collar.

That is what our meetings with Darko amounted to until New Year's Eve 1993, which we spent at his house, with the friends with whom we had gone to the convent. We listened to classical music and church hymns, then to the group Anastasija, then more classical music. It was still the Christmas fast, and we ate Lenten food. The only thing that reminded us that it was New Year's Eve was the tree his parents had decorated before they left to celebrate at a restaurant. The tree was large, sparkling, decorated with many colored lights and ornaments. Its gaudiness reminded us that it was New Year's Eve, even though we just wanted to spend the night as simply as possible, far from the New Year's Eve atmosphere in our homes or on the TV. At midnight, it was inevitable, however, that we would all wish each other a Happy New Year. Everyone wished each other a Happy Holiday with a hug, Srebra and I, as always, hugging everyone jointly, touching them with our faces. They grasped our heads with both hands and hugged us at the same time, which somehow seemed more natural. But Darko hugged me first, lightly, his hand across my back, wishing me a Happy New Year. Then he held Srebra's head in his hands, just below the ears, looked into her eyes, and said, "I love you." At that same moment, he kissed her on the lips. I felt his breath, there, on my left cheek, his cheek nearly touching mine, but he didn't move. He closed Srebra's mouth with a long, deep kiss, holding her head the whole time, which caused a pain in my temple. Our joint vein gushed; our blood had never poured through at such frightening speed; Srebra's entire body pulsed, and she transferred that throbbing into my head, then down to my chest. Afterward, she couldn't catch her breath. She dragged me to the bathroom, and we locked ourselves inside. I was overcome by uncontrollable laughter, but Srebra began to cry, quietly, controlling her voice. She was sinking into tears, I into laughter. We finally calmed down. We sat there, each of us half-perched on the lid of the toilet, and brushed our tears away. "He loves you," I told her, and she said at the same time, "I love him."

Someone knocked on the door. It was Kristina. She said Sanja had to pee. We went back out to the room. Darko was in the kitchen, cutting Lenten baklava at the counter. The others were sitting and listening to Kosta talk about a woman, their neighbor, who had kept her dead husband at home for seven whole days. "Her son," he was saying, "forbade anyone to tell the press, which is why you haven't heard about it. Listen: as soon as he died, his wife called his work, saying he was sick and wouldn't be able to come in. Then she called her own employer and said she was sick and they shouldn't expect her. She went to the store to buy food, then called her son and told him they had decided to take a trip to the village. They had some vacation days, and so he shouldn't try to contact them. Then she shut herself up in the apartment and spent all seven of those days with her dead husband, rubbing him with rakija to keep him from smelling. She stripped him naked, covered him with a sheet, and watched him the whole time, talking to him, telling him all sorts of things. She would turn on the television, lay down beside him, and make various comments. Once, God forgive her, she even wanted to have sex with him and, though she thought at first she wouldn't be able to, she took his hand and poked it down there, God forgive her. That whole week, we smelled something coming from their apartment, until it finally became intolerable and we called the police. When they came and opened it up—what should they see but the wife, dressed in her finest. She told the police, "You can take him now." She told them everything—I think she had gone crazy—and they took her away too. They called in a service to come clean the apartment, but I think it'll smell like a corpse forever; in our apartment we sit under blankets with the windows open. It's unbearable. Just think, that whole time, she thought he would come back, that he would be resurrected. "He was so good. I was certain he would rise again. He had no ill will toward anyone, and he was always helping people," she said. That was all true. None of the other neighbors in the building were like him. She said that, during those seven days, she argued with him about her unfulfilled dreams, but also recalled fond memories and did to him everything she had been unable to do, because he had been a very shy and good man, humble and pious." "God save and protect him," some of those who were listening said, and we slowly got ready to leave. Darko came in from the kitchen with a bowl of mandarins, and we peeled and ate them, all three of us looking at the floor. As we left, Darko said to Srebra, "I'll call you."

And he did call her. Srebra, melting with pleasure and love, held the receiver to her left ear, and every word she heard I heard as well, but I don't know if Darko was aware of it, perhaps thinking he was whispering expressions of love to her privately. But I did hear them, until it occurred to me that I could use earplugs so they could at least talk freely; I was aware of Srebra's discomfort in returning such tender expressions to Darko. She was embarrassed next to me, not so much by me, but more by the closeness of our ear canals and our mouths, so, no matter what they said, all four of our ears heard it. We couldn't see each other's eyes, except in a mirror, but our noses always smelled the same smells. We bought a whole bag of cotton earplugs, and whenever Darko called, I stuffed some in my ears. While they didn't completely block out the sound, they were like a wall between their intimacy and me. We met Darko nearly every day after class at the university, and after every Sunday service. We met too often for the situation I found myself in, though their situation was perhaps even more difficult. But while their love was new, they moved past my presence as easily as through a tightly stretched Chinese jump rope, giving themselves over to each other, even though I had to be there with them whether they liked it or not, and they had to be with me. That was the first time I was witness to a love affair. I watched how it developed, how their feelings changed, how their small sweet games of seduction, rejection, attraction, connecting, distancing, and drawing closer again played out. All this was taking place in their souls, almost without anything physical, because Darko was considerate of me, but I was still aware that carnal desire burned between them. I thought that if Srebra hadn't known before what it was for the clitoris to tremble with desire, she would learn now, since sex wasn't even required for that. It was enough for Darko to stroke her leg, or put his arm around her waist or even a bit higher, closer to her breasts. I think they were most aroused when, upon greeting or leaving one another, they'd kiss while, behind my glasses, I closed my eyes, the cotton in my ears, gritting my teeth. I wasn't angry with them, nor did I envy them. I just wanted to fall through the earth because of the unpleasantness, the embarrassment, the powerlessness. Most of all I was powerless, because I didn't want to be, but had to be, the third wheel in their relationship. Through no fault of my own, I was witness to their tender moments, although honestly, they were both very considerate, as considerate as two people in love could be. Perhaps it was Darko's faith that prevented him, in those intimate moments, from grabbing her hips or breasts or peeling off her clothes, and Srebra, I believe, just wanted, more than anything, for him to embrace her, and she him; to hold each other close while I tried to move my body as far away as possible from them and not make unnecessary contact. But it was difficult, because the spot where our heads were connected would ache. That piece of skin would stretch to its maximum taut-ness, and my temple would throb and throb. We would be struck anew by the strength of the pain even though we had felt it since childhood, since our birth, when, according to Grandma, we cried at every small movement of our heads until we passed out. We no longer cried but stoically endured the pain that was the proof of our Siamese deformity; I wore a back brace all the time, because my spine and neck hurt constantly, but Srebra wore hers only at home, because she was embarrassed Darko might run his hand along her shoul-der and feel the strap beneath his hand. We hadn't been to a doctor for a long time, but it was likely our backs needed physical therapy, if not an operation. At home, we hid Srebra's relationship with Darko as much as we could, although our mother eavesdropped on their phone calls or came into our room without knocking, asking where we had been, why we had stayed on campus so long, whether we were going back downtown, and with whom, and why, and all sorts of other things. Even though we were students approaching the end of our university studies, we still received no allowance, except for our bus passes and enough for a bun or something at school. Our father wrote checks for the books and things we needed for school. But we simply had no money to go downtown, for mascara, or even for sanitary pads, because we saved every penny anyone—usually our aunts—gave us, and counted them like young children.

The first time we were going to go out for pizza with Darko, we saw that we didn't have enough for even one pizza, let alone two. We asked our mother for some money to go out for dinner. "I don't have any money, but there's a bit of change in the ashtray—just take it," she said, annoyed that we had even asked her such a question. Our mother had been given the large crystal ashtray at work for International Women's Day, and it had stood for years on the dining room table, even though no one ever smoked in our house. In it was a small pile of coins, more than thirty of them. We spilled it out on the bed in our room. We counted all the money, and it turned out we had just enough for one pizza, the least expensive one. "We'll just say we already ate and two pizzas are too much for us," I said quietly. But Srebra shot back loudly, "Is she crazy? We're supposed to go downtown with these coins?" I was certain Darko would offer to pay the bill, because he was always generous, and he came from a wealthy urban family—his father was an architect and the vice president of the opposition party, and his mother was a councilor in the parliament. Still, we felt humiliated as we stuffed the change into my purse, which bulged as if the coins might tear it apart. We thought about how stupid it would look if we emptied the purse out in front of the waiter, making him count the coins and stuff them into his small change purse while everyone at the bar laughed because the ones over there with the heads had collected change so they could go out for pizza—mental cases no doubt—and what was that normal-looking guy doing with them? He must be crazy, too. But what else could we have done? Our mother lay on the small couch in the kitchen, angry at the whole world, though for no clear reason, except now, most likely, also because the ashtray was empty. Srebra reached a decision that day—the incident with the coins pushed her from the axis about which our lives had always revolved. Darko paid for the pizzas that evening, and when we got home, Srebra pretty much ordered me to give her my purse. She opened it and poured the coins into the ashtray. Our parents were already in bed, perhaps sleeping, but they surely heard the coins clinking, ringing out as they hit the crystal ashtray. Our parents didn't get up, and the next day, they said nothing. But that day at the university, Srebra said, "We're going to the administration office." I complied. Behind the counter stood the clerk, an old woman knitting a sweater. Srebra dragged my head along with hers up to the window and firmly asked how one could submit an application for a scholarship.

"For what kind of scholarship?" the woman asked. "There are two, one based on need, and the other based on merit. For those such as, such as…" She couldn't find the right word and said only, "There aren't any specifically."

"Both kinds," Srebra said, as if she had not heard the last sentence. "We're both eligible for need-based, but she's also a star student: all her grades are nineties and hundreds," I said, not wanting to present myself as a talented student with my Cs and the occasional B. "Then it would be best if you put in an individual request for an academic scholarship," the woman said to Srebra. "Those stipends are bigger." Srebra filled out the papers. "You will be notified in two months," the clerk said, then, leaning toward us and taking a good look, she said, "Why don't you go to the dean's office as well? When they see you, they might be able to help you with something. Plus, the dean is a member of the awards committee." When Srebra told Darko over the phone that she had submitted an application for a stipend, he said, "My mother will arrange it. She'll call the dean." In less than a month, Srebra received notification that she would get a monthly stipend through graduation, and the first installment would arrive the following month. We didn't say anything about it at home. Srebra wanted to take revenge on our mother for the coins in the ashtray. Although the stipend was hers, she gave half of it to me. "Why?" I asked. "Keep it for yourself; it's yours." "You're my sister," Srebra responded, and I felt my face turn red, my heart nearly bursting, and, a moment later, our joint vein surged. I felt like crying, sobbing, drowning in my own pathos. Instead, I said ironically, "Ah, I'm your sister now that you have Darko…that's why I am a sister to you now." Srebra didn't respond, just turned to some notes, and I immersed myself in a book by Ted Hughes, who had won that year's Golden Wreath prize for poetry at the Struga Poetry Evenings festival and who even came to Struga. On television, I saw him surrounded by so many people that I thought he might need bodyguards. Maybe the organizers were afraid someone would attack him, throw an egg or a tomato at him, because in literary circles, everyone knew he had been Sylvia Plath's husband, the poet who was so filled with despair that one day, she put her head in the gas oven and asphyxiated herself. I thought about how Srebra and I couldn't commit suicide that way, even if we wanted to, because a standard-size oven only had enough space for one head. We could have hanged ourselves, but what chandelier would hold two bodies, two ropes? And it would be difficult to shoot ourselves in the heads with a pistol, since that would mean me shooting with my right hand into my right temple, then passing the pistol to Srebra to shoot herself with her left hand in her left temple. But how could I give it to her if I was already dead? But if we poured hydrochloric acid into two glasses, and then said: "one, two, three, bottoms up"—that would be certain death. Why did such thoughts enter my head? Was it Christian to think about suicide? Srebra clearly didn't think about suicide, while I seemed to place the temptation before myself, contemplating the process. I imagined doing it with Srebra, and that somehow eased my spirits. But later, I would feel ashamed to look Saint Zlata Meglenska in the eye, and I would beg her to pray for me, for us. At Sunday services in Krivi Dol, I would feel wonderful, but the blessedness lasted only a day at most. My brain automatically repeated the Lord's Prayer before I slept, before an exam, before a date between Srebra and Darko, at difficult moments. It was somehow a part of my being, in the same way that the icon was never not in my pocket. Jesus Christ was most present in my life when I was at the edge of insanity or despair—or already inside it. But in my ordinary, everyday life, it was as though he wasn't there. I felt he had given up on us, and I no longer hoped that a large sum of money would fall from the sky so we could go to London to seek the best surgeon at separating Siamese twins. Even if we saved Srebra's stipend, we would need at least twelve years to collect enough money for such an undertaking. So we didn't save it, but bought new stockings and exchanged the rags of torn-up old tee shirts and underwear for real sanitary pads when we had our periods. We bought ourselves perfume and a few blouses that could be pulled up over our legs, went to the theater, and often insisted on paying the bill when we went out with Darko. At home, they noticed that we had gotten money somewhere, and one evening, we heard our mother tell our father that there were two bottles of perfume, some shampoo, and other new things in the cupboard. "Where are they getting the money from?" she asked. "They must be going out with young men." "God only knows," answered our father. "Who knows what they're up to, where they're going, and with whom? Sotir says he saw them getting out of a Lada—someone was bringing them home from downtown." Our mother added, "They've been a problem our whole lives. And it's your fault. You made them like this. You let them get away with anything and now look. People are going to talk. People talked anyway, but now they'll talk even more." Our father flew into a rage, almost shouting at her, "You think you know everything. You've all devoured me. Now it's my fault that you're all brainless." Srebra pulled me with all her strength, and we marched into their room. She shouted, "We are not whores. We are not. We are not whores!" Our mother only said coldly, "Go ahead and shout. Give Dobrila a laugh." Then Srebra began to cry, and I began to cry, and through her sobs, Srebra told them that she was getting a stipend, a stipend, because she was a talented student, because her grades were all nineties and hundreds and it was no longer possible to live with them—why hadn't she aborted us, since she did not love us? Why had she given birth to us at all? Srebra said all sorts of things in her rage. But I was silent. I let her blow off steam, free herself from the burden of her pain. I just moved my head in rhythm with her turmoil and alarm. For several days thereafter, we didn't speak to them. We grew even more distant from them, if such a thing were even possible. And Srebra's rage didn't end. One day, while they were at work, she had us climb up on the armchair, and from the empty space between the shelving unit and the ceiling where they kept blankets covered in plastic and wrapped in pages from the newspaper *Nova Makedonija*, towels, and a bathrobe, gifts for those starting an independent life in one's own home with one's own family—some of which would never be used—we took down the imported Ambassador brand fleece blankets our Aunt Milka had given us for our high-school graduation: green, beautiful, and soft. We brought them to our room and gathered up the greasy worn-out blanket that smelled of old and dusty fibers, which had covered us since childhood. We rolled it up, took it down to the dumpster, and then set the two new blankets on the bed, one next to the other—now we each had our own blanket. Now, when we lay down on the bed to read, we could each wrap ourselves up completely to our chests in our own blanket. Our mother noticed immediately, but kept silent. We were home less often, so we argued with her less often. We were at the university, or a café, or a bakery, sometimes at the movies or the theater, or at the home of one of our friends from the convent outing, where we talked while drinking tea and listening to soft Byzantine music. It was at one of those gatherings where I first heard that there was something called a chaste marriage, in which the husband and wife didn't sleep together. They didn't make love, but loved each other in other ways: through respect, understanding, conversation, prayer, confession, communion, liturgies, and everything else that belonged to the ascetic Christian life. These were people who loved each other, not sinfully, but sacredly, in their spirits and souls, but not with their bodies, so carnal desire was foreign to them. They did not make love even to produce children, but led a type of monastic life in the world. "But we'll have children, right?" Marina asked, taking Kosta's hand. Srebra's cheeks turned red. Darko shifted in his chair, and Srebra and I, seated on the small couch, just stared, bug-eyed. "There is nothing more difficult in the world than a chaste marriage," said Ivan. "I guess that is how we will have to live," Darko said, and everyone turned toward him, then toward us. Everyone already knew that Darko and Srebra were together, but they didn't know where to put me in that relationship, whether it was natural, given by God, and a blessing to be in such a relationship. Srebra said nothing, barely breathing. I gulped, stock-still. Darko and Srebra had never spoken about marriage, about children, or a shared life before. It was self-evident that it would be impossible. "Indeed. How are you thinking of living in the future?" Kristina asked, because we already knew that in the summer of 1994, even if they didn't graduate after the June term, Sneže and Ivan, and Marina and Kosta, were going to get married at the same time on the Assumption of the Blessed Virgin Mary at the Kališta Monastery near Struga, because they wanted Father Seraphim, their spiritual father and one of the best Macedonian scholar-priests, to marry them. Srebra and Darko were silent, as was I. We had no answer to her direct question. I liked the fact that such questions were discussed openly in this group of friends, that it wasn't friendship for the sake of friendship, that here, interpersonal relations developed, everyone looked after each other, a sort of tenderness reigned, a kind of love, something humane, warm, filled with trust. I felt we could depend on these people. I knew we could call and ask a favor or for their help. They were friends in the truest sense of the word. And now they were interested in the question of how we would live, because we also were looking forward to the completion of our coursework, when all that remained was our senior thesis before we were done. How quickly the years of study passed! As long as those too long years of fighting lasted across Yugoslavia—especially in Bosnia and the blockade of Sarajevo, where civilians were still dying—so short seemed our studies, for Srebra, at least, because she enjoyed it so much and lived for her studies; for me, because I didn't enjoy it at all, and wanted to race through and be free of it as quickly as possible. In the meantime, Darko had come into our lives, and, it appeared, did not want to leave, and Srebra didn't want to leave his. I had nowhere to go. I was dependent on their decisions and God's help. "I don't know," said Darko. "Don't ask us about that. It is all so complicated." So we closed the topic, and the discussion turned to the war in Bosnia. Andrej said that, naturally, he supported the Serbs. "They are Orthodox," he said. "Who should I support if not them?" Everyone looked at him flabbergasted, and most heads bowed or turned aside, as if away from some unpleasantness, shame, disgrace, from what else, I did not know—their faces red, some unknown spark in their eyes, hands sweating. My temple and Srebra's communicated with agitated beating. At the tips of all our tongues were words, statements, likely different ones, but from no one's mouth did the truth erupt, a truth that, this time, wasn't shared, wasn't universal but individual, conditioned by each of our conceptions, whether radical or not.

Kristina's little daughter began to cry. She had pricked her finger with the needle she was using to string beads. It seemed as though we had all been waiting for something to interrupt the conversation, and now, rescued, we turned toward her with advice or ran around seeking bandages or gauze, reacting more than the situation required, since there were only a few drops of blood on her finger. In the confusion, I managed to whisper that I wanted to go home. Apparently, Srebra didn't want to, but fortunately, Darko also wanted to leave, and said that he had to finish something for school—a difficult drawing. We left the apartment quickly and didn't come back to those gatherings again for a long time. Something had broken within me, and likely in some of the others as well, but I didn't know exactly what or in whom. I didn't feel the need to meet with them anymore. I longed to see Sister Zlata, but the others—Father Seraphim, the monks whom I met at one of the vigils at Saint Petka, and later met from time to time at our gatherings, and all those people "from the church," whom I liked with all my heart—now became distant from me; I preferred to think about them than see them, and whenever I went to church, I lit candles for each of them, but then tugged on Srebra to leave as quickly as possible so we wouldn't need to talk or go somewhere with them. That suited Srebra, because Darko always left with us, and we would go to a café. After a while, we also started going to his house alone with him, and while we listened to music in the living room—the three of us sitting on the couch—I would turn the pages of a book or photo album, shifting my body as far away from Srebra as possible, while he put his arm around Srebra's waist or put his head in her lap so she could stroke his face, or he would simply hold her hand. I pretended not to see all this, immersing myself in the text or photographs in my hands, but I could hear Srebra's breath—right there, right next to my cheek, by my left ear—as if it were my breath, broken, swallowing the quietness that served as their private conversation. They loved each other more and more. Physical desire was literally born from the love between their souls; the arousal of their bodies was not ignited merely by sexual desire. That drive I recognized from my nights with the clown, when I wanted anything at all to enter me, satisfy me, fill me with bliss, and then, when it was done, I felt empty and hated myself for my self-gratification, because that wasn't lovemaking, but simple masturbation. Darko and Srebra loved each other so much that it would have been the most natural thing for them to lie with each other, caressing and kissing each other, then at last, joining one another, blissful in the act of conjoining their bodies and souls, without a condom or the pill, because even at the outset they wanted to conceive a child; they were already three in one, and God was with them at every moment as well. But unfortunately, I, too, was with them, inseparable from Srebra, and now from Darko as well, aware of everything happening to them, but powerless. God forgive me, but several times I considered suicide so Srebra could be alone and finally live her own life. But what if, when my dead body was separated from hers, she died as well? What if something went wrong and they were simply unable to save her? After all, our blood mixed in our bodies across the link between our heads. If we had only conjoined legs or arms, we would have been separated long ago, since it would have been better to have only one leg or one arm and be free rather than to be whole, but have, in fact, nothing.

Srebra and Darko had been going out—or, more precisely, had loved each other—for more than a year and a half, when, on our graduation day, which Srebra had hurried along as quickly as possible, preparing me, too, for the final exam, Darko waited for us in front of the university. He had graduated several days earlier. It was a beautiful June day, warm, not too hot, the beginning of the summer of 1995. "I just came to congratulate you," he said. "Let's get together tonight. Go somewhere and celebrate." Srebra and I agreed to go to Café Kula, our favorite place in the evenings, and after standing around a bit with Darko, we left. "Do you feel a bit empty, now that we've finished?" I asked Srebra, with barely enough courage to say those words. "Yes, a little," she said, hesitating. "I wonder what Mom and Dad will say." We were walking toward the National Theater but didn't feel like hurrying home, so we stopped in front of the Kultura bookstore by the stone bridge. We went in. The mother of one of our high-school classmates worked there; she was always kind to us, and now we told her we had graduated. She congratulated us warmly and shared her regret that Biljana was dragging through school and still had some outstanding exams to make up from last year. "But you," she said, "even as you are, you've graduated." We walked along the stone bridge toward the Record bus stop, but I felt an emptiness inside that I couldn't express in words, nor was it clear to me why I felt it, because the fact was I had finished my law studies, which I had disliked for the entire four years. I had irrevocably lost that time to something I hated, something that had been the biggest compromise of my life. But now what? I saw no goal ahead of me. We didn't have the money for the operation we had longed for since childhood, or money to open a lawyer's office, and there was no one who would employ us, and Srebra wouldn't get her stipend any longer. What would we do? What would we live on? At home, we neither received nor expected money, though occasionally our father—sad that we had grown more distant over the years than one could even imagine parents and children becoming—pressed some money in our hands, without our mother seeing, when we went out. Accompanied by these thoughts, in complete silence, we arrived home. I knew I would find it unpleasant to say, "We graduated," like when you go to an office and people you don't know are there but something important has happened and you can't hold it in, so you say, "I graduated today," and those unknown people smile through their discomfort, not knowing what to say, caught in the midst of something, but then collecting themselves and saying, "Great, congratulations." Srebra, however, announced clearly and loudly, "Hey, we're done! We've graduated." Our father was sitting in the dining room watching the news, and Mom was on the couch in the kitchen making some sort of wall hanging. Our father mumbled something under his breath, so quietly that we couldn't hear what he said, then went back to watching television. Our mother looked at us and asked, "So who else finished? Did everyone pass? What about that professor who apparently fails students, except when he saw you like that..." She got up and set out some cold fried liver with eggs, bread, and salad of half a cucumber sliced in a small dish on the table for us. We sat and ate—without a word, without answering her questions—quickly, enveloped in shame, as if we were intruders in the home of these people who were, by chance, our parents. We went to our room, sat on the floor, pressed our heads against the bed, and kept silent, but inside us all the anger in the world grew. Fortunately, at that moment the telephone on the wall by the bed rang. We got up. Srebra picked up the receiver, and immediately we heard Aunt Ivanka's voice. She said she was calling to learn how we had done; she'd been thinking of us all day, wondering whether we had graduated, and she was as happy as if we were her own daughters. She said we had to go visit them the next day for piroshki so she could congratulate us on our graduation. Our aunt, our mother's sister, was always more maternal than our mother. We also called Aunt Milka, and she cried with joy and kept repeating, "Auntie's lawyers." We called our uncle, and heard in his voice how proud he was of us—he said he would immediately tell our grandma and grandpa. "We'll come to the village this weekend," I told him, and felt an urgent need, as I'm sure Srebra did too, to sit on our grandma's lap, to have her hug us—one with one arm, the other with the other— and we would say to her, "Grandma, sing the song about the galloping horse," and she would sing it. Then we would stand up and turn our faces toward her at the same time, and we would shower her with kisses, and in doing this, we would nourish our souls with love.

We felt much better that evening in Café Kula, as we drank red wine sitting on a bench and chair at our table, toasting the three of us, as Darko said. There were stars in the sky, quiet jazz came through the speakers, the tables were full. Darko leaned across the table toward Srebra and me. He fixed his gaze on her, trying not to look at me at all, and said, "Come on, let's get married." Then he repeated it: "Let's get married." Srebra seemed to have anticipated this and turned the proposal into a question, "Should we get married?" "Yes, let's get married," Darko said again, taking her by the hand. "How can we get married?" Srebra asked. "How can you get married?" I asked, in shock, managing to say something. And at that instant I was overcome by the most hysterical laughing fit of my life. I kept giggling, imagining it in my mind: Darko the groom, Srebra the bride, and I, with my head attached to hers, walking beside them in a long black dress. I choked with laughter and began to hiccup. Srebra, angry that I was shaking her head with my laughter, said in a loud, clear voice, "Yes, let's get married." "Hold on, are you crazy? How do you think you can get married? What about me? What am I going to do?" "You will live," said Darko, "just as you have lived at home until now, only now with me." "Yes, but at home we didn't sleep with our mother and father," I said rudely. But Darko replied, "If you love Srebra, you will do this, because God is looking at all of us." "That's exactly right," I said, "God looks at us and what does he think? How will you marry Srebra when she isn't an individual, when our bodies are bound together, and you can't have one minute alone together? Are you thinking about that?" "It's important for me to be with Srebra, without regard to anything else," said Darko. Srebra added, "And all that matters to me is to be with you, without regard to anything else." I took control of myself, and the laughter froze somewhere inside me. It had turned into a heavy lump in the center of my heart. I grasped the icon of Saint Zlata Meglenska in my pocket, squeezed it, caressed it, scratched it with my fingernails. "Are you aware of what you're asking of me?" I said to them. "Are you aware of the fact that this isn't how married life is lived, with a third person always present—never alone? Are you aware of what you are asking? What if I don't want to? Will you make me?" "Yes," said Darko. "If necessary," and he forced a smile. "But you are a good sister and you believe in God. You can make this one sacrifice in your life. And listen, I promise you I will do everything possible to get you the operation to be separated, even if we have to go to the ends of the earth! Do you think this will be hardest on you? No, Zlata, you are lying to yourself. It will be me. It will be hardest for me. I will be ridiculed by everyone I know. They will call me crazy, but I don't care.

I love Srebra more than myself, and I will marry her, without regard to anything else." Darko finished his speech, heated, red in the face, holding Srebra's hands in his own. "What sort of marriage is this going to be? Do you have any idea? A chaste one?" I asked, a crumb of hope in my soul. "Yes," said Srebra at the same moment that Darko said, "No." "No," Darko repeated. "We will have children, right Srebra? We will also have children? Wherever a couple is in love, God is there, and children." "And me," I said, as ironically as I could, unable to recover from the shock of the proposal, from the entire situation. "We will find a solution," said Darko. "There has to be one." He leaned across the table and kissed Srebra on the mouth, and then they rubbed their noses together, Eskimo fashion, as they did when they wanted the most intimacy between them, but, unintentionally touched me as well. I felt their breath on my face; an intoxicating sweetness came from their mouths and spread around our heads. From all the other tables in the garden, people stared at us, shocked by the sight, some with mouths agape, saying, "Whoa, look at that!" I abruptly stood up, pulling Srebra from the bench, and she moaned at the familiar pain in the spot where we were conjoined once again tearing at us like a knife. Darko left money on the table and we set off rapidly, as though escaping from a place marked, for me, by an evil deed—but the place of love's pledge for Srebra and Darko.

"We must tell our families," said Darko, his arms around Srebra's waist. When I thought about how Srebra would have to tell our parents, I thought that when our mother and father heard about this proposal, they would either die of heart attacks or begin shouting and not allow her to do it, for them to do it. I was certain they wouldn't agree to such a scandal, if for no other reason than what our neighbors and relatives would say. They wouldn't permit the scandal of their daughter with a physical deformity, unable to be separated from her sister, marrying and all three of us having to live together. I also hoped that Darko's parents wouldn't allow it, even though they were educated and in influential positions. It was his mother, after all, who helped Srebra get her stipend. We had never met his parents, but from the things Darko said, we knew they were decent people, his mother at least. She was a liberated, open, and modern woman, he said, and his father was, in any event, away from home for days at a time. He spent his time at the planning bureau or at party headquarters; he would likely run for president of the party in the next election. They had a lot of money, Darko was always generous, and their apartment looked like something out of a magazine, with modern appliances and comfortable armchairs and couches. "My father told me he would buy me an apartment when I graduated, and yesterday we went to look at one in Kapištec; it was very beautiful, eighty square meters. So we'll have a place to live," said Darko, as if reading my thoughts. "You are so kind," I said ironically, unable to hold it in. Srebra tried to say something, but Darko kissed her, again and again on the lips, while I stood there, eyes wide behind my glasses, lips pursed, waiting for the appearance of the bus that would take us back to our normal life. Our mother and father were still watching television. "You're home early," our mother remarked. "Srebra's getting married," I said like a gunshot, and Srebra, as if she had expected no less, said, "Yes, I'm going to marry Darko." We went to our room before they could say anything, but didn't close the door, just pushing it halfway. If the door wasn't closed, it was a signal to our mother that she could come in if she wanted to talk to us. Our father never entered our room, except when we weren't there; whenever we showed Verče, Lenče, or Aunt Ivanka to the door he would quickly go into the room and open the window to let in some air after the departure of our guests, who always smelled to him of something, as if they hadn't bathed, even though bathing took place only once a week in our house, too. Mom came in and sat on the bed, while we stood beside the small cupboard and acted as if we were looking for something among the decorations on the shelf. "What do you mean you're getting married?" she said to Srebra, while also looking at me. "How do you plan to get married with your heads like that? Is he crazy? What will your sister do? Is she going to be your witness?" "Yes," said Srebra, "if necessary she'll be our witness. Darko and I are going to get married. That is what we have decided." "You aren't thinking. Knock a bit of sense into your head. What will people say…a man living with two wives? Doesn't he have a mother and father, or are they all strange? My girl, I understand you need to go out and have a juice in a café so you are not shut up at home, but I don't understand you getting married when you're like this and incapable of marriage." From his chair in the dining room, our father added, "They have devoured the world…as if they're going to get married. This has become intolerable." He spoke in the plural as if I were also getting married. At that moment, I realized I had actually forgotten that we had finished our studies that day, that they hadn't even congratulated us, and that from now on, we would have to languish here with them, with no university, no Srebra's stipend, no work, no money for the operation, nothing. It occurred to me that it would be better to flee from this strange home, to go anywhere, to break away from our family. The marriage between Srebra and Darko would be out of love, and so, with them, I would at least live under normal conditions, in a normal apartment, and, in the end—with normal people. So I began defending Srebra—to her great surprise, and the shock of our parents— saying I fully supported the marriage, and that we would live together, and, I'd take three diazepam before bed if I had to, to sleep like a log so they could do whatever they liked. That's what I said, and Srebra held on to that thought. "Really, you would take sleeping pills?" she asked me later, when we were in bed, though we usually never spoke in the dark. "If I have to," I said. Our mother and father could be heard whispering for a long time in their room.

After that, everything happened very quickly. Darko and Srebra decided to hold the wedding ceremony on July 9, in the church in Krivi Dol, followed by lunch at Café Kula. They would invite our closest friends and relatives. Srebra and I raced from one boutique to the next looking for a wedding dress. Everyone looked at us in horror, not knowing whether we were joking. In the end, Srebra selected a beautiful white dress with a veil for her hair. As for me, I insisted we get a black dress for me, and I found one at the Una boutique. It was long, with bell sleeves, just like the wedding dress, but black. Srebra didn't dare contradict me. The engagement ceremony was short and almost funny. Darko and his parents came to our apartment without the traditional gifts. "That's how it is being done in our neighborhood," Darko's mother said, a fairly young, well-put-together woman. "Engagement gifts have become village stuff. Who can be bothered with it?" she said, smiling embarrassedly, as if sensing our mother would still be interested in such gifts. Darko's father took out an envelope and handed it to me. Inside were one hundred German marks. "For our new in-law," he said and laughed. "I do not know how this will all turn out," Mom said. "You have just the one son, but I see you didn't talk him out of it.

He decides to marry Srebra and that's it, with Zlata tagging along." "We don't have time to concern ourselves with such things," Darko's father said, laughing again. "The country needs to get itself in order, so let the young people live as they see fit. They will get the apartment together; they will find their way. I'm already looking for work for Darko, and with his salary they will make ends meet. We are here for them." "They are educated and know for themselves what's best," his mother added, and I didn't know whether to take that remark as negative or positive. Darko and Srebra exchanged engagement rings while sitting down so that I wouldn't have to stand up with them, but they were too embarrassed to kiss in front of the others. I closed my eyes anyway. Then they all left. Our mother and father had resigned themselves to their fate, or at least that is how it appeared. Our mother said to Srebra, "What do you need a wedding for? Look, now you're engaged. Just go to city hall and be done with it so people don't make fun of you." But Srebra said she and Darko wanted a small celebration with their closest friends and family, there was no reason to hide anything, and they wanted to get married in a church. The closer it got to the wedding—when the invitations had already been sent—the angrier our mother became. She said, "What are we going to do at the wedding? I don't have teeth. I'll be sitting there ashamed while people stare at me. Big shots from the party will probably be invited. Your aunts will come, your uncle, maybe your grandmother. That's enough. It will be best if we just stay home." I was shocked. It was true that for months, she had complained that she couldn't get used to the dental bridge she had been given after her teeth were destroyed by periodontal disease, and she usually didn't wear it at home but she wore it at work, which meant she could put it in for the wedding day as well. Several days before the wedding, Srebra and I were at the shopping mall and nearly ran into our aunt, the wife of our father's brother, whom we had not seen since the short meeting in the convent when we were visiting Sister Zlata. "Oh, what are you doing here? How are you? What's new?" she asked us kindly. I think she was the nicest person in our father's family, our might-have-been extended family. Without skipping a beat, Srebra told her she was getting married and added, nearly shouting, "Come, Come!" She explained where the wedding would be and to whom she was getting married. Our aunt looked at us in shock, confused, in disbelief. But she took the extra, unaddressed, invitation that Srebra kept in her purse. She didn't say whether they would come. "Tell Auntie Anka to come, too," Srebra called after her as she walked away. "Are you nuts?" I asked. "You think they are crazy enough to come? Aren't you the one that said you never wanted to see them again in your life?" "It's what Dad would want," she said.

On July 9, 1995, Srebra and Darko were married in the church in Krivi Dol. All our friends from the convent trip were there, as were our aunts, our uncle, and our grandmother. Darko didn't do many of the old wedding traditions. He did not "take" Srebra from her home, nor did we sing the traditional wedding song, "The Cherry Tree Has Been Uprooted," to avoid people laughing, as our mother said they might. Then we all went to the registry office. The registrar threw a fit and complete chaos broke out because we hadn't told her what the situation was and she hadn't known we were like this. "With those heads," she said, and had she known, she would've asked her boss if it was even possible to register Srebra and Darko's marriage, but now it was the weekend and there was no one to ask—her boss had gone to his cottage, where there was no telephone. We stood and waited for them to be registered. The registrar screamed, threatened, spoke spitefully; she didn't want to register them. Darko's father finally got so annoyed that he picked up the phone from the desk without asking, dialed a number, explained the whole situation to someone, and requested that the situation be resolved immediately. "We need to wait a bit," he said, so we waited in the hall while the registrar, shaking, closed the door behind her. After half an hour, another registrar came, but rushing in with him were several video and photo cameras. The registrar immediately began the ceremony, and there was simply no time to chase away the cameras, because Srebra and Darko had already said yes, and I bent down with Srebra so she could sign her name. Then she and Darko kissed beside my face, and Darko's breath smelled acrid from the acid that had collected in his stomach. We all left, making way for the other brides and grooms who were boiling with anger, waiting with their guests in the hallway. Darko's father swung at one of the cameras, but the cameraman was clever, and in just a few steps, he had run from the building with the others following him. We climbed into the cars and set off for the church in Krivi Dol. The priest gently pushed away the cameramen so they couldn't come in, and not even Darko's father argued with them there. The venue was so holy and solemn that even our father, who was fuming with rage, held his peace. Our grandmother cried with happiness and sadness, and for us, she was the most important person at the wedding. Our grandfather had stayed behind to take care of the animals. In the church, I walked quietly alongside Srebra, participating in the whole wedding ritual with Srebra's veil tickling my face. It fell across my right eye; the bridal crown grazed my head as well. Several times, we accidentally stepped on each other's long gown. Darko was glowing with happiness and from the candles shining in front of the icons; Jesus Christ and the Virgin Mary looked over us kindly. The corners of my icon, sewn into the inner pocket of my dress, poked me. I prayed silently to all the saints to forgive my sins and give me the strength to endure. We got back into the cars and set off for Café Kula, where the caterer was waiting for us, since the café didn't prepare food. The whole garden was reserved for Darko and Srebra's wedding. One of the cameramen had driven behind us, but he no longer dared to get out of the car, filming us through the open window as we got out at the parking lot by the shopping mall. "Where are you celebrating the wedding?" he shouted, and for some reason, I shouted, "At the Kula." Srebra pinched me on the hip, causing a bruise that lasted for days. We sat at assigned places at tables arranged in the shape of a V. We were on "our" bench, Darko on a chair beside Srebra. Grandma was seated next to me, then our mother and father, then all our relatives. Next to Darko were his parents and relatives, and at the ends—our friends. We ate and drank, a bit mechanically. No one was in a celebratory mood. The sounds of jazz came from the speakers. The afternoon was hot; we sweated under the parasols, drank, and brushed away flies that stuck to our bare arms. Srebra needed to go to the bathroom, and we set off for the small toilet in the café, which barely accommodated us in our dresses. "Are you happy?" I asked, but she responded, "Are you?" "Look, your wish from the fortune-telling game has been fulfilled," I said. "Do you remember? You wanted to get married at age twenty-three and have a husband whose name began with D who was rich. Now you just need two children and to move to London…that is, we need to move," I laughed. "You remember all that? I had forgotten," she said, and asked me, "So, when are you supposed to get married, according to the game?" "I was supposed to marry last year," I told her. Srebra gulped down her spit. We returned to the garden, our dresses a bit wrinkled, and saw them coming in from the parking lot—our father's brother and sister with their families, all dressed up, large presents in their arms, unsure in their gaze or their gait, with their children behind them, two younger ones, and our other cousin already grown up, clothed in shiny dresses and pants. They tentatively entered the garden, while Srebra and I stood frozen, like two stone dolls. They came over and congratulated us, Srebra and me, as if we had both gotten married. They kissed our cheeks, squeezed our heads, the children looking at us with curiosity and happiness. Then Darko stood up from the table and came over to introduce himself. He greeted everyone with kindness and sincerity, pinching the kids' cheeks, though he had no idea who these people were—we were too confused to introduce them to him. We didn't know our uncle and our cousins from our father's sister's side at all—and in that moment, amidst all the confusion, we saw our father, pale, mouth open, repeating his brother and sister's names, using their nicknames, as he had called them in his childhood, as tears fell down his cheeks; his hands shook; he kissed the nieces he had never met and turned to Srebra and me, introducing us: "This is your uncle and this is your aunt," then all the others in turn, while we pretended we were seeing them for the first time, that we hadn't even known of their existence, and had forgotten that once in our childhoods our aunt turned up, this dark-haired woman who now had a husband and two children. He also introduced us to our other aunt—his brother's wife, whom he was just meeting for the first time, but whom we had already seen three times in our lives. Then Mom came over, pale, almost yellow, on the brink of one of her fainting spells.

She collected herself, greeting everyone, quickly finding them places at the table, and having food brought over. They sat down, and we returned to our places, but our father stood behind them, behind each one for a moment, his hands on their shoulders trembling so much that it looked as though he was massaging them, each person individually, or two at a time. Tears ran down his cheeks while his brother, sister, and their families, who had been driven away from him, sat motionless, heads bowed, almost ashamed—but from what?—and they seemed to be waiting for the wedding to end as quickly as possible so they could leave, definitively, forever. Our other aunts, uncle, and grandmother went up and kissed them. Their arrival at Srebra's wedding constituted forgiveness. We were all convinced that from now on, both our father and the two of us would finally have a normal family—that they would make peace among themselves even though they had never personally quarreled. While our grandfather had been alive, it was his wish that the brother and sister not speak with their older brother. But that grandfather was no longer alive, so they could be brothers and sisters again. They could belong to one another again. This was an important event for all of us, a historic event for our father, even more important than Srebra's wedding.

The cake arrived at last. All three of us stood. Srebra and Darko cut the cake with a knife but didn't dare to rub it in each other's faces, as was the custom at weddings. The cake was melting on our plates, so we ate quickly, wanting everything to end as soon as possible, although that is what I feared most. I would then have to go home with Srebra and Darko to live with them and be a part of their marriage. The strains of "Moscow Nights" began to play. All three of us swayed by the table, not daring to dance as a threesome. Our mother was on her feet, a bit tipsy from the beer she always drank when we went visiting or at weddings or other celebrations, but even more by the presence of our father's family. She spun around the tables, dancing alone; her face was not joyful, but clouded and furrowed. That song was my only memory of the music that played over the speakers at Darko and Srebra's wedding. Our mother dancing, our father trembling in the July heat like a branch in the wind. Srebra's wedding was the most important day of our father's life. Srebra and I stood to toss the wedding bouquet. Although we stood with our backs turned, the bouquet didn't fly toward the guests but landed on my head, tangling in Srebra's veil. Some of the guests choked with laughter but stifled it immediately. No one clapped; no one yelled. Darko untangled the bouquet from our heads and handed it to me. It was all so grotesque. I thought it was good there were no journalists nearby. The guests began to get up to leave. Our father's brother and sister were among the first. They said goodbye to everyone, shaking hands like a departing delegation, and then nearly ran toward the parking lot and their cars, quickly vanishing. Our parents also stood to leave. Our grandmother pressed our mother to stay a bit longer. "Come on, we're going. It's enough," our mother said to her. "Whatever fate has in store for them now, so be it." We hugged our grandmother, our aunts, our uncle, but not our mother and father, though we sensed our father wanted to hug us. What prevented him at that moment? We were leaving our home, their home, forever. We parted like strangers. Now they would be alone in their apartment, in the kitchen by the small woodstove, in the dining room in front of the television, in the big room. They will rarely go into our room. They will not have to pay high telephone bills, or large bills for the electricity and water. They will continue to heat the boiler once a week, without exception. It will suit them. They'll be calm, their hearts beating evenly, their nerves growing stronger. Will they talk about us? Probably, the way one speaks about the neighbors' children, or people at work. Can one talk that way about one's own children? I don't know.

Darko's mother and father came up to us, smiled, and said, "Everything you need is in the apartment," handing the key to Darko. "Children, may you be happy," they said, including me along with the bride and groom. We got into Darko's car and set off. The apartment was absolutely beautiful—clean, bright, with beautiful furniture, all of which Srebra had chosen, with me offering advice. But I still hadn't grasped the seriousness of my role in their marriage, in their lives. Darko had selected the bed, the largest I had ever seen, and had it placed in the largest room. It had three pillows and two blankets, one larger, one smaller, all in a gold color that shone like sunlight on the bed. The wardrobe was big, running from one end of the wall to the other, and opposite it was a large vanity with a velvet-covered bench for two. Darko and Srebra were distracted that evening. We sat in the living room and stared absently at the television. All of a sudden we saw ourselves at the registry office when Srebra and Darko said "yes" and I bent down with Srebra so she could sign. The camera's zoom lens zeroed in, seeking the spot that connected us, and the reporter said, "Scandalous, but amazing. Love indeed knows no boundaries. Today this young man and the woman in the white dress entered into marriage, along with her Siamese twin with whom she is connected by this link between their heads." The picture was grotesque, a mirror in which we saw ourselves: the groom in his fashion-able suit, the bride with a veil on her head entangled in the hair of her Siamese twin sister dressed in a black satin dress. Their heads joined, fused forever. Then they showed Darko's father swinging at the camera, and the reporter commented, "Unfortunately, the vice president of the opposition party tussled with our cameraman. Is this the democracy he stands for?" That night, Darko slept on his back, holding Srebra's hand. There was no other touching, no movement; he was dressed in his pajamas, just like we were dressed in nightgowns we had slipped over our legs in just a few seconds, and in total darkness. I didn't take off my bra as I always did before bed. From then on, I always slept with it on, even though it pressed and dug into me. We couldn't fall asleep for a long time that night; from time to time, we swallowed the lumps in our throats, clearing them with broken coughs or an inhale, trying not to be heard. We fell asleep at last. That was the first night of Darko and Srebra's marriage. And my first night in their double bed.

The front page of Monday's newspapers carried only two stories, accompanied by large photos: one was of the taking of Srebrenica by the Republika Srpska Army; the other was the wedding of the "threesome." And once again there were attacks on the vice president of the opposition, Darko's father. Srebra wanted to throw the newspapers away, but I managed to save one. I threw it into the wardrobe in the bedroom and never looked at it again. For several nights we slept as we had that first night, but then one night, I heard Srebra ask Darko, "Do you love me?" Darko whispered, "I love you more than the whole world." "Then be mine," Srebra whispered back. Darko gulped. He didn't know what to say. I thought it was my turn to do something. I told Srebra, "I need to go to the bathroom," and we got up. In the bathroom—beautifully appointed with a small comfortable chair with velvet covering next to the toilet—I said, "I am going to take diazepam." "Are you sure about what you're doing?" she asked. "Yes," I said, "What about you?"

"I don't know," said Srebra. I took three diazepam from the small bottle in the cupboard and gulped them down with water. Then Srebra and I took care of our other business. By the time we returned to the bedroom, I already felt dazed. I fell into a deep sleep as soon as we lay on the bed. In my dream, I felt the mattress shaking below me. It felt as if I were on a boat, but I slept and didn't know where I was or with whom. When I awoke, Darko was already gone, but Srebra was waking with sweet sighs; her nightgown up above her thighs; she wasn't wearing panties. When we lifted ourselves to sit up in bed, she immediately pulled her nightgown over her knees. We stood up, and there, where she had been sleeping, were several drops of blood. "So, it happened," I said calmly. "It was so lovely," she said, laughing, "it was so lovely." It was good that Darko wasn't home, because otherwise, I think she would have wanted to do it again right away, whether I took three diazepam or not. She was excited all day. She could not sit in one place, but got me up, then sat me down, then pulled me around the apartment, until finally, she took a cookbook out from one of our bags, and we began preparing things. She wanted to greet Darko with a nice meal, and when he got home he pressed a hand between her thighs and his lips to her throat, on the side opposite our conjoined spot.

Every day, the television carried news of the massacre in Srebrenica. Darko tuned in to the BBC, which had more information. We watched and couldn't believe what we saw. Since Auschwitz—according to the history textbooks, anyway—there had been no event as monstrous in Europe. Srebrenica weighed on our lives like a heavy fog. Those nights, all three of us slept as if dazed. I don't know what Srebra and Darko felt, but I was afraid. I was frightened, disturbed, thinking of that most accurate description: man is wolf to his fellow man.

But life continued, and I don't know whether that's the fortune or the misfortune of the living. Collective tragedies, no matter how intense, cannot surpass individual tragedy. Or comedy. Now every night Srebra spilled three diazepam into her hand for me, and every night I felt a force rocking me in my sleep, as if I had fallen into a hole and was listening to breaths of pleasure and shouts from a distance, but they were right here in our shared bed. Darko wasn't home during the day. He went to work in a planning office. His father had found work for him immediately and could have found work for us as well, he said, but only if we wanted it. I did not want to work in an office, and Srebra and I agreed that she would prepare for the judicial exam and no longer torment me about exams or law books; that was over and done with for me, as was, in fact, my life as an individual. During the day, when I wasn't cooking with Srebra or we weren't out buying something, we sat on the couch in the living room. She would have some big legal book, and I'd read an entrancing novel. Those moments were lovely. The apartment was gorgeous, comfortable; the balcony looked out over the city center. Life in this multistory building carried on in a completely different way from life in our building on the periphery of Skopje: the neighbors barely greeted one another; each person hurried up the stairs; and in the elevator, if people exchanged remarks, it was only about the weather. At first, everyone looked at us strangely, thunderstruck, but eventually, they either got used to us or pretended that they had. If someone asked us anything a bit intimate, we answered without shame that we were born this way, Darko and Srebra had fallen in love and had wanted to get married, and I had agreed in order to bring happiness to my sister. But we said nothing about our nights, letting everyone think whatever they wished.

We rarely went to our mother and father's—only to pick up something. Our room gaped empty, bare, and our mother kept their things in our cupboards. What was surprising was that Dad began coming to our place more often. If he was somewhere in the city, or at the market or the doctor's, he would drop by, sit awhile, drink a beer, nibble on something sweet or savory if we had anything. He would offer to vacuum for us, or take out the garbage. He leafed through the photo album from Srebra's wedding, looking at each picture for a long time, transfixed, especially at those taken at the party at Café Kula, with his brother and sister. He borrowed the videotapes of the wedding to watch them at home with our mother, returned them, borrowed them again. We felt uncomfortable talking to him about anything other than the most ordinary things, like who was doing what. We spoke with our father about our neighbors, and with our mother about our relatives and Grandma and Grandpa. Those were our common topics. We had no others. From time to time, we would give our father the garbage to take out on his way home, or have him pick up some document for us if he was going to town. And we began to pack him a bag of things to take home, fresh vegetables or fruit, a piece of kashkaval, salami. It became the custom whenever he came; he came only in the morning, before lunch, when we were alone. He sat for half an hour, and then we would fill up the bag with food. We would give him money for the bus and he would leave, without exchanging a single word of importance with us in that half hour. Once, he handed us a small scrap of paper, and with a trembling voice he said, "Your mother has jotted down here what she needs." It was a grocery list, written in our mother's rapid handwriting: bananas, coffee, shampoo, two bars of soap, kashkaval, feta, salami. Srebra and I went into the bedroom. "Is she crazy? Is she crazy, or what?" Srebra whispered, but I elbowed her, saying we had to go buy the food. Our father was reading the newspaper in the living room. We went outside, and Srebra pulled me along, repeating in a loud voice, faster and faster, "Is she crazy, is she crazy?" Yes, she was, but we still bought her everything she asked for, and from then on, our father regularly came with a list, and we bought the things. We'd put everything in a bag for him, and he would leave. Mom never thanked us, not on the phone, and not when we went to visit, but sometimes, she would make comments like, "Those plums were not fit to eat," "I don't drink that kind of coffee, I only drink Rio," "That hair dye you bought me—I had to recolor it; white, white as if I were an old lady—where did you find that brand?" And other comments like that. I would snatch the phone when I saw the number, because I would just stay silent and listen, but Srebra would get angry. Our father was always embarrassed when he handed over the list from our mother, and sometimes said, "Your mother, well, it is becoming intolerable." These meetings of ours were strange, as if we were trying to get close, but it eluded us. His hands shook more than before, and his voice trembled when he spoke. Srebra and I were depressed when he left, but both of us kept silent. Srebra rarely told Darko that our father had been there.

After all those nights of diazepam and the bed shaking, it was obvious that Srebra would get pregnant, because I never saw any condoms, and there were no pills. We'd had only one gynecological exam in our lives, when we were fifteen years old and our vaginas had itched terribly. We scratched ourselves discretely and headed to the bathroom, and, ashamed or not, we washed ourselves with cold water. For a short time, the redness and itching had seemed to go away, but just for a little while. Then we itched even more, and had no choice but to go to the gynecologist, whom we told, even though she was still in a bit of a state because of the sight of us, that both of our vaginas itched. She said, "I don't have a table on which to examine both of you. Take these instructions, and go have a swab sample taken." We went to the laboratory, located near the mortuary. There, the nurse placed us crosswise on a bed, took swabs from us, and then we walked past the mortuary again to get the results. We both had yeast infections. The nurse told us the best medicine was to clean ourselves with vinegar and water, but the doctor prescribed tablets that were placed into the vagina, suppositories, and said we should shower regularly, ideally using baby shampoo. None of this was feasible in our house, not even washing with vinegar and water, because one bottle of vinegar had to last at minimum a half a year—we only used it for salad—and hot water was heated only once a week in the boiler, so we couldn't shower regularly. We used the vaginal suppositories, and for a while, the itching disappeared. But when the itching began again, we simply didn't go back to the gynecologist. So we itched, scratched ourselves, and washed ourselves with cold water. Now, when Srebra began to feel nauseous and dragged me to the bathroom to throw up—her head bent over the toilet bowl and my head bent over the stool with the velvet seat—she said she was probably pregnant, but was still not sure, and had to go see the gynecologist. Darko brought home a pregnancy test and gave the kit to her to place under the stream of urine while I sat beside the toilet on the chair bought especially for me, with its soft seat covered in red velvet, just like Srebra's on the other side of the toilet, where she waited when I was doing my business. The small indicator window displayed a white cross. The test was positive. Srebra was pregnant. All three of us looked at that cross in awe as if in church, and Darko, in his excitement, even crossed himself as he began to cry. He cried like a small child. He hugged her and kissed her; he hugged me and kissed me as well, but I boiled in anger, seeing myself on that small white cross on the pregnancy test, seeing myself crucified on that cross, on the cross of their love. And now this? "Each child is a child of God, Zlata. Ours most of all," he said to me. "Still," I said, "one never knows—she should see a gynecologist."

We went to a male doctor at a private clinic, where, in a comfortable, bright office, the nurse had already pushed two hospital beds together, and on the bed, there was equipment for conducting the exam. Both the gynecologist and the nurse were extremely discreet; they asked no questions, as if it were an everyday occurrence to have patients with conjoined heads. "Yes, you're pregnant," the doctor told Srebra. In the hallway, there was more emotion, ecstasy, sentiment. It wasn't clear to me how they could be so unaware, so clueless. Was it such a small thing that I had agreed (without anyone asking me or begging me) for them to get married and for us to live together? And now they wanted to have a child. Srebra couldn't contain her happiness. She wanted to dance with Darko but couldn't without me, so I had to hug him awkwardly, with my arms around both him and Srebra. We danced like a kind of sandwich, stepping on each other's toes, which made Srebra and Darko giggle with that seductive joy of lovers that particularly annoys those who aren't in love. Srebra was happy, but frightened. "Can I count on you?" she asked me a few days later, pulling me in front of the bathroom mirror to look me right in the eye. Her question confused me. We had never asked each other questions like out of a movie. We rarely said "thank you"; we didn't say "please"; we didn't wish each other "good night" before going to sleep in our shared bed; we didn't say "excuse me" or "pardon me" if we bumped each other unintentionally or stepped on each other's feet or jerked each other's heads, which happened often and always hurt. We simply did not use such phrases, the ones found in the Serbian handbook *The Book for Every Woman*, although we knew them and used them with other people. Indeed, it was only with strangers that we acted politely, but not with our parents, who themselves didn't behave that way. Not with our aunts or our uncle or with our grandma and grandpa. No one in our family used the words and phrases of good manners, and in fact, the first person close to us who used such words was the person closest to Srebra: Darko, who had been raised with good manners and who not only knew how to use silverware as if he had been born to it, but also never said "give me" without adding "please," said "thank you" for every small act, and excused himself for each clumsy thing that he might do to anyone. I don't know about Srebra, but at first, it really bothered me. It seemed to me out of a movie, and a sign that we were strangers, even Srebra and Darko, because we had always thought people who were close never had to use such phrases. It was normal to say to a close family member "gimme" and not say "thanks," let alone "thank you," because it was understood and didn't need to be stated. But Darko used such words, and it was strange to him that we didn't talk to him in the same way. Srebra had already begun to talk in that way with him. And now Srebra was asking me whether she could count on me, and her manners, that cinematic question, confused me. I was silent for several seconds before I finally said, "You can."

Srebra told our mother over the phone that she was pregnant. The next day, we went to visit them. Our mother

was dressed in her blue robe. It was the first time she had
been dressed like that in front of Darko. Both of us understood. When our mother was dressed in the blue robe with
the yellowish-green flowers, we knew she was sick, but the
illnesses she had were never anything concrete, they were
something unspecific, psychosomatic, menopausal, as our
aunt would say. Our mother had stopped menstruating at
forty-five and was showing early signs of menopause, but
even when she had still been menstruating, her health had
not been much better. Now, wrapped in her robe, she informed everyone in the vicinity that her body was weak beneath it, vulnerable, sick. We had come so Srebra and Darko
could tell her in person the news that she would become a
grandmother. Our father was muddled but well intentioned.
He poured a glass of aged rakija for Darko and drank a toast
with him, though he didn't say, "To the baby," or anything like
that. Our mother, pale, with matted hair, said to Darko, "So
now this, Darko… People will laugh. It's not as if they weren't
talking as it was, but now, with her stomach when they go
out walking…" Darko wanted to respond, but our father said,
"Well, you just know everything don't you?" Srebra and I
stood, pressed against the chair in the dining room like help-
less children. Our mother dragged herself to the kitchen and,
most likely, lay down on the couch, but we didn't have the
courage to follow her. Instead, we went into our former room
to take a few more of our things. I took some of my books,
and Srebra grabbed *The Book for Every Woman*. She wanted
to take it, but we both knew she couldn't—it belonged to the
apartment, to no one in particular, just like the other Serbian
book, *Natural Herbal Cures*. Those two books stood on a shelf
in our room and were shared among us. Our mother often
looked up recipes for medicines in them, although she never

made any. And she, Srebra, and I all read them, but never left them just anywhere—returning them to their place, which was an unspoken rule all of us respected, even our father, who sometimes checked something in them, too. Srebra wanted to take *The Book for Every Woman*, because it had an entire chapter dedicated to pregnancy, with explanations of all the phases in the life of a baby, practical advice, and even drawings showing how to nurse, how to wash the baby, how to swaddle it, and all sorts of other things. "What do I care," Srebra said, and she took it, putting it in the bag we were filling with books, and our hands knocked together as we stood on the bed to reach the books, which, as always, creaked so much we were afraid it might break, which our mother repeatedly warned us it would. Either she heard us, or something else was bothering her. She came into the room, and we immediately jumped off the bed. Although Srebra was a married woman, our mother treated us as if we still lived at home, and she said, quietly but decisively, "You are going to be the death of me. People will laugh; they'll shout: 'Hey look, the one with the head has a baby; how did that happen? It certainly didn't fall from the sky. They slept together, but I wonder who did what with whom?' They'll gossip about you, and won't you be shocked: you'll have harmed that child for the rest of its life. But that's OK, keep playing your games, idiots." Srebra was silent, but our temples had begun to pound, to thunder, as if the blood would burst through our heads. "How things are is our business," I said, while inside, I seethed with anger. Insults like that turn into anger and spite: "As if we care what others think," I said, my voice rising to a shout. "We are going to take care of this baby, and I'll be a hundred times better an aunt to him than you were a mother to us." I couldn't contain myself. Srebra sobbed loudly. The shaking in her body transferred to mine. She was trembling and crying, and in the dining room, our father said to Darko, "Leave them alone—it's women's business." But Darko came into our room anyway; he grabbed hold of Srebra, and the three of us abruptly left the apartment. The bag of books remained in our room.

I don't know how we got home. Srebra cried the whole way; her tears rolled down my neck and wet my left shoulder, but I didn't brush them away. I cried, too, but softly, without a sound. I cried for everything that had happened to us, while Srebra cried for everything that hadn't happened. The drive seemed to last an eternity. The streets downtown were closed, the textile workers striking, so we drove down side streets, and by the time we got home, we had calmed down, and were even at peace. We went into our apartment as though in a dream. I wanted to go to bed right away, but Darko poured us each half a glass of chocolate liqueur and himself a whiskey. "A toast to the new life," he said, and the sweet liquid slipped down our throats, awakening us, reviving us. Although I told Srebra she shouldn't be drinking on account of the baby, she answered that this would be the last time. We were gripped by excitement, joy, and sadness all rolled into one. We picked up the bottle and drank. We drank liqueur and Darko drank whiskey, and when we went to bed that night, we weren't conscious of anything. My head was heavy, and I felt it wasn't my head but Srebra's on my neck. I had the feeling that my soul was in her body and hers in mine. Darko was too drunk to lie by the wall, so he lay beside me. As I heard the sounds of Srebra falling asleep, my hand seemed to stretch itself toward Darko's body, toward his short pajama pants, where a peak rose. I reached through the slit of his underwear, and once I grasped it with my right hand, I couldn't release it. I masturbated him calmly and quietly, and he stifled his moans. When he finished, he turned and poked his middle finger into my vagina, giving me pleasure like I had never experienced. Although his finger was like the tip of the clown's cap, it was unimaginably better, moving in and out, turning around inside me seeking the most secret places of bliss. While Srebra breathed regularly in the sweetness of a dream, I reached orgasm with her Darko's finger. Then I fell asleep.

But the night had no end. Later, just before dawn, Srebra woke me, dragging me from the bed. "I have to get to the bathroom, I have to, get up!" We could barely drag ourselves to the bathroom. I tumbled down onto my chair while she sat down on the toilet. She sat there for a long time, but nothing came out. Then, suddenly, something splashed into the toilet bowl, like a small turd falling. Srebra jumped from the toilet seat, and I from the chair. "What's the matter with you?" I yelled at her, sleepily. "Blood," she said. "Look, everything is red." I wasn't wearing my glasses, and although I peered into the toilet, I could not see anything. "It felt like something fell out of me," she said. "Like a ball. Look, blood," she was upset, shaking, and I shook along with her. I cried out, as loud as I could, "Darko!" and as Darko awoke, we dragged ourselves to the bed. "Darko, I'm bleeding." Srebra trembled, trembled as never before in her life; we trembled as never before in our lives. I was completely awake, but everything was jumbled in my mind: me, Srebra, Darko, the night. I knew Srebra had lost the baby, but I didn't say it aloud. Darko must also have known, but he said it was nothing, everything was all right, and then he helped Srebra put on clean underwear while we sat, hunched on the bed. Then we got dressed. Darko started the car and we drove to the municipal hospital, where, at the entry ramp, they shouted to us that cases like ours weren't admitted at night, thinking we had come because of our heads. Srebra didn't look pregnant, and, while Darko explained everything, a group of nurses passed by, holding slices of burek. The smell filled the night, and it was like the atmosphere after a party. We followed them; there wasn't a single doctor around. They finally led us into a small room, but they didn't know how to lay the two of us on the bed, so they placed us crosswise. The doctor, who had been more curious about our heads than about Srebra's pregnancy, told her, "A piece of tissue from the embryo tore off and fell out while you were urinating." And while we stared at him in shock, he added, "Tomorrow, we'll abort it, and then it will be over." I asked in an unsure voice, "Can't the baby be saved?" and he looked at me and said, "What baby? It was a three-week-old embryo, a chromosomal mistake, a monstrosity. It's for the best that it turned out this way." Then he stood and told the nurse to give Srebra a referral for surgery and left. The nurse added, "Sometimes this happens for psychological reasons as well," and gave Srebra the referral. We immediately left, dragging ourselves from the doctor's office, bent over nearly double. Darko already knew everything; the doctor had told him the same thing, but without the personal commentary. Srebra was completely silent. In the operating room, we lay like two fallen branches, as if we had each lost an embryo. I didn't move at all; I didn't want to move Srebra even an inch. She was still dazed from the anesthesia. They hadn't given me any, although I had asked for it. They told me to close my eyes if I didn't want to watch. As it was, I couldn't see down to where the forceps removed my unformed nephew from Srebra's womb. I listened to the surgeon tell the nurse, "It will be difficult for this one to give birth after this," and the nurse muttered, "God listened." I wanted to shout at her, rebuke her for invoking God in that way, with her mean-spirited conviction that Srebra shouldn't have a child, given how she was, joined to me, but I didn't have the strength, and wanted to sink into myself. When they brought us back to the recovery room, they placed us on a bed beside the wall, and I squeezed up against the wall so there would be enough room for Srebra. Three more women were brought in, one after another: two didn't want to have children, so they had come alone to have an abortion; the third wanted one, but this was already her fourth spontaneous miscarriage. That was all she said, and then she sank into silent sobs. The two who didn't want to bear children and had been saved from it were having a lively conversation a half hour after their operations. They talked about life on Mount Vodno, about houses and apartments, furniture and gardens, their husbands, their work, and most of all about upholstery and wallpaper. They exchanged telephone numbers. They would be in touch to work out exchanging contractors. But their babies, along with Srebra's baby—unformed, undeveloped, tiny, strange, almost invisible—were sent to a garbage dump somewhere or to a cosmetics factory. Who knows? Darko came to get us that afternoon, after Srebra had completely revived, had come back to full consciousness and to herself, not only recovering from the anesthesia, but also from her confrontation with herself, with her loss, with her despair. She was silent the whole time, even when Darko asked how she felt, if she was all right, if she wanted anything. She was silent and dragging along beside me to the car. In the car, while the radio played, "Stay with Me, Stay with Me," a song I hadn't heard for years, she said nothing, nor did she say anything as we rode the elevator up to the apartment. When we got inside, I turned toward the bedroom, thinking she would want to rest, but she yanked me with surprising strength toward the living room. We sat on the couch, while Darko bustled about, asking whether she wanted some orange juice or something. She swallowed, cleared her throat, and said, loudly and clearly, "Sit down!" Darko sat. "I know," said Srebra, "I know." "What?" Darko asked in surprise, but my heart jumped. "What you know, too. I don't need to say it. You know I know. Right?" Both Darko and I were silent. It was clear to Srebra that I knew what she was talking about; the wild beating in our temples gave me away. My cheeks burned, giving off heat that Srebra could feel on her skin. "Take your hand out of your pocket; your icon will break—look how sweaty your hand is." She grabbed my free hand. "Look." Darko was sitting in the armchair, and, although he shifted nervously, he had had time to collect himself, and said as self-assuredly as he could, "I don't know what you're talking about." "You do, too," Srebra said, with a voice like a squeezed lemon: without force, but sharp, sour, and unflinching. "But your God forgives everything, right?" she said. After a few minutes—a full eternity—I quietly asked, "And yours?" "In my case, only the court decides whether to forgive. But that's no longer important. What is important now is that we get separated, Zlata. Once and for all. With Darko, or without him." Srebra wasn't saying anything new. After all, for our entire lives, we had been dreaming—privately, or together, even saying it aloud—that one day we would be separated, having the operation and finally living according to our own wishes. Or we would die. Though in our imaginations, there was never death. We dreamed of a successful operation, and we imagined ourselves alive, healthy, and separate afterward. Srebra was ready for anything now, for a shared death, or for mine, or hers. She could no longer endure our bond. No longer. It was too much for her, without a baby and without the husband whom she willfully distanced from her, because, as she said, she knew. But how? How did she know that the night before the miscarriage, drunk and unconscious of the consequences, we satisfied our basest passions? There were none baser; we had fallen into the greatest, most terrible, most shameful sin. "All right," said Darko. "Either with me or without me." That is how the conversation ended: unclear, unspoken, unexplained, yet at the same time clear and irrefutable. Darko picked up the phone and called his father. He told him about Srebra's miscarriage. No, no, he didn't want to talk with his mother. He told him that he had never before asked for anything, but now he had nowhere to turn. His father might have to call the president, he said, but the money for the operation must be found. "Whose?" "Srebra's," he said, and then added, "and Zlata's—they must be separated… No, no, that's not what the doctor said," he added, already annoyed. "Does someone need to have said that for them to be separated? Is that it? They're twenty-three years old. How long must they live like this? How long will we have to live like this? Call someone. You're the vice president, after all. The whole party is behind you. Surely someone has a connection to the monetary fund. Yes, it's likely expensive. We haven't inquired, but still, ask for the money. If not, we will take out advertisements to raise the money for the operation. Someone might be more humane than the party, right?" Darko was sarcastic, for the first time ever, and his father probably was as well, because Darko added, "Yes, I am a member as well, but only a member; you are the vice president, and you have power." He said some other things to his father as well, speaking passionately, convincingly, but his face was pale, and the receiver trembled in his hand. When the call ended, he was silent. He went into his study, where, in a corner, stood an icon of the Virgin Mary with a lamp and candleholder in front of it. After several minutes, he called us, but Srebra didn't want to stand. Darko persisted, begging us to come in, so we got up, and, wondering what he wanted, entered the room. He stood in front of his small shrine and read prayers for the forgiveness of sins, then he passed a prayer book to us, but Srebra wouldn't take it. So I did, and Darko and I read one prayer after another, and crossed ourselves, but Srebra didn't. I took my icon of Zlata Meglenska from my pocket, and passed it to Srebra to kiss, but she brushed it away. I didn't pass it to Darko, I don't know why, and he seemed not to notice. We read the Akathist Hymn to Mary, and tears fell from Darko's eyes. For a moment I envied Srebra, because he loved her so much, but then I remembered that she knew and could no longer love him. Thoughts swirled in my head. I missed Sister Zlata and I missed God. Before going to bed, I gave Srebra a sleeping pill, and I took one as well, of course. We slept thanks to the pills, not the prayers. Darko slept in the study, with the candle lit and the icon lamp filled with incense from Mount Athos, which he had received from his friends at the church in Krivi Dol. Srebra and I were alone again, sisters, but in the much more comfortable bed in Darko's home, rather than at our parents' house, but we were more unhappy than we had ever been in our lives, nearly on the brink of death. Our parents knew nothing about Srebra's miscarriage, although I knew she would call them the next day to tell them. "What has been written will unfold," I heard our mother say into the receiver, "Don't be upset, you silly fool, you are not the first and won't be the last. Besides, what would you do with a child, given your situation and how people talk about you?" Srebra's hand holding the receiver was clammy, but she didn't hang up. "We're going to have the operation," she said. "We're starting to collect money." "Where could we possibly find the money?" Mom said. "You haven't said anything about it for years, and now it occurs to you. What next?" "It didn't occur to us? It didn't occur to you!" shouted Srebra. "We aren't asking you for money; we'll find it ourselves." Our mother repeated her favorite saying: "Do whatever you want. You're the smartest girls in the world, and you do whatever you want; you don't listen to anyone, and now you find yourself in a fine mess." That broke the camel's back. Srebra hung up the receiver, then lifted it again. She called a taxi. "We're going home." "Don't!" I said. "That will make too big a deal out of it. Calm down, please. Darko will sort things out with his father about the money, you'll see." But Srebra was already pulling me outside, into the elevator, then down to the street where the taxi was already waiting for us. The taxi driver went crazy when he saw us. "You're them!" he gasped. "You're the ones. I let out a passenger here who told me about some girls with their heads stuck together, and now here you are…" "Yes, that's us," Srebra said. "Would you like to see how we're attached? Would you like to touch?" "No. That's not necessary," the driver said, and he started the engine. I immediately said, "To the cemetery in Butel." I could tell Srebra was boiling; she didn't understand why I told the driver to go to Butel. The driver did as I said, and after a long drive through Skopje traffic, he dropped us off at the cemetery entrance. There were a few heavyset women selling bouquets of carnations and daffodils. We didn't buy anything. Behind our backs they crossed themselves and moved away a bit, spit to ward off the evil eye, and prayed that such a thing would not happen in their families. We went into the cemetery. "Why did we come here?" Srebra asked. "To find peace," I said to her. "Both in ourselves and between ourselves. Here, where everyone is dead, will be the best place to find peace."

And I held out the little finger of my right hand to her, but she didn't give me hers. I recited the rhyme we said when we hooked pinkies to end a quarrel, but didn't add "cut," because Srebra didn't want to make peace, not this way, not so quickly. "Just think about whose grave we have never visited," I said to her. "Roza's. It's the right thing for us to do, come here once, together, as she knew us, before we're separated and have our own lives and don't think about her. She wouldn't even recognize us any other way, you know." "You actually think we'll find her?" Srebra asked sarcastically. "We'll ask someone; there must be some sort of manager. A registrar or something." But there was nothing. The guard said he was new and had no information about where anyone was buried. "You have to ask the family for that information," he said. "You don't just come like this to a cemetery. You could wander around all day, and someone might grab you and rape you; there's all kinds that come out here, and they come looking for all kinds, one head, two heads, just as long as they have somewhere to put their you-know-whats." Although he was young, he was giving us a lecture as if he were some old relative. "Have you been raped yet?" Srebra tossed back at him. But I was already dragging her toward the older graves, from the eighties. There was no order to the Butel cemetery, no way for a person to get oriented. We wandered among the graves, staring at the inscriptions and photographs. We rested on a bench, stood awhile beside a child's grave, a young girl, who had recently died at the age of three. Her poor parents hadn't made a grave but a monument—a throne on pillars, strewn with fresh flowers and wreaths and small plush bears and other animals, a white house of marble with red ribbons and balloons tied to all four columns. It was more like a birthday party than a grave. Tears fell down Srebra's cheeks. "I didn't bury my child," she said. "It was only three weeks old," I said. "It wasn't a child yet; it was an embryo." "It was a baby," she said. "My baby, and I didn't bury it." Our mission to find Roza's grave was a failure. Srebra didn't even look. She just walked beside me, absently, drowned in her own misfortune. I dragged her along the pathways. I felt Roza no longer meant anything to her, that she didn't remember her. Who knows whether she was even buried here. It would have been more logical for her to be buried in Triangla, which was closer to her home and not out at the end of bus route 59, all the way out in Butel. I pulled Srebra toward the cemetery exit, which we found only with difficulty. The guard waved to us. We hopped on the 59 bus and set off. We didn't go to our parents' apartment. That night, I dreamed about our father: He was wearing a long black overcoat (something he brought from his childhood home, something that remained from his life with his parents); his chin was stubbly; his hair was thick and straggly. He was lying dead in a hearse. I looked at him through the balcony rails and realized that he was not dead, just seeing what it would be like. Srebra cried out in her sleep. I woke, and woke her as well. She said a skeleton had been lying on top of her all night. She had grabbed its head—no its skull—under the blankets, thinking it was Darko's, but the skeleton wanted to enter her with a bone instead of his penis. Her head was covered by the blanket. She wanted to scream but had no voice. She wanted to pull the blanket off, but she didn't have the strength, and the skeleton's bones touched her through the blanket. A horrible nightmare. How much freer a person is to retell her disconnected thoughts when half asleep, not yet in control of her words, not thinking of the consequences of what's being said, completely free from shame and the pressures of conventional conversation. In fact,

Srebra was describing the weight on her soul. Darko, awakened by her scream, stood in the bedroom doorway, disheveled. He was aware of how hard this was for her, how much
she still loved him, but also of how the pain didn't allow her
to forgive him. God would forgive him before Srebra would.
That's how it is with people; their hearts are in their heads,
and their heads are in their hearts. Even for those whose head
is attached to another's. At breakfast, Darko asked her hesitantly, "Are we still husband and wife?" Srebra was silent a
moment, and then said in a tired voice, "Yes, we are. But until
Zlata and I are separated, I can't think about it. We have two
options: either we get divorced and Zlata and I leave, or we
wait until after the operation, and then consider what to do.
But I can't live with you as my husband until Zlata and I are
separated." Srebra spoke rationally, calculated and cold. Why
hadn't she thought so rationally before the wedding? Why
hadn't she pressured me, pressured us to find a solution—
money, a surgeon—and begun her own life, and I mine? Had
she been afraid? I had been. In Macedonia, we were written
off as a hopeless medical case. No one had given any serious
thought to our situation. All our family doctor said was, "An
operation like that is doomed to fail from the start. You have
a shared vein. How can you be separated? Who could perform such an operation? I've been a doctor for many years,
and I've never heard of such a thing." And that had been that.
Conversation closed. But since then we had read how, in the
history of medicine, there have been surgeries to separate
twins, both successful and unsuccessful. Back in the nine-
teenth century, a surgeon in a London hospital separated two
young girls, though, to be honest, they had been attached at
the shoulder rather than the head. Our family doctor hadn't
heard about that. But now we were gripped by a zeal, by a

fury, and we could no longer cope with how things stood, not on account of ourselves, because we were used to being two in one, but on account of the events that had taken place: Srebra's abortion and my nighttime drunken adventure with Darko. None of that could be brushed away or forgotten. I don't know whether Srebra really knew what had happened that night or whether she just sensed it; neither Darko nor I admitted to anything. But it seemed she had begun to hate me because of it. Throughout our lives we had always hated each other a bit, outwardly, in our relationship and in our words. We hated each other more than we loved each other, although in our souls we did, surely, love each other. I don't know how one couldn't love one's own sister; I don't know if blood can be the same as water. "For better or for worse then," Darko said, and kissed her cheek. Srebra said nothing. She could let him go if she wanted. We could go back to our parents if we wanted, but the fact was she didn't want to let him go. She still loved him, even if she couldn't forgive him, and we could not go home. "There's absolutely no way I would go back there," I told Srebra. "But if you don't want to live with Darko, we can rent a place. Or we can go to the convent." "Darko is my husband, and as long as he's my husband, we will live here," Srebra pronounced, and that decided it. Although she said those words with unspoken hatred toward me, I was relieved. On no account did I want to return home, though, to tell the truth, I did miss it sometimes. It was, after all, our home. We still called it *home*. We had spent our entire lives there, in that room, in that apartment, which—through all the good times and bad—smelled, nonetheless, of home. There are only two kinds of home: *Home* with a capital letter, the place one has come from, and *home* with a lowercase letter, which are the places one moves to. We moved from our Home as if we had moved to a foreign country, as if we had emigrated. The mix of pain and joy, sadness and enthusiasm; we were at the border between the old, familiar, somewhat terrible life and a new, unknown, certainly far lovelier life. For us, moving to Darko's apartment had been as if we had moved, or better yet emigrated, to America, or Canada, or Australia. It was clean, orderly, warm, with a constant supply of hot water, a full refrigerator, a washing machine, a dishwasher, new bedding, and sparkling pots and pans and dishes. I felt as if we had left our Home for sanitary reasons. Srebra's marriage had been for love, but also as an escape, a voluntary expulsion from the conditions under which we had lived. At Darko's, we had become more beautiful. We could shower whenever we wanted. To iron our clothes, we laid them on an ironing board, not spread on the couch in the kitchen. Our clothes had never been properly ironed before. We ate fresh vegetables, had as much yogurt as we wanted—not just a tiny little cupful. We cooked what we wanted, and Darko always left enough money in the drawer in the bedroom for all our needs: cosmetics, clothes, shoes, as well as for small pleasures such as books and CDs. We were finally washed and combed, with skin clear of acne, smooth heels, white teeth brushed with warm water. We were like two village girls who don't know what city life is like and are so delighted at having discovered it that they want to take every advantage.

We actively sought funds: writing letters and sending requests to hospitals around the world for days on end. Our father still came to visit, and we put groceries into a bag when he left, never mentioning our operation, although he saw the brochures from hospitals, our open address book with telephone numbers, letters, and stamps scattered on the small table in the living room. Whenever we called our mother, she told us bizarre things. She said that Aunt Ivanka had come to visit and had told her, "Mirko is lying in one bed sick from all those teas of his, and Lenka is in another, neither dead nor alive." After one of their visits to the village, she told us that, in a bedroom cupboard in the village, she found a nest with eggs inside. Now, who would have put it there if not Snežana, our unloved aunt? Our mother had fainted, and an ambulance came, barely saving her. Snežana had been at Aunt Milka's for All Saints' Day, and while she was there Aunt Milka lay down, unable to move for two hours. But Snežana released her, still alive. Aunt Milka said she would become anxious from time to time, and would feel like everything was collapsing. "Why?" we asked our mother. "Poverty," she answered. Yes, poverty drives people crazy. In Macedonia, more and more people were going crazy. Our mother cried, complaining that our uncle hadn't come to the village for the entire two weeks they were there. We defended him, saying it wasn't his fault—Snežana was his wife; after all, he lives with her, and the time he spent living with us was too short for him to love us more than his wife.

Darko's mother and family rarely came, but when they did they brought full bags of groceries, saying that they had been to the store for themselves, and had picked up things for us that might come in handy. Then all we would talk about was the operation. His father always said, "It will happen, it will happen; I'm working on it." Then one day he said, "Why don't you become members of the party like Darko? That would help things along, and, of course, it's easier to request money for a member of one's own party than for just anyone." "Everything is easier with a party membership card," his mother said. "And it's not only that, it's necessary—people need to belong somewhere. It's not like it was before 1991, when everyone could be a member of the party or not and it didn't matter, because as long as there was socialism, there was no opposition." That shocked me. But Srebra said, "If that's what we have to do, we'll do it." "Excellent," Darko's father said. "Come to our office on Monday. We'll take care of everything, and people will get to meet you and understand what I'm always talking about, and then it will certainly be easier to find the money." That evening, the three of us argued. I argued with Srebra, because I didn't consider it right to join Darko's father's party just so we could get the money; Srebra argued with me because she insisted that we join, officially. "What does it matter to us?" she said. "The most important thing is that we find the money; everything else is secondary." "Even if it means stepping over corpses?" I asked her, but she said, "Whose corpses?" "Morals are a corpse," I told her, but she said, "You don't even know what you're talking about. A corpse is the baby I no longer have. That is a corpse." Our quarrels always unfolded in parallel—we spoke next to each other because we couldn't look each other in the eye. This made it seem as if we were talking into the air. Our disagreements never ended or resolved. Darko argued with both of us: with Srebra, to convince her that even if she didn't join the party, he would still do everything to get the money and that it was dishonorable to become a member just for that reason and without ideological conviction; she would be using the party, and he was surprised by how Srebra had changed. Hadn't she been interested in politics? Hadn't she finished a law degree? Wasn't she the one who understood such things? Darko argued with me because, he said, I had no political convictions. I wasn't for things or against them; it was all the same to me who was in power and what happened to us. He said, "You only think about yourself. You read novels, and that's it." Then I reminded him that in Bosnia there was still shooting and killing, but no one here paid any attention to it any longer and he and his party hadn't lifted a finger to help. But he shot back immediately that that wasn't true—many volunteers in the Bosnian refugee organizations were, in fact, members of the party. We talked about all sorts of things that evening. I even heard myself say to him, "Your Orthodox people killed children in Srebrenica." But Srebra yelled at me, "His? So, you're not Orthodox?" "No," I said, "I'm of the Orthodox faith, but the Orthodox are those who ostensibly believe in God but only through their sense of national identity." The discussion lasted the whole weekend. We shouted, kept silent, pleaded with each other, ate, and cried. What topics didn't we cover! Whether Dostoevsky was a generally Christian writer or more specifically an Orthodox one. Was the Russian philosopher Berdyaev correct when he talked about the perfection of Christianity and the imperfection of Christians? Would it have been better for Yugoslavia to stay together? Who was to blame for the war: the Serbs, the Slovenes, the Americans, or Tito? Were young people in 1968, about whom we had heard from our parents, more engaged than today's youth? Should there be a death penalty? Is party membership necessary? We were wrung out from these long discussions—angry, calmed, exhausted. We didn't go to services at Krivi Dol that Sunday morning. We felt it would be a desecration to hear the holy liturgy with such thoughts in our heads. On Monday, Srebra dragged me from the apartment. She had resolved to get her party membership card, and I was also resolved—resolved not to get one. "Let's walk through the city first," I said, and instead of going straight downtown, we got off the bus by the National Theater. Something pulled me toward the National Gallery of Art, housed in the fifteenth-century Daut Pasha baths—its breast-shaped domes with their erect nipples poking into the air so seductive, so erotic. The cashier just said, "Go on" and let us in without paying. It was probably because of our heads; we were often admitted for free. It was usually the older women who worked as cashiers, and they, it seemed, felt pity for us, but then they would spit against the evil eye and pray that such a thing didn't happen in their families. We entered the left wing of the baths, behind the piano. On the walls were large paintings of radiating spheres by someone named Matevski—one of ours, a Macedonian who lived in Paris. Oh, how those spheres washed over me, how their colors—red, orange, yellow, white—struck me, leveling me. I had never seen such colors before; the globes were fully four-dimensional: a saturated color, a light gathered like a dewdrop, a concentrate of light, a well of light. My blood rushed to my head and my cheeks burned. Srebra, too, was enthralled by what she saw. I couldn't contain my delight. My heart was beating madly, and I couldn't calm myself. I took off my glasses and I could still see all those spheres, so dramatic that I could see them even without my thick lenses. Matevski became my Matevski, the Macedonian painter of my life. Srebra laughed hysterically, saying how remarkable, how impossible it was: "Look over here," she said. "He's painted our heads. Look how the spheres touch and intersect one another, and inside, there, that is definitely us." After we stood a long time in front of the paintings, we left dazed, picking up some posters that stood on a small shelf by the ticket window, and then tottered over the stone bridge, staring at them. We stumbled over each other, laughed, and almost sang, while the passersby looked at us then turned away, horrified by the sight and the atmosphere that surrounded us. "Do you still want to join the party?" I asked, when we had finally calmed ourselves and had arrived in the city center. "Well, why not?" she asked. "Come on, let's go to London or Paris. Let's find this Matevski, too, and let's get separated. Let's begin a new life." "Then will you forgive me?" I asked, and she began to whistle, to whistle like a lark. It was so lively, so filled with energy that I just let it go. It was the first time since the abortion that she had been like this, normal. We went to the party headquarters, where they had been waiting so long that Darko's father had been getting nervous. He presented us by saying, "This one is my daughter-in-law, and this one is her sister." Everyone greeted us, smiling, bright, clean-shaven, freshly combed, kind, not staring, only looking discreetly and with concern at our heads. Then, suddenly, with glasses of juice and Evropa chocolates, the forms were brought in. Srebra immediately filled hers out, but I just looked at mine, reading it but not taking the proffered pen with the party logo. Srebra signed hers and gave it to the secretary, but I said, "I can't join now." Darko's father's face turned red, but he said nothing. They served us coffee, and while Srebra chewed a chocolate, the party secretary said, "So, you are seeking funds for your operation. The country must help people like you, but look who's leading it: former Communists. Nothing functions as it should, but we are already working on it; the money will be found." "The money will be found," Darko's father repeated as he led us to the door. The others waved to us, smiling, saying, "Goodbye and good luck."

1996

"The money's been found," Darko said one day, several months after Srebra joined the party. "We're going to London." "*We're* going?" I asked, in surprise, not knowing whether "we" meant Darko was coming with us or only that Srebra and I were headed to London, the destination we had dreamed of for so long—not as tourists, but for the realization of our fate. "Yes, we're going," Darko said again, hugging both of us. "How could I let you go alone?" Srebra pulled me over and nestled beside him. She pulled his arms around her waist, while I stood within their embrace, restrained, motionless. "Everything's arranged," said Darko. "I've bought the tickets and have visas for you, well, not yet actually, because they wouldn't give them to me without you there, but my father went to dinner with the British ambassador and told him the whole story. The ambassador already knew everything, though he'd already talked to the hospital in London. You have no idea the network that has been assembled for you, how many people are preparing for your operation—diplomats, doctors, and journalists, the whole world. I wanted it to be a surprise, and now we can really go. Tomorrow morning at seven o'clock." Darko was speaking excitedly. We stared into space above his head, mouths open, our breaths intermingling. It was rare that Srebra and I smelled good to each other, but at that moment our throats, our viscera, emitted scents that were floral instead of sour. A warm bliss spread through our souls, as if some spirit (the Holy one?) had settled within us. Our hearts beat with excitement and a bit of fear, though we weren't thinking about the fear. It seemed that our departure for London predestined success, as if the trip to London was, in and of itself, the uncomplicated separation of our heads. No, we didn't feel the fear, uncertainty, or worry. All those feelings arrived later that afternoon, when we went to tell our parents the day had come for our trip to London and our separation. "What's wrong with how you are?" our mother asked. "You're risking everything for this stupidity. That operation is difficult, and no one is giving you a guarantee. But go, since you're so obstinate." "You know best," our father said. "Do whatever you want. You're not children." We sat in the dining room—Srebra and I, on the chairs we had always pulled side by side, our father and Darko sitting across from us—while our mother stood at the head of the table, where there was no chair, because it was leaning up against the wall. Darko drank rakija and said nothing. However, after our mother and father said what they had to say and we sat in silence with our chests full of that well-known feeling of powerlessness and anger, Darko said, "They're not children, and the time has come for them to be separated." Then he stood up, and we stood up after him, and, I don't know how, we said goodbye to our mother and father. We offered them our hands, then our faces, two for one. They quickly kissed us, me on the left cheek, Srebra on the right. They shook Darko's hand, and we left. I don't know why, but, as we walked down the stairs, I crossed myself just as we passed Roza's door. I crossed myself automatically, just as my mother did before every trip, murmuring, "Oh, Lord God! Oh, Lord God!" We left quickly. As always, Uncle Blaško was sitting on the balcony, and he greeted us, as always, with "Howdy Do!" Then we ducked into Darko's car and set off, hurrying home to pack. Early the next morning, Darko's mother and father came over. They hugged us, wished us luck, and shoved money into Darko's hand. He said, "Everything's already been paid for, right? The hotel, hospital, and operation?" They replied, "This is to help you get settled and to see a bit of London. You've never been there before." Our passports were stamped with three-month British visas—tourist visas—and Srebra laughed. I said to her, "Wouldn't you rather have a work visa?" and all of us laughed in the taxi as we drove to the airport in Petrovec with ecstasy, optimism, and high spirits. But as we passed our primary school, on the road to the airport, something tightened in my chest—sharp, like pincers. Srebra likely felt it as well, because both of us fell silent, and within us grew a kernel of worry and uncertainty mixed with a feeling of transiency, of nostalgia for our small pale red school, where, with conjoined heads, we had spent our childhood days. Now we were driving along the road we had gazed at through the school windows and from the schoolyard for eight long years. It had seemed to us then, as children, that this road led somewhere far away, to a brighter future, that we could flee along this road from home and into the world. Here we were, traveling along this very road, toward a brighter future in which each of us would find her own life, with her own head. "Will you ever forgive me for what happened?" I asked Srebra in my mind, while pressing the icon in my pocket. "God will forgive you; he's your friend," I heard her voice say in my head with its familiar cynicism. Then I imagined her voice asking, "Tell me this, at least:

Was it good for you?" "I don't know," I responded in my head again. "You can believe it or not, but Darko and I didn't have sex, not the way you think. Just with our hands," I thought, cheeks flaming. "Ah, hand jobs. What a good idea. When we're separated, I'll have sex with him like that too." That is how Srebra's inner voice spoke to me, while in the car it was quiet, Darko's hand resting on Srebra's shoulder. I turned my left shoulder away, as far as my head would allow. The radio was playing some psychedelic song by the group Dead Can Dance. Had Darko chosen the seventeenth of August 1996 for our flight to London on purpose? It was our birthday; we were turning twenty-four. For all twenty-four of those years, Srebra and I had carried our heads together. She had a husband and a dead child; I didn't even have that. We were living at the wrong time, in the wrong place, in the wrong bodies.

On the plane, Darko was in front of Srebra and me, seated beside a passenger holding a briefcase on his knees. Darko must have looked at him inquisitively, because the man turned and told him he was going to London to see how things were progressing with the Macedonian denar. He told him how, at any moment, the Royal Mint would be producing a gold denar with the crest of Macedonia on one side and storks on the other. "To commemorate the fifth year of our independence," he said. Darko said this was the first time he had heard anything about it. "Is Macedonian money really made in London?" he asked. "We don't have a mint or a printing facility for money," the man with the briefcase said. "London is the best place for that." It seemed that London was best for everything—for money and for separating heads. Heads or tails, the flip of a coin could settle the fate of a life, a country, or a person. Srebra swallowed a lump in her throat. I said nothing, though I suspect we were thinking the same thing. I immersed myself more deeply in Sabato's novel *The Tunnel*, and she into Seneca's *Letters from a Stoic*. Darko didn't mention his conversation with the man beside him, who, when we landed, immediately disappeared in the crowd. In London, a black taxi brought us to our hotel in Kensington, the Golden Star Hotel, a tall, modern hotel, nothing like the old architectural style of London. It felt familiar, resembling the Hotel Continental in Skopje, on the outside at least. Inside, however, the conditioned air suspended between the red velvet armchairs and couches was lapping against us. Everything inside sparkled: the elevator doors, the small hallway tables, the neckties of the men working the front desk, and the women's neatly pinned-up hair. The black skin of the porter's face shone like a diamond, completely in keeping with the sparkling chic of the hotel with its red carpet and silver plates piled with red apples. We were given rooms on the eleventh floor, one with a double bed and one with a single.

In a letter Darko received from the hospital, we had been informed that we would be seen the day after our arrival in London. We were free for the afternoon and could do whatever we liked. We could walk around, spend the two hundred pounds Lala gave us once long ago for when we would go to London for our operation, so that we, as she had said, could discover the city. How beautiful London was! "How beautiful London is!" Srebra cried as she pulled me this way and that to look at one thing, touch something else, try on summer dresses in one of the thousands of stores on Oxford Street. It was August, and London was filled with tourists. We were intoxicated with the city. For the first time in my life, I felt like a tourist. Yet, a moment later, my heart tightened as I remembered that we were in London for an operation, that it was here we would ultimately be separated. The flesh that joined our heads would be severed, and each of us would have her own head; each of us would live her own life. Or not. That's what frightened me, that it might not be life that awaited us after our celebrated operation, but death. "Didn't you want to get married in London?" I teased Srebra. "Weren't you supposed to live in London?" I said, reminding her of our fortune-telling game from childhood, but I didn't go on. Then she said, "Yes, and I would have a husband whose name began with a *D*, which I have, and we would have one child, the one we lost, and my *D*-named husband would be a multi-millionaire." Then she fell silent. "Well, I am a millionaire. You are worth a whole million," Darko said, and he laughed and put his arm around Srebra's waist, being careful not to touch me. She was returning to him more and more; she increasingly belonged to him again, and she said, "Still, the millions we've paid to come to London are not our own money. Macedonia paid for it," and we all laughed ourselves silly, far from Macedonia but with its money in the bank accounts of the hospital and the hotel, and spent on round-trip airplane tickets. Macedonia was doing something for us at last. It had given us the money so we could be apart from each other—as if we were two republics of Yugoslavia that had once been joined but would now be separate, though peacefully, without war, by mutual agreement—not like the Dayton Accords, but like the Geneva Convention. We would separate amicably, and, though a huge amount of blood would be spilled, we wouldn't see it. It would all take place in our sleep, under heavy anesthesia, and when we awoke, we would be independent, free, each with her own constitution, and then only the most cynical and most malicious people would call us the "former sisters-with-conjoined-heads." But we would be in the present with separated heads. How we philosophized and laughed. Standing beside the Thames, we were doubled over with laughter, though perhaps more from fear than with joy.

That first evening, after celebrating our birthday with Indian curry in a small restaurant by the Thames in the summertime light of the moon, we returned to the hotel around nine o'clock. Darko suggested we stay up a bit longer together, either in his room or ours. Our room had a double bed, so Darko came to our room. We turned on the television. Darko flipped through the channels, all eighty-seven of them. We hadn't known it was possible there could be so many. There were channels from all over the world, though most were in English. One of the British channels was broadcasting the show *Guess and Win* live, a quiz show we had read about in the Entertainment section of the Macedonian daily newspaper *Nova Makedonija*. Once, while crowds waited to apply to be on the show, standing on the stairs leading to the television studio, a young woman on the sidewalk began to experience labor pains, and by the time the emergency crew arrived, she had already begun giving birth. Her baby was born on a nearby bench, just about in front of everybody. The baby was taken to the hospital. A day later, the woman told journalists that her daughter would be called Victoria, not after the former queen of England, for whom bus stops and small souvenir shops in London are christened, but as a kind of moral victory over the quiz show *Guess and Win*. I remembered that incident because I had read it aloud to Srebra, saying, "Just look at those crazy English people." And now that very show was on TV, and the contestant was a young man, a very good-looking young man, with black hair, burning eyes, half-parted lips. On the screen, large red numbers flashed the amount he had already won, and the host announced that he needed just one more guess to win the grand prize, and now was the decisive moment for our contestant. She said, "All or nothing." If he failed to answer the last question correctly, he would lose everything, everything, and that would be the end of the show for the season. "Hey," said Srebra, "isn't that…?" "Who?" I asked, and I focused on the young man's tense face. I seemed to recognize him from somewhere, from some long ago past, but we both fell silent, because the man suddenly yelled, "Shit!" and the camera showed the word *Tajikistan* on the screen crossed out with a red line. The man struck his knees, saying, "Shit, shit, shit," and he nearly tumbled from his chair as his body gave way, and the host announced, "Unfortunately, the bed warmer from the Golden Star Hotel has lost the game." The answer was Turkmenistan, and the sum he had won so far flickered with a red line through it. Beneath it, in a black rectangle, was buried the main prize that the young man had hoped to claim. In the studio, he slumped in his chair, wailing, sobbing, and pounding himself on the head. Two people came up and helped him to his feet. The host came over and said, "Dear Bogdan, winning isn't important; what's important is that you played the game." She stretched up on her heels and kissed him quickly on the cheek, and then the two men led him away while the host closed the program with the words, "Our bed warmer from the Golden Star Hotel didn't win, but that's no reason for despair." She pulled a scrap of paper from a small envelope and read what was written there: "Every loss in life is a victory as well." The show ended. Srebra and I sat on the bed, dumbstruck, neither of us entirely sure what we had seen. "Hey, that guy apparently works here, in our hotel," Darko said, and Srebra exploded, "It's Bogdan! From Skopje—the guy from our neighborhood. We went to primary school together until he adopted a single woman and they moved to London. He was Zlata's friend."

She began to laugh, shaking my head with hers, and I was terribly confused. I couldn't believe everything we had just witnessed on the screen—yes, that really had been Bogdan, poor Bogdan who had solved crossword puzzles so passionately, who was part of our circle when Roza had been alive, who had adopted the single woman in our neighborhood and had gone off to London while we were in the village. That's what Auntie Dobrila had told us. And since then, over the next ten or eleven years, we had heard nothing about him. He contacted no one, didn't return to Skopje, and we forgot him. Now he had risen before our eyes on television in London, and—strangest of all—the emcee twice said he was "a bed warmer at the Golden Star Hotel," which was exactly where we were. Even though there were two other Golden Star Hotels in London, I had the feeling he was here, that Bogdan worked in this hotel, and I yelled in disbelief, "What a coincidence!" Darko responded, "There are no coincidences in life," which isn't something anyone would say about a situation like this, but that's what Darko believed, the same as anyone who has been touched by faith. Darko felt the presence of God and understood that coincidences don't exist, only God's forethought and human will. "How is it possible?" Srebra repeated, laughing nervously. I felt sorry for our Bogdan, who had been carried from the studio almost doubled over. I was sorry he hadn't won the grand prize of 500,000 pounds, which was, evidently, extremely important to him—as if his life depended on it. And, although his reaction had been merely to repeat the English word "Shit," as he struck himself, I recognized the same childhood pain as when he read his homework in school on the theme "When You Hit Rock Bottom"—the tragic story about his mother's death and their abject poverty. Yes, it was the same pain filling his eyes with tears. That money wasn't just money; it was an escape, a balm, perhaps precisely because of that loss in his childhood and the moldy sausages made from the pig he had written about in his homework. "We have to find him," I said, and it seemed so important I almost forgot why, in fact, we had come to London. "Yes," said Srebra, "we'll tease him a little." "No," I said, "we'll comfort him." "What's wrong with you?" Srebra asked. "Do you think he's waiting for our comfort? He may be already married; he may even have a child—maybe that's why he's so unhappy he didn't win the money. Besides, do you think he'll even remember us?" I responded, "Of course he does. Who doesn't remember us? Don't be an idiot. I can't believe he's seen anyone else with conjoined heads in his life." Darko just looked at us, and the expression on his face was a mixture of anxiety and curiosity. He said, "We can look for him tomorrow, when he has calmed down." And, at that point, we began to wonder about his extremely odd profession. "Bed warmer" is what the host had said, but we had no idea what it meant. We'd never heard of such a thing. For us, a bed warmer was the hot water bottle from when we were young that we called Hermes, which our parents slept with; or a bed warmer was the bricks our grandma heated in the woodstove, wrapped in cloth, and placed in our bed to warm our feet; or the Strumka bottle filled with hot water from the pot on the stove, which Srebra and I passed back and forth before going to sleep. But human bed warmers in people's hotel rooms—we had never heard of that before, and it wasn't clear what, in fact, such a bed warmer might do. Darko kissed Srebra passionately on the lips and, for a moment, seemed to consider staying in our room, but Srebra gently pushed him away and said goodnight, so he left. Srebra and I lay in the dark as we always had, but we no longer spoke a single word.

We lay on our backs, each with her own thoughts and breaths, both of us absolutely puzzled by the incident with Bogdan; blood pulsed in our temples. I pressed the icon in my left hand under the pillow, and, with mixed feelings, memories, and questions spinning in my head, I didn't fall asleep until deep in the night. Srebra fell asleep more quickly—surely Darko's kiss had calmed her and given her the peace she needed to sleep—but I kept vigil, while our whole childhood returned to my thoughts: all those moments with Bogdan, and, invariably, with Roza, and my recollections seemed to belong and not to belong to my life at the same time; I flitted in and out of my body, in and out of seeing things through my eyes; I looked at myself from outside, and from outside, I saw only myself, as though Srebra and I weren't connected, while from inside, I, as always, saw myself with her, and between those two perspectives, there was such sadness, emptiness, irreconcilability, fated always, it seemed, for destruction. I was still more disheartened by our twenty-fourth birthday, with the irrefutable reality of almost a quarter century passed aimlessly, senselessly, bound together. I fell asleep, feeling completely lost. I dreamed a strange dream that night: a naked man with no first name but the surname Micev. In my dream, I thought he was Dr. Micev, the famous psychiatrist from Skopje, whom our art teacher, Lala, had once mentioned, even saying, "If you can't endure having conjoined heads, at least speak with Micev about it. He'll know what to do." But in my dream, Dr. Micev was holding pieces of bloody meat in his hands. He was jumping up and down, and took aim at Srebra and me with the bloody steaks; slimy, ripped-out, dripping pieces of liver; bits of other organs and muscle; and no matter how we hunched down, ran away, or tried to protect ourselves from being hit, globs of meat fell on our bodies.

He was young, blond, dressed only in white underwear; bloody from head to toe. When I woke from the nightmare, Srebra was still sleeping. I pulled her to wake her up.

We had to go to the hospital for our first physical exam. It was Sunday morning, and the doctor was coming to the hospital just to see us. We had to be on time. We could not eat breakfast; both of us felt our stomachs turn at the very thought of food. Darko waited for us in the hallway, his face radiant, a secret expression in his eyes. He said nothing specific as we hurried to the underground station. We changed trains twice, reached the East Acton station, and then walked a short way to the hospital. The main building was an old structure, dating from the beginning of the twentieth century, with new wings added on. It was no accident that we were going to this particular hospital—it was the largest university clinic in Europe. Soon after it was built, conjoined babies had been successfully separated, though they hadn't been conjoined at the head, but at the shoulder. In the letter that Darko received from the hospital giving the date of our appointment—August 18, 1996—it said there was no guarantee they would actually perform the operation. The doctor wrote that he would determine whether to do the operation following an exam. With mixed emotions, we were now on our way to meet that person, our legs intertwining as we nearly ran. Srebra was laughing, almost hysterical. Darko followed us, calling out, "Hold on, calm down." I kept sneezing, from excitement I think. Srebra covered her mouth; we were anxious, frightened, and happy. Our nerves were nearly shot. Darko was pale; our cheeks were flushed. Were our parents talking about us? We had sent them a postcard with the short message: "Greetings from London," and now we were running to see our doctor, our savior, our executioner. "Hey, what about

Bogdan?" Srebra suddenly cried out, right at the clinic door, but Darko merely said, "Please, really, just calm down. Let's go find the doctor." At the reception desk, a black woman greeted us kindly. She skimmed through the letter we handed her, then called our doctor. He came in, tall, middle-aged, straight-backed, with an athletic build. He looked like a film star from the 1960s. His hair was black, slicked down. His complexion was a mix of European and African. When he saw us, he smiled broadly and said, "Are all the women in the Balkans so beautiful?" He then immediately added, turning professional, "You don't even notice that your heads are conjoined." Srebra and I pulled our hair back so he could see where our heads joined, then he led us to his office on the third floor of the left wing, jumping up two stairs at a time ahead of us. In his office, he had us sit on a leather couch and offered Darko an armchair, while he settled in the other armchair, and, with a remote control, lowered the blinds. Then, with a different remote, he turned on the television—a DVD player connected to a monitor, to be precise—and before us was a video of two sisters from an Arab country, around our age, with their conjoined heads wound in a scarf as they happily entered the operating room. On the video the doctor gave a brief account, and when this matter-of-fact narration was finished, the camera showed the doctor, an old man from South Korea, saying, "I decided to separate them when I considered that they had slept on their backs for thirty years, unable to turn over to get comfortable." Then a voiceover added, "The day after their operation and death, this doctor cried in his wife's lap like a child. But the twins' dream had still been fulfilled—they returned home in two separate caskets." They showed the caskets of yellow wood being lowered into the ground, one beside the other. Then our doctor turned off the film, raised the blinds, and looked at us. We were shocked by what we had seen. We had not expected such a beginning, such an introduction to our operation, which was our undertaking for salvation. It was far too raw, too painful and frightening, a slap in our faces, or, more precisely, a blow to the shared vein where we were conjoined. We sat speechless, lost, crushed, and exhausted. Darko cleared his throat while the doctor played with a pen, turning it over in the air. Finally, he said, "This could happen to you. This is, in fact, the most likely outcome of such an operation." Then he fell silent. We were also silent, shifting around on the couch. We had expected a different approach—encouragement, endorsement, agreement with our decision as we had explained to him on three large sheets of paper sent from Skopje—we had anticipated support. He said, "The worst thing is that I don't have a wife, so I don't know whose lap I would cry in." He laughed, loudly, ironically, almost cynically, and then stood up, walked behind our couch, took both of our heads in his hands, and said, "Be here tomorrow morning at eight. You'll be given a hospital room. We'll do a complete examination, and after that, I will perform the operation. There is no other solution. You can't live like this any longer. Still, you have to decide whose life we should save if forced to choose. And you both must give signed consent." He patted our heads, adding, "When we wish to change the fate we have been given, we must do it through our own accountability alone." We were confused, our faces flushed. Darko watched all three of us strangely, not knowing what to say. We stood, extended our hands to the doctor, and left. We had never seen a doctor like that before. He didn't fit our conception of the most successful neurosurgeon in Europe, one who could separate our heads successfully, as we had always thought. The worm of doubt gnawed our flesh, but we looked at it triumphantly, because our skin had thickened from the moment we decided to separate at any cost so now it was impenetrable, like armor, and didn't allow the doubt to penetrate beneath our skin, into our souls. We had no other choice—we had to believe in the good. We had to free ourselves from this evil in our life, in our fate. Surgically. What God had joined together, let the knife put asunder. That was Srebra's raw logic. She said: "If God made us like this—though I personally think the two of us are descended from monkeys—then this operation will correct his mistake." I squeezed the icon of Zlata Meglenska in my pocket. I stroked it and held it. I didn't take my hand from my pocket even in the doctor's office. All my strength, all my soul, all my hopes were gathered in the feel of the icon's soft, yet coarse, wood. God, how many years had I been inseparable from it. It was worn and faded from all my touching and squeezing and from the shapes of all the pockets into which I had shoved it every morning after spending the night beneath my head. My life was unimaginable without the icon, without this saint to whom I prayed automatically, though all my energy was concentrated in that automaticity. It was no empty prayer but a prayer-concentrate, a Hesychastic soothing of the soul. A human being was going to touch what God had ordained—our physical deformity. Orthodoxy didn't forbid operations, because a person needed his body to be resurrected, which is the reason that the holy fathers looked negatively at cremation. The body must be buried, the body must be healed, the body must give birth, and the body must be resurrected.

"He'll separate you," Darko said with conviction when we were outside. "He will separate you!" He was euphoric. He was shouting through the street that led to the underground—the aboveground, actually, because here at East Acton, the trains stopped above ground, and only later, at the third station, did they go deep into the earth, down into the depths of our thoughts. "Dead or alive," I said, although I didn't want to be cynical. "Alive, alive," said Srebra, "Oh, I'm so hungry!" But the choice we had to make cut between us like a living wall: Who would live if a choice had to be made? We didn't say a word about it. After a long ride, we got off near Hyde Park and went into a small, nondescript restaurant with a sign over the door, reading "We serve English breakfast all day." We were hungry, not from hunger, but from excitement, anxiety, fear, and joy. We ordered three English breakfasts: we each got a fried egg, sunny-side up, bacon, roasted sausage, broiled to-mato slices, a pile of boiled beans with hot red peppers, bread spread with butter, and coffee. Breakfast at eleven o'clock. We ate everything. Then we headed to the park. We came face-to-face with an enormous black marble Achilles. Bicy-clists and people running in different directions swirled past it. "Look!" Darko pointed out a family to us. The mother was running, and the father ran while pushing a carriage in which a three-year-old boy was loudly laughing, excited by the race. I asked why they ran even on a Sunday, when so much time was spent every other day hurrying about from here to there. But they were a family, and for them, that was something far more important than the running. At that moment, I made my choice: Srebra must live. We approached the Speakers' Corner. A man standing on a bricklayer's ladder was speaking loudly, shouting actually, screaming in defense of Jesus Christ. A typical, populist herald of God, so sure of both himself and God. Standing right beside him, though not on the ladder, was a Muslim man who contradicted the Christian in a quiet voice. He kept repeating, "You know, you know," which was the only thing that could be heard amid all the roar and commotion. An absurd scene, cinematic. Behind them, a young black girl in a pink dress was running around with her father, a large, imposing man. On the other side, a man sat on a chair singing meditative songs, then reading psalms from the Bible. While we were there, not a single person spoke about politics. I thought Macedonia should have something like a speakers' corner in the park in Skopje for politicians—though not just for them—so they could say whatever came into their minds, talking as much as they pleased. People could say whatever they wanted and lighten their souls. A speakers' corner for radicals, in every sense of the word. Perhaps Srebra and I should climb on a chair in Hyde Park and speak about our torment. Had anyone ever spoken in Macedonian from the Speakers' Corner in London? I said none of this aloud; after all, Darko was the son of the vice president of the opposition party in Macedonia—Srebra's father-in-law, who had found enough money for our medical treatment in London, although it wasn't clear to us how. Officially, the money had been given to us from the Health Insurance Fund, and had gone directly into the account of the London hospital.

We continued on to the British Museum. The Parthenon, Greek Gods, Egyptian mummies, Indian deities, terracotta from Taranto, the Rosetta Stone, and, at the end—Macedonian folk costumes from Galičnik. Everything was in the British Museum, the whole world, everything that had existed prior to us, artifacts from every civilization were preserved there. Everything was there, and everything not there was coming. Including us. "Look, they could put us here," said Srebra, "with the inscription 'Two-headed Macedonians, embalmed,' you in black, me in white, like on our wedding day." "It would be one of the most popular exhibits," said

Darko, and he laughed. All the museumgoers looked first at us, as if we were an exhibit that had stepped out of a display case, and only then did they turn discreetly toward the real exhibits, still affected by the sight, unsure in what era they found themselves. We were not invalids. We were not blind, not autistic; we didn't have Down syndrome. We "only" had conjoined heads that didn't immediately strike the eye. It was only after the fifth second they saw it, when our heads moved in unison in the same direction, and our bodies, always leaning to one side or the other, were pulled by gravity, gravity which, in our case, was always off-balance. But we were here in London, seeking an escape from the circumstances of our life. Just one more night, and we would be in the confident and capable hands of our surgeon.

That evening, we returned a bit early to the hotel. Along the way, we each had a Cornish pasty. As we entered the hotel, the woman at reception handed Srebra and me the key to our room with an expression on her face different from the one she wore as she gave Darko his. She looked at us with a smile playing at the corners of her lips and a secret in her gaze. We weren't sure why. We took the elevator to our floor. Darko said he would go to his room and then come to ours in half an hour. We went into our room, undressed—pulling our clothes down our legs—then popped into the shower. We dried off quickly, and, seated at the small vanity in our room, dried our hair with the hairdryer. I dried mine a bit and hers, then Srebra dried hers a bit and mine. We knew that this was the last time we would dry our hair in this fashion. We looked silently into the mirror, and in our gaze, everything was condensed, everything we had been silent about all our lives, everything we wanted to tell each other but didn't for whatever reason, everything was in our eyes, because other than in a mirror, we couldn't see each other. We loved each other, we hated each other, we were ashamed of each other, we felt contempt for each other, we were afraid of each other, we were close and we were distant. Everything was mixed up in our hearts, our heads; yet, surprisingly, it had all become unimportant, nearly meaningless in the face of our desire to be separated once and for all! Period. End of sentence. While the hair dryer blew on our hair, mixing the strands together, we were aware that, right in that moment, in the loneliness of a hotel room in London, we were separating, and it made us both happy and downcast, more out of fear than pain. Someone knocked on the door. "OK!" Srebra called out. "Come in!" she added even louder. A moment later the door opened, but it wasn't Darko on the other side, but a young man in strange attire, as if he were from outer space—from head to toe in a shiny silver woolen jumpsuit, with a soft hat that covered him from forehead to chin. Srebra and I gasped at the same time. Srebra said roughly, "Excuse me?" and the young man said in English, "You ordered a bed-warming?" At once I recognized Bogdan, not from our childhood in Skopje, but from the television show we had seen the night before, when he was sobbing and striking his head with his fists, yelling, "Shit, shit" after he lost. It was Bogdan, it really was. "Bogdan!" I cried, but he couldn't believe his eyes. Evidently, he had not known we were there. Darko had ordered the bed-warming as a surprise. Bogdan stood, holding onto the door, and said, "Zlata? Srebra?" Then he took his hat off and began to pull his arms out of the suit. "You're not going to warm our bed?" Srebra asked with a smirk, while I stared with mouth agape. He nearly jumped, saying, "If you want me to," but I waved him off with my hand. My heart nearly flew from my chest, and our hearts and temples pounded in a shared rhythm, which I thought might echo through the whole room. I don't know how we calmed down. I think it was when Darko came into the room, and, laughing, introduced himself to Bogdan. Bogdan, the childhood friend who had disappeared one day from our lives, was now here, with us, in a hotel room in London, as a professional warmer of hotel beds. It was a new profession—human bed warmers who lay down in specialized attire before the hotel guest got in. It was warm outside, but in the room the climate control had cooled it to sixty-two degrees, and the bed was cold. Some guests really did want a warm bed to climb into, so the hotel came up with this new job. Guests could order a bed warmer, who, hoping for a good tip, would warm it then discreetly withdraw. Bogdan was the only one in the hotel, and, apparently, in all of London, because it was rare for someone to want the service, and the manager had told him he would probably have to let him go because it was simply not worth keeping him on for those few occasions when a guest requested him. Many associations, organizations, and individuals considered the service controversial, but guests seeing the ad for the service hanging in the display case at the reception desk either reacted by laughing uncontrollably (which made the watchman in the hotel, a black man named John, also laugh), or with shock—arguing with the receptionist, defending human rights, intimacy, hygiene, human worth. One guest even said he would order the warmer to warm his bed, but would also fuck him, certain that the service was sexual, because otherwise, what normal person would warm a stranger's bed with his body, even if wrapped up in protective clothing from head to toe. Stories in the newspapers said that the hotel had crossed all boundaries of good behavior and was offering a service that encroached on an individual's bodily integrity. It was a scandal. "As for me, this isn't my first job and it won't be my last. I finished a technical school program, and since then I've done all sorts of things, working in pubs, restaurants, offices, laundries, now here. But I mainly work here just so I can say I have a job. Most of the time I solve prize crosswords (he looked at us knowingly, but also a bit shame-faced, saying, 'You know how much I liked *Brain Twisters*'). I play the lotto. I mail in prize coupons, postcards. I answer questions. England has tons of these things, and there are constantly new games. I go on quiz shows; yesterday, for example, I almost won the grand prize, but didn't. I'd be rich, and wouldn't have to warm hotel beds anymore. But then I wouldn't have seen you." "What about your mother? What's she doing?" I asked tentatively. "My mother? Are you thinking of Auntie Stefka? That's what I call her. I couldn't get used to calling her Mom. She's alive and well, and when her sister died, she married her sister's husband, her brother-in-law. He's an Englishman, a good guy, but I still call him Uncle. I couldn't get used to calling him Dad. They live in Brighton, and we see each other from time-to-time. I live here, in an area called Shoreditch. I rent a place and usually sleep there, except when I know a client wants me to warm the bed. Then I get an employee's room in the hotel." We spoke that night till dawn. About London, Skopje, the operation that awaited us. We all talked, but mainly Bogdan. That night, he was more talkative than he had been all the years of our childhood together, when he silently solved crossword puzzles and we played together and watched one another, at times timidly, at times aggressively, embarrassment and courage mixing like water and oil, depending on whether Roza was around. Srebra had barely any relationship with him when we were children. His presence annoyed her. But since Roza had accepted him as a friend,

Bogdan was often in our circle. How had I felt about Bogdan when I was a kid? I had been embarrassed and sorry for him, but I didn't ignore him. At school, I listened closely when he spoke in class. I was shaken by his essay "When You Hit Rock Bottom." I had never forgotten him, and whenever we met in the neighborhood, I was confused and couldn't talk. But it had always passed quickly, because Srebra would pull me away. We talked about Roza. Bogdan remembered every detail of their friendship and at one point said, "Roza was like a sister to me." We all fell silent. The memories came back and struck each of us like waves hitting a rocky shore, breaking our hearts with pent-up feeling, truths unspoken, thoughts unsaid. Until dawn, we combed through our lives as we never had before. We talked, laughed, kept silent, but we did not cry. Darko attentively pulled the threads of our conversation. He knew when to prompt us, when to stop us, and when to get us to open up a bit more. That night, Srebra and I passed through a ritual confession, a cleansing of our souls, a farewell to our joint heads, and looked toward a new future that would undoubtedly be bright. We went to bed, each of us calmed by her own collection of memories, her own personal history. Srebra and Darko kissed on the lips. Bogdan seemed taken aback when he saw them kiss right beside my face, next to my cheek. He said good night and left, with the promise that he would visit us in the hospital, where, he said, he would see each of us with her own head.

Before we entered the hospital, Srebra said we should phone our mother and father. "So they're not worrying about us," she said, and from that perspective, from abroad in London, it was natural they would be thinking of us, asking each other what we were doing, what we had done. "Let's," I said, and after inserting British pounds, we dialed their number in Skopje from a phone booth. Our mother always answered the phone, as she did now. "Where are you? Why haven't you been calling?" she asked, but her voice was lost. It was so muffled and raspy that we barely recognized it. I felt concern weigh on my conscience. Holding the receiver to our ears under our chins, Srebra said in one breath, "We're fine. We are going to the hospital right now. They've given us a room. The doctor is really good. He said he first has to do an examination and several tests, and then he'll do the operation." Our mother was silent for a moment, and then said, "Your grandmother died. Your uncle called this morning. So we are going there." She choked. In shock, Srebra and I couldn't utter a word. We heard our mother say, "Bye," and she hung up the receiver. Srebra and I stood in the phone booth in the hospital courtyard, lost, broken. Darko helped us go into the hospital. We were taken to a room with a large bed that had a special mechanism for raising and lowering our bodies, a bundle of shiny equipment beside it, a gorgeous magnolia out the window, and two green bonsai on the night-stands. The room looked more like a hotel room than a hospital room. It had its own private bath, with the largest shower stall we had ever seen, with an enormous showerhead and two small hand-held showerheads for rinsing. How could there be a stall especially made for Siamese twins and we had never seen such a thing in our lives? The nurse smiled from ear to ear as she showed us all the things in our room and in the bathroom, as though we were her guests and she had given us the nicest room, with a view of a green lawn stretching out beyond the hospital, which from the fourth floor could be seen in all its splendor. "Our grandma died," I said, barely audible. The nurse gasped and said she was sorry, but added that such was life: old people die, young ones live, children are born. She asked us if we needed anything. We needed nothing but our grandmother, alive, like when she'd held us in her embrace and sang, "This is the way the ladies ride, a gallop-a-trot." They left us in peace. We lay down in the enormous bed, each with her own thoughts and tears, staring at the television without knowing what we were watching. Darko tried to make conversation, but neither Srebra nor I could get words out of our mouths. That first night in the hospital, I dreamed we were talking to our father on the phone, and he asked us, "What does the doctor say? Is there any chance?" And just as I was about to say, "There is," Srebra moved the receiver to her ear and said rapidly, "There is and there isn't." Then our mother grabbed the receiver and shouted, "So why then have the operation? Why can't you just go on as you had before? You're just there for the hell of it. There are people who go around with no legs or arms. You have everything, but you still think it's not enough." But I repeated, as if in a trance, "We have nothing! We have nothing!" and Srebra added, "Please, I beg you." Then she put down the receiver, and in our anxiety, we both wet our pants. When I woke up, I immediately felt the sheet beneath me to see if it was dry. I thought about how our grandma must have already been buried without us, and how we would never see her again. The doctor came in. The tests began, conducted by a team of twelve doctors and nurses, both men and women. What did they not do to us? What did we not endure for those three and a half weeks of both painful and interesting experiences? We gave ourselves over completely, acting as if nothing hurt, as if nothing bothered us. "What obedient girls," a doctor said. "Very Balkan," added our doctor, and he laughed. He had this irony in him, as well as a sense of humor that made anything forgivable. He was a neurosurgeon, an intellectual who allowed himself both humor and irony, everything in the service of the relationship he was building with us. A nurse came in with a razor and said they would have to shave our heads. As the nurse shaved me, I felt my head getting smaller, as if it were becoming smooth and round as it never had been before. Even the nurse was surprised by what she saw. "You have such small heads," she said. "They're so Jewish!" When we looked at ourselves in the mirror, we saw two strange faces, unrecognizable at first. We each looked first at herself and then at the other, and saw how much the hair determines a person's look. Now, with no hair, we looked funny, almost grotesque. "Your hair will grow back, I guarantee," the nurse said and then bit her lip slightly, as if realizing that she shouldn't have said the words "I guarantee." While she might be able to guarantee our hair would grow back, she couldn't guarantee anything else—the outcome of the operation, for example. But she had guaranteed our hair would grow back normally, if… When he saw us, Darko laughed happily, looking relaxed. In fact, Darko laughed the whole time we were in London, as if he had swallowed some happiness medication. He tried to get us to relax, take away our worries, infuse us with hope. He laughed in a joking way or in a simple, childish way. He even went as far as to flick little stones and blades of grass at us. He scampered around, teasing, sparkling with optimism, trust, and faith in God. I think Srebra had forgiven him for everything, everything, and she seemed to have forgiven me as well, though she didn't speak to me at all. Over the course of those weeks, Bogdan rarely came to the hospital. I felt heavy in my soul asking myself why, but at the same time asked myself why I expected him to come every day like Darko did. Darko was Srebra's husband, while Bogdan was nothing to Srebra and me, after so many years in which we hadn't thought of each other. Why did I miss him after the one night in the hotel that we spent talking and talking and talking? Days later, an hour after we went into the operating room and were left alone to get accustomed to the room, to talk, and to see Darko, Bogdan also came. "Here?" Srebra was asking uncertainly. "Yes, here," the nurse confirmed, adding, "Don't worry, we'll sterilize everything again. Just relax and spend some time together." The operating room was enormous, like a high-school gymnasium. It was bright and equipped with the most modern medical instruments and machines.

It was Friday, September 13, 1996. "Friday the thirteenth," Srebra said that morning. "Yes, how did it happen to land on that date? Still, the evil eye won't get us," I said, thinking how our superstitions had come from our childhood, when, along with Roza and the other children, we would grab our hair whenever we saw a dead sparrow, or make a wish and count to three when an airplane flew over us, leaving a white line in its wake, or we would shout, "Pu-pu, mother from the grave, serpent in the grave," or we would say, "I swear to God," even when we hadn't told the truth, or we avoided utility poles and didn't walk under the wires lest some misfortune befall us, or we took care not to step over someone's leg because that would keep us from growing taller, or, in the village, our grandmother would tell us not to look at each other in the mirror before bed or we might be married off by a Gypsy, and we shouldn't light a fire before going to bed, because of the village superstition that the head of a match could make you wet yourself. There were many, many habits against superstitions from our childhood. But Friday the thirteenth had never been a part of that, for the simple reason that dates didn't interest us, especially during the summer, when time flowed like sweat in the Skopje heat, or like a village game, without end. It was September 13, 1996. Bogdan tumbled into our room, eyes aflame. How handsome he was! It was only now I noticed how good-looking Bogdan was, what sort of man he had become, his body firm under his tee shirt, which read "Love your shit as you love yourself," and his legs firm under his blue jeans. He carried a large plastic bag. He said, "Hi, I'm sorry I'm only just getting here, but I had so many things to do." Then out of the bag he pulled his hotel bed-warming jumpsuit and quickly put it on over his clothes. While we lay on the bed, propped up with pillows and staring at him, he hopped onto the bed. First he got in beside Srebra, pushing her over to my side, and covered the bed with his body in the jumpsuit. Then he jumped around to the other side, to my side, but I was already at the edge of the bed, so he lay down on top of me. Srebra automatically pulled her body as far away as our heads allowed. Bogdan lay on top of me, just for a second, then jumped up, saying, "There, I've warmed you and your bed. Now they can do the operation, and I can give back this suit because I'm not going to be a bed warmer anymore." I was confused, but Srebra laughed and said, "You're crazy." Then Darko came back into the room. He had been with us since early in the morning, and he sat down beside Srebra and stroked her face, and for an instant, his fingers also touched me. I immediately touched the icon of Zlata Meglenska in the pocket of my nightgown, and once again thought about how I would have to part with the icon, because we had been told very clearly we couldn't have anything on us, no rings, earrings, or anything. We would be under deep anesthesia and would be naked, and there could be nothing else in the room, not a scrap of fabric, nothing, not even my glasses, and when we awoke, we would already be in our room or some other room in the hospital where all our personal effects would be waiting for us. A crazy idea went through my mind. I took the icon from my pocket and handed it to Bogdan, saying, "Keep this for me until the operation's over." He took it and looked at it in his hand as if some image from his memory had flashed into his mind. He held it, seeming to not know what to say. "Just until the operation is over," I repeated, and he nodded. Soon the nurses came in and began to get the room ready. Bogdan appeared perplexed; he held the icon in his right hand, and with his left, he waved and said, "Good luck." Then he darted from the room. Darko first kissed me on the cheek, then bent over and kissed every inch of Srebra's face. His breath smelled of Orbit gum with a hint of watermelon. Suddenly, my mind seemed to expand, and I saw Srebra and me seated in Grandma's yard, holding big slices of watermelon, "the heart," as the older folks called it—the part they usually gave to the kids—and the juice flowed down between our legs, between our knees. It dripped all over us; our shorts were spattered; we ate and ate the red watermelon, and the smell of watermelon floated in my thoughts. I would fall asleep to the smell of watermelon, and perhaps Srebra would too, and we would wake with separate heads, separate lives. The nurse coughed discreetly; Darko pulled away from the bed, stood up, and said, "I'll have my fingers crossed for you." He left the room, and Srebra and I were silent. It was as if we both wished to say something. Yet we remained silent. It seemed obviously pathetic to say, "Forgive me" or "Good luck" or to make a joke, even ironically. So we were silent, and then the whole medical team was beside our special operating table, as well as another hundred or so doctors and nurses. Our doctor said, "There are a hundred people gathered here, just because of you," then he added, "Have you decided whom we should save, if we can only save one?" I said, "Srebra! She has a husband, she wants to have a child, she wants to be a lawyer…" Srebra interrupted me. "Zlata. Until now, she hasn't had anything of her own. Let her have her way for once." The nurse handed us a document to sign. I grabbed it as quickly as I could, and circled Srebra. Then I signed it. Srebra had no choice and signed it as well. Then our neurosurgeon angel stood over us and, with a smile, wagged his finger like at a child, saying, "Now don't you go and not survive on me." Injections followed, and a quiet, intoxicating plunge into sleep, into a state of peace, calm, blessing, nonexistence.

I did not witness anything that happened during this time, anything that happened to us, to me, or to Srebra. I heard everything from other people—Bogdan, Darko, our doctor. For the entire two days of the operation, Darko and Bogdan waited in the hallway. Only they know how they passed the time, which must have seemed to stretch into an eternity, an exhausting and powerless eternity. They slept in shifts on the benches in the hallway, and no one reproached them. On the contrary, a nurse brought them two sheets to cover themselves and offered them coffee and water. On Sunday morning, Bogdan left the hospital for a short time and took a bus to Manette Street in Soho, to the chapel of St. Barnabas, which the Macedonian Faith Association sometimes rented for holy services and whose chapel housed a center for the poor and homeless. The church was open, and a priest was celebrating the liturgy in Macedonian inside. It was the name day of Saint John the Baptist. Bogdan took my icon, clasping it in his hand throughout the service, and, as the city clock in Soho chimed ten, the liturgy ended. He looked around to see if anyone was watching, but the few worshipers were already leaving the church, and the priest wasn't behind the altar, so Bogdan walked quickly down the left aisle and stuck my icon under the left altar door, crossed himself, and hurried away. He had no idea why he did it. It just occurred to him. He thought that if he put the icon in a church, God would have mercy on Srebra and me, and the operation would succeed. At critical moments people do unconsidered things. I had told him to keep it for me, but he left it in the church. He couldn't carry the weight of the icon's might alone; he needed God's strength, and in London it was only at St. Barnabas where God was glorified in Macedonian. When he got back to the hospital, upset and worried by what he'd done, he was vacillating between repentance and approval of his actions. Darko was waiting for him in the hallway. "They're about to tell us," Darko said. "A nurse came out and said, 'It's all done.' We just have to wait a bit for the doctor to wash up." Indeed, after a short time, which seemed like an eternity, the doctor came into the hallway—tired, disheveled, unshaven, dejected, forever aged. He said to them, "Srebra did not survive." "Srebra did not survive, and Zlata is still uncertain. Her life is hanging by a thread, but the bleeding stopped half an hour ago, and we might be able to save her." No one said, "Srebra died," only "She did not survive." This wasn't clear to me when I awoke, and after avoiding the question, "Where is Srebra?" for a long time, I was told the same thing. "Srebra did not survive." "She bled every last drop," one of the nurses said. The doctor clouded over at the remark, and, holding my hands, he said, "We separated you. The vein was on your side. We transferred Srebra's blood to a different vein. There was no longer any connection between you. A hand could pass between your heads, but a moment later you both began to bleed. No matter what we did to stop the bleeding—and we did everything, everything—Srebra wouldn't stop. At one point, just at ten o'clock, her heart stopped, but you were bleeding less, and slowly you bled less and less until, at 10:25, it stopped. You survived. Srebra did not survive." I moved between states of unconsciousness—dream, or intoxication, I don't know which—a state of falling, almost hitting bottom in a deep chasm in which all that could be heard was the echo of a word: *No. No no no*... Later, perhaps the next day, Darko came into my room. He wept with his head in his hands, repeating, "Srebra did not survive. Srebra did not survive." The nurse immediately led him out. After that, the doctor wouldn't let either Darko or Bogdan into my room for several days. He sat beside my bed, always there when I awoke from half sleep, half unconsciousness. Before he would leave the room, he unlocked the door. In a moment between delirium and reality I thought, "I'm locked in," but, as if reading my thoughts, he turned and said, "Zlata, the hospital is flooded with journalists. There are even some from Macedonia. I have to protect you." "Where is Srebra?" I muttered, and it was that instant I realized that Srebra did not exist, that she would never exist again. "She's in the morgue. You will leave together. Everything is arranged. You need to get a bit stronger. Another two or three weeks." I would fall into the delirium of a therapeutic sleep and then awaken. A blunt pain throbbed above my temple, at the spot of the operation, but it wasn't physical pain, but spiritual, the pain of my— of our—life. For the rest of my life I would continue to feel Srebra's head next to mine. My head was wrapped completely with a thick casing of bandages. I was dazed, only half alive, without the strength to cry or to think. But in one of those eternal seconds, I remembered the icon. I desperately needed my little icon; it was the only thing I could grab onto, like a straw. Bogdan came in, his face frantic, aged, dejected. "The little icon," I whispered, "Did you save it for me?" He nodded, but didn't give it to me. I was too weak to ask him any more. I fell into a delirium and awoke for just a few seconds. When he next came, he gave it to me without a word. One side was chipped. A small piece of wood had broken off, as if it had been caught in a door. But I didn't ask what had happened, because I had no strength to ask. He told me Darko was gone; people from the Macedonian embassy had taken him away— he was at the end of his strength and had begun to fight with the journalists in the hallway. But he, Bogdan, was here, and would remain here, with me.

I knew nothing of what was happening. Darko hadn't gone to Skopje, but to the consul's house. He was waiting for the airplane that would fly us all back to Macedonia—me alive, Srebra dead in a casket, and him neither alive nor dead. Bogdan decided to go with us as well. It was all the same to me, I just couldn't believe Srebra no longer existed. All the time I was conscious, I wondered if our mother and father knew. Surely, they hadn't called to ask how things were going; I knew them too well to think that—they wouldn't dial a foreign telephone number on their own dime, even if it were a matter of life or death. They would wait for us to call them, after everything was finished, of course. But I hadn't called. Srebra did not survive. Surely they had learned from the media. After all, hadn't the doctor said that there were journalists from Macedonia? But Darko had called them. He told our mother, "Srebra did not survive." That's all. Then everyone cried and mourned, each in his or her own way. When I felt strong enough, I gathered my strength and called them from the hospital room. My mother's voice was barely audible. All she said was, "Ah, child." In the background, I could hear my father's sobs. I dropped the receiver. It was then that I, too, began to weep. I shouted and wept, I howled and sobbed. But

Srebra could no longer hear me. Had she not survived so I could survive? Hadn't we both signed the paper saying that she was to live? "Liars!" I shouted. "Liars!" "No," the doctor said, "the separation of your heads was the same down to the millimeter. But the vein was on your side. Her blood killed her. It gushed from the vein into which we had diverted it, refusing to flow properly; we could not stanch it. No force alive could have stopped it. No one from the entire team managed to compress the capillaries and stop the flow. But yours stopped on its own. At exactly 10:25, it seemed to just dry up."

My wound had been wrapped with tremendous care. I was ready to leave. Srebra's body was yearning for its grave in Macedonian soil. Accompanied by the Macedonian consul in London, we—Srebra in her casket, Darko, Bogdan, and I— left London by plane for Skopje. Journalists from around the world were at the airport, microphones and cameras focused on the plane. I made no statement. None of us did. We were silent, not looking at anyone. My head was wrapped in a special casing of different bandages. The lights from the cameras flashed in my eyes, which filled with tears behind my glasses. I don't know how we reached Skopje. A hearse was waiting for us. The casket carrying Srebra was placed inside and then brought directly to the chapel in the cemetery. We were ushered into a black Mercedes, and the driver discreetly asked the diplomat where we should go. "Home," I said at once. Bogdan gave him the address. There was no one in front of the entryway. Above, on the balcony, my father stood—a twig in black—swaying as if he might fall at any moment. It was as if he wasn't even there. Darko, Bogdan, and I climbed the stairs to the apartment. Dad stood in front of the door. Terrible scenes of pain and tears followed. My mother and father were withered, lethargic, with dark circles under their eyes.

My mother still managed to say to Darko, "You're guilty of this. You drove them to it." Darko said nothing and shielded himself with his arms gripped tightly across his chest. At first, they didn't recognize Bogdan. They had no idea who he was or what he wanted, thinking he was from the embassy. Then the neighbors began to gather and our relatives arrived. They expressed their sympathy to me, stroking my face. They were sorry for Srebra, and it seemed as if they were not particularly happy I had been the one to survive. It was clear in their eyes, not their lips, twisted in pain. Auntie Dobrila recognized Bogdan, who sat beside me on the arm of the couch in our parents' room, and she hugged him, then me, then him again. Darko stood by the window. The freezer gurgled, and the sound mixed with the sobs and cries in the room and through the whole apartment. Aunt Milka threw herself on the floor and cried, "Srebra! Ah, Srebra, where are you, apple of your Auntie's eye? Who will be the lawyer in our family now? You left a husband, a sister, a mother, a father..." and on and on. Auntie Magda and Uncle Kole also came, and they caressed my shoulder, saying, "Zlata, now Srebra's left us, too." When Roza died, he had said, "Roza has left us." Do I need to say the pain I felt after losing Srebra was twice as great as the pain of losing Roza? Just as my life was now twice as long, my pain was that much greater. When Roza died, I was a child. I wasn't fully aware of the enormity of what was happening, and never completely understood her death. It was as if she moved somewhere, as if she disappeared from my life, not into death, but to some other place. It was like when people move away, when there's sorrow and emptiness in the souls of those close to them, but not hopelessness as well. And the world is not so big; people may meet again sometime, somewhere. That's how Roza vanished from my life, at least when I thought about it now, having lost Srebra. The pain was similar, but not the same. I don't know. The burial was the day after our arrival in Skopje. The scenes repeated: sobs, my aunts fainting, our mother as pale as a dried-up rag, our father completely lost. I hadn't hugged my mother or my father even once. Everyone else embraced me, but not them. Grandpa didn't come. He was forbidden to, so as not to upset him in his old age. And he didn't have the strength after our grandmother's death, exactly forty days prior. My uncle, my mother's brother, came alone, without his wife or my cousins. What a curse had befallen us. Why had everyone in our fam ily started dying? Still, had my grandmother been alive, we would have had to bury her alongside Srebra. She couldn't have endured it. The burial was teeming with journalists. I said nothing. The priest, the same one who married Srebra and Darko, didn't stop chanting "Lord have mercy." Darko also said nothing. Nor did Bogdan. Not a word. Bogdan was sleeping at Auntie Dobrila's. No food was served after the burial. I won on that at least. "No one will eat or drink because of Srebra's death," I told my mother. "No one!" Everyone just went his own way. Darko asked me if I needed anything. He clearly needed strength and support. Evidently, his parents were able to offer it to him. I surely could not.

I don't know how the days following Srebra's burial passed, or—even more—the first nights. I lay in our bed alone, and beside my head, it was as if Srebra's head were there. But it wasn't, and that fact jolted me like an electric current. So many things went through my mind... I sought the house I had imagined in childhood that magically lulled me to sleep with its warmth and comfort; it no longer existed, but I still recalled how it looked in my dreams. Now it was only an empty house, lifeless, abandoned by its own tenants.

The time passed between delirium and reality, between our bed and the bench in the courtyard of our school, where, in the evening when the school day was done, Bogdan and I sat for hours, sometimes without uttering a single word. We sat and looked at the windows of our primary school, which hadn't been renovated in all these years, at the monument no longer sporting the bust of our patron, at the fountain that Cvetko, our art teacher, had made—it had been placed in the schoolyard with great ceremony, but water never flowed from it. Also missing its bust was the half-hidden monument to Josip Broz Tito in front of the windows, where recess had been held and where our teacher Stojna gave Srebra and me a doll named Leila to play with. That's where we made our one and only little umbrella out of matchsticks bound together with red wool thread, and our only International Women's Day card with grains of corn and wheat glued to it, which Srebra and I then tucked under the couch in the kitchen along with an egg slicer as a present for our mother on the eighth of March. How our hearts had beat, waiting for her to come home from work. When she arrived, we poked both our heads under the couch and pulled out the present to give to her. But she just laughed, broadly, loudly, saying, "That's just what we need—an egg slicer." But when Srebra and I had examined the egg slicer in its little yellow box in the Slavija store, we had thought how wonderful it would be to have such a thing at home, so that when we boiled eggs for Easter we would be able to place them under the knifelike wires, and the egg would split into ten beautiful yellow and white slices. It was this school where Bogdan had read aloud his essay, "When You Hit Rock Bottom." It was from this school that we had walked in rows of two toward Bogdan's little house to see his dead mother. From this school, we went to see the dead parents of other classmates: Natalija's father, Dejan's mother. Srebra and I returned to this school after Roza died. Bogdan remembered the names of all our classmates, all the teachers and principals. He knew exactly who had sat where, with whom, what sort of winter jackets they wore, what kind of boots, if they had sneakers, who wore glasses, who had lice. Bogdan remembered everything. He even remembered the song "I wander the streets…," which our classmate Juliana sang on every field trip and during breaks between classes. We sat on the bench, which had only two planks remaining, inscribed with names, arrows, hearts, and a variety of sayings. We looked at our childhood school, into emptiness, and Bogdan sang, "I wander the streets" in a quiet voice. I wanted to die, only that. I could shove my head in the oven or hang myself from the chandelier that had always hung from the ceiling a bit off-center in our childhood room, or drink a glass of the hydrochloric acid our mother used to clean the toilet bowl. I wanted to die instantly, for the ground to open beneath me and to simply fall, already dead, into my own grave, with no lead-up to death, no preliminaries. For the earth to close above me and for no one to think about me anymore— about Zlata with the head, the one who survived, while her sister, Srebra, did not. But I was alive, and all those thoughts and memories flooding my mind after Srebra's burial were my organism's self-defense. Life struggles for itself; like when your temperature rises and your body signals that it's unwell, fighting the attacking viruses with heat. That is why I had those senseless memories and suicidal thoughts. I was battling against the pain. The left side of my head was still bandaged, which intensified the feeling that Srebra's head was still there, bound with mine. Nothing could fill the feeling of emptiness I felt on that side. My left hand had been suddenly freed, but it didn't know what to do in space; it had not yet learned how to extend horizontally, wave, grasp, take. I missed Srebra. I missed her body right there, right beside mine, her hair intertwining with mine, her breathing next to mine. Srebra and I separated so we could stop being "invalids," and no longer have a "physical defect," but now, with my body alone in the universe, without hers, I felt that the lack of her body, of her head, was a deficit. I felt I was missing an arm, a leg, a head. Now I was truly an invalid. Bogdan understood my pain, but my emptiness was something he couldn't quite understand, the lostness, the powerlessness without Srebra's body next to mine. "You'll get used to it," he said, "but I can't guarantee you'll get used to the fact that she died." "Srebra did not survive," I corrected him. "Srebra did not survive the operation she wanted so much and had anticipated since she was a child. Much more than I, she had longed for us to be separated. It was her choice. At any price. But I don't know if she was really aware of the price." In those weeks, Bogdan went to his mother's grave several times. Alone. I went to Srebra's, most often alone, but usually ran into Darko, who would then leave. He was slowly but surely distancing himself from me. He would leave me alone with my sister. He asked me if I wanted to come over and get my things. I told him I couldn't; I didn't want to go back there—it would be too difficult. "Please, bring me the books, all of Srebra's and my books," I told him. The following day, he brought me a box with the books, along with several bags of my clothes and other incidentals, such as makeup. "I'll keep all of Srebra's things," he said, "in case you need anything." He also called my parents and asked if they needed anything—perhaps to be driven somewhere—but they always refused. Our father was in no condition to drive our beat-up Škoda. His hands trembled too much, and he was constantly on the edge of tears. He had no one else to drive him to the cemetery, and it was hard to get there by bus. "I have to pay fifty denars to go, and fifty denars to get home," I heard my mother explaining to Aunt Milka about why she didn't go to the cemetery more often. Then she wept, sobbing into the receiver, but my aunt always talked over her. I couldn't stand those scenes. I tossed and turned in the bed in our room. I lay there reading. Always the same things. Three books Bogdan brought me from downtown one day. "From Sonja, the used bookseller," he said. Three thick volumes of Marina Tsvetaeva in a Serbian translation: one volume entitled *Songs and Poems*; another called *On Art and Poetry and Portraits*; and a third, *Autobiographical Prose: My Pushkin; Letters*. Each was inscribed, "In love." I read the books in no particular order, without bending the pages. Tsvetaeva's songs, her letters, her notes, her prose, everything, everything. I understood her, and she understood me. It was a different type of reading, different from everything else. I read, but from inside it, as if in sync with the rhythm of her writing. Each sentence was also mine. Everything that was hers was mine, and everything of mine was hers. With one hand, I turned the pages of the three books, with the other, I squeezed the icon. It poked me with its broken edge as my life, stretched like a corpse between Marina Tsvetaeva and Saint Zlata Meglenska, slowly revived. My life wanted to survive. Today, I know I wouldn't have survived that period of my life without Marina Tsvetaeva and Saint Zlata Meglenska. I know. And not without Bogdan, although in the days right after Srebra's burial, I didn't know what I felt toward him. Gratitude, that is certain: a shoulder to cry on; support; a protector, although I don't know from what or from whom; someone to recognize that I existed, that

I had survived—something the journalists, with whom I didn't wish to speak, wanted to document more than anything. I wasn't ready. And never would be. Any contact with the media felt like a desecration of Srebra, as if I were becoming famous on her account, on her back, over her dead body. On television, I saw Darko give a statement about the money that had been designated for his wife's and her sister's operation. "Who will pay back the money, given that your wife didn't survive?" the reporter asked. "Will you sue the hospital in London?" Darko's face burned, and he said, "No, I won't. The chief neurosurgeon did everything possible, and even more. The chances for survival were very small, but both of them agreed to the operation. They signed off; each took responsibility for their separation." The journalist ended the conversation by saying, "Their risk, but our bill." I was stunned.

Bogdan told me he had to leave. He had to return to London and find another job. At Auntie Dobrila's, he just slept and gobbled down his breakfast. Auntie Dobrila would sometimes invite me for breakfast as well, usually when she was making cornmeal mush with yogurt and cheese. The day before he left, Auntie Dobrila asked, "Well, children, are you thinking about the future or not? How are you going to live with one of you in London and the other in Skopje? You've got to come up with a plan." The food stuck in our throats. We were startled by the thought. It was the first time we grasped the weight of the separation before us. Having found each other by chance once, there surely wouldn't be another chance. We left the apartment. In the entryway, on the stairs leading to the door where Roza used to live, Bogdan got up the courage to hug me. "Auntie Dobrila's right," he said. "How are we going to live from now on?" For the two of us, the question was of vital importance. "After all, when you were little, playing the fortune-telling game, didn't you get a husband whose name started with the letter *B*?" Bogdan asked. "Aren't I that man? The city was to begin with an *S*, and we're in Skopje now. I'm not a multimillionaire, but I will be. And we'll have only one child, although that's a pity." How was it possible Bogdan remembered the childish game we had played while he sat, immersed in the crossword puzzles from *Brain Twisters*? "Twenty-three years old," he said. "That's when you wanted to get married." "That's in the past already," I said, and felt how true it was, how our game had been tragically fulfilled, in the most tragic way possible. Except for me. B was here; he would be a multimillionaire; he was from Skopje even if he lived in London; and it wasn't so difficult to have one child. A wave of shame, fear, confusion, passion, and excitement washed over me, something I hadn't felt before that moment. My God! I felt desire. I wanted to caress Bogdan. I wanted him to have me. I wanted to have him. As if I would find a balm for my wound, for my misfortune, in that gratification. The excitement was stronger than I was. I dragged him down the stairs to the basement. The laundry room was always open, and inside, there was only an old wooden table and a few pails of cheese. Everything was dusty and covered in spiderwebs. I closed the door behind us. I kissed him. And he me. We kissed passionately, stroking each other. Then Bogdan laid me on top of the old dusty table. He penetrated me as if for the last time, but it was my first, the first time with a man's penis. We closed our mouths so we wouldn't cry out too loud, and through the small basement window I saw blades of grass swaying back and forth. It took us a long time to regain our calm. Our hearts beat like crazy; we hugged and kissed each other some more. I think we both understood we wouldn't be able to live without each other. And that was that, as they say.

Bogdan left. I stayed with my parents, lost, broken, and empty, but at the same time, full of love, Eros, and a feeling of belonging. I belonged to Bogdan. I would do anything to be with him. Just as Srebra had done everything to be with Darko. In fact, even the operation had been because of Darko. I had to return to London. But there was no way for that to happen. My checkups were with a neurosurgeon at the Skopje clinic. He said the wound was healing well and I was a world phenomenon and asked whether I was aware that such operations were extremely rare and were usually failures, but not in my case. "You survived," he said. "But Srebra did not," I said. "Yes," he said, "but it's unrealistic to expect both of you to have survived. You gambled with your lives and each other's. Russian roulette," he said. "That's what your operation was. That's the reality. Didn't you get separated so you could have a better, higher quality life? This is your chance. Now go do what you want. Be what you really are." Yes, everything was as the doctor said, but I didn't know who I was, I didn't know what to do with myself. It was as if my *I* was inseparable from Srebra's *I* and now that she no longer existed, I no longer had a singular *I*. The only thing I knew was that I wanted to be with Bogdan, wherever he was. I was drawn to him with my heart, my body, my life. My mother, father, and I scraped along in our sorrow, each in our own way, but most often in silence. My mother put on her blue robe. She wore it all the time, to let us know she was clearly not feeling well. Without Srebra, it was as if we had nothing else in common; her death alienated us even more. Surely, I was too harsh in my judgment, but I felt it would have been better had Srebra lived and not I. She and Darko would finally have been able to live like a real husband and wife; they could have had a child. Srebra would have become a lawyer, just as she had dreamed, and it would have pleased our parents. Everything would have been more normal had she been the one to survive. But I had no reason to live—I had just scraped through university in a field I didn't like. It was hard to imagine myself in a law office or courtroom. I had no prospects, no boyfriend, though I was at the age when I was expected to have one. I was twenty-five years old, and I had nothing. Had I died, perhaps my parents would have started to love me. They wouldn't have visited my grave, because it would be too complicated for them, just as it was to visit Srebra's. They couldn't manage to get to the cemetery by car or by bus; my mother was always sick with something; my father's hands trembled so much that he couldn't drive; taxis were expensive; buses were inconvenient, and so they'd remember me for their entire lives, and mourn for me, but wouldn't visit my grave. Over time, my father would start dressing in brown again when he went out; my mother would wear her robe at home, but would occasionally put on a black blouse and go out. That's how their lives would go on, filled with my death, as they were filled with Srebra's now, but empty of my life.

One day, when I returned from wandering aimlessly around the city—for the first time wearing contact lenses, which itched and brought tears to my eyes, beneath a pair of sunglasses, wrapped in a shawl, a hat, and a heavy cape, and looking down so no one would recognize me—I noticed that my mother had been in my room and had glued a calendar of naked women over the poster of the unforgettable Matevski exhibit of luminous spheres at the Daut Pasha gallery. The calendar was for 1997. One of the neighbors had probably given it to her. "Yes, I put it there, so you would know what day it is. New Year's is coming," my mother said, but I angrily tore down the calendar and ripped it up. Half of the Matevski poster came off with it; only one complete sphere remained on the wall. I recalled Srebra remarking that Matevski had painted us. "Our heads," she had said, as the two of us walked, exhilarated and joyful, across the stone bridge. I was boiling with fury, rage, and sadness. I could no longer endure this home that was not a home, the non-home to which Srebra would never return, even to visit.

It's said that when you really, really don't want something or when you want something very, very much, God the omnipotent takes notice. Toward the middle of December 1996, a letter arrived for me in Darko's mailbox. Darko brought it over right away, and I noticed that he had become even thinner. He was growing a beard, and was still dressed in black. "You don't come to Krivi Dol," he said. No, I couldn't go where I had gone with Srebra, where everyone would look at me with candid and sincere pity in their eyes. I went to Saint Petka every week, and there, standing awkwardly in the corner, I was alone with God. "I'm going to join the monastery," Darko said. "There's no more life for me out in the world." And with that he quickly left. The letter was from the London hospital. It was a polite, formal letter from the hospital administration, and it didn't fail to include this sentence: "Once again, we are very sad about what happened during the operation." Then, "As a gesture of support and of our condolences for the death of your sister, we would like to return the funds to you that were spent on the operation. The entire team has agreed to give back their pay for your operation, and through this gesture, we hope the operation can be considered a humanitarian act that will serve to contribute to the development of contemporary neurosurgery. We ask that you send us your bank account number so we may forward you the funds." I couldn't believe it. That money wasn't mine. It wasn't ours. The Health Insurance Fund had paid, not through any regular process, but through connections. If Darko's father weren't the vice president of the opposition party, there would simply be no way we would have gotten the funds. Not a single doctor in Macedonia signed any form authorizing an operation abroad. That agreement was signed via some personal and party deals in which neither Srebra nor I was included. That Srebra had become a member of the party was an act she later had no time to reconsider. She left any thoughts about her connection to the party for after the operation. Surely, without her signature, Darko's father's party wouldn't have helped us. Srebra had undersigned her death, and my life.

I called the hospital in England, and told them the funds weren't mine, but had to be returned to the Health Insurance Fund of Macedonia. I had nothing to do with it. Their answer, however, surprised me: the money couldn't be returned to a state institution, because they wished to make the return of the funds an act of moral support for me, and for my family. It was precisely for that reason that every member of the team refused payment, and they hadn't considered returning it to the fund. They didn't trust Macedonian institutions and didn't believe the fund would give it to me, so I could begin a new life. The fund had made the payment, but that was the end of their involvement. What could I do? I faxed them my account number. By the next day, they had paid me 200,000 pounds. I was confused and astonished. I didn't know what to do with the money. I called Darko, and asked him to meet with me. We met in a tea house in the Old Market. He hadn't yet left for the monastery. He had aged a decade. Only the eyes behind his glasses were still the same. I told him what had happened. Darko said he had to think. He called me several hours later, his voice trembling. He was upset. He told me he had spoken with his father and told him about the money. His father said there was no question: The money had to be divided, 50,000 pounds for me, 50,000 pounds for the party, and 100,000 pounds to be returned to the fund. If it hadn't been for his people, he said, the fund would have remained deaf to our entreaties. Darko added that his father said: "Zlata isn't aware of what we did to get that money released, the pressure my men had to exert on the people at the fund. I even had to meet with the vice-premier, although we don't get along. She isn't aware of the sacrifices the party made for her, even though she didn't wish to join it." And he added: "The money has to be divided with the party. We are anticipating an election campaign, and we need it." I was silent. Darko said, "That's what politicians are like. That's why I left the party. I don't want to have anything more to do with that world. Nothing." I had never found myself in a situation like that, involving financial machinations. The people in England had returned the funds, and their role in the process was done, but I, with 200,000 pounds in my account, felt poorer than I had ever been. I didn't tell my parents. I told no one except Darko. Bogdan was far away. He called me once a week, and in those conversations, we mostly exchanged sentiments of love, but we rarely spoke about our everyday concerns and activities. He told me he was looking for work but it was difficult to find. He said, "I have money, though; that's not the problem." I didn't tell him I also had a lot of money, too much for my needs. I couldn't tell him that over the phone. I did not take a single pound from the bank. I didn't know what the outcome with the party would be. But Darko's father did not give in. He called me personally and was quite cold, as if he hadn't been Srebra's father-in-law, and wasn't Darko's father. He told me I had to go to their office immediately so we could take care of the business. That's what he said: that I had to go. I greeted his team. The women looked at me with pity and curiosity. They expressed their condolences and offered me some juice. Darko's father came in, and, behind him, the president of the party. "How are you?" Darko's father asked me, but I declined to answer, shrugging my shoulders. I asked him, "You?" but he only said, "We're getting by," and then, professionally, he opened an envelope in front of him, took out a sheet of paper, and said, "This is all the information concerning the payment: bank, account number, address, everything. Take care of it today." The party president smiled kindly. He said in English, "Fifty-fifty," then added, "One hundred…," laughing at his quip. "One hundred and fifty thousand goes to our account, and we'll return 100,000 pounds to the fund. Don't worry about that." They didn't say anything else to me. They had called me solely to give me the banking information.

I took the information, confused and upset. I held it in my hand all the way to the bank in the shopping mall. When I went into the bank, I was struck by the smell of potato stew. Where was it coming from? People were pushing and shoving each other in front of the counter, with no respect for the queue. I stood with the piece of paper in my hand and waited, not paying attention to the movement around me. I finally found myself in front of the window. "I would like to transfer 150,000 pounds from my account to this account," I said, and handed the paper to a teller with longish hair, who was holding a cigarette in his left hand and a pen in his right. He looked at me as if I had fallen from Mars. "How much?" he asked. I repeated what I had said. Around me, people began to whisper, elbowing each other and staring at me. The teller looked at me in disbelief. "Come around back," he said, and let me in through the small door by the teller's window.

He walked in front of me, taking a drag of his cigarette, and knocking ashes on the floor. He led me to a small room with a table, two chairs, and a file cabinet. "Let's see what this is all about," he said. I told him that it was aboveboard. He remembered seeing me on television. "Who doesn't know about the Skopje twins who went to London for an operation!" I was wearing contact lenses and had dyed my short hair red. People no longer recognized me. He expressed his condolences. He said transferring the money was not so simple. The bank could move the money from my account to the account of the opposition party, but it couldn't happen just like that. There had to be an invoice. And had I been given a guarantee that the party would return the money to the fund? The fund could demand the money from me later or take me to court. Anything could happen. "There is no sympathy when money is in question," he said, "I work at a bank. I see things." He told me to think about it and then come back. I left, even more upset.

That evening, as I watched the evening news in my room on the small black-and-white television, listening as the voice of the anchorwoman doubled the voice coming from the dining room, where my mother and father were watching the same news program, the newsman announced the lead item: "Scandal! The surviving twin from the operation in London paid for by our Health Insurance Fund is now being bullied by the opposition party to transfer 150,000 pounds into its account! After the medical team in London decided to return the 200,000 pounds to the surviving twin as a humanitarian gesture, the opposition party, which evidently convinced the fund, through bribery and manipulation, to finance the operation, is now trying to take the money for itself! The party claims it will return 100,000 pounds to the fund and keep

50,000 pounds for the upcoming campaign. The surviving twin will only get to keep 50,000 pounds of the money the hospital in London gave exclusively to her." I think my heart stopped. The vein left to me after the operation gurgled non-stop, throbbing in my temple, my ear, my throat, my brain.

"Now that's a fine business!" my mother shouted as loudly as possible from the dining room, and then she burst into my room. She spouted off at me as if I were the one at fault for this affair. Harsh words were spoken that evening, many angry utterances and expressions of hatred, with an absence of affection, appalling attacks and insults. There was only one line all three of us were careful not to cross: naming Srebra. No one mentioned her. No reference was made to her in any context. Thank God we preserved her from our human baseness. That evening, I once again asked myself why I had been the one to survive and not Srebra. She had every reason to live; I had none. They should have cut my head in half, leaving only the side attached to Srebra's. They should have removed everything that remained in my head, removed it piece by piece, so the vein on which Srebra's life depended would remain untouched and the piece of skin and veins from my head would be left attached to hers. Her hair would have grown on that side to hide the wound. She would have been completely healthy and normal. Perhaps at night, my skin on her temple would have prevented her from falling asleep; it might have poked her until she pressed down on it, and that would have weighed on her, but she would have just turned on her other side and fallen asleep in Darko's embrace. Why hadn't Srebra and I agreed on that kind of operation? That kind of operation could even have been performed in Skopje. Without the money from the fund and without joining the party. Why had I been so selfish that I, too, wanted to survive?

Now I was alive but dead, completely dead. I lay on my back, just as when Srebra and I had lain there, and I felt that it was my grave. I would be buried alive in it.

The next day, early in the morning, I called Bogdan. I told him I was coming to London. I would try to find a way forward there. "Either with you or without you," I said. "With me," he replied. I went to the bank and took out every last pound. I hurried to party headquarters with 200,000 pounds in my purse. Inside, I pulled out the piles of money the bank teller had bound and numbered for me. I set exactly 50,000 pounds on the table. The only one there was the cleaning woman, washing the floor. She said everyone was in the president's office having a special meeting. "Here's their money," I said and left. I continued on to the Health Insurance Fund. There, I nearly created a scandal in the office of the director's secretary. She didn't want to let me go in. I took out the biggest pile of money. I was certain it was 100,000 pounds because the bank employee was a true professional. I left it on the table in front of her. "Here it is. I sincerely thank you for helping my sister and me get separated," I said to her. She said, "I had nothing to do with that." At that moment, the director came out, saw the money, and said, "But your sister didn't survive the operation." "Yes, but I did," I said, leaving. "But what am I supposed to do with cash? They'll put me in jail," he shouted after me, but it wasn't my concern. Then I went to the British Embassy. They already knew me there. They had tried to reach me by phone, they said, but my mother told them I had gone out that morning and she didn't know where. I was led into a large room, where I explained everything to them. The employee was stunned by the way I had handed the money in cash to the party and Health Insurance Fund. He said, "That's not allowed. You graduated with a law degree, didn't you? There are laws, administrative procedures, and regulations. You can't simply walk around Skopje with that much money, leaving it in offices." I responded that I was aware of that but it's what I had done, and I'd come for an expedited visa. I planned to go to London immediately, on January 1. I would not remain in Skopje. I planned to enroll in a graduate program but had to meet the application deadline. With 50,000 pounds, I was sure to find some program. "That's for certain," the employee said, "We'll see what we can do. I can't guarantee anything."

The media didn't stop reporting on the money. They had a statement from the president of the opposition party, who said that no one had asked me for it directly but that I had, of my own accord, given them 50,000 pounds. The director of the fund said, "Most likely, the surviving sister has some sort of mental deficiency, which is why she came in today and left 100,000 pounds on the table." I was the only one who didn't give a statement. I had raced around the city wrapped in a shawl and wearing a wool hat and large sunglasses, as I disbursed the money, then went home by bus. That evening, in addition to being on all the other news programs, my—our—incident was the topic of the program *Open Club*. Experts from various fields spoke about the situation with the twins, or, rather, the twin. Among them was Darko's father. The debate was sharp. Some thought the money should be returned in full to the fund so someone else could use it for medical expenses. There were so many sick and dying children in the country, but no one offered them help. Others said that, since Great Britain had given the money to me as a gesture of support and condolences, and not to the fund or the party, the money should belong to me—to serve, at least, as material compensation for the loss of my sister. One even said that England should take the money back and not play games with humanitarian acts or gestures, since Macedonia had not yet reached that level of thinking and what they'd done had only created difficulties and nothing else. A government official went after Darko's father, asking him why there was no documentation of the incident, why the request for funds hadn't been made public, and why there was no written verification that the fund had actually paid for the operation. Darko's father said he had met with the vice-premier and it was delusional of the public to think the government didn't know about the case. "I mean, how?" Darko's father said. "The vice-premier, the director of the fund, and I ate lunch together at Del Fufo and agreed to help the twins. But, to avoid kicking up a lot of dust, we decided we would bring the case to the public after the operation." "Yes, but you helped them because one of them, the one who died, was your daughter-in-law," another guest interjected. "Had it been someone else, you wouldn't have lifted a finger." All sorts of things were said at that round table. Afterward, viewers called in, and every single one asked where I was, why I wasn't participating in the broadcast, and then gave their own interpretations of the situation, radical, trivial, or even shameless. The impression it gave was that the fund had taken a bribe to pay for the operation and the opposition had hidden the payment. And the government had played dumb so as not to appear like it wasn't helping one of its citizens. Potato stew, just like the smell in the bank. I pulled the television's plug from its socket and didn't plug it back in before I left.

I received my visa on December 31, 1996. That night, I barely slept. My mother and father went to bed at ten o'clock. We didn't wish each other a Happy New Year, even after we awoke. On January 1, 1997, I went to Srebra's grave in the morning. I told her everything. I cleared the snow from her grave, and then with the snow made a small snowman on the grave. I tore out the two inside buttons from my coat to make his eyes. I drew a mouth on him with lipstick—smiling from ear to ear. I took the red hat from my head and I put it on him. I blew him and Srebra a kiss, and left. My plane was departing that afternoon. I put my most important possessions into my black suitcase—a few small things and some photographs. I was unable to unstick the poster of Matevski's luminous spheres from the door. I kissed Marina Tsvetaeva on the poster hanging on the door to the room, but didn't take it. I wanted it to be there if I ever came to that apartment again, that home, so that someone would be waiting for me with love. I took Tsvetaeva's books. And I put the small icon in my pocket, checking it three times to make sure it didn't fall out. I called a taxi. My father carried my suitcase downstairs. In the hallway, my mother kissed me quickly on the cheeks and said, "Oh, child!" My father wept beside the taxi. I felt sorry for him. For myself. For Srebra. For my mother. Everything in our lives was broken. I got into the taxi and left.

1997–2000

Bogdan was waiting for me in London. We kissed chastely, and our noses bumped. We laughed and rubbed them together, giving each other Eskimo kisses. A train would take us to Victoria station. An old woman who had been on my flight from Skopje got on the train. She was a granny dressed in a black knit vest and carrying a bag and suitcase. She sat down across from us and asked to see our tickets, pointing at them with her finger. We gave them to her. Then she mumbled in Macedonian, "twelve times two is twenty-four." Bogdan and I laughed, but didn't say anything. I looked at the London suburbs out the window, a hodgepodge of Dickensian houses and more contemporary structures. The Macedonian woman got out at the station before Victoria. We took another train to Shoreditch, an area in East London. Dark wood stairs led to the attic apartment of building number 130–132. Bogdan rented it a long time ago when he turned eighteen and Auntie Stefka, the woman he had adopted from our neighborhood, told him it was time for him to leave Brighton and confront London. The apartment belonged to a Turkish family, whom I never met. The windows looked down on the street and some neighborhood bars. In the evening, starting at around six, people gathered in front of the bars with drinks in one hand, briefcases in the other, to celebrate the end of yet another workday. Sometimes, Bogdan and I went down and had a drink: I usually drank tea; Bogdan, a glass of red wine. Although we had known each other since childhood and he was with me at critical moments in my life, it was only now that we were living together that we got to know each other as a man and a woman—as girlfriend and boyfriend. He had already given up the job as a bed warmer at the time of Srebra and my successful, or rather unsuccessful, operation. Indeed, how should I think of the operation—as a success or a failure? I survived, but I didn't consider the operation a success, because only I had survived, and not Srebra. The medical profession, however, looked more positively on such results. And, according to the media, the operation was a success. In similar situations, the normal outcome is for neither patient to survive, and seen in that light, ours had been successful.

I contacted the doctor at the clinic. He said that he could hardly wait to see me, and I had an appointment with him that same day. He told me I was in great shape. The wound had healed, and the world's shortest pageboy looked great on me, as did the color. He also noticed I was wearing contact lenses and said, "That's a change for the better." He said he would like to x-ray my head to see that everything inside was in order. Everything was fine. It was as if I'd never been conjoined with Srebra, as if we'd never shared a vein. "Externally, things are fine," I said. "But I feel an emptiness in the spot where I was joined with Srebra. It's as if I'm missing a piece of flesh, as if I'm missing that part of my head." He nodded, and said, "That's normal, but with time you won't have that sensation," and I wondered how he knew, given that he had never had a Siamese twin with whom he was conjoined above the ear.

"How do you feel psychologically?" he asked. "The worst I've ever felt in my life," I said. "I have nightmares, and during the day, my conscience gnaws at me, and I don't know how to deal with it. I have crying fits and bouts of despair. I feel lost. Sometimes, something like hysteria comes over me, or I fall into a depression. I can only function normally when I'm with Bogdan. I'm afraid I'm not going to be able to live like this." The doctor nodded like he understood. "Should I see a psychiatrist?" I asked. He looked at me awhile, thinking about how to respond.

"In conventional medical opinion, cases like yours can't proceed without psychiatric intervention," he said. "I'm personally against it, however. I am more in favor of people finding their own way, their own remedy, depending on their individual natures. Think about a time when things in your life were good, when you felt happy. Was it in yoga class? Or during meditation, if that has been a part of your life? Perhaps the Hare Krishna chant fills you with hope. Or Sunday mass? Try to recall the happiest moments in your life and repeat those experiences, those feelings. In painful moments, we should return to the things that have offered us support, and when we felt truly ourselves." He was serious and no longer joking around. I left his office with an open mind, like a book waiting to be written. I told Bogdan about it. He said, "That's good advice. Look, you're in London. You're with me. Take your time, relax. You've weathered the worst of this crisis. After a while, you'll see that everything will be better. And if you need help, do what the doctor said. I'll do everything I can for you. Everything I couldn't do for my mother."

I still wasn't accustomed to sleeping on my side, but after passionate lovemaking in all sorts of positions he dreamed up, as if pulled from the Kama Sutra, Bogdan turned my back toward him and pulled his body close to mine, curving into an arc, hugging me with his right arm. That is how we fell asleep, in a constant state of excitement, because I felt his penis against my body all night, and I would fall asleep only when he began to snore. I would carefully pull myself from his embrace and turn onto my back. I'd then sleep with my legs spread and my hands on my chest—sometimes crossed, the way Sister Zlata showed me long ago—but I had nightmarish dreams in which my head would fall from my neck and roll away. I was still alive, but without a head. Bogdan told me I would sometimes cry out in my sleep and wake him. He would shower me with kisses, and then, a moment later, spread my legs and penetrate me without foreplay, and, panting, he would come before I was fully awake. He would make Turkish coffee, we would have breakfast, and then he would leave. "To go chase work," he would say, but it wasn't quite clear to me exactly what he meant by that. He would return in the afternoon with a whole pile of supermarket catalogs filled with coupons for prize games, or magazines with prize crossword puzzles or announcements for quiz shows. He was obsessed with them and not looking, evidently, for any serious work. His auntie Stefka put money in his account once a month. "Like a paycheck," I said, but he replied, "Yes, that's what it looks like, but it's only pocket money. She's still trying to make up for telling me when I was eighteen years old that she was tired of being an adopted mother and I should become independent and find my own apartment in London."

I decided to do what Bogdan said. Take my time. Find relief for my soul. But I could not do it alone. I felt torn inside, in my very center. Some kernel inside me had begun to sprout, to grow and blossom, but its scent was not beautiful. Everything was mixed up inside: Srebra, God, Bogdan, love, faith, and now sex as well. It was as if I were not one being, but many rolled into one, each one ashamed in front of the others. They reproached one another, sinned, made mistakes, set stumbling blocks in each other's path, mocked and destroyed one another. How immature I was, how inexperienced both personally and with others. I had never seen farther than Srebra, and now, left to myself, I fell from one existence into another. The icon of Saint Zlata Meglenska poked me in my pocket, and Bogdan's penis under the blankets. I always felt the absence of Srebra's right ear beside my left. I nearly fainted, horrified, whenever I saw myself alone in the mirror. My nerves and my soul churned both day and night. I didn't know how to pull myself from my accumulated pain and impotence. I contemplated what event had meant the most to me, what my moment of greatest happiness, peace, and spiritual fulfillment had been. The chipped edge of the icon in the pocket of my sweat suit jabbed me again, as it had at the doctor's. There was no question: it had been the short stay in Sister Zlata's convent. Without a doubt, that is where I had been the happiest, the most satisfied, the most fulfilled; Srebra's head and mine were conjoined, but we had such joy in our souls. We both felt it, though Srebra didn't want to demonstrate her happiness the way I did. It was there I discovered my song, the *Cherubic Hymn*. It was there that I felt blessed, blissful, because of God's presence within me for the first time. The convent would cure my sadness. I didn't intend to live a monastic life, like Darko, but I would go to the monastery for a period of time so I could return to life. To my life with Bogdan. I needed a long church service, confession, Communion, a conversation with a priest, a stroll with a radiant nun or monk, who, with downcast eyes, would call me *sister*. I didn't know where to seek such salvation in London, a shoulder like that to cry on. The only church in London Bogdan knew about was the chapel of St. Barnabas in Soho, where a Macedonian service was held occasionally. I needed something more. I needed someplace more authentic: a spiritual community. I needed brothers and sisters in God, who, I thought, would know how to heal me with their love—not corporeal, but angelic, and as deep as the universe—from my loss, from my own conscience, from my pain. There are no accidents in life; I was sure of that. And one day, at the Liverpool Street station, I was checking to see what track the train to Hyde Park was on, and I noticed a group of two women and three men walking toward the ticket window. One of the men was carrying a sign in English that said, "Essex, Monastery of Saint John the Baptist." Those words spun in my mind for several hours while I sat in Hyde Park looking at the lake, drowning in my depression, my mind otherwise empty. I repeated the word Essex, as if it were connected to something I knew, but I couldn't remember what. And then it came to me. I remembered that once, during a service in Krivi Dol, the priest mentioned the name Essex as he listed all the patriarchs and bishops in the world while blessing the bishop at the monastery in Essex. That place name had stuck in my mind, but I had forgotten about it. Later, I asked Bogdan where Essex was, and whether he had ever been there. He answered that, around the time he and his adopted mother settled in England, they had gone to Essex with her sister and her sister's partner. They had gone to the church there, and inside, it was just like the church in our neighborhood where his mother had taken him for holidays before she fell ill. There were candles burning, and the scent of icon lamps; there were icons, the women's heads were covered with kerchiefs, the mens' were bowed. Bogdan said they just went in and listened for a few minutes before going to eat at some big restaurant—he didn't remember where. "It was only later I found out that the only Orthodox monastery in England is in Essex, but I never went back," he said. "Do you want us to go?" he asked. I wanted to go, but alone.

It was only thirty-five miles from London. I took a train to Witham, then a taxi to the monastery. Evening service had just begun. I made my way to a corner on the left side, where I pressed my head to the wall. I, too, wore a kerchief, black with white dots. Huddled in the corner, I felt my head open. I felt my scar slowly dry up, and then, without blood or pain, the flesh where our heads had been conjoined opened, and flowing in, almost like a physical sensation, like a warm and summery gust of wind, the evening service entered: all the prayers and hymns, each sound around me came in, and outside there wasn't a single sound; my head had become their sanctuary. Of its own accord, the door of my head, a well-insulated door that didn't let in sounds, closed behind them; the incision from the operation vanished. It smoothed over, invisible. It no longer existed. Only the most luxurious sound remained, the voices of the nuns and monks from the monastery. Songs to God's glory and prayers for the human soul. I sat transfixed until the last person left the church. I turned around. On the wall behind me, where my head had been pressed, was a small fresco of Saint Christopher. The child Jesus was on his shoulder and he said to him, "Why are you so heavy, child? It is as if I were carrying the whole world on my shoulder." Jesus smiled, and through the expression in his eyes, told him who he was. I pressed my face to Saint Christopher and Jesus. I pressed the icon in my pocket. I felt secure. This was the corner that would revive my life. Only here could I save myself from myself.

I felt ready to go to the University of London and inquire

about the Centre for Migration and Diaspora Studies, which had opened a few years earlier and was still interested in having foreign students attend the graduate program, even though I was more interested in sitting in the apartment by the window and looking out at the building opposite us, reciting the Lord's Prayer to exhaustion.

The building had four floors, the same as Bogdan's. The ground level was all glass but stood empty; it had probably been a restaurant or bar. On the floor above that, there were windows with the blinds lowered, and on one of the blinds was the word *Stone*. The only visible thing through the windows on the next floor up was a table. Everything else was hidden by curtains. A small open tower had been built above the apartment on the top floor, containing a spiral staircase that led up to a terrace. The terrace was gorgeous: potted coniferous plants, green when everything all around was gray, snowless, but also without sunshine, wintery and melancholy. There was a small table and two armchairs on the terrace. A man would appear on the terrace, sit in one of the armchairs dressed in his housecoat, then stand, touch the plants, enter the square tower, and descend the stairs to his apartment. The terrace was bordered by a low metal fence, but on the far side there appeared to be no fence between the building and the gap. There must have been, however, a small addition, a paved landing of some sort, because the man would walk up to the fence, jump over, pause a moment, then return. He would continually repeat that strange ritual. I often saw someone else at his place, drinking something, probably tea or coffee. One day, standing at the window and watching the strange, perhaps even mad, neighbor, I saw the person sitting with him stand up, go to the back edge of the terrace, jump the fence, and not return. He disappeared. Had he thrown himself off the terrace? Or was he the strange guy's neighbor from over the fence and had simply gone home? I never found out. There were no emergency sirens, and the man from the terrace went down the stairs; he didn't appear again that day. But he did appear in my dream, when I dozed off watching the BBC on television and I imagined myself going into the building across the street.

Entering the building, I had to pass through the glassed-in area, which appeared empty from the outside. But inside, there was, in fact, a large glass booth in which a uniformed policeman was sitting. There was an ashtray filled with cigarette butts and a box of Multivitamin Juice on the table. When he saw me, he asked sadly, "Why?" "Why what?" I asked, stopping in front of him. "You don't know?" he said, "This is the Suicide Center." It had the required registrations and permits. There were so many suicides in East London that the government had decided to legalize it, and this was the center for suicides. On the ground floor, those who wished to commit suicide were greeted and their names entered into a ledger. They were given leaflets and brochures, and then sent to the psychosocial services office on the next floor. There, a psychologist, a social worker, and a representative of the Queen worked with the client, for hours, to try to dissuade him. They solved his problem symbolically. They gave him an empty matchbox, some paper, scissors, and glue. He wrote something on the slip of paper, and then cut up each unhappiness pushing him to commit suicide. Then he glued them onto the matchbox, constructing a palace, cabin, automobile, anything that could be made with a matchbox and several torn sheets of paper. Some were thrilled by the task, others barely managed to make anything. The agency gave him something to eat or drink; they ordered a pizza,

Chinese food, sushi, whatever. The state paid for it. If the suicidal client held out against all the persuasion and was still intent on committing suicide, he was sent to the next floor. There, the person he loved most in life waited for him: his first love, a school friend, his favorite teacher, his best-beloved grandmother, his craziest cousin, his idol, his five-year-old sister. That significant person tried to persuade him to step back from his intention. He was hugged, kissed, begged on hands and knees. Sometimes, a stronger step was taken: a slap or a punch. If the meeting also didn't help, the client went to the top floor. There was no one there. The kitchen was locked, and the other rooms were empty. He could do whatever he wanted. The windows were hermetically sealed. Some who reached those rooms would fall to the floor, crying, shouting; others prayed; some threw themselves against the walls. Still others climbed directly up the small stairway in the tower and stepped out onto the terrace with the coniferous plants. The owner of the house sat there. He greeted the client warmly, invited him to sit down in the armchair. Then he went down for tea or coffee. He'd hand him a cup and ask sincerely, "What would you do if you were alive again?" The client usually said nothing. The director would say, "You're the master of your fate." The client either went back down the stairs in the tower or over to the back edge of the terrace, where he would throw himself over the fence.

I woke up, numb from the dream. It was so long, so detailed. It had a beginning, middle, and end, which was rare for my dreams. I looked through the window. There was no one on the terrace. I went into the kitchen to make dinner. Spaghetti with ground beef and tomato sauce. I looked through the window in the kitchen. From that angle, the apartment looked directly into another apartment, whose blinds were always raised. In the living room, a young woman was ironing clothes, while in the kitchen, in a sweater and boxers, a handsome young man sat in front of a laptop. Then she went upstairs to the bedroom and put on a short black dress and high boots. She put on perfume and came down. Only then did he look up. He stood, slapped her behind, and pulled on his pants. They left the apartment. My spaghetti was overcooked. Too much so for Bogdan's British stomach. I boiled some more. Then he came home and kissed me like he always did. We ate, and he told me some friends were coming over that evening—members of an association they had recently formed—the Society of Young Pro-Western Immigrants from Eastern Europe. "You now belong with us," he told me. "You will see what outcasts these people are. They're all educated. They are the brains drained from the Balkans. They want to meet you." "What does the association do?" I asked, but he answered vaguely, "Everything. They help new immigrants; they research jobs, stipends, opportunities for education. They look for apartments, organize cultural events, everything. They will help you, too; you'll see." "I already know what I want to do. I told you, I'm going to enroll in a graduate program in migration studies. I have 50,000 pounds from the operation." "Well, wouldn't it be better to get a stipend and not spend that money? We might need it. You'll need it in the future," he said, correcting himself. "No," I said. "This is exactly what the money's for, for graduate school, and that is what I'll use it for." That evening, four men came over, all about twenty-five or twenty-six years old. The other men couldn't make it, and as for the young women, they had remembered they had Pilates that evening. They sat around the kitchen table. One was from Romania, another from Moldova, a third from Ukraine, the fourth from Serbia. They all spoke English. They were formal and stiff. They spoke about Leo, a guy who had recently come from Moldova and lost his passport at the British Museum. "Without a passport, he's going to get kicked out of the country pretty quickly. He needs help," said Bogdan. "Didn't they find his passport at the museum?" I asked, standing by the refrigerator. I had the feeling that I was not exactly welcome at the table with them. All four, except Bogdan, began to laugh. I shrugged and went into the bedroom. I put on warm clothes, and then with just a wave, I left.

I set off toward Bunhill Fields, which was not far from the apartment. Bunhill Fields is an old memorial graveyard, where, in past centuries, the nonconformists of London were buried, among them Daniel Defoe and William Blake. Defoe's monument was tall, imposing, almost unnatural among the low broken tombstones of the other dead. In a row beside him stood a small sagging stone, Blake's memorial. He was buried with his beloved Catherine. On his cenotaph, some admirers had left dried figs, café sugar packets, and an earring with a little blue fish. Those items on top of Blake's marker took root in my soul. The gesture of those who had left him sugar, figs, an earring, filled me with delight. I had nothing to leave. I decided to go to Blake's cenotaph whenever I could. I felt, in the instant of my encounter with Blake, that Srebra was also present. I felt as though I were at Srebra's grave and had left her figs, sugar packets, and an earring. Blake's grave would serve for years as my substitute for Srebra's. Only when I could stand, or better yet, lie atop her grave in Skopje would I forget about Blake's grave in Bunhill Fields, that cemetery for nonconformists, the outcasts. In her life, Srebra wasn't an outcast, she wasn't alone, and the two of us were cast out together. But she became one after her death. She became an outcast because she did not survive. She was nonconformist to her life. When I got back to the apartment, Bogdan was alone, engrossed in the computer, and didn't even notice me.

In the days that followed, I gathered my strength and went to the Centre for Migration and Diaspora Studies. I offered them the 50,000 pounds I had been given because of my head for graduate studies. They accepted me. I started at the university in the fall of 1997. There were ten students in our class. Black, yellow, white, like that song from my childhood. Different ages. I was quickly included in the group. Every morning I could hardly wait to get to school. It was completely different from the Law Department in Skopje. The students had homework. We had to write essays on migrant policy, but in unusual ways. We had to describe our own experiences in relation to life in a foreign country, comparing the way of life, manner of thinking and acting, from both sides of migration. What interesting stories and reflections I heard that semester! I had to tell my own story, about my confrontation with Otherness. When I returned to London, I had resolved I would never tell the story of my life with Srebra and everything that had happened. Although the media wrote a great deal about our case after the operation, only two photos appeared, taken the day I was released from the hospital. In both, my head was wrapped in a swathe of bandages as if enclosed in a capsule. I was wearing my glasses, and my eyes were downcast, so my face hadn't been captured completely. I wasn't afraid of being recognized. I told Bogdan I didn't want anyone to know my history. He agreed. I told my mentor at the university the same thing, even though I had had to tell him our whole story. He promised he would never tell anyone and would protect me if necessary. With these assurances that Srebra's name would not be dragged into public view via the ravenous curiosity of the press, I was able to live like a normal person. So now, as we analyzed Otherness, there was no expectation I would tell my personal story, though I knew of no greater Otherness than Srebra's and mine. Nor a greater loss than of that, which, paradoxically, we had wanted to free ourselves. I spoke about the coexistence of Macedonians and Albanians in Macedonia or, more accurately, the lack of co-existence. The parallel worlds in which Albanians constantly felt like immigrants, and Macedonians constantly reinforced this feeling. I spoke about how I didn't know Albanian, even though I had studied in a bilingual high school. About the fact that my former homeroom teacher, a Macedonian, mar-ried an Albanian and was disowned, with an announcement in the newspaper, by her parents, her brothers, and her sisters. And she even taught the Macedonian language. My fellow graduate students had their own views of everything that came from the "other side." The Bulgarian, Marija, whom I met the first day, told us in the very first class that she had four friends from Yemen in London with whom she had studied English in a prep course. They later enrolled in med-ical programs, but had remained friends. She told us how the first time she went to visit them, she was dressed modestly in a long skirt and big sweater, because they always dressed that way, and they even wore headscarves. When she rang the doorbell and they opened the door, they were wearing shorts and shirts with spaghetti straps. "Then the Otherness could be seen in reverse," said Marija. "I was to be seduced, and they were my seducers," adding, "I had brought them some Bulgarian Turkish delight, and they had chocolate rum can-dies for me. 'We have Coca-Cola and whiskey,' one of them said. 'What would you like to drink?' And, quite befuddled, I said, 'Both.' So that night, everyone drank Coca-Cola cut with whiskey, and we laughed and danced, but one of the

Yemeni girls got sick and threw up in the toilet, and then I decided to go home, forever freed from the stereotype of the Other hidden behind clothes."

Boris, from Ukraine, read an interesting essay:

> Just as the body rejects a foreign object, each nation rejects and discards the foreigner who wishes to work inside its living organism: like the dental prosthesis I never got used to in childhood or the contact lenses that cause my eyes, even after a full decade's acclimation, to become scratched and bloodshot. Great Britain rejects me, discards me, kicks me. It does not want to accept me as an object to which it could offer new opportunity. Perhaps it is still early. I have only lived here for two years.

It appeared Boris had a talent for writing and contemplation; perhaps that's what led him to study migration.

The title of Ervin from Bosnia's essay was short: "On the Train" followed by a colon. Then:

> Three guest workers in stocking feet. The men with raspy, inaudible voices. The woman with fat oozing out on all sides. Cheap jeans, short sleeves. A mouth without sense or self-censorship. "I'll fuck your ass; he says his nuts hurt not his asshole. You still want to feed the workers? If you only give 'em burek, they won't finish in one day." "They nibble, eat, drink, munch, go to the bathroom, laugh, and then they're quiet again." "Oh, my leg hurts something awful,"

the woman keeps repeating. The men mumble something unintelligible, uninterested in her torment. "I love that Bosnian kefir, but not the buttermilk." "Kefir isn't any good, it's too thick, I have to thin it with water." Sajko, probably her husband, says the word for chitlins, *kukurek*, and starts to laugh; everyone laughs. The woman's body is a naturalist painting—black disheveled hair permed into curls. When she comes back from the bathroom, she smells like flowers, carrying the scent of her floral wipes.

We all laughed at what Ervin had written. Later, I learned that he had come from Bosnia two years before, from somewhere near Srebrenica. He had fled before that fateful July. In my mind, the thought *just before Srebra and Darko's wedding* flitted. Ervin kept saying, "I can't believe I'm in a secure place, that I am safe. I'm so safe here that nothing could happen to me." He buttoned up his soft fleece jacket and ran his hands along it as if it gave him full protection.

Peter, the Hungarian, one of the most spiritual and cynical students, always ready to comment on any topic, said that he had analyzed—theoretically, of course—the excrement of immigrants and of the native-born, and had come to the interesting determination that the excrement of primitive tribes weighs 250 grams, but Europeans' only weighs 100 grams. And he added, "Currently, in Hungary, our excrement also weighs 250 grams, but that number will fall drastically when we enter the European Union." He said the excrement of English people, because they are in the European Union, weighs 100 grams, but that of immigrants weighs between 300 and 350 grams. "And that's normal," he said. "Immigrants shit a whole lot more, in both the literal and figurative sense. Not only are they under more stress, which accelerates their metabolisms, but they are always dissatisfied, and from countries of primitive people." We all looked at him in shock, but he was convinced of his theory.

Raluca, the Romanian, had lived outside of Romania for years. She had completed high school in Vienna, university in Berlin, been married and divorced in London, and was now in graduate school. She said she would read to us from the diary she had written on her most recent trip to Bucharest:

> On leaving Vienna, the train was already filled with Romanian guest workers who had short-term work permits. Sitting next to me was a middle-aged woman who spent several months every year looking after an old woman near Vienna. Every time she went home, to Braşov, she brought four suitcases (two fake leather, two cloth) filled with various products: coffee (a hundred packages), special salami, candy, processed cheese (three slices for ninety-nine cents), chocolates, pita, kashkaval cheese, laundry soap, etc. Seated across from us was a younger woman, now on her second marriage to a man in Vienna, filled with self-confidence, certain of her good looks. Her daughter, a teenager, is now living through a second relocation. Although she had originally not wanted to live in Vienna because children in Vienna didn't play outside, now she didn't want to stay for long in Romania. While at her grandmother's during vacation, the daughter sent her mother

a message, "I miss our refrigerator." Her mother was traveling to Romania to get her. Also in the train car, a young man, who had been living and working in Vienna for six years, found another young guy who wanted to drink, and the two of them drank and sang until the young man had drunk so much he became psychologically and physically violent (while smoking in a non-smoking car) and even attacked me twice: first, two ping-pong paddles fell out of his bag (above my head) and struck my elbow; and then, before he got off, even though I had moved out of the way, he didn't fail to hit me—accidentally—on the shoulder as he grabbed his bag. I arrived in Bucharest with two bruises.

A Slovenian woman, Alenka, told us what happened in Ljubljana one day when she was contacted by a nongovernmental agency and asked if it was true that she translated from Romanian. She had been taking Romanian classes at the university for years, and had been to Romania for summer courses several times. She said that she occasionally translated, and agreed to help them. They told her to come to the Youth Crisis Center in the southern part of the city. There, waiting for her, was the coordinator of an NGO committed to protecting women who were being trafficked, and a fifteen-year-old Romanian girl named Rodica. Rodica was twenty weeks pregnant. She was carrying a girl who would be named Petra, after the father, Petar—a fifty-seven-year-old Bosnian Serb who bought her parents a house in exchange for her. That was the official version given to the police. For Rodica, Petar was the first man in her life, the man who bought a house for himself, for her, and for their baby in her village in Romania. Petar worked as a seasonal construction worker in Slovenia. They came from Romania by car. Her father brought her across the Hungarian and Slovenian borders, because he was also traveling outside the country, to Austria. There were no problems; her father told the border guards he was bringing her to her mother in Austria, who was in the hospital, sick with cancer. Her father continued on to Austria, but she and Petar stayed in Slovenia. They went to register at the police station, and there they remained: he in custody for the seduction and mistreatment of a minor, she in the Youth Crisis Center. As the interpreter, Alenka had to take a trip she hadn't planned on that day: from the crisis center to the gynecological clinic. Rodica hadn't showered for days and stubbornly refused to do so at the crisis center. Her body filled the exam room with the smell of rotten fish, or more specifically, dead fish thrown onto dry land in the hot sun. Her genitals exuded an intense odor, steaming vapors. The doctor said everyone had to work like crazy to air out the room after the examination. Alenka stood behind a curtain and translated, but the smell penetrated the material and into her clothes. But it didn't disgust her. She didn't feel like vomiting. She had taken a liking to Rodica. She trusted her. "Maybe I was crazy," she said, "but I believed her. She was kind, beautiful, and mature. Maybe as mature as I was when I was fifteen and in love for the first time, when it seemed like it would last forever." The psychologist—a blond woman—tried to help. "No," she said, "Rodica isn't going to commit suicide. But she can't stand being without Petar any longer. I don't know what the wisest course of action is." Rodica was fifteen, pregnant, and, out of stubbornness, refused an IV. She refused food and liquids. She thought the baby would survive without them, and she had no real relationship with the baby. She loved it, but she loved Petar more. She carried his photo in her purse. White-haired, but strong. Now, beside his photo was the ultrasound of their baby. While they were performing the gynecological and psychological exams, the coordinator from the NGO bought shampoo, shower gel, a toothbrush, and toothpaste. The inspector, who was with them the whole time, dressed in civilian clothes, gave her a Fruitabella bar. The nurse gave her underwear and slippers. But she just wanted a telephone card so she could call her mother, whose number she didn't know. Her parents' number was in Petar's cell phone. A bit strange. Why didn't she contact her sister's fiancé, a Slovenian? Was her love for Petar real? "Love for a man of below-average intelligence, a lost man from the dregs of society, living in Slovenia in a barracks without water or a bathroom?" the inspector said. Did he really buy her, or did he love her, too? Once, when she was sick he cried, she said. Now she was crying. She was looking for Petar, who was already in custody and likely would get a long prison term for the seduction and ill-use of a minor. Rodica remained at the gynecological clinic. That whole time, another inspector was walking the hallway, dressed in civilian clothes, as if waiting for his wife to give birth. The nurses and doctors were obligated not to reveal that Rodica was under police observation. Alenka and the coordinator left. A few days later, the coordinator came to Alenka's house so she could give him some books in Romanian to give to Rodica. He was very grateful to her. He told Rodica there was no way she and Petar could see each other again until she reached the age of majority. The baby would most likely be given to a foster home. She couldn't go to Romania, because her father was evidently mixed up in the whole business. Petar would rot in jail. The story of Rodica and Petar would not have a happy ending.

All these stories were a sick revelation for me. Some were connected with emigration, others with human fate, which knows no borders. Did something similar await me? Had I also become an emigrant the moment I left Macedonia? Apparently so. In exile because of my parents' lack of love, in exile for hygienic reasons, in exile because of my love for Bogdan, in exile because of Srebra's death. Paradoxically, I had emigrated to the place where Srebra died—where she had not survived. London, the city, in every sense, of our separation.

Bogdan and I were in love, and if one didn't take into account my spiritual torment over Srebra's death, how the loss overwhelmed me, the guilt I felt because I had lived and she hadn't, my conscience gnawing at me, my abrupt departure from my parents' home, and the endless questions connected with our relationship and family, if one didn't take the dark side of my soul into account, then I was as happy with Bogdan as he was with me.

He would often say, "Oh, love of mine, I know what loss is. You know my mother died when I was a child. At that moment, something was torn not only from my soul, but from my body as well—as if an organ was removed. And even though I got a new mother, one I picked myself—which is no small thing—that part of me has always remained empty." I knew that I, too, would always feel an emptiness where Srebra had been. What could possibly fill such a void? Bogdan said, "Some fill it with drugs, some with alcohol, some with religion, some with politics, and in each instance, to the extreme. But it doesn't help." He filled the emptiness with crosswords, prize coupons, quizzes, and various other games that were entertainment for other people but income for him. And what about me? How could I fill the emptiness Srebra's death left in me? When she was alive, both of us longed for privacy, for solitude, to be without the other. But now, when I had privacy, I didn't know what to do with it. In the bathroom, while I hunched on the toilet seat, I behaved as I had when Srebra was present: I tried not to make any sound except what was unavoidable, I peed quickly, in one stream, I shit just as quickly, my hands always on my knees, hiding me—from whom? I needed time to free myself from my self-imposed restraints and feel the freedom that existed behind a closed bathroom door where no one could be if you didn't want them to be, and there's no excuse for someone to come in while you're in there, except if you allow it. Once I grasped the freedom of the bathroom, I slowly got used to it. I locked myself in, and showered for hours, sat on the toilet, changed pads, looked at myself in the mirror, combed my hair and studied how it grew, rubbed my body with all kinds of lotions, waxed my legs, polished my nails... What didn't I do locked in the bathroom, even when Bogdan wasn't home? The bathroom became my refuge, where I discovered my own identity, an individual identity, like everyone else's, no longer one part of a pair of Siamese twins. Surely Srebra would have discovered herself in the same way had she lived and I hadn't. Surely she would have wanted to get pregnant again. I still didn't want that. I wasn't ready for motherhood. Nor, I think, was Bogdan ready for fatherhood. Although we weren't young anymore, we felt unprepared to be parents. We didn't talk about marriage. We lived for ourselves together and for ourselves individually.

I plunged into my graduate studies, which turned out to be extremely interesting. Since the courses were connected with themes of migration and migrants, they required field research, attending conferences, participation in projects, and travel. My mentor at the university proposed I study émigré writers. I was in touch with literary institutes that had information on this topic, or which organized events with émigré writers. The University of London's reputation opened up many doors to me—to festivals, conferences, literary events. And housing and travel costs were always covered by the university. The university was clearly spending my 50,000 pounds. I also received a stipend of 500 pounds a month from an NGO that helped East European graduate students. That was enough for me to split costs for bills and food with Bogdan. He paid the rent and didn't want me to give him money for it. In that way, he maintained his independence and I mine: we lived like boyfriend and girlfriend, but not as man and wife. It was as if he were simply treating me to a roof over my head.

I began to delve more deeply into the politics of migration. Even as a child, I had read and had favorite writers, but I'd never attempted to write anything myself. Of all the authors I read, it was Marina Tsvetaeva, who, although for the briefest time, was the most present in my life, and I bought everything, in any language, I could get hold of. She was a typical example of an émigré poet—both in her own country and throughout the world. "We are interested in contemporary emigrants," my mentor said, "not those of the past centuries." From the theoretical works I read, I learned that a person is unaware that he is living at the same time as thousands of dispersed writers who had left their countries for political or personal reasons: writers who still wrote in their mother tongues; writers who had changed languages; bilingual writers; writers who stopped writing; writers who began to write after they emigrated. A huge topic opened up before me. I began to meet émigré writers. London was filled with émigré artists. With each conversation, I grasped again and again that we both are, and are not, born as citizens. It's not only the soil upon which we were born that defines us, but all the ground we've trod, all the air we've breathed, all the people we've met, all the languages in which we've tested our power of transmutation. The person who writes is half chameleon, half stone. Before he dies, a worm in his soul says in his mother tongue: "Who are you? Who were you?" He dies before answering the question. The émigré writer has no answer to that question.

One day, when I returned from school, Bogdan's friends from the Society of Young Pro-Western Immigrants from Eastern Europe were gathered. Pizza boxes, plastic plates, and cans of beer were strewn all over the place. Bogdan quickly began to straighten up. His friends even more quickly began to stuff some cards on the table into envelopes. I went into the bedroom, and while I was changing my clothes, they cleaned everything up, said goodbye to Bogdan, and left the apartment. "Did they leave because of me?" I asked him. Although they often came over, I still hadn't become friends with them. They always left quickly, as if avoiding my presence. I didn't know why, but I avoided theirs as well, even though they were immigrants, the same as us, and their narratives could, at the very least, have served me in my studies. But there wasn't a single writer among them. They either were, or were studying to be, economists and programmers. They worked a bit here and there, but didn't have steady work. None of them had an internship or employment, but supposedly, through the help of their society, they would obtain this from their employers. That's how Bogdan explained it to me. It was clearly difficult to succeed in London. It was more difficult to find work than to study. "Why don't you enroll in a program, too?" I once asked him, because it was surprising: here was someone who knew everything, who solved crossword puzzles in just a few minutes, who was the first to find answers in quizzes, but who hadn't finished college. "Auntie Stefka felt it wasn't necessary to have a university degree in the West in order to succeed. Under capitalism, it's not education that's important but resourcefulness. In socialist countries," he explained, "so much revolves around one's studies, but here, it's important to make your own way, hustle, make a deal." His adoptive mother's way of thinking was a bit odd to me—Balkan somehow—but I didn't say anything. We rarely saw her and Bogdan's stepfather, who had once been the partner of Auntie Stefka's sister. Stefka married him when her sister died. That didn't mean Bogdan didn't go to Brighton often to help her with this or that, as he said, but he never slept over. He always came home by train, bringing fresh fish that he bought at the main fish market. Perhaps I didn't see Auntie Stefka more often because she could no longer be characterized as Macedonian, as the single woman who had been adopted by Bogdan and then one day left with him unexpectedly for London. She was no longer the beautiful woman with a bun who lost her parents in a fire and had, as a result, been left alone. She had been dignified and kind, the youngest single woman on our street. She was extremely annoyed when I greeted her in Macedonian and immediately said, in English, "We only speak English here." I was stunned, but Bogdan reassuringly stroked my hand. Whenever I mentioned anything about Skopje, about the neighborhood, about the people whom she had also known, she looked through me, as through a glass door. She simply didn't react, either with her body or her voice. She said nothing about Srebra. She completely ignored my story, as if she didn't know it. In fact, in her home we only spoke of the present or the future, but not the past. Bogdan's stepfather, an older, kind-hearted Englishman whom Bogdan called "Uncle," made us such strong Irish coffee that I would be dizzy the entire train ride back to London. Bogdan and I didn't talk about those visits to his adopted mother, whom he persisted in calling Auntie Stefka, and his stepfather. We never talked about them. In moments of sadness, he thought only of his real mother, whose photograph he kept in the bottom of a globe vase in which we never put flowers. There the small pale photograph of his mother sat, photographed with him in her arms, a smile on her face, and with such pride—as if saying to the world, "This is my son! Bogdan! The personification of his name—God given!" Occasionally, Bogdan would look at the photo through the glass, as one looks at fish in an aquarium, but he never took it out. And, though he never explicitly forbade me from taking it out to wash the vase, he would always prevent me from doing so, saying gently, "Don't. She will die again." That sentence frightened me. I didn't want to be her killer, so I left her inside, and only wiped the outside of the vase. Inside, the dust was piling up, and one day a spider appeared, but the photograph was clean and remained there, at the bottom of the vase, at the bottom of Bogdan's heart.

Bogdan and I lived together happily, with no quarrels or complaints. His tenderness and passion knew no borders. He literally carried me in his arms, listened to me, comforted me, understood me. He was the love of my life, and he said I was the love of his. "I can hardly wait for you to finish graduate school so we can have a child," he said. "But you do know it takes three years?" I laughed, and that night, as usual, I took a contraceptive pill. There were times when I, too, could barely wait to finish school so we could have a baby. A small beautiful child with a modern name: Maya, David, Dora, Sergei.

It had been two years since I had been to Skopje. From time to time I called my parents. My mother always picked up, so I never got to speak with my father. These were informational conversations—what I was doing, how university was going, what Bogdan was doing, what they were doing (nothing), what was new (what should be new?), if they went to the cemetery (well, your father's hands shake so much he can't drive the car anymore, and it takes two hours on the bus). They had been there on All Saints' Day, had brought things and cleaned the grave—a lot of grass had sprouted. Then I would change the subject and ask how Aunt Milka was doing (sick, hit with ten injections), how Aunt Ivanka was doing (she's upset at Lenče and Mirko and has gotten so thin you can hardly recognize her), Verče (who knows what she's doing, she only goes from work to home), Lenče (back and forth between the hospital and home—she beat her mother again, turned her black and blue; Mirko taught her all of that, mark my words), my uncle (he doesn't call; Snežana doesn't let him). "Does Darko call you?" "No," she said, "he doesn't call anymore; your aunt Ivanka told me he's gone off to the monastery and become a monk; she saw his father at the bank, God preserve him... Oh and yes, I met Miki and his girlfriend; ugh, she's worse than you: dark, skinny, a nothing! A ponytail tied up with a rubber band!"

I listened, laughing with self-irony. She had always thought I was ugly, worthless, Srebra and I. Probably from the time we were babies. Worthless. Like bats, but with conjoined heads to boot. Perhaps that's why we never had our pictures taken as babies. Only beautiful people get photographed. These were the things my mother talked to me about on the phone—always distressing, always filled with negativity. Everyone was on the verge of death or at a critical moment in life. If it was summer, it was hellish, you couldn't breathe. If it was winter, it was cold, the radiators had frozen, and she just hung around at home with my father. They were sinking in their own misery.

Two full years after my move to London, I said to Bogdan, "I can't put it off anymore. I have to go to Skopje." "Go," he said. "But I'm not going. I'll wait for you here." I bought a ticket and left on the first plane to Ljubljana. There were no direct tickets to Skopje, so I decided to go from Ljubljana to Skopje by train. It was the beginning of November 1999. I had bought a few presents in London and a lot of food for the trip. I had a long trip ahead of me, and I ate a lot while traveling. The evening before I left, I prepared a bag of food: some chocolate, juice, water, bread sticks, salty snacks, chocolate milk, a banana, a tangerine, and the next day, before I left, I also put into the bag a sandwich I packed in foil and a plastic bag, along with a folded napkin. I ate almost the entire trip. I ate and read. My stomach got full, but I simply had to empty the bag before I arrived, filling it again with the remains and wrappers. To lighten it. To lighten myself. On the train from Ljubljana, the young man sitting across from me took a loaf of bread and a small wheel of kashkaval from his backpack. Everything was neatly covered in plastic wrap. He took out a knife—a real one, long and sharp—from a black leather case, and on the little table by the window, he cut two pieces of bread and four pieces of kashkaval with precision. He made himself a sandwich, wrapped up the bread and cheese in the paper, returned the knife to its case, and bit into the sandwich. I thought: what precision, cleanliness, polish, order. The man was from Slovenia. My food was not as beautiful. I had a feeling that it didn't have an enticing aroma, but stank. How much can one manage to eat during a train trip from Ljubljana to Skopje? Nearly twenty hours of nibbling, chewing, sipping. I recalled there was a town in Slovenia called Litija. When I was young, instead of playing catch or volleyball on the schoolyard during gym class, we played "Partisans and Germans." I was called Sister Lita, and Srebra was Sister Kerol; we were orderlies for the wounded Partisans. Lita was short for Litija. I had read that name somewhere, probably in an atlas, and had dreamed up the character Litija, but I don't know how. Beyond the schoolyard fence ran the Kumanovo–Belgrade highway. One day, our classmate Olivera said that she wanted to run away from home and that was the road she was going to take. She said she was going to run away from the smallness of her home (her mother and father slept in one bed, and she and her sister—a younger sister who often wet the bed—slept in the other). Her grandmother slept on the narrow bed in the kitchen. The grandmother knew Russian so well she could translate an entire movie into Macedonian. She would turn her back to the television and translate aloud while Olivera followed the subtitles to see if she was correct. She was. We wanted to leave home along that road, too, and go somewhere far away, out into the wide world. Srebra had gone into the widest world, into the heavens, but I remained in London. And now I was traveling toward Skopje, toward the source of my entire life, which had clearly been running dry but was now reviving. I took out a book to read. Since I had moved to London I only read books in English, for the simple reason that I had no more books written in Macedonian. I had decided not to bring anything back from Skopje besides new books in Macedonian. I didn't know what awaited me at home. Yes, I thought, *home*. My home was still in Skopje, at my parents' apartment. I longed to go to Srebra's grave, to kiss it, caress it, and tell her everything. Although I often went to Blake's grave in Bunhill Fields, which had become my substitute grave for Srebra's, I was still aware that it wasn't there, but in Skopje, in the cemetery in Butel, where Srebra—her remains and her spirit—was buried.

Sometime after we passed Zagreb, a woman with a long tormented face and a black ponytail came into our compartment and immediately called someone on the phone. It sounded like a child, but I didn't know if it was hers. She spoke to him for a long, long time, explaining how to fry two eggs and top them with a slice of salami. She gave precise directions: "The eggs are in the refrigerator on the balcony; use the silver pan; don't put in too much oil or they'll get greasy and then you can't eat them; two minutes is enough…" Again and again the same instructions. At the end, she said several times, "Enjoy your meal. I'll call you when I'm coming back. If Baba let's me." She was speaking Bosnian—was *Baba* his grandma or father? Who was this woman with the sunken face calling? I looked at her, but couldn't understand what was going on with her, clearly something unhappy, clearly one of those personal sorrows and misfortunes that slowly destroys a life and compound, until nothing remains but a pile of bones and a puzzled cranium staring into its own emptiness.

The guy with the sandwich got off in Belgrade, and in Niš, a fortyish woman, who was trying to look much younger, got on. She was wearing a thong—a black cord peeked out of her pants, and each time she bent forward to get water or something from her backpack, the cord became more and more visible, shaking with her ample hips, which didn't narrow at the waist but seemed to continue right up to her breasts, where they came to a sudden halt: she was as flat as a board. That made the black cord beneath her pants seem to be both thong and brassiere: her ass and bosom together in one place, drawing attention. It was like a spread in a porno magazine where many small pictures are set close together to create the image of a single body. For a woman like her, who had just come on the train but had already taken off her boots and stretched her legs onto the seat opposite hers—then curled them up on her own—for a not-so-young woman like her, the montage was comprised of her ass and her absent breasts, which the black thong highlighted like a product advertising two for one. It wasn't sexy. With every bend forward, as the belt of her jeans dropped below the level of the black horizontal string, the thong's vertical string exuded the foul smell of dried excrement. I was nauseated. I burrowed deeper into the poetry of Czesław Miłosz.

Nobody was waiting for me when I arrived in Skopje, which was understandable, because I hadn't called my parents to let them know I was coming. I don't know why I wanted to surprise them. Some streets were closed to traffic because of a large strike led by impoverished workers. Taxi drivers had to wind their way across the entire city in order to continue on to the far side. It occurred to me that I didn't have enough Macedonian denari for a taxi. I had to walk several stops on foot, carrying my backpack. Outside, it was slippery, cold, and dark. I finally found a bus. I arrived home exhausted, hungry. I rang the bell for a long time. I didn't have a key to the apartment. My mother finally opened the door, and after a quick greeting with two glancing kisses on the cheeks, she said, "So now you've chosen to come? Your father just got out of the hospital today." We stood leaning on the chairs in the dining room, facing the wall on which the needlepoint of "The Goose Girl" was hanging. My father, pale, weak, face sunken, hair white, was bent over following his recent hernia operation; I had just arrived from London, not having slept—tired, hungry, and unwelcome. I was silent. I didn't know what to say. Not one inch of the apartment was my home anymore. When I went into "my" room, I curled up on the floor and didn't know what to do with my hands, with my heart. I had to go to the bathroom. There was no hot water in the boiler. It was cold; the heater couldn't warm the room, which hadn't been heated for two whole years. I wanted to leave the door open so warmth could come in from the kitchen and dining room, where my parents warmed themselves by the wood-stove, but I didn't dare. I kneeled before the radiator as if before God. The room didn't dare open itself to me, to warm me. I was a stranger to it. In the bathroom, the little window was open a crack; the handle on the shower had been pulled off; the water sprayed in all directions. I turned on the boiler. I kneeled in the tub, and with barely tepid water, attempted to wash my body. Then I stood up, but let the water run off me for a moment longer. Whenever I showered standing—alone since the operation or with Srebra when she was alive—the water never seemed to go down the drain, but instead spilled onto the floor, and then we had to use all our energy to mop it up, pushing it toward the drain. With my father's heavy, un-comfortable, plastic red-brown flip-flops on my feet, I stood naked in the tub. I shivered as I mopped up the water; then I opened the window wide to dry the floor more quickly, so my mother could again cover the floor with old newspapers, place a plastic sheet over them, and then, over that, a small mat or rug, the best of which was the blue plastic bath mat that Srebra and I had rolled up and carried home from the department store "26 July" as a victory for home cleanliness. On the floor, prior to that purchase, there had been only a long coarsely woven rug (most likely from the village, per-haps from my mother's trousseau). That rug had red, green, blue, brown, white, and black stripes, but was mainly red, a red carpet for celebrities, a simulacrum of something a family of property would have. I knew that rug down to the tiniest detail. I had thought it no longer existed, but then noticed it rolled up behind the washing machine. I stretched it out on the floor and lay down on it, but I could neither laugh nor cry. I rolled it back up and shoved it behind the washing machine. I went out. My father was lying on the couch. Pale, withered, he didn't look like the father I had known two years ago. After Srebra died, he had completely withered. He tried to smile when I came into the kitchen and sat on the chair by the window. Srebra's and my double chair was no longer there. I didn't dare ask where it was. I sat on an unfamiliar chair and ate bread, ajvar, and cheese. "Why didn't you let us know you were coming so I could have prepared something?" my mother whined. "You don't just show up like this from abroad." I shrugged. "How is Bogdan? Why didn't he come?" my father asked. "He sends his greetings," I said, "but he has work and couldn't come." In that moment, it occurred to me that Bogdan hadn't had work for two full years, except for his quizzes, games, and prize crosswords, and the pocket money his mother sent for the rent. He was always busy with something. He was gone for hours at a time, and when he was at home, he was immersed in the computer. If I approached, he would jump up from his chair, hug me passionately, and nearly always carry me to bed, where he'd undress and caress me almost to unconsciousness, until both of us felt even greater desire for each other than before. But a moment of doubt flashed in my mind when I said he was working and was very busy before it disappeared, because I was too upset being here, in my home, in our home, in my parents' home.

My mother had tucked all the photographs of Srebra and me into framed needlepoints hung in the dining room. Most of them were photos from Srebra's wedding, but there were also a few of just the two of us. We didn't have a single picture of the four of us: Mom, Dad, Srebra, and me, even though the photographer had twice asked to photograph us as a family at the wedding. Our father had said, "Do we really need that, too?" So we were left with no family portraits except for some black-and-white snapshots from a family vacation, in which my mother and father are wearing bathing suits, and Srebra and I, with our long hair intertwined, are dressed in shorts and the tank tops with the straps long enough for us to pull up over our legs. Once we got a bit older, the four of us together were never photographed again. My gaze passed over the photographs, wedged in the framed needlepoints. I leaned against the chair in the dining room, staring as if I were watching the TV, when I was, in fact, looking below it, into the glass cabinet that held the smallest imaginable cups, which I had always thought were children's coffee cups. That's what Srebra and I had used them for, pouring in real coffee to read the grounds and learn whom we were going to marry when we grew up. Srebra and I had been extremely curious about whom we would marry after we were separated in an operation in London. But now, as I stood looking at them, I realized they actually belonged to a tea set, for serving the milk that was usually added to Russian, Indian, or Turkish tea. There was also a small dish for sugar cubes. Srebra would never know that we had been mistaken about the miniature cups. And about many other things as well. Must I even recall the things we are ashamed of? In the bathroom: pages from independent newspapers under the blue rubber mats. On the wall-mounted steam heater: a rag from old work clothes, most likely a coat. On the hanger: my father's belt. (Sometimes, we touched and studied it carefully, hesitantly. It seemed to be some secret connection between us; or was the belt, in some odd way, the parental link between our father and us?) When we were children, children with conjoined heads, how many times had he threatened Srebra and me with, "I am going to take off my belt," and we had fallen silent, petrified. We became perfectly still. Once, he actually did take it off when Srebra and I asked for the rulers with a 1983 calendar printed on them, which our mother brought us from work. We weren't allowed to bring them to school so no one could take them from us. They were kept in our parents' room, probably in the same place as the folder with the pictures from Animal Kingdom. One evening, Srebra and I dug in our heels. We wanted to get our rulers and draw with them, so we went to their room while they were watching television in the dining room, and we climbed up onto the armchair to look for them in the cupboard. A small porcelain ashtray tumbled to the floor and shattered. Srebra and I quickly closed the cupboard and climbed down, but our father had heard the crash and came into the room, took off his belt, and hit the two of us on our behinds, shouting, "You have devoured the world! Voracious creatures!" Then, as he left the room, his shoulder knocked against a ceramic boy that hung on the wall beside a ceramic girl—a pair that was made to hang on a bathroom door because both the girl and boy had their pants down. They were bathroom signs, but in our home, they hung in the dining room. The boy fell and shattered, and that's when our mother jumped up from the chair in which she had been sitting, sullen with furrowed brow, waiting for our father to punish us, and shrieked at him, "Are you blind? Aren't you paying attention? It was so nice there on the wall." Our father, in a rage like we had never seen before, ran up and slapped her, then left the house—probably going down to the garage. Our mother cried, sobbing, saying nothing, and Srebra and I felt such pity that we forgot about the belt on our backsides. We were shocked by the slap our father had given our mother. Then Srebra and I repeated—I to myself, Srebra half-aloud—"Pervert." *Pervert*, a word that in our childhood was a synonym for idiot. Who knows how its use, clichéd and crazy, had become embedded in the membrane of our brains.

I lived through those two weeks in Skopje ascetically: one *pastrmajlija* for the three of us for lunch; half an egg, margarine, and a bit of kashkaval for breakfast. I bought fifteen Turkish pastries at the pastry shop near the church, but they sat somewhere in the big room for days without being eaten. My mother, dressed in her blue robe the whole time I was there, kept telling me there was a cake in the freezer. "But," she said. "It would have to be thawed." Even when there was something, there was nothing. Post-socialist asceticism. A stomach-grumbling diet program. I was chronically hungry. I went downtown, walked from the Bit Pazar market to the center and from the center to the flower market, where I bought flowers, and then walked back to the Bit Pazar, buying burek, a small meat pie, or a sesame bun along the way. I ate and walked, walked and ate. I lit candles in the church of Saint Dimitrija. I prayed, and a feeling of home, of comfort, washed over me. Oh! How much I had missed in London that smell that doesn't exist anywhere except in Orthodox churches—the smell of icons, frescoes, candles for the living and dead. Then I took the bus to the cemetery in Butel, where I sat on Srebra's grave and arranged flowers around her stone. I brushed the marble with antibacterial towelettes; I sat and spoke to her. I told her everything, without shame, without a speck of the anger or irony that had always been present in our conversations. I told her about things in London, how Bogdan was, how things were in Skopje. I told her Darko had gone into the monastery, had taken his orders, and that was why he wouldn't be coming. I told her what I had eaten that day, what our mother and father were saying. I told her Mom had not taken off her blue robe. I remarked on their habits and ego trips, sometimes with laughter and sometimes with tears. I asked her how often they came to visit, rhetorically answering, "Only for All Souls', right? Dad can't drive. His hands shake, he doesn't see well, and buses are expensive. It costs 100 denari each for them to come. Things are expensive, you know..." I laughed like a fool, because I knew Srebra would have laughed too, had she been alive. If anything connected us and made us close, it was the non-parental way our parents acted, to the point of absurdity, surrealism. I told her our parents had been at the pig slaughter in Bulačani a few days prior. They had come home with two bags: one with meat, liver, and cracklings for them, the other with ears and trotters for piftija pork aspic for Aunt Ivanka. The next day, our father brought Aunt Ivanka her bag, but the day after, at 7:30 in the morning, our mother realized that they had mixed up the bags, and he had given Aunt Ivanka their bag. Cries and shouts. At 7:30, she called Aunt Ivanka and in a weepy voice, told her that they had mixed up the bags. At twelve o'clock, our father set off to the school with the correct bag, where he met Aunt Ivanka, who was clutching our bag. The handoff took place. Suppressed shame in his eyes, a bit of anger and scorn, something right out of the movies. I told Srebra how I imagined Aunt Ivanka and our father meeting in an empty parking lot or under a dark bridge at night, exchanging the bags as if they were exchanging money and drugs. I began to laugh again. Perhaps Srebra was also laughing in her grave. But the people at the surrounding graves looked at me and crossed themselves, spitting into their jackets against the evil eye—"*Tfu-tfu*, God protect us from such a thing"—just like it had been when Srebra and I were conjoined and people gave us a wide berth or spat against the evil eye, praying that such a thing wouldn't happen in their families.

On the way back from the cemetery, I walked several stops. In front of a social services center, or something like that, I came upon something I had never seen before: a truck filled with small roasted chickens. A woman was standing in the midst of them and with a long two-pronged fork, was doling out one bird apiece to people gathered around the truck. People were pushing; some took two. Then, with chickens under their arms or pressed to their chests, they walked past the center's door. Weak, sunken bodies and faces, collapsing skin and bones, big empty eyes—but their voices, with supernatural strength, shouted, begged, and fought for their lives. It was like a concentration camp. I pressed myself against a post to watch them wait, then take the chickens. Some also grabbed the cardboard boxes a man with bright red hair in front of the center was handing out. I was watching them fight for their lives.

I thought I had returned to Skopje only because of Srebra, because her grave was in Skopje. I had lied to myself every time I stood by Blake's grave and looked for Srebra in my thoughts. No, Srebra was born in Skopje, she died in London, and we buried her in Skopje, in Macedonia. She returned to the land she had come from. And me? Who knows where I will end up, who knows where my end is. I wanted to see Roza's parents. I had never felt as strong a desire as I felt to go to Roza's home, after fourteen long years. I wanted to go inside her home and find some part of her, something that spoke of our childhood. It was already late when I returned from the cemetery. Along the way, I stopped in a store to buy coffee and a box of chocolates. The following day before lunch I stole away from home and rang Roza's parents' doorbell. I hadn't stood where I now stood, glued to the spot in front of that door, for years, ever since Roza's death. Roza's mother opened the door. I went inside. Her father was there, too. We sat in the dining room. The whole time, I looked at the shelf where Roza and Mara's red and blue kaleidoscopes had been kept. They weren't there any longer. How warmly Auntie Magda and Uncle Kole welcomed me. I sat and listened as they talked about Roza, about the fateful day before leaving for Greece when Roza stood in the opening between the kitchen and dining room and argued with them. She wanted to go with her grandmother, her grandfather, and her sister at any price. They tried to convince her not to; after all, they were going to Greece that summer for vacation, but Roza insisted, and they let her go. And then what happened, happened. I wanted to tell them about my chain, about the culprit of this tragedy. I couldn't find the strength. But my eyes flooded with tears. I told them I had never gotten over Roza, ever. I told them I lived with Bogdan, whom they had loved when he was a boy. They mourned Srebra and they mourned for me. Auntie Magda gave me a photo of Roza. There was Roza's swarthy head with its thick, curly hair. Had she lived, she would have been a beauty. Perhaps she would already be married, with a young child to whom I could have brought a present from London. Roza was dead. Just like Srebra. My tragedy was fresher, and seemed greater. But is one tragedy greater than another? A comedy can be greater than another comedy, but a tragedy? Never. Every tragedy is tragic to the extreme. There can be no comparisons, and while at first glance, the number of victims seems to determine the degree of tragedy, each individual person mourns most for his own: if the one closest to you perishes, that is the greatest tragedy. Roza died when we were children; when no one else in our lives had passed away. She was my first tragedy. My, our, second was when our grandma died. Srebra was the third. Tragedies don't form a hierarchy. They are arranged alongside one another, not above or below. I said goodbye to Roza's parents, thinking how hard it would be for me to go there again and face, all over again, their tragedy, our tragedy.

When I got home, my mother asked where I had been. I told her. How angry she got! Her face grew dark and crumpled, and she sat like a bundle of unhappiness by the oven, in which her pita was baking. She sobbed: "What made you go to their place? No one goes there, and *you* just up and go. Were you looking for a mother? Who on Earth did you think you'd find?" She sat and sobbed, talking and stroking her robe, but I couldn't listen to her. I went downtown. I walked through the Old Market, looked in the shop windows, tried on shoes, poked around in the nearly forgotten goldsmith shops and shops selling pillows and slippers. One of the salesmen told me not to go into an Albanian café by mistake, because they might slip something into my coffee or Coca-Cola.

"There are good people among the Albanians," I responded. "Yes, that's true," he said. "I work with them every day, still—watch out. You don't really know them." I laughed at his advice. Then, in Saint Dimitrija, I lit candles for my relatives, both living and dead, for my friends, and for my enemies. I kissed the icon of Saint Dimitrija—the protector of our home, the saint our family celebrated—whose celebration our lack of love and our misunderstandings had desecrated many times in our lives. I kissed the Holy Mother of God, delivering my life to her before God; I kissed Saint Petka so she might also pray to God for me, for us; I kissed Saint Nedela in her beautiful dress; and then I set off across the stone bridge. I walked along the quay, the wind whistling and tossing the late autumn leaves. Reaching the post office, I called Bogdan from one of the phone booths there. His voice, at first confused and muffled, became dear and tender. All I wanted was to get back to him, nothing else.

That night, after my mother and father fell asleep, I went into the kitchen to put water in the cup that had been always in my room when I lived in Skopje. My footsteps were silent. I recalled how, when I was younger, I wanted to try to walk silently, but Srebra, out of spite, stomped. We'd then pinch each other and shout through our tears and laughter. I went into the kitchen and stepped toward the light switch. There were exactly four average-sized steps from the doorless opening from the kitchen to the dining room to the narrow wall with the light switch. I knew exactly where it was, but the darkness infused my feet and hands with a slight uncertainty. I stretched out my left hand, and just as I touched the switch, a sharp twinge pierced my body, in my gut. I barely managed to sit down on the couch across from the wood-stove and electric stove. I heard a nearly inaudible, dry, curt, resolute, determined, sharp "Go" in my mind. The next day, when I awoke in the old, dilapidated bed, I couldn't connect what had happened with the actual room. It seemed I had been hallucinating. Two weeks passed quickly. On the day I left, rivers of people were flowing to the voting station to cast their ballots for a new president. "Are you going to vote?" my mother asked before I left. Aunt Ivanka was over; she had come to say goodbye. "What does she need to vote for?" my father said. "Tito," my mother said. "Tito Petkovski will win, mark my words." "Well, I'm not voting for him," said Aunt Ivanka. "I'm voting for Boris Trajkovski; he's our neighbor and is a fine man, too." I didn't vote. I quickly said goodbye to my mother and father with parting kisses. My aunt kissed me three times, dampening my cheeks. She pushed a box of Napolitanke cookies and a bottle of rosé wine for Bogdan into my hands, as well as some coffee and an orange towel in a bag. She said, "I don't know if we'll see each other again, Zlata. I'm leaving. I can sense it. I didn't give you anything, child, neither you nor Srebra." I hugged her. I climbed into the white Mercedes taxi. Then onto a bus for Ljubljana.

All night I listened, half-awake, to new folk songs broadcast over the speakers. In Ljubljana, I took a taxi to the airport. Then a flight to Munich and another to London. I arrived the evening of the following day. Bogdan was waiting for me at the airport. I didn't want us to take a taxi. I wanted to enter London slowly, returning to my *second* life, because after Srebra's death this life couldn't be called anything other than a second one. Two trains took us to Shoreditch. Bogdan pulled the suitcase, as I walked on the sidewalk behind him. I thought, *like an Albanian woman in Skopje*, and smiled. Bogdan turned around as we were passing a multistory building under construction that had stood unfinished for months, without anyone working, and a torn protective fence. Bogdan stopped, turned toward me, lowered the suitcase, and whispered, "Let's go in." Without waiting for me to say yes or no, he pushed me and the suitcase into the brick building. He set the suitcase by the wall, and then pulled me up the stairs to the next floor. The whole place was empty and dusty. Holes gaped in the outer walls with no windows and in the inner walls with no doors. There were construction materials, boxes, and pails strewn everywhere. Bogdan unbuttoned my coat, feverishly pulling me toward him, and kissed me. At first I didn't even realize what he was doing, what he wanted, but quickly I felt the desire to touch him, and I unbuttoned his jacket and shirt. I groped toward his body until I found his skin, soft, warm, desirable, while we kissed each other madly. We caressed each other. Our passion was vast, immeasurable. He leaned me against the corner of one of the unfinished rooms and spread my legs. He filled me with his desire, and then with his sperm. Panting, we stood looking at each other silently, kissing. We buttoned each other back up and went downstairs. He picked up the suitcase, I set off after him, and we went home. That night, we slept deeply, cathartically cleansed of our absence. We were together again, happy again. I was fully convinced that God could not have sent me a greater happiness: the Bogdan from my childhood was, in fact, my fate, and, like his name, was "God given," the gift of a new life. At the cost of Srebra's life.

One day, when I got home from the university all excited to tell Bogdan I was going to America—the department was sending me to New York to research émigré writers from Eastern Europe living there—he wasn't there. His laptop was on the kitchen table. I decided to look up New York, to see what awaited me. While surfing the Internet I was suddenly pricked by a curiosity I had never felt before. I'd never opened Bogdan's computer before. I never read his email. Indeed, I never looked through his files. His computer was always turned off when he wasn't in front of it, but it had now been on. Had he forgotten to turn it off? Had he rushed off somewhere and forgotten to take it? The worm of curiosity began to eat into me. The chipped edge of the icon poked me in the side. I closed the browser and opened his documents folder. There were recognizable titles: crosswords, prize games, quizzes, computer games. That was all clearly Bogdan. But one file was named *PS*. Strange name for a file. I opened it. Inside were long lists of passport data, divided into two columns. On the left side were passports from a wide array of countries: Moldovan, Romanian, Macedonian, Bulgarian, Serbian, Albanian, and Croatian passports. On the right, the same faces with British passports. In two parallel columns: the same faces, sometimes the same date but different places, dates of birth, or different last names. Some had both a different first and last name, but each person had two passports. There were more than 120 sets. It didn't make sense to me. I looked at all the names, dates of birth, and passport numbers. For some, the name was different in the first column, but the date of birth was the same, or vice versa. In each case, there was some error or change. What were all these people with two passports doing in Bogdan's computer? I asked him as soon as he got home. We didn't keep secrets, so it wasn't hard for me to ask. "Let me just go to the toilet," he said, ducking into the bathroom. He flushed twice. He washed his hands.

"We're preparing these for a quiz show. It's a new show we're pitching to the BBC. It'll be called: *Guess My Nationality!* You know, like the show *Kviskoteka*, where play ers have to guess which is the real person: the pilot, the trainer, or the stewardess. Each contestant says, 'I am so-and-so, a pilot,' and based on what they say about themselves, people guess which one is the real pilot. Well, this is something like that. For the first episode, people will have to guess whether the person is Moldovan or British. Then we'll have a show for Macedonians, Slovenians, Ukrainians, Albanians. People will have to guess whether someone is British or from one of these other countries. We'll include many nationalities. It'll be quite a show. The facts will be scrambled, so the game is harder, but the prize will be a trip to one of the countries." He spoke so convincingly: excited, almost feverish, with his cheeks flushed, that he seemed a bit off, almost unnatural. I looked at him in disbelief, and he sensed it, asking, "What?

You don't believe me? Ask the guys in the society. We're making the show together, and you know how much money we'll get for it? Everybody in Europe will watch it, maybe even Americans. Who knows, maybe there the show won't be about countries but about states. Like, is he from Arizona or Florida?" Bogdan threw in all sorts of other things, but I was already tired, and remembered I was going to the States in two weeks. I told him, and we immediately switched topics. He turned off the computer and put it in his bag. Then we lay down, but for a while, we couldn't sleep. Both of us cleared our throats, held our breath. Our mouths were dry and we had to gulp our saliva, but I finally fell asleep. The next day, when I awoke, it was as if nothing had happened.

I stayed for a full month in New York. Arriving in the city, I saw a huge billboard that read, "Don't take your organs with you to Heaven! You won't need them!" In the center of the city, demonstrations were taking place: Vietnam War veterans were seeking pension insurance. Why did the Vietnamese man standing next to me seem so frightened when he saw these old men demonstrating? Next to me on the subway traveling out to Astoria, where the university had put me up in a small apartment, was a young girl with an angelic face, blue eyes, and arms that flapped around as though they were her wings. She said something, but it was as though her tongue were wrapped in cloth. She clearly had some kind of mental illness. I thought—if she gets married someday and becomes a mother, what will her days be like? Who will clean, wash, and iron? Someone has to clean the sink; someone has to put gel into the toilet bowl, then take the scrub brush and swirl it around in the gel's blueness that smelled like the ocean, flush, then clean the lid and seat. (My mother cleaned the toilet several times a day, running a wet rag, paper, or her hand along the seat, and whenever Srebra and I went to the bathroom, whoever was doing her business always got her bottom wet when she plopped down on the seat. Whichever of us was seated on the trash bucket would laugh.) What man would do all those chores while his wife was preoccupied, lost in the clouds, ill, artistic, forgetful, absentminded, depressed, unhappy, and not herself, but without money for a cleaning woman? She was so beautiful that every man would want to marry her. I wanted that husband to be not only good and attentive but also rich enough so this angel could fly rather than wallow in the everyday.

New York amazed me. It was so open, bright, cosmopolitan. I walked and walked along the endless avenues. I met many interesting émigré intellectuals in the city. One of the writers gave me his Croatian novel, in which he had described his craziest experience—becoming the operator of a security gate in front of a medical center. As he stood in front of the ramp, waiting for a taxi following his prostate exam, drivers asked him to raise the bar because it wasn't opening automatically, even though it was supposed to. There was no taxi. Nearly every minute, a driver approached and wanted to enter the hospital grounds. Everyone thought he was the security gate operator, and they asked him, some politely, some angrily, to lift it. He had set his briefcase with his laptop by the wall beside the gate, and there he stood: a short man, dressed in a suit, raising the gate with both hands, jumping a bit to lift it higher, so the cars could pass through. He stayed for the whole day. In the evening, the real operator arrived. That day, he had gotten a call that his wife had gone into labor and he'd run lickety-split to the maternity ward, where he stayed all day. He had taken part in the delivery, a medical technician had helped him give the baby a bath, and then he brought the baby to his wife, who nursed it. They were happy, they loved one another, and the man forgot that he was supposed to have been at work. No one thought about the fact that he was the operator of the security gate, or that the remote control was still in his pocket. So this Croatian intellectual had served in his place for the whole day. His taxi never arrived. That evening, when the new father returned, he couldn't help laughing when he heard what had happened, but the Croatian intellectual had already gone home on the bus. At the end of his book he wrote: *I felt like Saint Peter opening the Heavenly Gates.* New York's major bookstores didn't carry the book, but he was convinced that he had achieved great success with it. "I'll write the next one in English," he said.

In the States, students were like peas in a pod: with sparkling eyes, quivering voices, sweet smiles—they looked like future monks who have been touched by a deep sense of God's blessing. It was the same for students from abroad who came to study. However, immigrant students who moved to the United States with their parents, for economic or political reasons, were different. They always looked worried, with circles under their eyes and a weary gait. They often held down jobs in addition to studying. There were several poets among them who sought their identity and roots in their verse. They questioned who they were and where they were from. One female poet, who had been born in New York, said while eating a sandwich, "They have to be careful in determining who should get citizenship." When I looked at her quizzically, she added, "I have nothing against immigrants. My brother has immigrant friends from school, but he doesn't bring them home, because you have to know where people's loyalties lie, who they belong with."

New York was the promised land of the *Snack*. "I love

snacks!" my NYU professor of migration said, passing me a small dish, from which I took some chips and dipped them into a green sauce with garlic and a tasty mix of spinach, kashkaval, tomatoes, and eggs. *Snack* was like a life philosophy. Without *Snack* it probably wasn't possible to survive in America. There's no household in New York where people don't snack at least once a day. In the homes of immigrants, you eat as well as you do in the Balkans. Several families of the émigré writers I was assigned to visit welcomed me, treated me to their hospitality, and sent me on my way as if I were a member of the family. The families of a Bosnian writer, a Ukrainian biographer, and a Slovenian travel writer. One day, I got hit with terrible diarrhea, which devoured my body for several days. I called a Romanian poet, who was also a doctor, and he told me not only exactly what to get from the drugstore and how to drink the solutions and medicines, but also that when I was better, I should come visit him—it would be a treat for him, his wife, and their son. When I was better, I went to visit them. They lived in a beautiful house in Queens, near a Russian Orthodox church. His private clinic was in the back of the house. I thought it was just the sort of house I imagined when I was a child and had trouble falling asleep. Now, though I hadn't thought about it for years, I was seeing a real-life version. The poet's wife, a blonde, who, though no doubt a beauty in her youth, had aged prematurely. She had prepared a wonderful dinner. She laid out the most beautiful tomatoes and the best sheep's cheese, with no trace of the sweetness that marked all New York food. We ate as if we were in the Balkans. But the doctor and his wife no longer loved each other. He called her names like "dumbo," or said, "The meat isn't cooked enough," and whenever she said something back, he added, "Yeah right, whatever." Their son didn't come near the table, loaded with roast pork, potato salad, tomato salad, and a wide variety of white cheeses and kashkaval. At the kitchen island he took a frozen hamburger from the freezer, put it in the microwave, then went to the living room where, sitting on the couch, he wolfed it down with a can of Coca-Cola. The poet gave me two of his books in English, self-published. They weren't bad poems. Once again the same themes, just like those of all the other émigré writers: identity, roots, native land, questions about language, language-fatherland, nostalgia. I had enough material. I could return to London. The night before I left, my mother called me in a dream and said, "Zlata, I'm ready. I am going. I will die. I ordered grilled meat, ate my fill, and now I'm going." Then the receiver went silent. In my dream, I asked myself if she really had left. Then she repeated that she was going. I woke up early to catch my plane. When I arrived in London, the first thing I did when I got to the apartment was snatch up the dream book from the third bookshelf, above the row of novels by Victorian writers that Bogdan brought me as a surprise from Brighton. In the dream book, it was written that, when you dream of your mother's death, you really want to free yourself of her, spiritually. The telephone represented communication that was blocked or discontinuous. That was all true. I still called Skopje every three weeks, but each conversation was just like all the others: They were sitting around, watching television. Was anything new? Nothing. They hadn't been to the cemetery for a long time—they would go, they would—Aunt Ivanka was quite sick, she was in bed, wasn't eating or drinking, things were hard, very hard...and on like that. Not a single bit of good news, not a single optimistic occurrence. The next time I called, my mother told me my grandfather had died. He died the day after I called the previous time. He had already been dead twenty days, but I was just finding out. I said nothing. That day, I walked from East London to Kensington and back, but my soul was not lightened. Srebra, Grandma, Grandpa. My family was getting smaller and smaller. I had more and more dead in heaven.

Bogdan began to buy me expensive presents: necklaces with Swarovski crystals, a Gucci watch, lingerie from Palmers. Brand names had never meant anything to me. My clothes were from the Old Market in Skopje or from discount stores in London. He said his auntie Stefka had finally received the inheritance from her sister, so she could live even better with his stepfather, and so would we, he added. It was all the same to me. I saw Bogdan's adopted mother so rarely, and when we did, her insistence that we speak in English added to my feeling that it was better if I didn't see her. Bogdan continued to go to Brighton nearly every week, returning in the afternoon. It seemed to me like something they had agreed on: he would visit once a week, and she would give him pocket money until the following week. But now he said Auntie Stefka had given him so much money that he wanted to arrange a surprise for me and—*ta-da*! He pulled airline tickets from the drawer and said we were going to China. He had always wanted to see China, and now we were finally going. Not only that, he had signed me up for an interesting festival of writers and journalists, saying he wanted that to be a surprise as well. When they had heard I was from Macedonia, they accepted me immediately, and invited him too, arranging everything except the travel costs. "So," he said, "everything came together nicely." "We're going to China!" I was very surprised, and although I had never dreamed of going to China, I was still delighted. It was lovely to think that Bogdan and I would be abroad, together, for ten whole days.

I went to the bank to withdraw some money. I still had money in my account, although the university withdrew a set amount each semester. At the bank, my attention was drawn to a thin older man with a tipped-back hat above his eyebrows. He was trying to convince the teller to move money from his wife's account into his, because his wife was in the hospital. He wanted to know if, were his wife to die, he could take the money out of her account. He would not have that right. The bank employee was telling him to bring in his wife's bankbook so they could transfer her funds (140,000 pounds!) to his account, and then, if his wife came home from the hospital (the employee said, "God forbid she should die!"), they would move the funds back into her account. But if she didn't come home, the money would remain in his. The teller said to the man loudly, as if he were deaf, "Go home, get her bankbook, and come back before one o'clock." The old man, nimbly, happily, flew through the door shouting, "Right away! I'll be right back!" He was already back and standing in line before I was done getting my account in order. Everyone looked at him. Evidently, he lived near the bank, or perhaps he had his wife's bankbook with him before, but acted as though he had gone home to get it. My God! Was this the greed that sickens the heart? Why was the man so happy? Will he be reborn with his wife's 140,000 pounds? Will he be young again, in love, alive? What could a man, his wife on the brink of death, do with her 140,000 pounds? Who knows? I took my 500 pounds and left. I thought even that might be too much for China. I stroked Saint Zlata Meglenska in my pocket. At home, I called Aunt Ivanka at the clinic in Skopje. I just managed to get her on the line. She said, "Don't you go wasting money; your mother will say you call too much."

In China: A Buddha draped with a red cloth. Surrounding

him are drawings—portraits of some poet or other. A man observes the statue, cigarette in hand. "Where is your husband? Where is your husband?" the interpreter's voice shook. I ran up the stairs to the room arranged with wooden conference tables. I snapped a picture of Bogdan through the window. "Here he is," I said, showing the camera screen to the interpreter. The young, baby-faced policemen watched me. When the time came and the Buddha revealed himself, they would be blinded by his power and flee in panic, but later these human pawns would be transformed into secret police. That's what I thought. For five days The Festival for Journalists and Writers was ceremoniously opened and then for five days, ceremoniously closed. The bed of Mao Zedong is wide enough and long enough to accommodate all his descendants. They gave us cigarettes, and in China, when a cigarette is offered, you have to take it!

The only pagodas now were cake molds. Since we were guests, we didn't pay an entrance fee for the People's Park. The people paid. They spat on the ground; we spat into trashcans. The golden rice wine no longer brought to mind the color of the field in which it grew, but rather the five-story building grown beside it. The vice president of the Association of Chinese Writers presented us with silk pajamas: pink for the women, brown for the men. They seemed to symbolize him saying, "Sleep!" Sleep and dream about freedom of literary expression, human rights, Chinese writers freed from political jails, the return of the dissidents—not as prodigal sons but as victors. Sleep, and don't look around and don't write about what's happening. Only write about beautiful things; write lyrical dreams.

At night, in Bogdan's embrace, I thought that the States smelled like Amai body lotion, and China like jasmine tea and toasted sesame oil. America wastes, China stockpiles. The villages were without villagers and the villagers without villages. A village with one percent agriculture and sixty percent industry was declared an eco-village. A rabbit made of rice huddled amid the pigeons in a village center. Naïve art? Handouts or hands out? As we traveled by bus along the highways through southeastern Chinese cities with silvery metallic centers and rusted yellowed outskirts, memories of Skopje and the village welled up in me. I had never seen a bonsai in Skopje or the village, but I learned that in China, forty years ago, a bonsai had been as valuable as a television. The mother of a Communist leader whom everyone called a "loser" had been a Buddhist, so the Comintern built her a personal temple in her garden. The former mayor of the village, now eighty years old, had been offered a rich pension and a house, but refused them. Our interpreters greeted him with respect. A small girl sang while she peed. Then she filled a dirty sink with water, stopped the drain, and washed her hands. Bogdan said that's what the English did, too. I had never seen anyone do that. That's how the English wash their dishes, too. I had once seen Bogdan's stepfather set the coffee cups in the sink. He washed them, took them out to dry, and only then did he drain the water. There were still tiny bubbles from the detergent on the cups. In our hotel room in Shanghai, the bathroom was made completely of glass. Bogdan and I were embarrassed in front of each other. When I went, I saw that my toilet paper had turned red like the Chinese flag.

Bogdan told me his back hurt and asked me to massage it. Whenever I gave him a massage, he pointed to where it hurt most, so I could apply more force exactly in that spot: always under his right shoulder blade. I thought I should mark the spot with a brand or tattoo, a pen mark at least.

Then I could get the aching spot into a small circle to collect all the tenseness of the day, all his—our—stress, fear, worry, and memories, and then, with no preliminaries or false starts, I could direct all the energy of my fingers directly at that small atom of resistance and knead it, squeeze it, press it, and poke it, like dough for a round Christmas loaf, until he cried out in pain and didn't want any more. I laughed as I told him what I was thinking about. He said, "You're absolutely crazy!" Then we watched TV, but all we could find were stations in Chinese—we couldn't even find the BBC or CNN in English. During one of our walks, our interpreter Cristine acknowledged that the Chinese don't get foreign channels for political reasons. The further God is tossed aside externally, the more He is missed internally. Cristine zealously prayed at the temple for Buddha to save her from herself.

The festival organizers did not allow us to leave our hotel at night. They guarded the hallways until they thought we were asleep. However, along with the guests from Germany, New Zealand, the United States, and France, we agreed to go out after ten o'clock, by which time the organizers had dragged themselves off to their rooms. We would gather at the corner of the hotel, and then, snickering quietly and walking quickly, set off toward the outskirts rather than the city center. After walking for a long time, we would catch sight of the small ragged huts and barracks in which poor people lived with a well in the yard and no electricity. All the settlements we saw were the same: garages turned into small shops or cafés with a television hung from the ceiling and karaoke for the locals, a few products spread out on two or three shelves. There were sunken faces, the smell of burnt food, young boys and girls dressed in a youthful, though kitschy, fashion, a scattering of small houses with leaning roofs, always whitewashed, with bricks that crumbled at the touch, the sound of screams, and babies crying from inside the huts—rooms without kitchens, without anything. In front of the houses by the water pumps, there would be a burner here and there, a few pots, banged up from years of use. Poverty…poverty away from the gleaming skyscrapers of the massive corporations nestled in the city center, each one full of working men and women, but children almost nowhere to be seen, except standing in a row behind a schoolteacher or on a school bus.

Whenever I passed a younger woman alone or with a child, I thought about how it was likely she had been sterilized, having the right to give birth only once in her life but never again, even if she were to become pregnant. Her womb would be punctured with a needle and everything inside would be pulled out. Her life would be destroyed. Communism with the hands of capitalism; capitalism with the face of Communism. There's no greater perversion of the world order. Bogdan and I were stunned by the spirit of China, which destroyed everything in its wake to build a new China, but preserved, through artificial means, its tradition for the eyes of the world: eleventh-century Buddhist temples and pagodas were destroyed and new ones built with cheaper materials and then presented to tourists as authentic. It was only when we were taken to a huge film studio—a movie city where more than half of the films in China were made, though not only Chinese ones—that I saw what China had been like before. It had everything: color, pagodas, and temples, while outside the studio those things were gone. The state destroyed and then the state built, through imitation, the monuments of culture. A perversion of artistic impulse. We ate on golden plates, with silver chopsticks. We drank from golden goblets and drowned in crab, lobster, shellfish, and the tastiest meat dumplings, but around the corner, an old man—prematurely old at fifty—squatted silently, like all the Chinese whom the golden hand of state structures hadn't touched, and splashed himself with water from a bucket. It was absurd for me to seek émigré writers in China. The writers there who had written candidly and critically were already emigrants, either out into the world, or in their own country—condemned to eternal exile inside themselves.

I was shaken by our trip to China. While Bogdan wasn't indifferent to what we saw and experienced there, for him, it was a lovely trip because we were together day and night. He bought me presents, kissed me in front of everyone, making the woman who interpreted for us call out on the bus, "Look how in love they are!"

The first night after our return from China, I dreamed about Aunt Ivanka all night. In the dream, it seems she is crossing somewhere. Like she's crossing from one side of a cube, something like a cardboard box, to the other. Then I dream about the room with the iron beds in the village, where Aunt Ivanka and Mirko usually sleep. It's Aunt Ivanka's room, and it's the same as it was in real life, except filled with flowers in flower boxes. They are like a garden from when she was alive, but now it is my uncle who waters and tends them. In my dream I see the mirror above the bed. In the past, Srebra and I had peeked through the window, and I do that now, alone, but instead of the street, I see only a strip of asphalt, like a small path. The room is bright, happy somehow. It occurs to me that I can take photographs of the house, from all angles, to have as a keepsake. I could even videotape it, but I don't have a video camera with me. Then I see Bogdan. He has bought himself a suit, from Greece I think, but inside, there's only a corpse whose heart seems to burst while it lies on a table. Nearby sits Aunt Ivanka; all that's visible is her head: big, healthy, beautiful, with the lovely hairdo she had in her best years. She says she'll wash the corpse, she'll move it. I say that I'll wash it, but Aunt Ivanka stubbornly tells me to leave it to her and she will put everything in order. I awoke in a sweat. A fever was eating at my heart. In the afternoon, just as I was thinking I should call my mother, the phone rang. It was her. She had never called me herself before. It was as if there was an unwritten rule that I would be the one to call, because I had money. And yet here she was. I knew something big had happened. Something bad. She wouldn't have wasted money on a call for good news. "Your aunt Ivanka is gone," she said. "Yesterday, at the hospital." I was silent, shocked by the news. My mother hung up the phone. I felt lost and alone. Bogdan had gone to Brighton. I left the apartment. I pressed the icon in my pocket until it almost drew blood. I took the bus to Soho, and on Manette Street, I found the chapel of St. Barnabas. The chapel was closed. There was no notice, no announcement about when there would be a service. I could have rung the bell at the house where the homeless center was—it was an integral part of the chapel. I didn't ring. I stood awhile and then left. I called Aunt Milka from the first phone booth. She had been crying before she lifted the receiver. I started to cry as well. Only then was the pain within me freed, and through my tears, it found a path. How much I missed Aunt Ivanka all of a sudden. In her summer dress—her only dress, an orange-brown one—coming breathless into our room. Ours, mine and Srebra's. Aunt Milka told me, between her tears, that Aunt Ivanka told her a few months ago she was going to die, and they wouldn't see each other again. She said the same thing to me the last time I was in Skopje. She had been preparing herself for a long time for the grave: clothes, comb, everything. She had prepared herself to go. She told Aunt Milka that she had hidden the money she got when her company went into receivership; it was for Lenče to finish her studies and have money to feed herself. She had thought of everything. Perhaps she knew her diagnosis and had hidden it. Who knows? She held her fate in her own hands and simply waited for her day of departure. She bought a new jacket for "Then." I wondered where she bought it. What was in her mind as she carried it home and hung it in the closet, new, with its label still on, waiting for her? When exactly had she gone to buy it? I felt terrible, absolutely lost. I went into Saint Paul's Cathedral. I found a seat in the corner, sat down, and wept, stroking the icon of Saint Zlata Meglenska in my pocket. Ah, if there were a single Macedonian church in London, would I have gone more often, perhaps feeling the bliss, the blessing of God's presence in my life again? Women with their heads covered, kneeling on the marble tiles; mellifluous voices, the strong scent of icon lamps; young women kissing the priest's robe. Warmth. Home. I could have gone to Essex, but I always put off going there because it was there, in the monastery, that I had overcome the pangs of conscience that gnawed at me after Srebra's death. Saint Christopher with the baby Jesus on his shoulder had somehow freed me of that sin of conscience, and when I left, I no longer felt guilty about Srebra's death, only the guilt that I survived. If I went there I would feel a new pang, because I no longer felt the one caused by Srebra's death. I could not confront once again my feeling of guilt that I had survived and not her, even though the doctor told me several times it couldn't have been otherwise. The vein had been on my side since birth, not on Srebra's. Bogdan was in Brighton to get money from Auntie Stefka, and I was in London, alone, with Aunt Ivanka's death thousands of miles away from me. I couldn't have gone to her funeral. She was to have been buried the day my mother called me. Everything about her stayed with me. Memories, warm and beautiful. Srebra and I pounding out poems for homework on her typewriter, which had almost never been used. How she gave us money before we left for London, fifty pounds to help us get settled. The time we were outside in a green field with Verče when we were little...maybe Lenče had also already been born. We were making wreaths out of chamomile flowers. I think Aunt Ivanka was happy then. The time she lay on our small bed in the kitchen and cried and cried because one of Verče's ovaries had been removed. How she would sometimes come alone. She'd sit on our chair in the kitchen and cry, complaining about Mirko, Verče, and Lenče, saying she would leave them, that she could no longer reason with them. The time Srebra and I went with her past the Gypsy quarter and we saw two girls wearing one skirt. Srebra and I and the girls exchanging stunned glances: we had conjoined heads, they were conjoined bodies in one skirt. The last time, before I left Skopje and she had dragged herself over to our place to bring me a bottle of rosé for Bogdan, and some coffee, Napolitanke cookies, and an orange towel "to remember me by over there in London," she'd said. The time she bought Srebra and me the most beautiful blue cardigan sweaters with shoulder pads, which we wore for years. How she took over the task of buying Srebra and me the dresses Grandma had promised us when we were young but hadn't managed to buy before the end of her life. What a weight on her mind! Couldn't our mother have secretly given Grandma the money, or bought the dresses herself for Grandma to give to us and thus ease her soul, free herself from her promise? Why did everyone, seemingly with intent and a dose of derision, fail to lift a finger, letting Grandma torment herself with a promise she couldn't fulfill, even though she wanted to? Every time we saw her, she mentioned it to Srebra and me, and we felt a twinge of awkwardness in our hearts. Those little dresses grew bigger than we were, bigger than love itself, becoming a symbol of our fate—all that we couldn't have. Our grandmother never made enough money to buy them for us. As we tended the tobacco, diligently threading the leaves in the root cellar, propped against the ice-cold earthen wall with pillows, our hands yellowed and gummy—which we'd later wash with pinkish cream from a round box as the strings of tobacco dried beside the quince below the house—Grandma would say she'd buy us the dresses with the money from the tobacco, but tobacco was always a source of Macedonian pain, unprofitable blackness under the poor's fingernails. After we stopped planting tobacco, Grandma still didn't give up on her promise. She never gave up until she died; she simply had no means to fulfill her promise. And the dresses didn't give up on Grandma. Nor did Srebra and I give up, because we always felt as if we were wearing those dresses and they were the most beautiful clothing, in which we enwrapped our souls. It was Aunt Ivanka who finally bought us real dresses—blue-violet mixed with other colors, and big flowers. They were simulacra of Grandma's dresses, but to us, Grandma's two little potential dresses were never equaled. Today, it would be so easy to buy the promised dresses. The stores overflow with dresses. Perhaps it was the same then, but for our grandma it was as impossible, as if God were somehow personally opposed to the fulfillment of her promise. So the dresses turned into fate. The agony of poverty was cultural, social, and political self-sacrifice from which all that survived was love. Srebra did not survive,

Aunt Ivanka died. Love became another name for the dresses and vice versa. Like fate. Like when she made beer cookies, piroshki, pizza, cake; like when she offered them to us with all her heart and soul. How many things I didn't get to ask her, how many things I didn't give her. I called Verče. She was heavy with grief. She said, "Mama was seriously ill, and she didn't recover. It's obvious that she had decided to die. She didn't have anything left to live for." Verče said Aunt Ivanka died because she couldn't change anything. "My father, most of all," she said. My uncle Mirko, who destroyed her life, turning it into garbage, bringing junk home from all over the city, stockpiling it in each room, under the beds, in the empty freezer, and in the drawers, not allowing any of it to be thrown away or cleaned up. He gathered old plastic bottles on his black bicycle from around the television station and university, plastic bags, cans and jars, yogurt containers, Tetra Paks of milk. All of it was in their apartment, where no one went anymore, even though my aunt wanted so much to have company. She wanted everything to be clean. She was a home-maker who couldn't perform her job, because whenever she attempted to tidy up and throw out at least some of the garbage, Mirko slapped her, and then Lenče, in the panic and insanity of a manic state, beat her like crazy, punching Aunt Ivanka until she was exhausted. That's why she decided to die. To save herself. My uncle had looked for a burial plot for Aunt Ivanka while she was still living: somewhere in one of the villages, anywhere, as long as he could bury her as cheaply as possible.

On the day of her funeral, my younger uncle came to see my mother in Skopje. He ate breakfast there. It had been such a long time. It was Aunt Ivanka on her deathbed that resolved their quarrels. She had always been the balm for our wounds. I heard the burial was brief. No one came except the closest family members and a neighbor from the building. My mother gave her a towel and some stockings. Aunt Milka made such a scene and cried so hard that people visiting other graves looked at her in disbelief. She was shouting, "Where will we be welcome now? Lenče is ruined, Verče is ruined." My mother said to me, "Maybe it's really hard for her; it is her sister, after all…but such is life." I didn't ask whether it was hard for her. She said, "Maybe that's what they do in the village, but this is Skopje. Nobody carries on like that." It cost fifteen hundred denari for the priest who performed the service at the burial. They barely scraped it together. That's approximately twenty pounds. Enough for a short list of items I'd buy at the Tesco. That's all. Verče wore a black scarf around her neck. My aunt, our youngest uncle's wife, called her husband, four times. Lenče had lost so much weight that my mother was convinced she would also die soon. I dreamed about Lenče a few days after Aunt Ivanka's funeral. In the dream, she had committed suicide. The dream book interpreted that as a life change—the beginning of a new life. Perhaps that is why Aunt Ivanka died. So Lenče could start a new life.

Bogdan was completely loving and supportive. Once I got over Aunt Ivanka's death—if one can get over a loved one's death at all—I turned once again to my studies. I read and read, analyzed, interpreted, and delved deeper into the works of Eastern European émigré writers. I discovered the works of Albahari, Škvorecký, Hemon, Ugrešić, Drakulić, Kadare, Herta Müller, Miłosz, Goma. I reread the plays of Goran Stefanovski and many, many others. Most of them left their native countries in the early 1990s, largely because of the war and political conflicts in the former Yugoslavia. I compared them with younger émigré authors. My master's thesis seemed to write itself, employing my hand as its amanuensis. For months, that's all I did: write and write and write, preparing meals for Bogdan and myself in between. He usually wasn't home, but when he was, we ate, lay down together, made love, then went to the market or the movie theater, or just for a walk around the neighborhood. We still fell asleep in each other's embrace as we had on the first day. I was so calm with him, not jealous of anyone. I loved him, and he loved me, but we were both free to carry on our own lives—I with my studies, he with his quizzes, crosswords, and games. He won money often, but also other prizes: a knit sweater, a leather belt, a box of groceries from Tesco, and a shaving kit. His mother, his adopted one, continued to give him money, and we lived well, modestly but pleasantly.

Bogdan began to dream of having a house. A house with a garden in which our child could play. "In West London, with English grass and a privacy fence." Although I thought he was joking, he assured me that he really did want to buy a house and would soon have enough money to do so. "I've been saving this whole time," he said. "And I almost have enough." Had he been saving from the money he got from Auntie Stefka? "That," he said, "and everything else." When he left, he always took his computer with him. "What's happening with that quiz show of yours?" it occurred to me to ask him one day. "We're still waiting for a license," he said. "It's not so simple." Whenever his friends from the Society of Pro-Western Immigrants from Eastern Europe came over—who, incidentally, still didn't have regular work though they had been looking for years—I often wanted to ask them about the show, too: how it was going, what was happening, but they were always laughing so loud, drinking beer, and smoking while talking about their home countries, always bringing up negative things and mocking them with cruel irony, so there was simply no space for me to join the conversation. I went on writing my thesis in the bedroom.

In December 2000, I received my master's degree. My defense generated considerable interest in the department. Lots of professors who weren't directly involved in migration studies but were interested in the topic came to watch. At the end of the millennium, Great Britain didn't know how to treat its immigrants, let alone Eastern European émigré writers. The crisis in the former Yugoslavia was essentially over. The country no longer existed, nor were there any dictators left in the Balkans. From time to time, though, writers from that area would still turn up at the Foreign Office, alongside the many immigrants from Asia and Africa, and the ones from India, who came as if they were coming home and, because they wrote in English, quickly became British writers. The writers on whom I had based my thesis were scattered across Europe and the United States and, almost without exception, continued to write in their mother tongues. But those who did switch to the language of their new country gained visibility more quickly. I tried to prove in my thesis—using studies of writers who had emigrated from Eastern Europe to the West—that language was still an ideological determinant of national literatures, and integration of these authors was most often understood as assimilation. If they changed their language, they got the attention of publishers and readers more easily, but the authors whose works were translated—or even worse, untranslated—remained outsiders in their new cultures forever. These authors were divided between two homes. They lived in a new country while maintaining ties to the old one, but the literary public was more interested in single-country authors, and looked at authors who hadn't changed languages with contempt. People who are native-born are frightened by otherness, while immigrant authors are also a bit frightened of the otherness of the native-born. There were two parallel worlds in which the national and transnational writers saw eye-to-eye and joked around politely, but an important criterion for their meeting was a degree of dissidence and political exile from "those raging primitive Balkans or the lands beyond the Carpathians."

My frank, and, I might add, sharp defense of my thesis provoked a long discussion. From his seat in the amphitheater, Bogdan made a time-out signal. My mentor finally concluded the discussion, and praised me for what I had accomplished over the previous three years. He congratulated me on my degree, handed me my diploma, and joked that from now on, they would no longer take money from my account. He then revealed my secret, which, at the very beginning of our studies three years before, I begged him not to reveal. I had told him where the money for my education came from, about Srebra, about our operation, about everything, and he had promised that he would keep silent, but he hadn't said until when. And now, with the degree in my hand, he felt it would be a glowing conclusion to the ceremony, and revealed my secret to all the gathered colleagues and students. Hundreds of eyes stared at me, shocked, with disbelief, fascination, and rapacious curiosity, like the eyes of the journalists when Srebra and Darko got married, or the ones outside our hospital room whom the doctor personally locked out to protect me, or the ones in Skopje when the politicians speculated on television about the money for our operation. I recognized that rapacious curiosity, that feverish frenzy to hear more, to learn something else, something perhaps more piquant than what they had already heard. My mentor didn't stop there; he told them everything. He had remembered every single detail: about the operation, about Srebra's death, about the affair with the money, and about my return to London—how I had come into his office with my short-cropped hair and the scar from the operation still visible... He told them everything. He was blabbing like a granny at the village well. I watched him and couldn't believe it. Inside, I felt Srebra's rage—not so much mine as hers—and I took the microphone and said I didn't wish to accept my degree from the University of London and they could take the diploma and shove it. I took it and tore it up—though that was hard to do because it was thick and wound with a gold thread. "I don't need your diploma, since you don't understand dignity and respect, since you don't know what privacy means," I said, and then stormed out of the amphitheater. Bogdan immediately left the room, calling after me, "Are you crazy? Do you know what you've done? You just trampled on three years of study. You trampled on everything you accomplished. Are you nuts? Maybe that's okay in Macedonia, you can be proud, but here in England, do you think they give a damn? That they'll respect you more? No, they'll forget all about you, like you never existed!" He said all kinds of things to me, but I just laughed. I laughed out of some supernatural joy. I took the icon from my pocket and danced in the hallway, kissing it, then Bogdan. He was angry, but he eventually softened. He seemed to understand that what I had done wasn't so bad. That in some way, I had defended Srebra's honor, and we were dancing in the hallway of the University of London, and Saint Zlata Meglenska, who usually frowned, seemed to be smiling at me. I kissed her darkened face. Bogdan kissed me, and we went home together. I didn't take a birth control pill that night, or any of the nights that followed.

2001
ZLATA

In February 2001, as we watched the morning news on the BBC, listening in shock and disbelief to the report that soldiers in the Macedonian Army and four members of the Albanian National Liberation Army had actually exchanged shots in the village of Tanuševci and staring at the unbelievable headline on the screen, "Crisis in Macedonia," I felt nauseated. I ran to the bathroom and vomited. When I came back, Bogdan was still watching, engrossed. It was clear—there was armed conflict in Macedonia. "They're going to kill each other. Albanians and Macedonians just can't live together," he said. That's what all the film coverage and commentaries demonstrated in the days that followed, and for several months thereafter. One particular event circled the globe: An interpreter was killed, along with representatives of the United Nations Protection Force, while traveling in an armored vehicle through Skopje streets. The interpreter's husband cried as he spoke. She had left behind a two-month-old baby. She hadn't needed to work, but a colleague had other obligations and begged Mimosa to take her place that day. Both women were daughters of a Macedonian mother and an Albanian father. Because I was upset by these events, I hadn't noticed how often I felt sick to my stomach. I bought a pregnancy test. I was pregnant. Bogdan was elated. "Just a little bit longer and we'll buy a house," he said. He wanted us to tell Auntie Stefka together that she would be a grandmother. We went. Bogdan reminded me they only spoke English at their place. I told her in English. She smiled. "I won't have much time to look after my little grandson, but I heard you refused your degree, and so you will be a housewife and will take care of your child. That's not so bad, you know." I don't know why she talked to me like that. She didn't like me; nor I, her. We acted like strangers. I wished Bogdan's real mother were alive, the dear woman who, in my childhood, cleaned the entryway to our building and only talked about Bogdan: how much she wished for Bogdan to study hard in school, to make something of himself. But Bogdan didn't finish college. His adopted mother considered it a waste of time for such an intelligent young man like him; he could make a living from the knowledge he already possessed. Bogdan did earn a bit from his knowledge, but she didn't hesitate to give him money, regularly, every week. She gave him some more money now, and we went out. We walked by the sea. It was yellowish, clean, sharp, and gentle. A feminine sea. I rolled up the cuffs of my pants and raced beside it. Freedom, love, challenge. I got wet. Cleansed. The smell of history is the smell of caught cod. Some motorcycles were parked beside the ramparts and the buildings from a bygone era, and sandy-haired young men in tee shirts emblazoned with various statements of rebellion shouted at each other as if digitally amplified. Then, sudden movement, hard turn of the bikes. You'd think they were driving through a desert and not through narrow cobblestoned lanes that were older than their ancestors. I dreamed of Grandma that night. After such a long time, she finally appeared in my dream. I told her I was pregnant. She didn't believe me at first. I told her I was just at the beginning of the pregnancy. She put her hand on my stomach, and a warm, kind smile of love spread across her face. In the same room, Aunt Ivanka lay seriously ill. Verče, apparently, hadn't had children, nor, it appeared, had Aunt Milka. The dream was bizarre; I couldn't figure out what it meant, even with the help of the dream book.

I carried my pregnancy in the nicest way possible. I liked to lie in bed and read books. Not just by émigré writers, but more broadly—I read classics, Victorians, a return to Marcel Proust. I discovered contemporary British authors. And I kept returning to Marina Tsvetaeva, whose books formed an ever-increasing pile, in a variety of languages, as I bought whatever I could find connected with her, ordering books from bookstores. I kissed her photograph in its glass frame, and whenever I was sad, I took her in my hands, pressed her to my breast, hugging her. I held her in my embrace, and was comforted by her face, with its eyes wide open, and her sad, barely visible smile. The glass covering the picture was warm, almost like a human touch. My stomach grew, and during an exam at the hospital, the gynecologist asked me if we wanted to know the gender. Bogdan did, but I didn't. "That's fine, but I do have to tell you that you are carrying twins. We'll keep the gender secret, since that's what you want." Knowing my medical history, the gynecologist followed my pregnancy carefully, and at each appointment reassured me that the twins weren't joined anywhere, only to my umbilical cord. The babies began to move in my womb, back and forth, left then right. I felt their heads under my fingers, restless and playful, as they stretched my belly to their will. My stomach had a different rumble than it had before, with a distant sound, as if it were their guts rumbling. Sometimes, I heard strange voices, as if they were crying or cooing inside me. We were three in one. One day, I colored my hair with henna. I lay on the bed with a shower cap on my head and one of Bogdan's winter scarves tied over it. I looked grotesque with my stomach protruding from my sweat suit and the turban on my head. It was a good thing Bogdan wasn't home. What would have happened had my water burst then? What if I had to call for emergency help? I could hardly wait the sixty minutes so I could shower and be ready once again for anything.

My moods shifted, and I noticed that I was thinking more and more about Macedonia, perhaps because of the still-raging conflict, or because I was thinking of motherhood, the language my children would speak, and the past behind me. I longed intensely for Skopje, though not just Skopje. In my dreams, I saw the convent and Sister Zlata, my friends from the monastery. Sometimes, I thought of Darko, and how I didn't know which monastery he had gone to. I missed my relatives, Srebra most of all—Srebra in her grave. Whenever I touched the icon of Saint Zlata Meglenska, she seemed to be telling me that she wanted me to come home to Skopje. I even thought that, now that I was pregnant, my parents might accept me. I thought I might bring gladness into our home, and something would change in our relationship—at last, they would love me. It was as if I had forgotten that my mother continued to talk mainly to herself, as my father remained silent, only cursing at my mother from time to time, while watching television. The food would be bad, even if we ordered in, because everything would end up in the freezer, whether intended for the freezer or not, to be thawed bit by bit to get as many meals out of it as possible. It was as though I had forgotten that I would still have to wash my face in the kitchen sink, where, in normal homes, people washed dishes, vegetables, and fruit, and that the boiler in the bathroom would be a battleground, because the number of baths my parents took had been set by the pattern of their parents. When Srebra and I lived there, we suffered so much under those abnormal living conditions. Those conditions always made us sad and ashamed, and we always thought we could change something. And now, as I pressured Bogdan to travel to Skopje, I thought we would be able to start over again at the beginning, love each other more, understand each other, and be a family. I thought we would rebuild our relationship on a better foundation and reset our unlove. In the end, we were all marked by Srebra's tragedy, a tragedy that bound us more than blood, but we would also be marked by the birth of my babies, who would cleanse that blood forever, down to the smallest drop. To be at home at least until I gave birth and perhaps until the babies had grown a little, enough to breathe Macedonian air and have the Macedonian sun shine on them. Surely, I had fallen into some sort of pregnant mania, but it was stronger than I was. I thought about Skopje for hours on end as I lay in the bedroom, where, between bouts of reading, I'd set aside my book and daydream, imagining with open eyes how lovely it would be to marry Bogdan in Macedonia, at Saint Petka, and then give birth in Macedonia so I could write "Skopje" in the children's passports under "Place of Birth," and to have them christened at Saint Petka. Then, after we finished life's most significant rituals—marriage, christening—only then would we return to London.

I was obsessed with the idea, especially because Bogdan also wanted us to get married before I gave birth. "Perhaps in Brighton," he said, but something pressed on my heart, and I said I didn't want to get married in Brighton, where there wasn't a single Orthodox church. "Then at St. Barnabas," said Bogdan. "I'll find out when the Macedonian priest will be there and we can work something out." He couldn't locate the priest for a long time. "Bogdan, let's go to Macedonia," I said. "Let's get married there, have our children there." But he answered, "Are you crazy? Everyone is fleeing Macedonia, but you want us to go there? You see what's happening there."

When Bogdan told me he had found the priest and that he agreed to marry us on September 1, after the holiday of Saint Bogorodica, I was overcome with spite and said, "No! I don't want to get married in London! I don't want to give birth in London! I won't! I want to go home!" "Home?" repeated Bogdan. "This is our home." "No," I said. "This is where we live, but Macedonia is our home. That's where we were born, and that's where I want our children to be born."

My obsession with Macedonia, the obsession to return at such a critical moment in our lives, was perhaps a post-master's–degree crisis. I don't know. But I simply felt our place was there, and it was there that I wanted to say, "I do." It was there—really there, not in some improvised church— where I wanted to feel the bride's crown on my head, and give birth to our babies. For their first cry to be in Macedonian and for the midwife to say, "*Mašallah*! How beautiful they are." And then, forty days later, the priest who had married us would christen them in the name of the Father, the Son, and the Holy Spirit, and he would clip the babies' hair then hand them back to us—one to me, one to Bogdan. It was a film I saw playing, not merely flickering, before my eyes; it was so real to me, just what I dreamed of.

Toward the end of August, with my large belly I called the chapel of St. Barnabas on Manette street, to tell them that the September 1 wedding was canceled. Then I reserved plane tickets from London through Budapest to Sofia. There were no other routes available. Many flights to Skopje had been canceled due to the armed conflict in Macedonia, and foreign correspondents, observers, and guest workers who were working abroad and were worried about their families, were all trying to get there on the regularly scheduled flights, so I simply couldn't find two free seats through Munich or Ljubljana. I knew there were buses from Sofia to Skopje, and was certain we could find our way. I called Skopje and told my mother that we would be arriving on September 11, would be getting married, and would then live with them until after the birth so we could christen the children. "We have money," I told her. "We'll pay for food and the bills. The room is empty anyway." My mother replied, "A pregnant woman needs to stay home and not go wandering around." I acted as if I had not heard her, and just said, "The tickets have an open return. We can leave whenever we want."

When Bogdan came home that day, I confronted him with my fait accompli. The wedding in London was canceled, which meant that if he really wanted us to get married, he would have to come with me to Skopje. "What can you possibly be thinking, traveling in your seventh month?" he asked. "Do you think they'll even let you on the plane?" "I'll wear a billowy dress," I said, "I'll hide it somehow." "And a bus ride on top of that? Couldn't you find a better flight rather than two planes and then have us banging around on a bus to Skopje?" "I'll tough it out," I said.

Bogdan was angry and concerned. It was rare that I displayed such willfulness without trying to reach a decision with him. He was upset, and that whole evening, he flipped through the TV channels without speaking to me. "Just so you know, I can't stay in Skopje long. I have to get back. The quiz show is most likely going to begin taping in two months," he said, after his long silence. "That means, just until the babies are born," I told him, then added, "It's not a problem, you can come back if that's what you need to do." "So that's okay with you? You would stay there without me, married with two babies, at your mother's, waiting for the christening! Rather than give birth here normally, and then for us to go to Skopje for a visit later after everything has settled down..." "Bogdan, please...please," I begged. That irritated him even more. He took his computer and left, slamming the door. That night, he came home very late, just before dawn. He was calm. As if he'd made peace with his fate.

I bought a colorful, billowy, Asian-print dress, which spilled freely over my belly. It was black with red flowers, and made me look a bit thinner, lengthening my belly rather than emphasizing its width. We each packed our own bag. Mine was lighter than his because he wouldn't, of course, travel without his laptop. Ours was the first flight on the morning of September 11. At the airport, the clerk gave me a strange look, staring right at my stomach. "What month are you in?" she asked. "The fourth," I said. "The fourth? Why is your belly so big?" "I'm carrying twins," I said, but she still looked at me in disbelief, measuring my belly with her gaze. She was probably wishing she could snap a picture of what a woman looked like in her fourth month of pregnancy with twins. Maybe I really was in my fourth month. She didn't know how big the belly of a pregnant woman got when she was carrying two babies. Even though she had her doubts, she let me on the plane. In Budapest, there was just enough time for me to buy a miniature Givenchy perfume set so I could give a small bottle to my mother, one to Aunt Milka, one to Lenče, and one to Verče. I had already bought my father a pen with *London* on it. As we boarded the plane, a young gate agent said, "Ma'am, you can't travel. It's quite obvious you're far along in your pregnancy." I tried to convince him, but then Bogdan lied for the first time. He told him that I was in my fourth month carrying twins, which was why my belly was so big, and I had already traveled from London to Budapest with no problems. The man requested a letter from a doctor, adding that I couldn't fly without one. I didn't have a letter. It occurred to me that I had my health book from England, but inside, it clearly stated what month I was in. I told him I didn't have anything with me. "That is so irresponsible!" he shouted. "That is so irresponsible. You're pregnant, traveling to Sofia, and you don't even have a doctor's letter or health card with you. You're risking your own life and the life of your babies, and you could care less!" More passengers and agents, mostly women, clustered around us. They sized me up; one agent who wanted to see how big I really was beneath the dress even touched my stomach. This totally infuriated me. Only Bogdan was allowed to touch my belly, in which our two twins floated. The belly of a pregnant woman is sacred territory. A new life—two new lives—were growing inside. And now some nameless person wanted to measure those two lives with her hands. Instinctively, I pushed her hand away and began shouting at everyone to leave me alone. The pilot, copilot, and flight attendants were walking past us onto the plane. The pilot looked at me for a long time, trying to read me and see what was hidden behind my glasses. He said, "Let her on. My wife gave birth at home, so I have experience with women in late pregnancy. If we have to, we'll deliver the babies." Then he gave a rather crude laugh, ducking through the employees' entrance with his coworkers. The other airport employees then left me in peace.

The flight was pleasant. Our babies kicked me every which way, and each time I would bolt up from my seat like a shot. Bogdan watched me constantly, keeping a vigilant eye, as if that could somehow prevent any complications. When we got to the airport in Sofia, there was unbelievable chaos. We waited a long time for our bags. The bus for Skopje was scheduled to leave in an hour and a half. That was just enough time for us to take a taxi to the bus station. We finally got our bags. Bogdan dragged both of them, and we climbed into the first taxi we saw for the bus station. The taxi driver demanded double the usual fare. He swore and shouted, "*Macedonians*—whatever that means. As if there is such a thing. I can't understand people who don't even know what they are. What Macedonians are is Bulgarian." When we arrived, we gave him the money he demanded and got out. As the driver pulled away, he raised something he was holding in his hand, but he took off so fast we couldn't see what it was. I reached into my dress pocket. I didn't have my icon. The wide pocket of my dress was flat. It must have fallen out in the taxi. And, apparently, the driver noticed it on the seat and raised his fist so that we could see, but didn't stop, angry because of our argument in the taxi. He had simply chosen not to give it back to us. Quickly he disappeared down the narrow streets. Without thinking, I set off after him, but Bogdan stopped me. It was useless. We wouldn't find him. It was one of those illegal Sofia taxis whose driver uses a fake taxi plate and doesn't belong to any company. My icon of Saint Zlata Meglenska, who had been my inseparable, indivisible companion since childhood, was gone forever. I sat on my suitcase and wept. For my whole life I had been connected with that small chipped icon. And now it was no more. It would likely meet its end tossed out of the taxi's window into a dump, or resting in the glove compartment under the driver's documents and chewing gum. No one would ever love it as I had. But that was already in the past… We needed to catch the bus for Skopje. We barely found two empty seats next to each other. Just as we left, the driver turned up the volume on the radio, and we heard that something terrible had happened in New York—an airplane had hit the World Trade Center. The announcer's voice was shaking, and although we didn't really know Bulgarian, Bogdan and I understood that the twin towers in New York had been destroyed, there were many dead, and the greatest terrorist act in the world had just occurred. Everyone listened to the report. Conversations fell silent as we all focused on the radio by the driver's seat, all of our ears pricked. We were all shocked, in our own way. There were remarks, exclamations of disbelief, astonishment, shock, and some, also, of joy. A passenger near the back of the bus shouted in Macedonian, "It's what they deserved." And someone from the middle responded in Bulgarian, "Right you are, brother. Let them get a taste of it, too." I pressed close to Bogdan, twining his hands around my middle. We whispered to each other about how terrible, how simply unbelievable it was. From the shock of this news, I almost forgot about the loss of my icon.

We slowly made our way to the Bulgarian–Macedonian border. On the Bulgarian side, the driver stopped, switched off his engine, and collected five German marks from each passenger. Bogdan and I didn't have any marks, so we gave him ten pounds, which seemed like a lot to us, but he said that's how it worked if we wanted to get across the border quickly: he'd give the border guard the money and they would let us go, or we could wait at the border for two to three hours. And after what had just happened in the States, it would likely be longer.

It happened exactly like that. The border guard examined our documents, took the money, and let us go through without customs control. A long column of vehicles wound ahead of us, and the bus crawled through the zone between the Bulgarian and Macedonian borders. I could see the Macedonian flag billowing on a small white building. Outside the building stood a cluster of police and dogs. Bogdan, who was sitting anxiously by the window, nearly shouted, "Look over there. Look how many dogs there are!" Other passengers on the bus were also shouting, still in shock from the news of the attack in New York. It appeared that something was happening at the Macedonian border. Suddenly, a man was standing right beside my seat. He was a passenger on the bus, dressed in a black leather jacket, white tee shirt, blue jeans. He had a dark complexion, several days worth of stubble on his chin, uncombed greasy black hair that was disheveled and pushed to the side. He was holding a package about the size of a box of cookies wrapped up in brown tape. With no introduction, he began talking quickly: "Take this. Jesus Christ. Take it already. Stuff it under your dress!" I looked at him, shocked. "Go on, stuff it under your dress. It's big enough. Don't look at me like that, you whore, stuff it in there before I do it myself!" He was shouting and pushing the package at me. "What's that look for? I'm talking to you!" Although he was panic-stricken, I recognized his voice. He had been the one who responded to the news from New York by calling out from the back of the bus, "It's what they deserved." Bogdan grabbed the package and threw it to the ground, shouting, "Stop it, you idiot!" The man, nearly mad with rage, turned bright red, bent down, grabbed the package, and, as he was straightening up, pulled a knife from his pocket. The blade flashed before the stunned passengers. Everyone turned toward us. I don't know how Bogdan's body found its way on top of mine, but at the last second I heard Bogdan's cry and the passengers' shrieks. The driver hit the brakes, and the bus came to a halt. I pushed Bogdan off of me. Then I saw the knife plunged in his chest, and while everyone around me screamed and jumped up, my cry lodged in my throat and I was lost in darkness. I lost myself from time and space.

I came to in a small hospital room. They told me I was in Skopje. Everything with the babies was fine. I felt my stomach. They kicked at me. For a moment, I fell into a kind of bliss, but the next instant, I jolted: "What about Bogdan?" Silence. Just like in a movie, the nurse didn't know what to say. "The young man…" I understood. Once again I fell, sinking into myself, into my own grave. I don't know if I was in the hospital for hours, days, or months. I came fully awake the day two police officers came into the room. They were kind. One was younger; the other had gray hair. They expressed their condolences and asked me how I was. "When is your due date?" I couldn't remember. They told me they had been following the whole incident, and the killer was in jail. He was captured immediately, right at the border. A "known criminal," they said, "dealing in drugs, cigarettes, alcohol, and now a murderer as well. He won't get less than twenty years in prison!" There had been drugs in the package. "Where's Bogdan's body?" I mustered the strength to ask, and they told me it was already in the morgue. When I was better, I would be able to bury him. "Does his mother know?" I asked, and they told me she knew. It had been their duty to notify her. She was shocked, but had said she couldn't come. "We barely understood each other," they said. "She couldn't find the words in Macedonian." "Your parents know, too," they said. For a minute, no one spoke. Then the older one said, "We are here to ask you about something, but you're the one asking us questions." He meant it as a joke, but I was confused and in an exhausted dreamlike state, likely caused by sedatives. "What?" I asked. They told me it had also been their duty to examine and confiscate our luggage along with the killer's. Everything had been sent for expert analysis, including Bogdan's laptop. "We found something we can't explain," the older policeman continued. "There were thirty files on your partner's laptop with falsified passports. And in your suitcase, in the large folder containing the ultrasound photo of your babies, were the passports of four Macedonian citizens, but not Macedonian passports, falsified British ones." He fell silent. I looked at him, stunned. Then he added, "There weren't any passports in his suitcase, just in yours." I kept staring at him, but nothing made sense. I was too weak to grasp what he was saying, but somewhere, as if through a tunnel, my mind went back to the time in London when I came across the file with passport data. Bogdan had assured me that it was for the new quiz show, and I had believed him. Now Bogdan was dead, and I decided to keep believing in him until the day I died. "They were for a show that Bogdan was pitching to the BBC," I said. The officers looked at me quizzically, surprised and sympathetically. "The passports had already been counterfeited," the younger one said. "We found the people in our international database. Counterfeiting passports is a felony. You're being charged for being an accomplice and for the cover-up. Do you understand what's happening? What's happened?" the older officer asked me paternally. I didn't. I was only aware of one thing: I lost Bogdan on that bus, Bogdan had died, the man with the package had killed him, and had I taken the package, Bogdan would still be alive.

Once again, I lost myself between dream and reality. I

don't know how I got to the cemetery for Bogdan's burial from the hospital. I know there were lots of police officers at the burial. We buried him near Srebra's grave, and the only ones there were my mother, my father, Verče, Auntie Dobrila, and I. Aunt Milka couldn't come—or more precisely, my mother convinced her not to come. My mother's relationship with my uncle had once again cooled. The burial took place as if in a parallel universe. I simply walked beside Bogdan's coffin. No. I didn't walk, my belly simply carried me forward. The officers walked behind us in silence. The hired men lowered Bogdan's coffin into the grave. I covered my mouth with the palm of my hand, kissed it, then lowered my hand: a last kiss for Bogdan. The grave was marked with chalk: Bogdan Majstorovski 12/5/1972–11/9/2001. His mother hadn't come. I telephoned her later. She said she'd been unable to get a flight. I said nothing, crying. She cried, too. Then she hung up.

Immediately following the burial, two police officers grasped me and led me, gently, almost tenderly, to a police van with barred windows. They showed me the warrant for my arrest: concealing falsified travel documents. I tried to break free and get out of the van, but a young police officer said it would better for me—"and for the babies," he said—if I were calm and obedient. If I wasn't guilty, the remanding judge would simply release me, the officer said. But the remanding judge didn't release me. "The passports were in your bag, in a folder with your babies' ultrasound pictures. Surely they didn't get there on their own," he said. And it was impossible to prove the laptop was only Bogdan's. "Furthermore, in the hospital you told the officer that Bogdan was creating some sort of quiz show with that data, which means you knew about it, but didn't report it. You can't be so naïve as to believe he wanted to make a show with passport information. How is that possible when it's quite clear: on the left side are citizens from Eastern Europe with passports from their countries, and on the right side is the data that would be needed for their new British passports. And those new British passports weren't issued by the government, but manufactured, counterfeited. With special paper, a special printer, and well-studied passport numbers. And a large number of passports! Those passports were made somewhere: a basement, an apartment, somewhere secure. Perhaps in your home?" "No, no, no," I insisted. But it didn't help. I wasn't helped by the lawyer representing me either, a former colleague of Srebra's and mine from the law faculty. He had been a member of our class. He had been an excellent student, who, needless to say, remembered us. He told me he had been following our situation, including the affair with the money for the operation. I simply couldn't prove I wasn't guilty. Because of my late-stage pregnancy, the officials granted me house arrest. Three months. So I couldn't flee the country. With newborns, it would be even more difficult. I had no choice.

They drove me in the police van to my parents' apartment. It was the first time I entered their home since arriving in Skopje. I was taken from the hospital to Bogdan's burial and from there straight to the interrogation. An officer helped me out of the van as the neighbors watched me from their balconies with varying expressions of astonishment. I was led to the entryway and then into the apartment, where I signed some documents and was told that I couldn't leave and I couldn't have visitors. My mother and father stared fixedly at us; I could barely stand, and when the police officers left, my mother said from the hallway, "Turn off the light." I went into my room, lay on the bed, and panted, my heart beating, and it felt as though the vein that had joined my head with Srebra's was beating too, yet Srebra no longer existed, Bogdan no longer existed, nor did Aunt Ivanka, Roza, Grandma, or Grandpa. Nobody. There was no one left alive any longer. So many deaths were connected with my life; so many people had died on me. It was as though I was the one person in the entire world chosen by God to have all of her close relatives killed. The one person who should remain alive while all those around her were dead. Inside, I carried two lives, the children Bogdan would never have, and I was the wife he would never have. I lay in my old bed in Skopje, and our babies kicked in my womb, and I wished I would vanish, go somewhere far away—into the void, if such a thing existed. For days, I just lay there, only getting up to get the food my mother prepared for me. She was pale, gloomy, wrapped in her blue robe. I carried the dishes into my room and ate there, alone, leaning against the sewing machine. Then I leafed through books, photo albums, listened to old cassettes, and, in moments of despair, remembering that Bogdan had been killed right before my eyes because of me, I sobbed with my head in the pillow. I don't know if anyone has ever shed as many tears as I did for all those near to me. And I couldn't even visit their graves. When my mother heard me crying, she would come into my room and say, "Go ahead and cry now, since you're smarter than anybody; after all, you know everything." Once again, I showered only on Sunday evenings, and on Wednesdays rinsed myself with water from the green pot. One day, my father brought me a letter the postman had left on top of the mailboxes because the number of the apartment was missing from the address. It was for me. From Bogdan's mother in England. It was only three sentences: "Admit your guilt so the matter will be closed and we won't be harassed here. They might search our place, and as Bogdan's mother, I could be extradited. I beg you, Zlata, confess!" I had nothing to confess. I didn't have even the smallest amount of guilt, and still didn't believe that Bogdan could have been involved with counterfeiting travel documents. Surely I would have noticed something! Something more concrete than the file on his computer. Bogdan wasn't that sort of person. He was so good, so humane, filled with understanding and love. He carried me, he loved me more than anything in the world. But lying on the old bed I had shared with Srebra, alone with my thoughts, I slowly put together the mosaic of our life in London, which was forever changed, and the consequences of which, evidently, my unborn twins and I would carry. Yes. Hadn't I noticed the list of passports on Bogdan's computer? And like an idiot, I had believed he really was creating a TV show with the young men from their Society of Young Pro-Western Immigrants from Eastern Europe. It was likely they had been counterfeiting the passports together, creating programs and selling the passports for large sums of money. But where did they do all of that? Where? We had no secret compartment in our apartment in London. We didn't have a basement or an attic. Maybe where one of the other guys lived? Or in Brighton, at his adopted mother's? The idea flashed through my mind. Maybe that was where…in the basement of the large family home where first Bogdan's aunt lived with the partner whom she had never married, Bogdan, and Auntie Stefka. Then, after his aunt died of cancer, Auntie Stefka married her sister's partner, who became Bogdan's stepfather. There was surely space there for the computers, printers, and special machines for counterfeiting passports. Where else would the money have come from that Bogdan received from his adopted mother every week for years? And why else would she write a letter telling me to confess so she wouldn't be interrogated and pursued in England? I didn't know, but the possibilities rolled around in my head, even though I refused to believe they were true.

I spent the final weeks of my pregnancy under house arrest. I exchanged barely a word with my mother and father. For days at a time, I lay in my room and only got up to get the food from the dining-room table that my mother had left for me. It was understood, though unspoken, that I would eat in my room, as if I weren't even allowed to leave that room while I was under house arrest. My father kept silent and grew thinner. My mother talked to herself, always saying horrible things. We didn't have a memorial for Bogdan the first week after burial or for the fortieth-day commemoration. I wasn't allowed to go out, and my mother and father didn't go to the cemetery even to visit Srebra. My mother went to church only to light candles. I wanted to tell her, "Light one for Roza, too," but kept silent, because Roza had not been mentioned for years in our home, as though she were a taboo subject, especially since my mother couldn't stand Auntie Magda.

My mother still cooked the same foods—beans on Friday, potatoes and meatballs on Saturday, stuffed peppers on Sunday, fried dough on Monday, Tuesday, and Wednesday... Always minimal: three small drumsticks for three people, three stuffed peppers, or one pastrmajlija baked on a large baking sheet. I was pregnant, and, aside from all my other pains, hunger sometimes took hold of me. I'd empty the plate placed on the sewing machine table in my room, and missed my grandma's stews: rice and macaroni with small bits of meat (there were always nice bits of meat for Srebra and me), potatoes and rice with roasted meat, thick pancakes, round loaves of soda bread, leeks and meat spiced with red pepper, boiled wheat ground with walnuts and sugar, baked apples, baked squash, French toast, peas our mother sent her. My mother moped around the apartment for days on end talking to herself: "What's happened to us, why not to someone else? Just funerals, just blackness. And it wasn't chance: Snežana must have been hexing us her whole life. She wants to exterminate us. May her heart be devoured. May she never see the light of day." My mother cursed my aunt, the eternal culprit of all the misfortunes that befell our whole family. As soon as she married my uncle, she began to demonstrate her—uncommon at that time—new-age interests, and perhaps talents as well. Who knew? She read books about white magic, about black magic, and about life beyond the grave. At one point, she believed in reincarnation, but then in resurrections and God, and then, at some other point, in Satan. She gathered magic spells, and then tried to perform them. In the village, we often found small nests of twigs with a single red Easter egg, or a person made of straw with red lipstick flecked along the length of its body. Whenever my grandmother found these items, she simply tossed them in the woodstove, and let the fire burn them. How beautifully the twigs of the nests sputtered as Grandma crossed herself in front of the paper icon of Saint Nicholas affixed to the wall. We children were never afraid of our aunt's interest in witchcraft, but it apparently frightened the adults. And now, listening to my mother cursing and damning her, now that I was grown up myself, a secret fear splashed over me like her words. I thought, what if she—the wife of the uncle we loved most in the world, the one who took him from us, so we only saw him once over five or six years—really had the ability to kill those close to us? Perhaps at her house, all of us were miniaturized in straw with our hearts pierced by a toothpick. And perhaps that was why we were all slowly dying off, one after the other. First Grandma, then Srebra, then Grandpa, then Aunt Ivanka, and now Bogdan. There was no love lost between my mother and my aunt—they couldn't stand each other. Why would she kill Aunt Ivanka—if in fact she had—by planting an illness in her body, as well as her soul? Making it so Aunt Ivanka simply didn't want to get better, resigning herself to her fate, her death. Why spare my mother if she really could perform death spells? Srebra and I had a strange relationship with our aunt. When we were little and our uncle married her, we both wrote little songs entitled "My Aunt." I wrote about an idealized aunt with blue eyes, blond hair, a slender figure, sweet smile, steady hand, and a quick step. My aunt really liked my song. Srebra's song was more realistic: my aunt has brown eyes, is heavy, nearly two hundred pounds, with dark brown curly hair that she never brushes, is the biggest lazybones in the family, and only knows how to make cakes with ten or a dozen eggs in them. When the domestic impulse for baking a cake took hold of her, both we and Grandma knew that for the next few days, there would be no fried or poached eggs. My aunt would go all out: mixing things, filling several pots, and using up all of Grandma's golden reserves of oil, sugar, and flour. And when she set the cake in the refrigerator, everything would be left unwashed and scattered. She would go off into her room, lock the door, and fall asleep, snoring more like an old man than a young bride. That was our aunt in Srebra's song, or, if not exactly a song, a poem. When our aunt read it, she became terribly angry. She tore it into tiny pieces and screamed at Srebra, "This is on your head, and it's too bad Zlata will also have to pay because of you." Srebra made a sign that she was a bit cuckoo, but the incident was soon forgotten, or at least we thought it was forgotten. But if she killed Srebra, why did she also kill Aunt Ivanka? Aunt Ivanka was the one who got along best with her; she understood her more than anyone else. She always let her have her way and helped her out. She took our cousins with the gorgeous olive-green eyes out for walks, the ones who, when they grew up, became completely estranged from us and never contacted us again. They didn't even come to Srebra's or Aunt Ivanka's funerals. True, I wasn't at Aunt Ivanka's either, but it was hard to come from London the same day as the funeral, but from somewhere in Macedonia—surely not. Aunt Ivanka got along with everyone, and wanted to please everyone to the best of her ability, but my mother was convinced that part of my aunt's mission as a witch was to kill her, too. But then why had Bogdan died? After all, Bogdan had never even met my aunt. As a child, he surely noticed my uncle when he lived with us while studying a foreign language, but do chance two-second meetings with grown-ups, our friends' uncles, really remain in a child's memory? Bogdan couldn't have been one of my aunt's victims. Did she forever hold on to the little song idealizing an aunt that I wrote when I was young, but then decided to do something to me, anyway, taking what was most important in my life: Bogdan? Then I thought about Roza. Could she have taken Roza from me as well? Surely not. As far as I can recall, I didn't see my aunt between the time I was given the chain with the little cross and when I lent it to Roza. In other words, the chain couldn't have had a spell on it. I hurled such conjectures at my mother, who continued to say Snežana wouldn't rest until she exterminated the lot of us. "Just mark my words," she murmured to herself. "She will mow us down like the plague."

Verče once told me she had run into my uncle in Skopje. She said he was wearing a completely moth-eaten suit, with one button hanging by a thread and another one missing, his pants wet from snow. He was wearing thin-soled shoes, and hadn't shaved for days. He was waving around the yellow briefcase he had bought while living with us and studying. Srebra and I often played with that briefcase. Hundreds of times, we put it on the couch and opened and closed it, arranging his pens, papers, notebooks, and lecture notes inside, arguing over who got to carry it to the big room and back. My uncle continued to use that briefcase, the same one, for years. If my mother wasn't at home constantly, I would have called my uncle to tell him that Bogdan had died, although he didn't know him. I would have told him that I would soon give birth and that I had graduated but refused to accept my master's diploma. He would have thought that incomprehensible; he had tried to get his degree, even when he was older. No one understood what I had done. I overheard my mother say to my father, "They can't prove she was making passports, too, but even if they let her go, what will she do? How is she going to make any sense of her life? She doesn't have a job in London, and with just a Macedonian diploma, who will hire her? She squandered her prime years on her degree, and then she didn't get her diploma out of sheer stupidity and self-indulgence. There's nothing for her to do here, either; there are so many lawyers just sitting around. No one is waiting to hire her as a lawyer." My mother embittered my soul, and in such moments, I even thought about pleading guilty so they would put me in jail to give clarity to my present and my future. But then I thought about what would happen to my babies, and I was afraid they would take them from me—I had a law degree, and I knew that, in Macedonia, in the women's section of Idrizovo prison, there was no place for babies. Then I would see, suddenly, how angry I was at myself. I wasn't guilty of anything. I'd had no idea Bogdan was actually working in some sort of counterfeiting passport factory. I cried for him and was angry at him; so many feelings were mixed up inside me. I was on the brink of a nervous breakdown, and the night my water broke I shouted as loudly as I could, "Mom!" I yelled again, and then my mother and father woke up in the big room. They got up, sleepily, and I told them to call an ambulance. My father looked for his glasses behind the television. His hands were shaking more than mine. My mother said that ambulances don't come for women in labor, so it would be better to call a taxi. My father called a White Mercedes taxi—theirs was the only number he had written down on a piece of paper—and I quickly slipped on a robe and left the apartment. My father held me by the arm and lifted me into the taxi, telling the driver to take me to the maternity ward. "The state hospital or the one in Čair?" the taxi driver asked, and my father said, "The one in Čair," but I said, "The state hospital." My father asked me, "Do you have any money?" I just nodded. It was a good thing that I'd put my wallet in the bag I'd prepared for the hospital. When we arrived at the state hospital, I paid the driver and then told the first orderly I met in the hallway that my water had broken. He looked at me—he probably hadn't seen such a large belly in a long time—and asked, "Where's the orderly from the ambulance?" When I told him I had come by taxi, he clicked his tongue and yelled, "Alone? By taxi? At two o'clock in the morning? After your water broke?" He was shouting and looking at me in confusion, even as he helped me lie down on a gurney in the hallway.

I gave birth by Caesarian section. I gave birth to two girls. No parts of their bodies were conjoined. Two normal girls. One weighed six pounds, the other five pounds, nine ounces. "Twins," said the midwife when I awoke from the anesthesia. "Mašallah! May they live long and healthy lives! What are you going to call them?" "Marta and Marija," I said like a shot, even though those names hadn't occurred to me before. Soon, all the nurses came to see Marta and Marija. Especially after they learned there was no father, that their father had been the one in the incident on television—the man killed on the Sofia to Skopje bus, with whom I was returning to Skopje from abroad so we could get married. "But aren't you under house arrest? Something about passports you had with you?" asked one of the medical technicians boldly as he helped me swaddle the babies. "Yes," I said, "but I'm not guilty. I haven't done anything." Some felt sorry for me; others gossiped about me. The other mothers in the room avoided talking to me. On the second day, a nurse came flying into the room and shouted, "Hide the pacifiers! There's a delegation from UNICEF coming!" The delegation had to see that all the mothers were nursing their babies and weren't using formula or pacifiers. But a lot of us were having difficulty nursing and we all had supplementary bottles and pacifiers that we dipped in sugar water to soothe our crying babies a bit. When the delegation left—quite pleased with how we were bonding with our babies, pacifiers still under the pillows—several police officers came into the room, sent by the court of inquiry, and, immediately behind them, my lawyer. "I had no intention of escaping. I couldn't give birth at home. I had to break house arrest to get to the hospital." Apparently, I was supposed to have notified the investigative judge immediately. At two in the morning? How, when the only number I had was for his office, which opened at eight? But if it had been during day, would it have occurred to me to call him? The police said they would wait for me in the hallway;

I was supposed to leave the hospital that day with Marta and Marija. My lawyer sat down beside me, and, as if trying not to wake the babies sleeping in a small crib beside my bed, whispered as quietly as possible that he had some information. The London police had searched the apartment, but they found nothing in particular, which demonstrated that the passports hadn't been counterfeited there. But where then? Where? I should try to remember all the people Bogdan hung out with, who he brought home, and most importantly, where he went by himself. "He hung out with Siniša, Jan, Georgi, but I only saw them when they visited us. They were all members of the Society of Young Pro-Western Immigrants from Eastern Europe, and it's hard to believe they would be involved in such things." "And you?" my lawyer asked, looking me in the eye. "You studied migration. Bogdan could have dragged you into the business. Tell me." "No," I said, looking him in the eye as well. "No, I really thought Bogdan was working on a show about nationality." The lawyer rolled his eyes, as he had the first time we spoke. He looked at me as though I were an idiot, which I had been. Marta and Marija awoke, and both began to cry at the same instant. My mother and father came into the room. My mother immediately took some holy water from her handbag and spritzed Marta and Marija, who began to cry even more. "What are you doing?" I shouted at her. "It's okay. That's what you do with babies," she said, as she lifted Marta and my father lifted Marija. The lawyer politely said goodbye and left. Then we also left the hospital, under police escort. My mother and father had come by bus. Now all of us, along with the babies, went home in a police van. There were journalists and cameras everywhere. That very evening, while Marta and Marija slept in their little bed made from two armchairs pushed together, with a pile of sheets and blankets over them and two sprigs of basil beneath them, I watched myself on the small television in my room getting in the police van with Marija in my arms, my mother carrying Marta, and my father carrying my bag.

"Look carefully at this young woman!" the newsman said. "Five years ago, she went to London with her Siamese twin to have an operation to separate their heads. Her sister died; Zlata Serafimovska survived. Today, five years later, she is charged with counterfeiting passports in England with her partner, who was killed as they returned to Macedonia. The husband-to-be and father of these two babies is dead, and only Zlata Serafimovska knows the whole truth. Will she reveal it?" The journalist shouted as the video showed me covering Marija's head and ducking into the van. But I was now in a secure place, under house arrest but in my own room with my two little daughters.

Everything that ensued could have been anticipated from a legal perspective, but I was nursing two small babies, and I had no more tears in my eyes. In my dreams, God and Bogdan were mixed up. It seemed like they were playing a joke on me. Bogdan sometimes laughed coarsely; sometimes he cried and shouted, "Mom! Mom!" In my dreams, I often watched as I flung myself from the roof of the building that had stood across from our apartment in London. Every dream was a nightmare, every night was long—long and broken by Marta and Marija's crying. I nursed them in a state of delirium. I stroked them as if they were plush toys, and not babies, not my children. During the day, my father walked them for me—first one, then the other—from the kitchen to the balcony and back, again and again, and my mother wandered around the apartment, cooking something or other. Marija and Marta, one after the other, pushed their

cherubic faces into my mother's, which was both old and in-
fantile at the same time. They slobbered one cheek and then
the other. My mother laughed and said, "You little bitches."
In Macedonian, dirty words are, for some reason, pet names
for children: s*hitbox, pisspants, bumhead, farter, little bitch*. My
mother didn't take them outside even once, and, although I
had given them the money and begged them to buy the double carriage, it just stood in the big room, and neither she nor
my father wanted to push it. "You don't take children outside
for forty days," she told me, so we languished in the apartment all winter. I had two heaters going in my room, and
covered Marta and Marija with a thick blanket, but my soul
was colder than it had ever been. I still ate alone on the sewing machine table in my room, watching Marija and Marta
as they lay on the couch. Once, Marija made a terrible mess
while being changed, like in a movie. It was surreal. First, she
pooped all over my hand, because she was naked and hadn't
yet been swaddled, and then on the changing mat on my
bed. I shouted, surprised. My father came into the room, and
Marija spattered us and the floor. We cheered her on, laughing. We were happy because she had finally managed to poop
after five whole days—we had given her a small bottle of
chamomile tea and sugar. We felt fortunate, happy, surprised.
It was the first time in my life I'd heard my father laugh like
that. I laughed all afternoon, adding fantastic elements as I
reimagined the incident: Marija is pooping, the excrement
flies in every direction, I crouch down, hiding, so she can't aim
it at me. How much I missed Bogdan at times like that. The
incident freed me, making me feel my awareness that I was a
mother, and Marija and Marta deserved to have a mother, in
the full sense of the word, and not an absent nurse who just
vegetates beside them.

Sometime before New Year's, my house arrest finally ended, and I was free while the legal process played itself out. It was a full nine months before I was called to a hearing, and after several proceedings, I was found guilty of being an accomplice to a criminal activity—concealing travel documents—and sentenced to a year in prison. "A whole year!" my mother said, and then gave me one of her lectures: "Your children will forget you. A year is a long time. Who will look after them? Your father and I are old. We can't take care of young children. This is what happens when you carry on with a criminal. He was in your home and you didn't recognize him. You went all the way to London, and ended up with a Macedonian guy. You couldn't find some Englishman, someone local. Even as a child, it was obvious what sort Bogdan was, sitting in front of our building with those silly crossword puzzles and looking at everyone like he was out of his mind. Even then, you could tell what sort he'd be. But it wasn't her fault. The poor woman was taken away young. But the single woman he adopted wasn't stupid; she knew why she was going to England. She was interested in business, and she taught her child. Now you need to just take it and shut up. As for the children, God will have to look after them for you." What my mother said wasn't what was important to me. What was important was that Marta and Marija were still babies, and my house detention had ended along with my nine months of freedom. I awaited my fate. My lawyer said he would do everything to prove I wasn't guilty on appeal. He convinced me to show him the letter from Bogdan's mother to help redirect the investigation. "See who has a bee in her bonnet," he said, and he was convinced—as I was—that Bogdan's mother knew about the crime and had possibly participated in it herself. My lawyer pressured me to tell him everything connected with my case—I must know something, something I was hiding, he said. "It's obvious…I suspect you don't want to expose Bogdan's parents for the counterfeiting, or his friends from the society. Your children will be given to a children's home if your parents can't take them," he said. "A whole year in prison awaits you." He was essentially convinced there was no way to prove I wasn't guilty except by informing on Bogdan's mother. At the hearing, I defended myself with silence. I didn't have the strength to speak. Bogdan's image inside me kept me from mentioning his mother's house as a possible factory for the counterfeiting. She never contacted me again. Why didn't I name her? The woman had never liked me, nor I her. Nothing else was found in our apartment in London, and the case was closed. Everyone now waited for the decision here in Macedonia. In the meantime, the owner of our apartment in London cleaned and rented it out to some other people. Who knows what happened to our things? Most likely, Bogdan's mother took them. I couldn't contact her to find out. Bogdan's laptop was the only piece of evidence the Macedonian authorities had, but it didn't contain a single name of a possible accomplice. All that was there were the data from real East European passports and false British ones. And the four passports inside the folder with the ultrasound pictures of Marta and Marija in my suitcase. I don't know. I promised myself I would inform on Bogdan's mother if it became clear to me that I couldn't live without Marta and Marija. Or not. To find the ability to denounce someone…you need to be born with that sort of character.

With a lump in my throat, I asked my mother if she would bring Marija and Marta to visit me while I was in prison. "If not," I said, "it would be better to give them to a children's home. Surely, the people there would bring them to me, or hear from my lawyer. It won't be unpleasant for you."

"*O tom potom*," my mother said, using a Serbism for "more about that later." She would use Serbian phrases whenever she wanted to express something important, something that ostensibly didn't exist in Macedonian. Marija and Marta still hadn't been christened. I told my mother to go to the church and beg the priest to come to our house to christen them. The children could have gone to the church, but I wanted to be there for the christening. My mother got dressed, all in black (at home, she always wore her blue robe). I asked her why she was wearing black, and she said, "So people won't say, 'Look how she dresses after all those people she buried: a daughter, a sister, her parents, and a future son-in-law.'" Even when she went to throw out the garbage, she dressed in black. It disgusted me. I was more and more annoyed with having to stay in my old home. I missed our London apartment, and more than anything, I missed Bogdan. I loved him, I desired him, I was angry at him, but he was dead. Gone forever and not coming back.

The next day, just as my lawyer arrived to announce that my house detention was to end that day, the priest arrived with all the things he needed for the christening. I recognized him immediately. He was old and confused, but he still had a big belly. It was the same priest who had given me the chain and cross, and the little icon of Saint Zlata Meglenska. Now he had come to christen my daughters. "Very lovely, Marta and Marija, Christian names. But how can we do this without a godfather? The children must have a godfather." He cast a rather rude glance at my lawyer. "If there's nobody else, it'll have to be you." My lawyer found himself with no way out. There was no one else, so he agreed. We christened Marta and Marija on the dining-room table. Marta always cried more than Marija, but at the christening, Marija was the one who kept crying, and I simply could not calm her. Marta looked inquisitively at the priest, reaching toward his beard. The ritual was short, and when it was over, the priest took his money, gathered the items for the christening, and we stepped out into the hallway so I could see him off. He said, "I recognized you. Terrible things have happened to you, child. Do you still have the little icon I gave you? I haven't seen you since so I could tell you either to bring it to church so I could bless it, or to throw it away. May your eyes be shielded from it. It turns out a Satanist left that icon at our church. He left other, similar, icons later, at night, apparently, in front of the church door. One of them—Saint Petka, I think—was spattered with blood. I didn't know that when I gave it to you. I thought someone had left it for his own soul's sake. Later on, we discovered that it was the Satanist. One time, he even desecrated our church door, scribbling all sorts of things on it. He's now rotting in Idrizovo." Then he bit his tongue, remembering that I, too, would likely rot in Idrizovo. He didn't wait for a response. He walked through the door, his cassock flying behind his old, large body. I closed the door. I stood in the hallway, looking at myself in the mirror. I looked at myself through my own eyes, hidden behind my lenses, wide and powerless. Tears appeared in the corners of my eyes. I stood for a long time without being aware of it. My lawyer's voice, as he was leaving, brought me back to reality. "Good luck," he said to me. "Good luck," I told him.

During those nine months people rarely came to our house. Ties with family and friends are so relative. What we understand as closeness, seems inconceivable later, as if we're demanding too much, as if we have no shame. Estrangement is a virus of this new century. Not even babies seem to want their aunts, uncles, and guests to change their diapers. They are restricted to their parents, who are bound even by law to care for them while they are young. They don't want the day to come when aunts, uncles, or someone else would ask for some sort of favor, reminding them that "I wiped your bum." In fact, there's no greater injustice than to throw at people the fact that you helped them when they were babies. Which is precisely what my uncle said over the phone: he had wiped my bum when I was young, mine and Srebra's, when we were in the village and he was in school, but now I don't want to help pay for his new house. And I had spent all that time in England. I was stunned. Does a person need to make a list of all the people who fed her, swaddled her, bathed her, carried her, put her to bed, and so on, when she was a baby? Then punctually settle their requests to pay back the debt? Even if, at the time, there had been no debt, but pure, overarching, genuine love. I had loved my uncle unconditionally, but the time came when he began to love me conditionally, reminding me that he had wiped my bum, mine and Srebra's, when we were little. It was good that Grandma and Grandpa weren't alive. Surely they turned in their graves, and not just once.

2002–2005

On September 11, 2002, while the world remembered and paid respects to the victims of the twin towers in New York, and we returned from the cemetery following the one-year memorial for Bogdan—my conscience gnawed at me that a whole year had passed since his death—a police van was waiting for me in front of our building. I gathered my most important things. It was quite an emotional scene with my babies; they were only ten months old, but they seemed to understand that I was leaving them, that I had to go without them, to prison, and I would be able to see them every two and a half weeks, to hug them, if, that is, their grandma and grandpa brought them to see me. They cried and kicked as if they knew. My mother and father shut themselves with Marija and Marta into the big room, and I crossed myself before stepping outside. Then I went as if I were going to face a firing squad. In my cell were Kristina, Anka, and Jasminka. Four months later, a woman named Marina was also placed with us. Kristina, a professional thief who targeted old women, was pregnant. She had already robbed four old women by following them home from the bank. "There's no better place to pick a pocket than on a bus or in an elevator," she said, laughing. "And old Macedonian women, pension-ers, are weird and stupid. Especially the ones who get their pensions deposited directly into their accounts. They go to the bank early in the morning and take out the whole check. So they can make ends meet. They don't put the money in their wallet, but stuff it, along with the receipt, in the bag they usually take to the market. But after they withdraw the money from the bank, they don't go anywhere else, just back home. It's really easy to follow them, get on the bus after them. They go into their building, their legs aching, and they press the button for the elevator. You joke with them politely, but you should also look a bit concerned. You get into the elevator with them and then take a map of Skopje from your pocket and ask them in English if this is the right address. There's supposed to be a dentist's office here in the building, and your tooth really hurts. You ask if she knows what floor it's on, and, as the woman looks confusedly at the map, you reach underneath, thrust your hand into her bag, take out the money. Then you fold up the map and leave the elevator say-ing, 'No, it's the other entryway. Thanks, goodbye,' and you go back down in the elevator. She unlocks her door, still in a daze because of the strange encounter in the elevator, and at home, after she's taken off her shoes, had a glass of water, and sat down in an armchair to catch her breath, she remembers her pension and looks in her bag, but there's nothing there." That's how Kristina spoke, laughing, in her sixth month of pregnancy. One day, however, the husband of one of those pensioners was already at the door, waiting to fetch a newspa-per as soon as his wife returned with her pension, and she said to him, "Take some money, and buy bread, too," and dug into her bag, but there was no money there. Her husband raced to the elevator after Kristina. He grabbed her and struck her so hard that her jaw hurts even today. Luckily, he didn't break any of her teeth. Then he held her tight and yelled at the top of his lungs, "Help! Police!" The old woman had already called the police…so now here she was. "But you just wait and see when I get out of here," she said. I was a bit afraid of her, because there was something vengeful about her. "When you give birth, you won't think about that anymore," I told her, but I wasn't convinced that would be the case. Anka was in jail because she had been caught at the border with cocaine in a small cooler. They hadn't believed she was merely returning from a vacation in Greece. Jasminka had beaten her mother, an elderly woman, into a coma. The mother had woken from the coma when the canary she loved more than anything in the world alighted on her breast. Jasminka's father had thought to bring the canary with him to the hospital. The canary died exactly forty days later. Jasminka's mother and father found Christ and became true believers. Jasminka felt a little of their influence, and perhaps during her six-month jail term she would become a better person. Who knows? One can only hope.

When I told my story, nearly all of them recalled the media coverage of our operation. They asked me about everything: why Srebra hadn't survived, how Bogdan had died. Bogdan's murderer was in the men's section of the same prison. "What will you do to him if you see him?" Anka asked. "I hope I never see him again," I told her. What would I do to him? I didn't have long nails to plunge into his face. I didn't have the strength to beat him up. I didn't have a knife or a pistol to kill him. And it was a good thing I didn't, because at home I had two children who were nearly orphans. I wasn't sure my mother was giving them enough to eat, making cereal every three hours, boiling soup with chicken and carrots, giving them Humana formula made properly, according to the directions. I had more faith in my father, but I still told him a hundred times that the children needed to eat every three hours. God, how I missed them! The only ones who might not be able to grasp what it means to miss their children are those who, for whatever reason, have no children. My soul ached in my body, my heart weighed like a stone in my breast, the vein left to me after the operation rushed like a river. My entire being longed for the fruits of my womb. Every two weeks, my father came to the prison, bringing Marta and Marija. My mother usually didn't feel well, so she stayed home. I always worried that they had forgotten me, that they would cry when they saw me, that they wouldn't love me. On the phone, I sang them the little song I had made up just after they were born, which I had sung every night before they went to bed: "Tick tock, tick tock; I am here, knock knock. Marija and Marta, go to sleep now with this song, and someday you'll grow big and strong." They recognized the song. It was my connection to them. I told my father to sing it before bedtime, too. At first he said, "Oh, come on, that's nonsense. What won't you think of next?" I insisted, however, and told him he could at least do that for me; after all, they were his granddaughters. I didn't add that I was his daughter. He probably did sing it to them, and when they came to the prison and I sang it, they blinked, confused as to whether it was time for bed or they were listening to an echo of their mother from a past they didn't understand. That little song remained our strongest link while I was in prison. If the meetings were happy, the separations were so painful that, afterward, I lay down, physically sick, with a mouth full of bile and pains in my stomach and back. My periods lasted two weeks, but the prison doctor always had the same answer:

"A psychosomatic reaction." I read every book in the library: the textbooks Srebra and I had used in primary and secondary school; I reread Stale Popov's *A Patched Life*, *For Whom the Bell Tolls*, and Koneski's poem "The Embroideress." I read and read. I sank into myself, into the things I read, but there wasn't a single book by Marina Tsvetaeva in the library, and all the books of hers that had been in our apartment were who knows where—lost forever. My life was a lost life.

Marta and Marija had their first birthday on November 7, 2002, a Thursday, not a visiting day. I called them and sang "Happy Birthday." They cooed and said, "Mama, Gamma, Gampa." I asked my mother if she had made them a cake, and if they were going to blow out the candles. She said, "How are they supposed to know it's their birthday and blow out candles?" "You didn't make a cake?" I asked again. "I didn't close my eyes all night; my ears were buzzing so badly I thought my head would burst, and now I'm supposed to have baked a cake? I can barely move. If your father hadn't given me a massage, I would have gone out of my mind." I didn't respond. I thought, *We will celebrate other birthdays, my children. You'll see. This is your first but not your last.* It didn't make me feel any better.

Four months later, a young woman turned up in our cell who seemed somehow familiar. Marina. I had thought so much of Marina Tsvetaeva, and now God had brought a different Marina, either out of spite or as a joke. Tall and strong, with black oily hair and black-framed glasses. She was so familiar it seemed like I had seen her just the day before. I remembered that this was the girl who had adopted the single woman from the building next to ours when we were children. She had a mild mental deficiency and always walked with her feet pointed outward, with a slight limp, leaning on the arm of her adopted mother. I had never asked myself how a child with a developmental disability could adopt a mother at all. Perhaps one of the clerks in the town hall pushed her toward the single woman with the dignified, suffering look— the woman who always dressed in a navy-blue suit, tidy, quiet. Or perhaps the girl's psychological problems weren't so great. She didn't go to our school, nor did she go to a school for emotionally disturbed children. She went to school in the Kozle district, near the Institute for Respiratory Diseases, where her mother worked as a nurse. They always walked arm in arm, her adopted mother gently holding Marina's hand in hers, elbows linked. And now Marina was here, in the women's prison. She had killed her adopted mother. Most terrible of all was that she had kept her mother's body at home for nearly three weeks, until the neighbors called the police because of the unpleasant odor emanating from their apartment. The neighbors had smelled it the whole time, but hadn't thought it was anything so terrible. Marina's mother died from a blow from a blunt instrument, and Marina kept watching TV in the living room, next to her dead mother, who was already decomposing. She went to the store, cooked, ate. At the police station, she confessed that she had struck her mother on the head because she wasn't obeying her. Marina didn't realize what she had done. She spent only one day in our cell before she was taken to the Bardovci Psychiatric Hospital. I don't know if she recognized me when she saw me. I don't think so. She was lost but somehow carefree. Our encounter was strange. She was someone who had practically been my neighbor, someone whom Srebra and I had often run into on the street as she came home from school with her mother, but we had never played together, nor been friends. When I thought about it, I understood how excluded she had been from our lives. She never left the house alone; even if she could have, she had no friends. We all avoided her. Even Srebra and I considered her abnormal. It seems absurd, when lots of people considered us mentally deficient simply because of our conjoined heads, but we lived far more normal lives than Marina. My father confirmed the story for me—a bit sketchily—when he came to visit with Marija and Marta. But I wasn't listening to him. I just hugged and kissed my little angels, as they clapped my face and said, "Mama, Mama." My strength began to fade. Blisters developed in my mouth. My waking hours, even more than the nights, were despondent, disturbed, and lonely. One night, Father Ilarion—Darko—appeared in my dream. When he saw my distress, he said, "Ask." I replied, "I don't know what to ask. I'm at the bottom." Or did I say, "In hell"? I don't know. In his eyes I saw both understanding and a possible answer. Had I become too distant from God? It was a bad time in my life. When I woke, I went off to clean the bathroom—if that's what you'd call the rickety shower stall at the end of the hall. I had decided to be the good fairy that cleaned the prison while the others slept. I mulled over the dream. Why had Father Ilarion appeared to me? Why as a monk and not as Darko? Or as Srebra's husband? Disgusted with myself, I thought about what we had done to Srebra, falling into the sin of that sweet liqueur and arousal in the middle of the night, only a few months after their wedding. We destroyed Srebra's life. Yes, we killed her before the operation. She lost the embryo and had decided we needed to be separated at any cost. She didn't survive and now Darko was in a monastery, I was in prison, and Srebra was in her grave. With all my other dead. And my girls were growing without me. They had grown from babies to toddlers without my witnessing the changes.

Toward the end of the winter of 2003, my lawyer dashed into my cell, and, in an excited voice, told me he had heard from London that the counterfeiting factory had been found in the basement of Bogdan's mother's house in Brighton. The British police weren't stupid; of course they would eventually search the house of his mother and stepfather. They found everything they needed to take Bogdan's mother and stepfather into custody: special equipment, scanners, inks, codes, paper, printers, an entire factory where more than two hundred British passports had been counterfeited, with stolen identities, fake data, and photographs. And the materials for laminating documents were inside a black leather trunk. I was stunned. Wasn't that the trunk Bogdan had taken with him when he left Skopje for London with his mother? That's what Auntie Dobrila had said at the time: Bogdan carried a suitcase like something from olden times, a black leather trunk. Srebra and I had immediately thought he must have packed his crossword puzzle magazines so he would have them in England. "Both the police and members of the British immigration service took part in the raid, and they seized 20,000 pounds from your deceased partner's mother." My lawyer said they wouldn't escape a ten-year prison sentence. "And the most important thing," he added, "is that your partner's mother said you had no connection to the affair. They never dragged you into the business, and it had been Bogdan's wish that it remain a family secret." I was relieved, but I had served more than half a year in jail for no reason. Just when my children needed me the most. I had no intention of letting bygones be bygones. I told my lawyer I would seek damages from the Ministry of Justice because I had been charged without cause and my daughters had suffered because of it. I wanted moral satisfaction for the more than a half year of my life spent without my children, stuffed into a cell in the women's section of Idrizovo prison. He agreed, most likely because of the percentage of the damages he would receive. I hadn't had a good lawyer the entire time. Although he had been one of the best students in our law school, he was not a good lawyer. Otherwise, why hadn't he refuted the so-called proof brought against me in the charges, particularly since it had never been proven I was an accomplice in Bogdan's criminal activities? "I don't need a lawyer to seek damages," I told him. "This time I'll do it myself. Even if I have to go to the European Court of Human Rights in Strasbourg."

I was released. When I stepped outside, it was a cold spring day, the fifteenth of April, 2003. I took a bus to our neighborhood. Marija and Marta—now a bit grown, a year and a half old, with silky hair, almost like Srebra and me, but with Bogdan's eyes—were waiting at home. We hugged, they laughed, and I cried. I cried and I laughed. My mother and father kissed me briefly on the cheeks. Through the window of my room I saw that the linden under my window had been cut down. I had never noticed that its roots were in the garden of the classmate who had been Srebra's and my guardian angel in first grade, walking us to school and back. Then one day, other kids started calling him the "guardian of two-headed shit," and after that he avoided us the way the other children did. He had a crease between his eyebrows when he frowned. From behind the curtain on the balcony in the big room we secretly listened as he played hide-and-seek with other kids. His mother and father cut down my linden, mine, the archive of every moment in our lives. I felt sorry for the linden.

I was finally free, with no restrictions on where I went or with whom I spoke. People began coming to see me. Verče and her husband and child, my former monastery friends—

prompted by Darko, now Father Ilarion, to come and offer me support—and Lenče, just back from the Bardovci Psychiatric Hospital, where she had spent three entire weeks because she hadn't eaten for a week at home. She had become aggressive and sworn to her father that she would kill him. "She's probably sleeping with him," my mother said, "You'll see. He cut all her hair off." My mother had apparently "caught them in the act" once when she came back from the market and dropped by their place. I didn't believe her, although I had thought Mirko was sexually abusing Lenče for years. Once Srebra and I had dropped by unannounced to visit them, and they almost didn't open the door for us, and they were alone. Aunt Ivanka was at the doctor's, and Verče at school. The big room smelled of semen. My mother thought Lenče was guilty as well—she wanted it, she was flesh and blood, after all—and that Aunt Ivanka knew and had even said, "Mirko gives her pills and uses her." At the moment she said it, she was calm, pumped full of medicine. Other friends from primary school, now married with children, also came by. My mother got terribly anxious when guests came, but she played the part of hostess in front of them. Whenever someone announced a visit, she would whisper, "May they be struck blind." When I asked why she was cursing, she would answer, "I was talking to myself." She told me that, during the months I was in prison, she had grown sicker and I was unaware of the torments she suffered, with two small children on top of it all. If it hadn't been for my father, who knows if she would have survived. She heard a constant rushing sound in her head, even now. It had been pressuring her for months; her head was going to burst. No medicine helped. "But if it's written that you're going to die, there's no turning back. That's it," she said, and then, filled with tremendous self-pity, she'd lie on the couch in the kitchen and read newspapers. The blue robe was threadbare and mended in many places, but she didn't take it off. Now that I was home, she no longer took care of Marija and Marta. They were still deeply attached to my father, but they avoided their grandmother, playing with her only when she said, "Hop up onto my truck. Brrr, drive Chucky the punker, drive!" Then they would laugh and squeal, "Taki the pankel, Taki the pankel," but I didn't know who this punker was who had entered our family's lexicon. There were moments I felt I didn't even belong with my own children. I used all my strength to try to wipe away the time I had spent in prison, and I said, loud and clear, that the topic of conversation was closed, that what happened, happened, and I didn't want the word mentioned in the house. My mother only nodded, not sure that she could keep from mentioning the prison again. She would say things like, "If you hadn't lived with that swindler over there, you wouldn't have lived as a prisoner here." My family was the most radically pessimistic, and had the least initiative, of any in the world. My mother lived with a focus on her death, not on her life. Not even Marta and Marija—babies left, God knows how, for her to look after—could change her outlook or give her a new outlook on life. No, she found no meaning in anything. She had no goals, no perspective on herself or on us. Objectively, it was perhaps understandable: in her lifetime she had lost a daughter, a sister, her parents, her future son-in-law. But hadn't I lost a sister, an aunt, a grandmother and grandfather, a husband-to-be, and also my best friend? I recalled how I once thought tragedies were incommensurate. Now I was no longer certain. My mother was clearly in despair, or, as the monks would say, suffering from melancholy. With her pessimism and negativity, she was a servant of the devil; she had none of the joy in life that is given to us by God. She was negligent toward us, resigned to her fate, submerged in her own dark, gloomy place. Heading down, not up. In her view, there wasn't a single good person in the world. And as for bad people, Mirko, for example—she would say that it would be best if "someone drove a pick into his head and was done with it." She would offer, only verbally, of course, a hundred euros to the person who would kill him. My skin crawled when she said such things. Marta told me in her baby language that "Gramma's gonna die." When I asked her why she said that, she was silent, but Marija added, "Gramma's gonna die, but Grampa won't." I thought that my mother had filled the heads of eighteen-month-old children with her own sickness, telling them, "Grandma will die," and now they were repeating it. Our estrangement created a closeness between us. We would quarrel and not speak for days, but then begin talking again. When we sat down to eat and I saw only two fried fish for all of us, I would say somewhat jokingly to Marija and Marta, "Look, your grandma is like Jesus, feeding the multitudes with just two fishes." Marija and Marta didn't get it, but they would laugh, because I was laughing. My father would then say, "Yeah, yeah, you know everything." Surprisingly, after I got back from prison, we ate at the dining-room table. I would eat with the children first; then my mother and father would eat. Marija and Marta had highchairs that my father had bought used at the auto market, where all sorts of things, not just car parts, were for sale, and they now stood next to each other where there had been a chair, now relegated to the big room, next to my father's bed, where there was also a sack of flour. Perhaps my father transformed himself at night from a wolf into a billy goat with white paws so he could ritually devour my mother. But it was my mother, not my father, who stored the sack of flour there. As for my father, he kept his shoes in the garage, and when he had to go anywhere, he went downstairs in his slippers and put his shoes on in the garage. When he returned, he took off his shoes in the garage and came back up in his slippers. He did it out of unspoken spite, because I had told him that his shoes didn't belong in the bathroom where we all washed up and that Marija and Marta needed to live in a clean place.

How much fortitude and time I needed to get accustomed to life in that apartment, where living had never been comfortable. The television was usually on while we ate, which had always annoyed me, but I didn't have the strength to argue. Once during lunch, the Serbian program *The Heart of the Problem* caught my attention: a mother was talking about losing her eight-year-old daughter, and how her husband committed suicide because if it. Then they showed an exclusive photo of the girl's murderer—a seventeen-year-old boy, the girl's neighbor and her brother's friend. Then the boy, Dragan Spasoević, calmly described how he tricked the girl into coming to his apartment, how he raped her, and how, because he was afraid she would tell on him, he killed her. First, he said, he put his leg on her chest and choked her. When he thought she was dead, he went to the basement to find a suitcase or a trunk, but he couldn't find one. When he got back, the girl had dragged herself to the door. He got scared, knocked her down, and strangled her until she was definitely dead. He said all this calmly, and with regret, although the psychologist doubted both his conscience and his regret. Later, he began to pray and draw icons, to seek God. The criminologist whom the program consulted said it was just a tactic to get released on good behavior from prison before the end of the twenty-year sentence, which his lawyer insisted was too long, but Larisa's mother felt was disgracefully short. The murderer's parents still lived in the same entryway, and were watching the live show, so the host suggested to the reporter that he go and speak to them on air as well, but a producer notified the host that they were out of time. We all watched the show without touching our food, and by then, Marija and Marta were covered from head to toe in chicken stew. I felt terrible after the program. I didn't know how to free myself from the brazenness of the sin. I turned on the boiler to wash the girls. Later, after they fell asleep, I took a shower, scrubbing myself with a goat-hair brush. I had spent the last of the money from England, but I had hopes in my pending recompense from the Ministry of Justice for having been sentenced without cause.

I wanted to take Marta and Marija to the cemetery. My mother and father hadn't gone while I was in prison. We all went together by taxi. The candles blew out in the breeze. The ritual bread my mother brought crumbled apart on Srebra's grave. We ate some there, then at Aunt Ivanka's grave, then at Bogdan's. My mother said you should go to the graves of deceased family members first, then to the graves of others. According to her, Bogdan had never been a part of our family. But Bogdan and I had been a family for four years, in our London apartment in Shoreditch. He was everything to me: husband, child, mother, father, friend, teacher, and student. Plus, he had been the father of my children. But apparently that meant nothing. The bread made my mother sick to her stomach. Bogdan's grave was overgrown and untended. My mother brought a spoon to Aunt Ivanka, because she had dreamed that Aunt Ivanka called her, asking her to bring a spoon; for Srebra she brought apple juice, but for Bogdan, nothing. I had no food with me. I took Marta and Marija to him. I told them, "This is your daddy." They touched the photograph embedded in the stone with their little hands and repeated, "Daddy, Daddy." I stood there, not knowing what to feel.

I was never able to feel close to my dead loved ones in the presence of my parents. A few steps from Aunt Ivanka's grave, which had nearly collapsed from negligence (I was angry with Verče for not finding time to visit her mother's grave), beneath a glass shelter like a carport, was the grave of a five-year-old child. It looked like a table covered in tulips, with a white cross in the middle. I squeezed Marta and Marija. I would do anything to keep them alive and healthy. Aunt Milka told me over the phone that she would go to the cemetery on All Souls' Day and perform the rituals—she would mourn for Srebra, she would mourn for Aunt Ivanka and Bogdan. "Even though I never met him, since you loved him, I love him too. May God keep little Marija and Marta healthy." Then she added that she would ask Grandma and Grandpa if they were together up there, beside God, and she would cry so that others would see.

I made a cake for Marta and Marija's second birthday. My mother covered it with yellowish paper from Marija and Marta's drawing pad. Then she sat on the couch, vacant, gloomy, and silent. Every day, her spitefulness took more of a hold of her. She would lie down on the couch and pretend to sleep. She'd curl up, alone, restrained, untouchable. It was as though she were an artist, a Bohemian who didn't care what others thought of her, or how her granddaughters would see her. She would barely utter a word. A crushed expression on her face. She didn't want to make soda bread for me. She said she didn't know how, she'd never made it before, and my father didn't eat that kind of bread. She made a loaf of white bread, and I said thank you. But in my family, it was almost rude to say thanks or any other kind, polite word. Especially to my mother. She was insulted: Her nostrils flared, bulging out over her mouth. Her eyebrows furrowed, her cheeks grew sulky, taking on a yellowish tinge. They were still soft, like a baby's. Her eyes emitted an austere, injured expression. The image of the angry victim. She no longer laughed like she once had, a laugh that could overtake my father's anger. Only when she called Marija and Marta, "you little bitches," did she laugh with her old laugh as Marija and Marta repeated the word "bishes." On their third birthday, Marta asked me if I could give birth to a puppy for them. I laughed. Maybe I really was a bitch, but I couldn't give birth to a pup. "But Grandma calls us little bitches," said Marija. "Out of love," I answered her. Nothing was clear to them. I never understood our odd family estrangement. There was a connectedness between us, an absurd closeness, which we continuously destroyed. I asked myself what I'd think about all this when my mother died. Would I be sorry? Would I hate myself? Would my conscience be clear? I gave her everything she never gave to Srebra or me. I bought her everything she never bought us. The money that we never had when we went into the city, needing new clothes or makeup for our problematic skin. I kept reinforcing my self-confidence, which she kept destroying. She had grown numb to the outside world and was on the brink of an internal abyss. Long ago, when Srebra and I were children, we went on Saturday outings to the Matka Canyon, outside Skopje. My mother fried peppers and put them in a yellow plastic container. A little cheese, a few tomatoes, bread, and that was our picnic lunch. We would climb into the Škoda and silently—if you didn't count my mother's cautions and my father's curses—make our way to Matka. I remember the river. The riverbed and beach were rocky, but I don't recall ever swimming there. Everyone said Srebra and I would drown if we got in the water, that the river was not the sea, that we wouldn't float, and anyway…how could we swim with our heads like that? There were many families like ours, but their children swam. We sat on the shore, throwing stones into the water, angry at the whole world and waiting for evening to come so we could go back home.

My mother still went looking for my dirty clothes to wash them by hand, even after I forbade her from washing my clothes. She searched through my cupboard and left tea strainers inside, saying she would continue to use the orange one, which was more than twenty years old, black, and dirty, but if I wanted to use these, they should be kept in my cupboard. She counted my money, looked at each thing I kept in the cupboard, to see what I was hiding. Is this how she tried to get to know me better? Rather than having a frank conversation, she concocted some mystery about my simple life, then shared her evidence with my father. She was, however, a secret, safe mediator between my father and me. My father and I were uncomfortable when we were alone together. In fact, we were never alone. Marija and Marta had managed to erase the emotional distance between us once and for all. That didn't mean that we spoke, but our attention turned toward the children, so we didn't question our relationship. Before, my father used to drink wine or beer with lunch. He'd buy a case of beer and a barrel of Golden Delicious apples; he smoked pork; we ate white bread. But now they bought everything ready-made. They waited for others to give them things. They took little pleasure in anything. My mother no longer made rolls, vanilla cookies, *tulumbi*, steamed cookies, halvah, apple cake, Russian salad, or her pudding cake. At a time when everyone else was starting to consume more, purchasing things wholesale at supermarkets, my parents lived more and more ascetically, even though Marta, Marija, and I were also living in their home. I wanted us to live as normally as possible, to keep something extra in the refrigerator, to have bananas, grapes, and chocolate, both for them and for us. There was no love between my parents and me. Just as it had been when Srebra was alive. Did I also carry my mother's genes? Would I become like her, full of meanness? That's what Aunt Ivanka, when she was alive, used to say in secret: She is full of meanness. But when all was said and done, I didn't have spare parents. And my mother didn't love me in a motherly way. If I clutched my back, she asked, "What's the matter with you? Does your back hurt?" with bitterness, roughness, an absence of love. She got more and more annoyed by my, and perhaps also Marija and Marta's, presence in our—in their—home. As a matter of fact, she didn't *want* to love me, and she most often succeeded. Once, she sat in her room for two full days, angry and stubborn, not making lunch, because I told her to not scrape the pots with a fork, because I had just bought new ones downtown. She closed herself up in the big room as if she were a child. She didn't want to pick up Marija and Marta at day care; she didn't eat the beans I prepared; she didn't speak to anyone. A day or two later, though, I went shopping with Marija and Marta, and she came with us. She picked out hair dye. I bought it for her, along with a few bags of pretzels and two beers, so she could drink with my father, and that cheered her up. Only by taking her shopping could I buy her smile. My father barely survived living with her—he was like a flower in an arid climate. I remembered how he came to Darko's when Srebra was alive and how Srebra and I filled his bag with the groceries on my mother's list, how he would be silent, closed within himself. He would take them, carrying them home with barely a word. He was more and more like her, but fortunately, not in his heart, only in his mouth. He gossiped with her about the neighbors, anybody who passed by, all their acquaintances. My mother filled his mind with her mean thoughts, but Marta and Marija protected him from them. They were always ready to hug him, to watch cartoons with him, to call "Grampa, Grampa," and to offer him pretend coffee in small toy cups. But not her. Good Lord, how could such a mother have given birth to Srebra and me! But I didn't have a spare mother, just as I didn't have a spare sister, or a spare husband.

But perhaps my parents' lives wouldn't have fallen apart if they had been able to work for the rest of their lives, or at least another ten years. Both of them were sinking, my father without his job in the glass factory, my mother without her typewriter in the YU-Tire repair shop office. They had been satisfied when working, fulfilled. My father had a belly full of good hot meals in the cafeteria, my mother had her customers (my mother had always talked about her customers, her *stranki*, but Srebra and I had thought they were her foreigners—*strantsi*—and we'd always wondered what language she spoke to them), the paper she brought home, the stolen coffee, the evening paper *Večer*, and the half a gevrek that was hard by snack time. And she had her stories about events at work, about Pavlina the engineer, about Comrade Director.

But now, the two of them were pensioners, and we all lived together. I received the compensation for my jail sentence for criminal activity I had not committed. Marta and Marija went to kindergarten. They were growing—they talked, they asked questions—but I still couldn't find work, and, rather than work in a boutique or café, I preferred not to work at all while looking for something fulfilling that would make me happy. The compensation was enough for me to live a normal life and have the means to support my children and my parents.

On July 9, 2005, I woke up thinking about how, had Srebra lived, she would have been celebrating her tenth wedding anniversary. Surely, she and Darko would have had a child, maybe two. I chased the thought from my mind. It was the hottest day of the year. Two days later, when the heat had lessened a bit, I went into town with Marija and Marta to light candles at Saint Dimitrija. I took them to get ice cream at Café Malaga. They tried stracciatella gelato for the first time. On a television outside the café, the lead story on the six o'clock news was about the tenth anniversary of the Srebrenica massacre. A memorial service was being held for the eight thousand dead. Serbian president Boris Tadić placed a wreath. Mothers lay on the graves like exhausted swimmers in a crying marathon. On the Serbian channel, Professor Gojko Djogo pounded his chest with Serbian innocence: "I would hide both Mladić and Karadžić if I could," his voice resounded. The mothers wept. Images of men and boys, walking like skeletons to their executions under the watchful eyes of Dutch soldiers. Marta and Marija ate stracciatella, unaware, thank God, that life held more tragedies than happiness. One of their few tragedies already had a name: "Daddy." The time would come when I'd have to tell them about Srebra as well. And about our conjoined heads. How I had survived, but their would-have-been aunt hadn't. About their father's murderer. About my innocent guilt, for which I'd received compensation that enabled us to eat stracciatella gelato. Still, I could never go back in time and be there when they started to use the potty or said their first word. At the small table beside us sat a slightly older couple with a baby in a carriage. The husband was wearing a tracksuit and held a cigarette in one hand while occasionally rocking the carriage with the other. From his mouth came words that soiled our ice cream: *cunt, cunt-sucker, fucking cunthead*. Someone owed him 1,500 euros. Malevolence poured from him, a clear reflection of the world in which he belonged. His wife, prematurely aged, black-haired, petite, and with a ponytail, looked at a bunch of papers in a binder, and, with her right hand, typed numbers on a black calculator. He was talking to her, but she didn't seem to be listening to him, and only rarely did she respond to something he said. The ice cream melted in the dishes. I wiped Marta and Marija's faces clean, and we left.

On November 5, 2005, two days before Marija and Marta's fourth birthday, someone broke into our storage cellar during the night and took everything he found: my empty suitcase from London, a pile of bags and backpacks, a box filled with bottles of oil, jars of winter preserves, and a sleeping bag. My father discovered the burglary when my mother sent him for onions. When he told us, my mother fell apart. She shouted and wrung her hands. She fell on the dining-room floor, gasping, then lost consciousness. I immediately sent Marija and Marta to my room. I told them to stay there and not move. They began to cry. They didn't understand what was happening. My father called the police. A half hour later, a young police officer appeared at our door. He went with my mother and father to the storage cellar. They filed a report, and the police officer left. My mother came upstairs, still in hysterics. She got a sheet of notebook paper, and, with a trembling hand, wrote: "11/5/2005 storage cellar opened then closed again, twenty kilos of oil stolen along with a suitcase, two bags, one large and one small backpack, six jars of ajvar, three jars of Russian salad…" She listed everything that the thief had stolen. If only we knew who it was.

After that, she fell apart completely. She barely ate or drank. She didn't cook. She did not have the strength for it. Nor did she take off her blue robe. My father bought her a container of blueberry juice, from which neither Marta nor Marija dared steal a drop. She didn't get up to blow out the candles with them on their birthday. Marta called from the dining room, but her grandma did not come. Marija said, "Grandma is sleeping." My mother was lying on the couch, and she looked empty, pale, sunken, as weak as a reed. She would gain strength all at once and get up, go into the big room, climb up onto a chair, and look through the wrapped blankets and wool afghans on the shelves, lightly touching them, almost as if caressing them. She would then open the cupboards and take out objects she had never used: new pans, a ceramic meat dish that she had been given one year at work for Women's Day, crystal fruit bowls. From under my father's bed she pulled out an entire set of fish plates. She counted the plates, looking at the fish, and when Marija and Marta ran around shouting, "fishy, fishy," she chased them away, saying, "Don't break them." Under her bed there was an unopened mixer, a new violet bedspread, and new shoes. She would take each object in her hand, stroke it, touch it to her face, and then return it to its place. Then she'd put down the cushions on the foldout beds, come back into the kitchen, lie down on the small couch again, and watch me while I cooked. In a barely recognizable voice, she'd tell me not to add any more salt, to cut the onion finer, not to fry the beans too much, not to waste so much oil. Marija and Marta fled whenever she looked at them. My father sat in the dining room watching television, and every once in a while, he said, "God help us.

She's being eaten alive over the storage cellar." My mother took a sheet of paper from a large notebook, a diary from 2000, and wrote in Serbian in large block letters, "I'm writing a letter to you, but since we're not together, what's a letter to do?…" On December 18, 2005, she died in her sleep. My father had gotten up early and, as usual, lit the woodstove before we awoke. Then he went out for bread. As usual, he went shopping early so he wouldn't run into anyone from the neighborhood. Once, watching him from the balcony as he hurried along the street, head bowed, racked with shame, I bit my lip. That morning, Marija and Marta woke at seven. They slept in the other bed in my room, and they'd climb in with me so we could hug and tickle each other. It was a Sunday morning, and we lazed about. At around seven thirty, they went to see their grandpa in the dining room so they could watch cartoons together. At eight, I came out of my room. My mother still hadn't gotten up. At eight thirty, I told Marija and Marta to go wake Grandma, because she had been sleeping a long time. At first, they didn't want to. Their aversion to her had grown as she became ever more locked in her world following the storage cellar break-in. But they went. I heard them yell, "Grandma, Grandma, get up! Mama's calling you." "Hey, Grandma, it's snowing outside." When we didn't hear her voice, my father and I went into the room. She was calm, pale, and already cold. She had died in her sleep. My father went crazy. I did as well. I automatically ran to Auntie Dobrila's. I told her…though I have no idea what I said to her. I know she came, said there was nothing to be done, and that there was no point in calling a doctor. "She's very cold," she said. "It looks like she died in her sleep." Then she rang our neighbors' doorbells. Soon the apartment was filled with neighbor women. Auntie Magda wasn't there.

She stood on the stairs and called, "Zlata, Zlata, bring the children to me." I brought them to her. They didn't want to go, and they struggled, but Auntie Magda got them inside somehow. They knew her. Whenever we met on the stairs, she patted their heads, and I had told them that Auntie Magda was Roza's mother, but Roza had died. An ambulance arrived, and the medics confirmed the death. They gave my father and me injections to calm us, and left. I don't know who took charge of the funeral. There were only a few people there: some neighbors, Aunt Milka, my uncle but not his wife, Verče with her husband, Mirko, and Lenče. Almost the same people as had been at Aunt Ivanka's funeral. Aunt Milka fell to the ground, crying, sobbing, and wailing. "She buried a child, a sister, a son-in-law, and now she's gone, too. Who will protect us, who will watch out for us? You were like a mother to us, our oldest sister. O Lord, have mercy." Aunt Milka said all kinds of things in her pain. The rest of us cried silently. A strong wind was blowing, and snow gusted from all sides. After the burial, we shared the memorial food quickly and went our separate ways. Only then did I go get Marija and Marta from Auntie Magda's. I entered the forgotten world of Roza. On the floor of the dining room, where Roza, Srebra, and I had once played, Marija and Marta were playing. Dear God, how many people in my life were already dead! Was this just?

In the week following my mother's death I was like a ghost. I won't even speak about my father. Marija and Marta went to school, and we didn't pick them up until closing time. I sat at home, in a timeless zone. I forced myself to prepare things to eat, and I thought about my mother. In the large room, I stood and looked: I saw the row of blankets kept for years on her shelves. I opened the cupboard and looked at all the things my mother had preserved for who knows when. I lifted the couch cushions, and beneath them, in boxes, faded with time, were the unopened mixer, the fish service, and the violet bedspread. I put her new shoes on her feet so she'd have them in the grave. I looked at all these objects, so important to my mother, and something within me grew, as if sprouting directly from my pain: I would bring these things to her grave, these things that had been so important to her. Let death warm her more than life had. After we conducted the seven-day commemoration, I asked the cemetery administrator whether it would be possible to buy another gravesite next to my mother's. "For your father?" the clerk asked. "Yes, you can have it. But, as you can see, there aren't many more spaces. People buy them for themselves." I paid for the plot. As we were getting ready to go to the cemetery for the fortieth-day rituals—just my father, Marija, Marta, and I—I began putting into the taxi the bags filled with all the things, unused, but so beloved by my mother. My father looked at me inquisitively. "Where are you taking all that?" he asked, and I said, "We're bringing them to Mom. They're hers." In the trunk I put all the never-opened blankets (gifts from aunts for Srebra and my graduation), unopened sets of dishes, the unopened mixer, all the boxes of chocolates and packets of coffee she had received from guests, the jar of honey I brought from London the time I visited alone, everything, everything that she had kept for some other time, saying, "Just put it there." Everything about which we had said, "Open it. You can't carry it to the grave." And she'd replied, "You never know." Everything. We would put everything in the grave so she could take it with her. I never knew if I came from a poor family or a miserly one. I decided to give my mother everything she had saved, saved for herself or someone else, but not for us.

I paid a gravedigger to dig the plot I had purchased right

beside my mother's. "If possible, dig it so there's no barrier between the two graves," I said, as he looked at me strangely. "You're not Satanists are you?" he asked. My father, sweating with shame and anger, snorted through his nose. For the first and last time, he shouted at Marija and Marta, who were circling around the grave: "Calm down! You have devoured the world." When the gravedigger finished, I filled the empty grave with the cherished items that my mother had preserved for her future. After we covered the grave with earth, I leveled it. I told Marija and Marta to stamp the dirt down with their waterproof boots. Then the priest came. He recited the memorial prayers, crossed himself, and left. We left as well, walking by the graves of Bogdan, Srebra, and Aunt Ivanka. Marija and Marta patted Bogdan's picture, repeating, "Daddy, Daddy." At Srebra's grave, Marija and Marta said, "Auntie," and for the first time I said, "Yes, this is your aunt." At Aunt Ivanka's grave, they said, "Let's go home; we're cold." In the taxi, Marta asked me, "If a dog dies, does it become a toy? Does it still bark?" "No, it doesn't bark anymore," Marija said importantly. "It's peaceful, and you can keep petting it." Indeed, that would be a good way for toys to be made. Create children's toys from dead animals. Embalmed like Egyptian mummies, they would never die in a child's embrace. But what about dead people?

2012

This year, on November 7, Marija and Marta will turn eleven. They are so much like Srebra and me as children that the older residents in our neighborhood are shocked when they see them. They experience a sense of déjà vu, even though the girls' heads aren't conjoined. The girls' eyes are just like Bogdan's, and it's only there that I still see him. The girls are in sixth grade. Their math teacher is Violeta, the same Violeta who taught Srebra, me, and Bogdan. She was the youngest teacher then, and we teased her in a mean way—scribbling on the radiator ribs in white chalk, because we knew she got cold easily and always leaned against it. The white marks on the radiator rubbed off onto her black skirt. Or one of us would pull out her chair just as she sat down. She'd fall, get up, start crying. She never reported us to the principal. Marija and Marta say she's very nice and everyone respects her. There are other younger teachers now, and the students joke around with them instead, taking pictures with their cell phones, while the teachers shout and threaten to send them to the principal.

We live with my father. He's old and forgetful. He doesn't wear anything—no sweater, shirt, anything—that doesn't have a breast pocket, even at home. He carries his glasses there and an old pen with the word *London* on it that I brought him from London a long time ago. He stands on the balcony every morning waving to Marija and Marta as they head off to school, and then, at noon, when they come back, he's back out on the balcony waiting for them. Sometimes, he'll come inside and say, quietly, "They're not here. Where are they? What's with those children?" Then, when he sees them coming, he runs back in and says, flushed with excitement, as if they were guests who hadn't visited in a long time, "Here they come!"

I work as a journalist for Radio Global. It's a radio station that, in 2006, after much bickering and a tug-of-war with the government, got permission from the Council of Radio Broadcasters to broadcast in Macedonia. It was founded by someone who came back from the United States with a PhD in media management. When I applied for the job, he told me, "Our station will be different because it'll be global, not just Macedonian." He added that the radio's editorial offices would never close; there would be three journalists on duty three nights a week, collecting news from foreign agencies, and then immediately—at most, fifteen minutes later—broadcasting that news in Macedonian to a Macedonian audience. Therefore, it was important for each journalist to have an excellent command of a foreign language: English, French, German, Chinese, Russian, Japanese, Arabic, Greek, or Spanish. We also had a journalist, Avni, who spoke Albanian, because our director wanted to comply with the Ohrid Framework Agreement, which had provisions for the wider use of Albanian in the country. He hired other journalists who knew languages not represented in the editorial office. "We want world coverage," the director said. "You journalists will establish connections with your listeners, anticipate the kinds of comments that will be called in, and you'll encourage them to call." "But what if we hear, at two in the morning, something like a terrorist attack in Paris?" I asked. "Everyone will be asleep. Wouldn't it be better to use it as the lead story on the early morning news?" "You really think so?" he said, staring at me in astonishment. "Believe it or not, there are many people, too many, who aren't asleep at two in the morning, for one reason or another," he said, adding, "If they already can't sleep, they can at least be the first to hear breaking news. We will be instant radio, no matter how American that sounds. We'll announce news from the global to the local, which is why we call ourselves Radio Global." I accepted the job. I didn't have any other opportunities for employment. I had graduated in law with very low scores. I didn't have a master's or doctorate. I had never gone back to request the torn-up master's diploma on migration studies from the University of London. But I knew English, and the director wanted people with a great deal of life experience. That's what he asked, looking at me skeptically, "Has anything really happened to you in your life?" "I had a sister, a twin. We had conjoined heads. We lived like that until we were twenty-four years old. Then we went to London for an operation and Srebra did not survive. Later, I returned to London. There, I completed a master's thesis on migration in literature, but I refused the degree because my mentor revealed my life story to everyone, which I had wanted to keep secret. My boyfriend was killed at the Bulgaria-Macedonia border. He was a counterfeiter of passports, but I didn't know that. I was framed. I was pregnant. I gave birth to twin girls. Ten months later, I had to leave them and go to prison. I spent seven months in Idrizovo. Then I sued the state, and was paid 20,000 euros in compensation for false imprisonment. Marta and Marija are now five years old." I told him all this in one breath. He looked at me, jaw-dropped. "Oh, that was you! Then you are quite aware," he said, "that every pain is both local and global. Yours is precisely that." And he hired me. All my colleagues have interesting life stories. Most often, they had returned from abroad because of some turn of fate or because they were consumed by nostalgia. They're all interesting, open, spirited. Everyone has a degree, some from Skopje, some from universities in the world's largest cities. We are all about the same age. They have families and children, either scattered around the globe, or here, in Skopje. Some hurry home after work, others go anywhere but home. I'm one of those who never goes for coffee or lunch in town, but hurries home, where Marta and Marija wait for me. They were five years old when I started. My father gave up the big room for us, and we partitioned it with a bookshelf so I could have a desk with a computer and a bed. Marta and Marija have their own corner where they sleep, play, and study. My father sleeps in the small room. He never complains. Because I'm a single mother, our American-Macedonian director gives me some privileges. I work four hours a day, from eight till noon. But three times a week, I have night duty in the editorial room. I collect a wide variety of news items, which I translate as quickly as possible and then report to our listeners. They call in immediately with comments and questions. Even I couldn't believe how many people in Macedonia are awake in the middle of the night. Cups of coffee, cans of Red Bull, and coffee-filled Ferrero Rocher chocolates keep me on my feet. Of course, there are also my two colleagues, with whom I often laugh, not for any particular reason, except exhaustion and too much caffeine in our veins. Night brings people closer than day does. But it also divides them. Impure friendship is a contamination of one's inner space, a poison that requires removal and purification from the toxic substances: a path, a prayer, a cleansing of the body and soul. Loneliness can be an ascetic cure for the heart, the soul, and the mind. But our friendship at Radio Global was pure, equitable…an eco-friendship.

We had mounted ten clocks on the wall of the office like those in hotels that show various local times: one set for Skopje, one for London, for New York, Beijing, Tokyo, Moscow, and other cities around the globe. Radio Global was the first station in Macedonia to learn on November 5, 2006, that Saddam Hussein had been sentenced to death. On February 15, 2008, we broadcast the proposal suggested by UN moderator Nimitz for renaming Macedonia: The Democratic Republic of Macedonia. "Like the Congo?" a listener asked. "So will our language be Democratic Macedonian? And will the people be called Democratic Macedonians?" Some of our listeners thought it was the most acceptable proposal. They thought that once the name question was resolved the country could turn to economy, employment, and human rights issues. I was at work when the news came in that Kosovo had declared independence. It was only two days after the Nimitz proposal for renaming Macedonia. While reporting on air, "After dreaming for thirty years of becoming its own country, Kosovo today declared its independence," I recalled when Serbra and I were teenagers—standing behind the curtain separating the kitchen and the dining room, twirling the ends of our hair and tugging at each other's—and a TV anchor said that Kosovo was refusing to abandon its desire to become its own republic. A few days later, some relatives came to visit from Prishtina and said, "There's no living with those damn Shiptars." I had been completely baffled, but Srebra was upset. Our temples were pounding. Srebra said that, most likely, the Albanians in Kosovo were saying the same thing about them: "There's no living with these Serbs!" I didn't know why people couldn't live with each other. "So let them separate!" I said to Srebra. "They can't. They have conjoined heads just like us. Still…" She was silent a moment before adding, "With surgical intervention they might. But blood will flow, and people will die." That same year, at midnight on July 23, 2008, just as I was starting my shift in the editorial office, I learned that Radovan Karadžić had finally been captured. He had been living in Belgrade under an assumed name as "a spiritual explorer, with white hair and beard, dressing in black clothes, a doctor of alternative medicine and contributor to the magazine *Healthy Life*." It was the biggest farce of the twenty-first century. That criminal with an intellectual's face who, behind tear-free glasses, watched death take those he'd condemned. He had wandered around for thirteen years, traveling by bus and appearing at seminars. He had written articles, eaten, drunk, slept, dreamed. What had he dreamed of all those years? Did he have nightmares, or, under his assumed name, Dragan Dabić, did he have no ugly memories from his past? "The greatest psychopath of the new century has been arrested." That's what I said on air, and a flood of calls immediately came pouring in from listeners who were still awake. Some rejoiced; others felt pity for him. The year 2008 was also the year the Summer Olympics took place in Beijing. The editorial office heard the news that, at the last minute, the president of the Chinese politburo replaced the little girl who was to open the Olympic Games with a song with another little girl, a prettier one, who, instead of singing, was simply going to lip-synch. The girl who had actually sung on the recording had crooked teeth and was deemed unsuitable to display to an international audience. I asked the listeners what they thought—would the Olympics be the greatest anguish in that girl's life? What impact would this event have on her? What would happen to her when she grew up? One listener said that it would be a good topic for research and someone would surely remember her and seek her out after ten or twenty years to learn what effect this political move in China had had on her life.

On March 25, 2010, I received a call from an editor at the *Economist* asking if I wanted her to send us an article they'd just published called "What's in a Name?" before it went online. I translated it live on air, encouraging my listeners to phone in with questions and comments at the end. According to the *Economist*, and to our radio station, that article received more worldwide commentary than any other. That day, we broadcast only news. No one felt like hearing about entertainment, but the listeners who called in still gave extremely amusing commentary. Or, perhaps more accurately—tragicomic. We all laughed at our own expense. On August 30, 2010, the BBC reported from a collapsed mine in Chile that the miners had made their first phone calls. Psychologists had advised the families to sound as positive and optimistic as possible. Each miner was allowed a one-minute call. Reality around the globe was becoming more and more like science fiction. Reality in Macedonia even more so. At noon on September 13, 2010, just as I was about to leave for home, all of Skopje's media outlets received an interesting tidbit of information: "Residents of Volkovo, just outside of Skopje, are to receive garbage cans." Those of us in the editorial office laughed: What, they didn't have them before? The government constantly flooded Macedonian media and its citizens with slogans: Start a family. Have a third child. Choose life. Open your heart. Realize your potential.

Knowledge is strength; knowledge is power. Macedonia—timeless. Macedonia—snow-covered. Read more. Be kinder. And on and on. I asked Marija and Marta if they discussed the slogans at school, and if so, how people reacted to them. "We don't talk about them," Marta said. "But some of the teachers repeat them when they try to give us advice. Especially the one that goes, 'Knowledge is strength; knowledge is power.'" "They seem to think that one is very insightful," said Marija, always more critical than Marta, through her laughter. "What about when our gym teacher called on Mia today and asked her to repeat that dirty sentence after him?" Marija said. "What sentence?" I asked. Marta turned red, but Marija bravely stated, "'Maxi-maxi, prick like a taxi.' Is that normal?" No, no it wasn't normal, just as nothing else was normal. Especially when you're a journalist, you're bombarded every day with all sorts of information, and you see that it's not just your country, but the whole world that is turned upside down. Still, you feel the most sympathy for your own country...not for your country as a country, but for the people in it.

Sometimes at work, we went to extremes with our journalistic cynicism. Once, Gjorgji, the journalist who covered German-speaking regions, said, "Just imagine that Macedonia made an agreement with Germany to exchange our entire populations. All the inhabitants of Macedonia, absolutely all of them—children, young people, old people, everybody—move to Germany, and all the residents of Germany resettle in Macedonia. That would be really crazy!" We laughed at the suggestion. It seemed absolutely crazy, but it would have been a great way to change the world order. Our name would no longer be so important. Everything is relative, just like history itself. "The Germans would still call themselves Germans, out of inertia, and Macedonians would call themselves

Macedonians, but we'd be in Germany." "Or lost Germans," added Keti, quite taken with the idea. And that night, when she was on air, she proposed the idea to her listeners for discussion. I was awake; being awake all night three days a week had totally altered my biorhythms. I couldn't sleep even when I was home, so, with headphones so as to not wake Marta and Marija, I followed the nighttime news and conversations on our station. So many people called in with comments, saying lots of crazy things. Some were already offering their home to the Germans who would be resettled in Macedonia; some asked whether they could take their car, their bike, and their computer with them or had to simply leave everything behind. Keti led her listeners through the labyrinth of our game. She was interested in what they thought best: Should the exchange include possessions, and what about pets, or the villagers' sheep, or pigs awaiting slaughter? The fatalistic listeners said it would be best if the exchange were carried out without those things; people should only take clothing and medicine and start over from scratch, with whatever the former homeowners had left them. I laughed that night. But when I turned off the radio, I was bothered by the question that I've been obsessed with for years: Is it possible for a person to get over the death of those closest to her and laugh, joke around, and just talk once again? Is time really the best medicine for everything? Is life stronger than death? The dead are, in fact, dead only when someone thinks about them. When we aren't thinking about them—caught up in the current of our everyday lives—they are as alive as those whom we simply haven't seen in years, out of negligence, inability, or for some other reason, like my uncle. Forgetting protects us from death. It's absurd, but true.

When I went to work the next day, I learned that Avni had

submitted his resignation. He felt the proposal to exchange populations was too similar to what the Serbian Academy had proposed for an exchange of populations between Serbia and Kosovo. Our academics had also once had a similar idea about Macedonians and Albanians. Although this had been a joke, we understood that Avni was genuinely offended. The director said the incident could cause us to lose our license. "And then," he said, "you'll just blame it all on God."

I was heading home from work across the stone bridge. I was surrounded by the roar of construction equipment; the city is littered with construction sites. Along the bridge there were tables piled with shredded cabbage. The vendors were shredding and shredding cabbage. They were selling special knives for chopping and shredding cabbage. Beside them lay half heads of dirty cabbage. The outer leaves hadn't been peeled away and they were unwashed. What do all these people selling knives do with all the waste? Do they bring it home and eat nothing but cabbage for days on end? Boiled cabbage, cooked sauerkraut, cabbage salad, cabbage a hundred ways... I thought of my uncle Kole. What a pro he was at cutting cabbage. I hadn't seen him in years. Aunt Milka came at least once a year. She would sleep at our place, on the couch in the kitchen. We would get Lenče and go to the cemetery, visiting one grave after another. She would go back home sick. The crying, sobbing, and memories took so much out of her that, two years ago, I told her not to come to the cemetery with us anymore. She never came again. How much I missed her. She was alive, and I didn't have much family left alive in my life. I decided to go and visit her for a day. I would walk to the village and visit the graveyard. I would light candles for Grandma and Grandpa, and see their house, which I hadn't been to for years. It now belonged to my uncle, and

I could just imagine what shape it was in. I went. Marija and Marta had a school trip that day to the village of Pelintse. I got off the rickety Yug-Tourist bus and headed up the path to Aunt Milka's house. When she saw me, she couldn't believe her eyes, and kept hugging me, kissing me, and crying. My uncle was still at work. I called my other uncle and told him I wanted to go to the village and the cemetery, but to see the house as well. "Can I have a key?" I asked him, although I wasn't certain he would give me one, especially since we had not seen each other in so many years, and because he had been angry at me when I didn't lend him money for his new house in the city. He had chided me over the phone, saying that he had wiped my bum when I was little, mine and Srebra's. "I'll come with you," he said. We hugged when we met. We walked down the village path toward the graveyard, and my uncle said, "Do you remember when you and Srebra were little and I asked you what you would be when you grew up? You said, 'a writer,' and Srebra said, 'a lawyer.'" "I didn't become a writer. I can't write, even now. Writing is a solitary act, and I still feel Srebra's head beside mine. And she'll see what I'm writing. I feel embarrassed and uncomfortable, so I can't write," I said, ashamed. "Here we are," my uncle said, waving his hand as we passed through the half-closed gate of the cemetery. And what did I see! The cemetery was full of weeds and garbage. Grandma's photograph had come loose and blown off among the other graves. It was lucky that my uncle found it. The photo's frame and the glass covering it were broken. I stood by the grave while he tidied up, and I felt they were truly gone. *They're not here anymore*, I thought. Surely, they must have found their place in heaven at last, close to God. Are they together with Srebra, my mother, and Aunt Ivanka? Maybe even Bogdan as well? That's how it should be. In heaven, one's loved ones are surely together. Grandma and Grandpa's house was full of garbage. Layers of trash: entangled nets and strips of rags, clothes, towels, sheets, odds and ends—bottles, vases, sanitary pads—everything broken, trampled on, destroyed. The dignity of our family home—desecrated, despoiled, soiled, disgraced. A house full of garbage. The house of our childhood, the home of our spirit. I didn't have the strength to speak to my uncle. I couldn't. I kept silent, gulped, took pictures of the walls, which had remained more or less the same, with the same paintings, photographs, and decorations. That was all that remained of the house. On account of my uncle, I didn't say a word. It felt as though my outer voice had gone mute, as though all that remained was this, my inner voice. I returned from the village that evening exhausted, upset, and filled to overflowing with an emptiness from which I might burst. Marija and Marta were already home; they hugged me, then went back to Facebook. I told my father what had happened. He said, "What in your mother's name drove you to go there?" Then he bit his tongue, because my mother's spirit was also there. She had grown up in those rooms. It was from there she set off on her life's path to Skopje. My father went back to watching television. I noticed that they were rerunning the series on the brave men in vests and white shirts—young Macedonian revolutionaries from the time of the Ilinden Uprising at the beginning of the twentieth century. When Srebra and I were children, that series was broadcast on Sunday evenings, when we had our bath. Srebra and I always managed to wash up in time to catch the beginning. Usually we lingered in the bath, taking turns rinsing off in the thin stream of water from the shower. To our mother, it seemed like we took hours, and she would bang on the door and yell, "Come on, what are you doing in there? Did you drown?" We usually watched that series with our father, in silence. Mom was always the last to bathe, and then she did the laundry by hand. With her hair still damp, she would hang the clothes on the balcony before calling Srebra and me to help her empty out the tub and battered green pot that served our family's hygiene loyally for so many years. Six months after my mother's death, I threw the pot away. Now my father was watching the *Our Years* series with a certain sadness in his eyes. To Marta and Marija, though, it was boring. They're always on their laptop, or messaging with friends on Facebook, or watching fantasy movies about new-age vampires.

In 2011, from the end of April through the first of the May holidays, I was on duty three nights in a row in the editorial room, because Vesna had begged me to swap days so she could go to Spain with her husband. There was one breaking story after another: the wedding of Prince William to Kate Middleton, the killing of Osama bin Laden, the announcement of the beatification ceremony for John Paul II, and the death of Ernesto Sabato, author of *The Tunnel*. The tunnel that led to my life without Srebra. I had read *The Tunnel* on the plane to London when we were going to get separated. Srebra had read Seneca's *Letters*. That tunnel was the blood flow of my subconscious. "How beautiful they are!" sighed Marija and Marta, watching Kate and William's wedding on the Internet. They liked nothing more than to be on Facebook gathering new friends, posting everything and anything, and liking things. I'm only on Facebook because I'm a journalist, and our radio station cannot ignore social networks. I don't post anything personal. I never talk about myself. Nor do I have the time to—so many things are happening every single moment of the day. Tragedies and comedies from across the globe penetrate my life instantly, the moment they occur. I lie in wait for them, eyes and ears at the ready. On top of that, 2012 is a leap year, which means one extra stack of information from the 366th day. One extra night without sleep.

Today is Saturday, August 18, 2012. Yesterday, I turned forty. Marija and Marta made me a cake by themselves, the first cake they ever made. When I praised them, telling them they'd baked me the most beautiful cake of my life, they said, "We found a recipe on Facebook; that's why we call it Facebook cake." We laughed. "Can we bring some to Auntie?" Marta asked, "It's her birthday, too." "And we'll bring some to Daddy and Grandma," added Marija. On our way out, we met the postman, who had a package for me. I opened it right there in the doorway. Inside was the collected works of Marina Tsvetaeva, a new, English edition. I couldn't believe it. "Haven't you heard of Amazon?" Marta asked, and she and Marija giggled. "Grandpa paid with his credit card." I hugged and tickled them. Then we all laughed together, my father, too. We went to the cemetery. At each gravesite we left a piece of cake on a paper plate, with a plastic fork, a white napkin, and we lit a candle. As we stood in front of the graves, it seemed as though I heard a birthday greeting from each one. Congratulating me on reaching forty, for surviving the curse of death that had clearly marked my life. My father didn't wish me a Happy Birthday; he did not know how. Srebra and I had always been upset about that, but no one had ever wished him a Happy Birthday in his life. Now I forgave him. I gave him two pieces of cake.

This morning, when we got up, Marta and Marija turned on their laptop first thing, like they always did. They're sitting at the table, whispering to each other. I sent their grandpa to the market to get tomatoes, cucumbers, and a watermelon. I am making pizza. They tell me they can wait for breakfast. They're very excited about something on the laptop. One shouts, "Look! That's how you count." The other whispers, "No, like this, from right to left." "But do you count it even if it's already circled?" It sounds like they're doing some sort of math problem, which seems odd, since they are still on break for another few days. I don't usually peek at their computer, except when they're not at home. Then, out of fear, like every other mother of eleven-year-old girls, I check their browser history, but I've never found any suspicious websites. My father comes home from the market, and Marta and Marija take the computer to their room before coming back so we can eat. We always eat together if I'm home. The dining-room table is the center of our life. We sit there at least once a day, three times on weekends. Sometimes, before a special meal, I recite the Lord's Prayer, but I'm the only one to cross myself. In our family, God is my business. That's what Marta and Marija say, joking with me. They praise the pizza. I peel a cucumber for them. I twist off the top of the cucumber, and from its headless body I drag the poison from its veins, up through its open pores. The poison is white, from the bitter gut. Foam bubbles around the cucumber's twisted neck, and the water in its body grows sweeter. I divide it for them. I think, *This is how you pull bitterness from a cucumber, but from life?* Beginning in my childhood, the death of those closest to me has been the bitterest foam. Tonight, with my full forty years, I confront my past, my whole life. I don't shut my eyes all night. No, I do not have a spare life. But in this one, I have people to live for. Unfortunately, my children have also tasted the bitterness of our family misfortune. Let them, at least, eat unbitter cucumbers, and when they grow up, may they drink only sweet coffee.

After breakfast, Marta and Marija say they're going

outside, but they want to know if Grandpa still has chalk in the garage. "Of course I have some," he says, going down with them to get it. Then he comes back, since one of his Turkish television series is about to start. "What do they want the chalk for?" I ask. "They're going to draw something," he responds, which surprises me. I go out on the balcony. In front of the building, on the sloping lane in front of Uncle Kole's garage, Marta and Marija crouch on the pavement, chalk in hand, and count aloud, over and over again. I strain my eyes, narrowing them into slits, because that's how nearsighted people see best. My lenses stick even closer to my eyes, and I'm not mistaken, I can see quite well. In front of Marta is a big square with the number *23* inside it, and around the edge are circled: *B* for her husband's name, *R* for rich, *S* for her city, and *2* for children. Marija had an even bigger square with the number *22* inside, and circled around the edge, *D* for her husband's name, *M* for multimillionaire, *L* for her city, and *1* for a child. No, my eyes hadn't deceived me. Marta and Marija are playing the fortune-telling game.